I0822381

A King Shall Rise

A. Corrin

To my father, whose ideals have become my own;

to my mother, who believed in me from page one;

and to my brother, every bit a Griffin King.

Credits:

Cover illustration by Eva Soulu–www.evasoulu.com

Book Design by Veronica Scott

OTHER BOOKS BY A. CORRIN

Jonathan Trilogy:

Jonathan, Prince of Dreams (Book 1)
Jonathan, Guardian of Dreams (Book 2)
Jonathan, King of Dreams (Book 3)

CONTENTS

Chapter One:

Good and Evil

"The greatest trick the Devil ever pulled was convincing the world he didn't exist."

–Verbal Kint, *The Usual Suspects*

When he was eleven, something traumatized Brody: an event that would forever-after set him apart from others.

He lived in a small town, a town so small that parents saw walking home from school as a safe responsibility, even if the walk was two-and-a-half miles through countryside as Brody's was. He and his friends liked to follow the railroad tracks until the number three train with its cargo of lumber came thundering along, and then they jumped aside, hooting and hollering at the piercing whistle that the conductor blew just for them.

His friends parted ways as Brody went, dashing off down long dirt roads between fields of corn and rolling pastures glowing in the sun. When the tracks curved east, Brody hopped off onto a dirt path through thigh-high grass. A little stream burbled along beside him, moseying under the tracks, and the path descended to the water's edge before veering crookedly into some dense alders and cottonwoods.

After picking through the stones at the little stream's fringe for a salamander or some fetching rock he could add to his collection, Brody squared his shoulders and entered the woods, whistling loudly. He was afraid of those woods–the hissing trees, the squalling birds, the groaning trunks swaying in the wind. Once he had come upon a possum on the trail and it had made such a sound of fury, showing all of its jagged little teeth, that he had run the other way and come home hours late after getting lost. Another time, a tree branch had fallen in a gale with a sound like a gunshot and landed so near him that the wind of it had tousled his curly black hair. Experience suggested that the woods were a dark place, possibly haunted by ghosts that wanted Brody's spirit to join them. The whistling was to drown out any spooky sounds he might hear and trick the ghosts into thinking he was unafraid because as everyone knew, ghosts didn't go after brave people.

But on this day, his whistling did not quite drown out the sound of monsters. Echoing around the trunks that were gouged by white-tail antlers shedding felt, over mossy mud patches imprinted with raccoon tracks, through thickets of cane that one of Brody's friends said witches used to switch kids with–echoing through those woods came screams.

The screams were shrill, female, broken into senseless syllables as the woman babbled something. She seemed to be pleading–shrieking helplessly–and then crying out for help. She was desperate. Brody's whistling ended abruptly and he froze, feeling the blood drain from his face. What should he do? Was he imagining it? Was someone lost? He was still a good mile from his house and he wasn't sure he could find where the screams came from if he came back later with help... Well, the least he could do was sneak toward the commotion and see what was going on.

Brody turned his backpack so that it was on his chest and unzipped it. He left the trail, stepping lightly, every now and then dropping a pencil or his straight-edge or one of his cherished baseball cards onto the ground so that he could find his way back. There was no way he was getting lost again.

The wind was a trickster that loved to throw noises around and confuse the unwary–but Brody was anything but unwary. The screams were a lot more nearby than they had sounded at first and soon Brody was tucking himself against a maple, its smooth bark cold to his cheek and steady to his twitching fingers. He showed one eye to peek at the scene beyond.

Hikers often cut through the woods to the river upstream and then beyond it to Eagle-Eye Summit, or turned west to get to the freeway. Brody's parents would chat with friendly hikers who came knocking seeking water or directions and Brody loved to listen to their stories over his mother's tea and fruit salad. Brody beheld two hikers, a young couple, before him amidst the trees, but something was horribly wrong. His heart began pounding so hard that his pulse thundered in his ears.

The male hiker lay prone half-slumped against the roots of a tree, his unresponsive body kicked and punched viciously by a crazed, drug-addled derelict, who was swearing the most obscene oaths, his slobber flying everywhere. The woman, slender and fit, avoided the man with quick, darting side steps, keeping him always in her sights as he paced and spun and circled the area. But though she kept the madman in her periphery, much of her focus was on her companion. She wept and screamed her impotent fury at the stranger. Her outrage and anguish, bordering on hysteria, spread slowly to Brody, like drops of acid that ate a hole in his chest. He began to stir.

The woman made to go to the other hiker, but the derelict charged at her and drove her back. She raised her fists to ward him off and the daylight glimmered off of a wedding ring on her finger. It matched the one her fallen companion wore.

Brody began breathing heavily, alarmed at the sight of such unreasonable violence. Finally, as if throwing caution to the winds, the woman stepped over her husband's body with a fierce and protective scream, shoving the crazed transient in the chest. Brody realized that she had given up hope of help coming and chosen to go down alone, fighting. The man spat a slew of foul words in her face and took her arms, twisting around, trying to unbalance her. Brody couldn't be sure, but the man seemed to be attempting to *bite* the woman.

Something ugly and unfamiliar filled that hole in Brody's chest, mingling bitterly with his pain and his fear. This was an anger he had never felt before; an anger that was both fierce and wild. *Rabid.* That's what it felt like–like the rabies that the bats would sometimes get around his house, that made them fall to the earth and scream and hiss as if they wanted the world to suffer with them.

Without remembering how he'd gotten there, Brody found himself standing just behind the criminal with his baseball in his hand. He struck the man hard in the back of the head, and the crazed transient grunted, released the woman, and turned almost casually on the spot. He was a lot scarier up close, all filthy beard, matted hair, stained teeth, drug-devoured flesh, and round, dilated eyes. He spoke to himself in slurred, disjointed sentences that made as much sense as if he were reading aloud from several different books at once.

"Stop," Brody said softly, quailing under that mad stare, fury burning beneath his skin.

The man's speech became more rushed, more forced. He reached up and struck himself powerfully in the side of the head. Brody flinched, but held his ground, narrow chest out, chin up, standing as tall as he could. He still held the baseball. The woman had rushed to her spouse and examined him, saying his name, sobbing. In his periphery Brody saw her embrace the body, her hair hiding the kiss she tearfully planted on its cheek.

That hot, squirmy, and unfamiliar sensation filled Brody in a burning cloud. It was like anger, but more powerful. Like grief, but it stung sharper. His cheeks flushed. The man's voice was rising. Brody's attention snapped back to that bestial face. Yes. *That* was the focus of the new emotion in him. "Stop!" he commanded loudly, scornfully.

The man wailed and lunged at Brody, raking his throat and upper chest with filthy nails. Brody stumbled back, arms trapped against the man's body, the skin of his neck and over his collarbone raw. The woman rose up beside him suddenly and dealt the derelict such a well-aimed kick to the side of the head that his muttering cut off. His attack became a cringing stagger and Brody was able to pull away, unconsciously massaging his fresh scrapes. The derelict had his back to them, his hands over his face. His every exhale was an explosive scream, as if something were trying to burst out of his chest through his lungs. His filthy hands scrabbled at his face. Red-black liquid began streaming down the man's arms, shining on his sleeves, pattering down onto the earth.

"Oh, Lord," the woman breathed over Brody's shoulder.

The tormented man tottered back around to face them, blood staining his entire, tortured face red.

Brody screamed. The woman screamed. The criminal screamed, and then collapsed not four strides away from the fallen hiker, gibbering feebly at the dirt.

"Run, boy, come on! Run!" The woman pulled at him. Brody leaped up like a shot hare and fled into the trees. He was too shaken-up to follow the path he'd made for himself, but luckily his instincts steered him true and he burst onto the main trail and practically flew all the way to his house, the woman right behind him.

A little over an hour later, Brody sat on the edge of a hospital bed, gazing dully at the electrical socket in the wall. He was trying to come to terms with a harsh truth:

There was true evil in the world.

His whole life he had been sheltered from it. His father didn't even talk about the war. Evil was just an ugly villain that the good guys always vanquished, like in his comic books. But no, not really. No hero had saved Brody today. No hero had rescued that hiker before the derelict had beaten him to death. No one had used supernatural abilities to turn the druggie into a docile human being before he'd clawed his own eyes out and bled to death right there next to his own victim.

Beneath the gauze over the bloody scrapes on his chest, beneath the antibiotic cream and the stitches, Brody's heart beat ponderously. His innocence had been claimed that day–a third victim of the awful ordeal. He grimaced when his wounds flared in pain. How could he have thought that commanding the crazy man to stop would've caused him to obey like an unruly puppy? He had always believed that being brave was what kept the monsters away, when actually being brave *attracted* monsters because brave people were *in* the way. A thrill of fear chilled him as Brody reconsidered all that he had once believed. And his mind kept returning to the sight of the derelict's face–the mask of blood–and the frightening intensity of the volcanic anger that had almost driven Brody to crush the man's skull.

Brody lay on his side on the hospital bed, shuddering, his every cell in upheaval. He'd been in shock earlier until he'd spoken with a few shrinks, but now he was drifting into a dark nightmare of memory and uncertainty.

His father came in, a stocky and ruddy-faced, pleasant-voiced older man with a slight limp. He wore his old leather jacket and a fond smile as he studied his son. He knew Brody had been through a lot and he now faced the unenviable task of all fathers in a difficult position such as his own, when one wrong word could make all the difference: he had to reassure, comfort, and encourage his child. Someone he loved more than life itself really needed him right now.

Brody's dad knocked on the open door gently and said softly, "Hey, trooper."

Brody did not uncurl but craned his head back to look at his father from an awkwardly twisted angle. "Pa," he murmured. A tear ran from the corner of his eye and pooled in the hollow of the bridge of his nose and upper eyelid. "Pa, why'd he do it?"

Pa came in and sat beside his son. Brody sat up and leaned against him, sniffling. "Brody," Pa started, "Every decision in life is as simple and as difficult as yes or no. The fight is in making that yes or no worth it in the end. Some people make a bad decision because it's the easy way out, or the only option they think they have, and then later, when they're paying for that decision, all of the pain and evil that's collected in their souls pours out and hurts others. That man was addicted to bad drugs. And that poor hiker paid for it–both of those hikers did. It's a lot easier to choose to be bad or cruel than it is to be good, noble, and brave."

"I thought I could be brave and good," Brody said, "But it didn't change anything. I almost..." He didn't finish the sentence. How could he admit to his father, his *hero*, that he would have killed the man, crushed his skull with a baseball, if the hiker hadn't pulled him away?

Pa gazed at the wall. Memories from his past drifted in to haunt him. Sounds, sights, and smells–a bullet clipping his hip, the sound of commands, and the enemy whispering to each other from amongst the trees. "In the war, I thought *I* was a coward."

Brody looked up sharply. His father never spoke of his time in Vietnam battling communism.

“I wanted to go home as soon as my boots hit the rice paddies. I was scared all the time; scared of the whispers in the jungle, scared of what the red peril was turning people into and what it was driving them to do. There were other men in ‘Nam who were a lot more courageous than me.” His face screwed up into something pained. Then his voice became restrained. Angry.

“Then I came home and breathed free air and there were folks calling me baby-killer. Throwing things at me. And I realized *I* wasn’t the coward. They were–kids afraid of what they didn’t understand. Afraid of reality. Angry at the way things were. They didn’t know me. They didn’t know what I’d seen and why I’d chosen to serve. But if I had to fight again, for this messed-up country and its screwed-up people, and the ideals it was founded upon, I would.”

He made eye-contact with Brody, whose cheeks were a little pink as he imagined people daring to disrespect his Pa. “True bravery isn’t for yourself, son. Bravery is for others. The world needs more of that.”

“Why should I be brave for the world?” Brody scowled. He fought back his tears. “It’s full of–of–darkness and selfishness and–and–”

Pa rested a hand atop Brody’s head. “Not all of it, son. It’s gonna get harder the older you get and the older the world gets but you gotta find an ideal and cling to it! Let that ideal, that vision, be your anchor. See its beauty! That woman you found? The hiker? She told me how brave you were.”

“I tried telling that man to stop,” Brody said. “And then...I tried to be brave, but something else happened instead. It didn’t feel right.

It didn't feel good here." Brody touched his chest over his heart and fresh tears spilled from his eyes.

Something in his father's eyes told Brody that his father knew what else had happened; that the hiker had told him about what Brody had done with the baseball. But there was no disappointment or disgust in the man's eyes, only love, and maybe sorrow.

"You protected her, Brody. You saw something wicked and the good in you was repulsed by that." He looked away again. "Sometimes that repulsion turns a man into something else." He blinked and gazed down at his son. "But that fire that you displayed out there gave *her* the courage to protect *you*," his Pa replied. "*That* is what bravery does. *That* is what makes it so powerful. Now can you imagine if the whole world was that way?"

Brody fell silent, mystified. Something in his chest, deep beneath the scratches, grew warm. His father saw this and knew that he had said the right thing. He stroked Brody's ear, making the boy smile and wriggle.

"Let your words be your first weapon, son. Speak loud, speak honestly, reprimand injustice. When your words fail and the monsters push in, use your fists. And above all, live life for a reason–and live it bravely."

Chapter Two:

An Ideal

"Here I stand. I can do no other."

–Martin Luther

His father's advice was the steel in Brody's spine even many years after the traumatic incident of his childhood. At twenty, Brody was smart and idealistic. He had a wordsmith's gift and spoke in a soft, contemplative voice, like a man of much wisdom.

For all of his promising attributes though, the heart in Brody's chest beneath the scarred flesh was sour with bitterness. In the time it had taken Brody to finish his remedial education, graduate high school, and see himself into college with the intention of becoming a prosecuting attorney, he had been made fully aware of the darkness in the world. Corruption, crime, selfishness, hate, all were commonplace, and Brody found his ideals harder and harder to cling to for hope.

This story really, truly begins on the first day of the second semester, in Brody's Humanities 101 class, a room filled with chattering students squeezing into their folding chairs and glancing expectantly down the amphitheater-style rows at the professor's podium. The professor, a woman with shoulder-length black hair, glasses, and skinny legs to juxtapose her generous bosom, wrote notes on the chalkboard spanning the length of the wall. The click and cough of the chalk tried to pull Brody in, but no. Not this time.

He would not be roped into another pointless discussion. He would just take his notes, read the text he was assigned, and then go back to his crummy apartment before bojutsu lessons and then work.

Brody preferred to sit in the back of classrooms, where he could see everyone and where his voice would carry best. His unfair reputation as an argumentative loner meant that he sat, more often than not...well, alone. He sat with one leg on a knee, scanning the notes he'd taken on the previous night's chapter, *Early Settlements of Man,* his notebook open flat on his collapsible desktop. With his other hand he idly massaged the knotted ridge of scar tissue sticking above the collar of his crisp button-up.

"They still hurtin' you or something'?"

Brody's head snapped up. A woman unslung her backpack to sit in the seat beside his. She was more alluring than pretty, though she was that too. From her very skin seeped confidence and a kind of cynical distrust of the world around her, displayed in her half-smile and the steady feline way in which she moved.

Her hair glowed white-blond. Black mascara heavily rimmed her blue eyes, cerulean eye-liner traced the corners, and indigo shaded her lids. Her leather jacket, black boots, and torn jeans all grumbled "rebel," but Brody couldn't help but feel an immediate attraction to her. There was something about her that made him feel bold.

She raised her eyebrows. "Good talk." And she began rummaging in her bag for her binder.

What? Oh! She had asked him a question!

"Uh, no. Sorry–no, they don't still hurt. It's just a habit of mine. I apologize if it creeps you out. Sometimes I forget I'm even doing it."

She studied him, those eyes deep and searching. "How did you get them, if you don't mind my asking?"

Brody chewed on his lip, his insides trembling in an internal chill. "I...was in a fight." *With a madman. Who pulled his own eyes out.*

She gazed at him in the same unblinking, enigmatic way that felines watch their humans' facial expressions. Then a smile exposed dazzling teeth and she said, "Gnarly."

It was Brody's turn to give her a look of appraisal. "If you say so," he said with a strange smile. Who was this girl? He wondered at her sins and virtues, her secrets and stories.

This girl seemed the diametrical opposite of what Brody found attractive. He was drawn to women who personified noon in early spring, when the clouds in the sky match the lambs leaping below; women who were as roses in a scented bouquet, morning dew still crystalline on their petals.

But this stranger was like a night on a foggy moor, cold, wild and distant. She was the last leaf in autumn, buried in the snow, still beautiful in speckles of orange and brown, but skeletal–a shadow of something glamorous.

Brody gave his head a shake. His mind often wandered like this, more and more often of late, concocting vivid daydreams as if piecing together a picture book of someone's life in his imagination. Perhaps it was a result of the trauma of his childhood, but Brody had a highly developed *intuition*, if that's what it could truly be called. With a quick observation and a short conversation, Brody could get a decent read on someone, and his evaluation of their character usually manifested vividly as pictures in his mind.

"My name is Brody," he said, holding out his hand, "Pre-law, biology minor."

She grasped his hand with her own and let him shake it, returning his grip firmly.

"Sylph. I'm here for business." Her lips pulled back into the broadest smile she'd given him yet. "'Pre-law.' You want to be a lawyer?"

"An attorney, yes." She wrinkled her nose and he laughed. "Not all fights are won on battlefields." That was something his father used to say.

"But some are," she said shrewdly.

Brody shrugged and smiled. "Hence the minor."

When the professor indicated that class was about to begin, Brody turned his attention to scrutinizing her. He tended to see his professors as wise, old owls. And for the most part, they didn't disappoint, their countenances a little grizzled like an old bird's plumage, their tweed coats covered with chalk dust, pince-nez making their eyes round and sage. As Ms. Gupta spoke, however, Brody began to second-guess.

She gestured at one of her bullet-points on the board and said, "As humans evolved and settlements grew larger, moral values began to evolve as well. We saw the development of the concepts of 'good' and 'evil' that we have today. They helped to keep crime in check and allowed for the proliferation of the human race..."

Brody, having swiftly read all of her bullet points already, had been holding his hand up for minutes now, but the professor waited until her point had been made to her satisfaction and the other students were busily copying her words down before calling on him.

"I don't understand. You're saying that morals are not an intrinsic trait of humanity?" That couldn't be right... Morality was an obligation. A need. A *desire.*

Ms. Gupta smiled wryly, as if squaring up to a challenge she'd faced before. The kindly, old owl feathers began to molt to reveal the vulture beneath.

"Moral values have survival benefits to the larger group," she said. "They are conditions that developed so as to ensure the flourishing of the human species. To say otherwise implies the existence of something like a *soul*, which, of course, cannot be proven."

Students twisted around to gaze up at Brody. His mind raced with counter-arguments.

"But what about the success of dictators, who survive well by being *im*moral? What about self-sacrifice, when a person puts their own lives at stake to save someone else's? Or what about the fact that we protect the weak? How does any of that ensure the survival of humanity?"

Ms. Gupta shrugged. "All beneficial in some way. Morals are often defined by the wealthy, the patriarchy, or other influential institutions, often in a way that benefits said groups and proves disadvantageous to marginalized groups."

"As if 'marginalized groups' don't also have morals?"

Ms. Gupta's eyes narrowed. Her smirk drooped. Someone down below said, "Huh," impressed. Brody plowed on.

"If what you say is true, then morality is an illusion–social opinion! Someone who commits murder isn't *bad* or *wrong*, they're just guilty of breaking a taboo! And if there is no universal moral standard, no right or wrong, then there is no truth. But your objection to absolute, inarguable, universal moral truth is, itself, what you believe to be a truth–so what you've been saying is contradictory, and a waste of all of our time." Students murmured and took down what he was speaking with frantic wags of their pens.

"Enough," Ms. Gupta said coldly, shaking her head and waving her hands as if he were a fool. "If you can't be respectful–"

"Respectful?" Brody cried indignantly, his temper rising. "You teach a fallacy!"

And that was why Brody was sent from the room an hour early.

Brody's job involved working the night shift at a karaoke bar called *Jitterbug*. It had supposedly been around since the twenties, with each new owner remodeling until it looked like it had ten coats of paint and was trying to rekindle the glam of flapper girls and bootlegging with stale disco and ashtrays.

As he slouched about his rounds stuffing dirty dishes into the heavy bin pressed against his hip, Brody had to admit, however, that, even now in the early 2000s, *Jitterbug* had its own kind of funk. The karaoke singers, mostly college kids, weren't all bad, and in the slower, down hours he could usually find a good tune on the old jukebox.

When he got a lapse in customers to clean up after, Brody dropped a couple of coins in the jukebox, searching for something to take his mind off the day's earlier, embarrassing debate. The more he thought about it, the more appalled he was at the offensive close-mindedness of his professors and the gullibility of his classmates. He settled on Johnny Cash's *Boy Named Sue* with a grumpy grunt.

"Boy, you have got to start picking your battles."

At that familiar cynical voice, Brody turned, then laughed dryly.

Sylph sat at the bar right behind him, looking identical to the way she had in class, only this time with a black-tasseled purse instead of a book bag. He was reminded of a leopard with a studded collar–all curving lines, graceful poise, and sharp bite.

"It was a battle worth fighting to me," Brody said softly. "My father always taught me to find an ideal and use it for strength, and here Ms. Gupta says things like that are just...an evolutionary means to an end."

"You and your Dad close?" Sylph's voice was gentle.

"Oh yeah," Brody said, picking up a near-empty glass of dark beer and swirling it around. "It's been hard going to school away from my parents."

Sylph elbowed him in a reassuring way. "Why don't you take a break and tell me about it?"

Brody raised one eyebrow at her. "Really?"

"Sure. What are a couple of malcontents for but to listen to each other bitch and moan?" She smiled disarmingly. Brody felt as if his footing was unsettled. *A couple of malcontents?* Did that mean she thought they had things in common?

Brody worked through his lunch break when he could, when his boss was too busy to notice. But today he bought himself a ranch-doused salad to eat and a glass of lemonade. He almost bought Sylph the coconut-vanilla mimosa she wanted but she gave him a withering look and pulled a few neat bills from her purse, handing them to the bartender, who bobbed his head in time to the next song on the jukebox. It was almost ten o'clock, time for the louder, faster music concocted by some aspiring DJ.

Sitting together in a private corner-booth with a secluded view of the dance floor around a stack of chairs, Brody and Sylph chatted easily about their families. Sylph pressed him to go first, so he told her about his childhood: the times he was lulled to sleep by crickets, the time when, during the Independence Day parade, they had brought a ferris wheel to town and he could see all the way to the eagle nests by the mountains.

He paused to take a drink of his lemonade, a little embarrassed at how chatty he'd been and how quickly he'd divulged precious, personal memories. He hoped that she would start talking and share something about herself, but instead she urged him to keep going. Her eyes fixed on him, sparkling with a bright, curious, sultry light, and he couldn't help but continue.

He told her about the pets he'd found: stray dogs, a raccoon, a robin and some salamanders, his mother's meals and singing voice, the fascinating stories that the hikers told on their way through the woods, and most of all, his father's anecdotes, lessons, and lectures. By the time he was done he felt heartsore, but...*fresh*. As if he had been squeezed free of hurts he'd been sponging up over time.

Feeling quite thankful to Sylph, and realizing that he had dominated the conversation, Brody gestured to her. "But what about you? How's your relationship with your family?" He took a big bite of salad so that he wouldn't be encouraged to interrupt or interject.

Sylph's eyebrows rose into twin lines of bitterness over a face that obviously had no fond memories of her own to recall. "When I was younger, my dad would always tell me this bedtime story about a girl who became a monster. Maybe the girl wasn't always this way. Maybe, once, a long time ago, before memory, she was pure and innocent. But her innocence made her gullible. She was tricked, taken advantage of, and her innocence was stripped from her. Over time, all of the poison in the world seeped into her veins."

The story resonated with Brody. He sat there, listening, a small leaf of lettuce clinging to the end of his fork and dripping ranch on the tabletop.

"Her children, all who came after her, were twisted into creatures of lust and blood by the monsters of the world. And so it's been to this day."

"Your father told you this story?" Brody asked, somewhat repulsed.

Sylph's carmine lips twitched. "He wasn't the best guy... But he'd been through a lot. And, looking back, I like the story. The 'happy ending' was that, even after all that had happened to her, the girl became strong. After all that she'd lost, she didn't go down, and neither did her children. The moral was that the real world is still full of monsters like the one in the story. Sometimes the monsters are even beautiful and their weapons are deceit and indifference." She sipped her mimosa, hand gripping it tight.

The lettuce in Brody's mouth suddenly seemed basted in vinegar. He looked upon the girl across from him with compassion. She was wounded like he was, scarred on the inside, in her heart and mind. Outwardly, she was bold, defiant, challenging a world that had treated her father with such distaste and apathy. She was like a black wolf, beautiful and proud, with one paw stuck in a trap, snapping and snarling at the hunters trying to approach.

Chewing slowly, Brody waited for Sylph to continue. His heart went out to her. For all of its dank, dark hovels the world had points of light, too–good things to believe in, and to strive towards. Did Sylph know this?

"I don't trust anyone," Sylph added, fixedly watching the dance floor as it became more crowded.

"*I* don't put my trust in flesh and blood," Brody hastened to assure her. "My dad taught me to find something and believe in it. An ideal."

"A daydream," Sylph countered dismissively.

"No. An ideal is something pure and perfect. It's not what we are, it's something that we strive to be. Something we live and die for."

Sylph looked back to him. She was amused. A lioness, at ease in her kingdom, watching a cub play mighty king. "Mm-hmm. And what's *your* ideal, O Silvertongue?"

"I..." Brody pressed his lips together. He thought of his father, kind and wise, and then of himself, an eleven year old clutching a bloody baseball, murderous wrath consuming him. He tapped his fork against the edge of his bowl. "I don't really know yet."

"No?" She smiled. The strobe lights came on, throwing rainbow spots on everything. A Backstreet Boys song began playing to the delight of the wriggling bodies on the dance floor.

The music's beat urged Brody to move along. Sylph looked beautiful there across from him, her pale eyes sparkling, her skin glowing crimson or turquoise or plum as the lights moved over her.

Suddenly, she stood up and took his hand and her lips were touching his ear so that he could hear her say, "All *I* know is that *you* like to argue."

His every cell was aflame and his every nerve directed at the warmth of her cheek against his and her ghostly, silky hair cool on his neck. Then he was pulled onto the dance floor, snapping out of his trance just in time to realize that he really couldn't dance, before Sylph's swaying hips, recalcitrant smirk, and hypnotic eyes pulled him under again.

Chapter Three:

Melancholy

"'Meaningless! Meaningless!' says the Teacher[...] 'Everything is meaningless.'"

–King Solomon, *Ecclesiastes 1:2*

Brody's dreams haunted him that late night.

Whether it had been the unfamiliar combination of dancing, an obliging sip or two from Sylph's second mimosa, and leaving for his apartment an hour later than usual, or whether it was just stress, Brody could not escape the cocktail his brain stirred up.

He was shaking hands with his father, and his father was smiling proudly but sadly, shutting the front door of the house. Brody knew it was a farewell, but he didn't want to leave. He raised his arm to knock and stay with his parents for just a bit longer, but now it was too dark to see. He stood on springy loam. The stars were out. A few coyote pups cackled somewhere distant.

The moon arose over jagged treetops as if lifted on strings for a theatrical play, illuminating the empty meadow that he was in. The bright, lunar light suddenly became long, silvery tresses–a fan of smooth hair spread over his naked chest.

Now he dreamed that he lay in some elegant bed in a large room with dark moldings and a healthy fire in a marble fireplace across the room. Sylph slept beside him, her hair fluttering with her breath. She was softer in sleep, like an arctic fox in fur of white, instead of the angry wolf he'd likened her to before. Their closeness felt right to Brody. He had never been with a woman so intimately; he'd never fallen in love before. But in this dream, he was and he had.

Brody got up carefully, not wanting to disturb her, and went to tend to the fire, stupid with sleep. A large, thick white fur rug was spread before the grate. Only–

The rug lifted a large head to look at him with eyes like two suns. It wasn't a rug, but an enormous creature with a cruel beak and wings folded close to its leonine body.

Brody stumbled back, suddenly burning with shame at his nakedness, burning as if that pair of blindingly-bright eyes were searing him–but no, it wasn't the monster's eyes, it was the fire from the fireplace. Reaching out to him, consuming him, melting him alive–

Starting awake to reality, the absurdity of the dream was fully realized after Brody's heart had ceased racing. He clutched at the pillows beneath his head, squeezing them in his fists, frowning but smiling at the ceiling invisible in darkness above him.

He had about an hour before his alarm to wake up for school would go off. Returning to slumber for such a short while would only upset his sleep cycle, so Brody sat up, still snickering at himself. Him? Sleeping with Sylph? In the trappings of a manor from a fairy tale? And the creature! Brody had recognized it as a griffin, but he had never seen its like outside of storybooks and fables. Why would one appear in his dreams now?

Brody began to dress as sunlight warmed the bedroom of his cramped apartment. All the place had to offer was the bedroom, situated so that it faced the main street outside and all of its noisy traffic, a bathroom sporting rust and grout, a living-room-slash-kitchenette, and a closet here and there. He barely had elbow room, but it was all Brody could afford and at least it wasn't a high-crime part of the city, although there were robberies now and then.

The bizarre dream kept returning to Brody as he nibbled toast and sipped OJ over an essay he was trying to write for one of his classes. And then his thoughts turned to Sylph again. Last night had been the most fun he'd had since arriving in the city. She was a wonder, and she really *was* attractive, in a suave, mysterious sort of way. He chuckled again. Though he wasn't sure he was ready to romance her, and certainly not in the way his dream had suggested, he supposed things could shift that way soon.

While he sat there, getting crumbs all over his paper, thinking over how grand it was to finally have a friend in one of his classes, a knock came from the door by the kitchenette.

Concerned, he arose slowly, dusting off his hands. Was it the landlord come once again to accuse him of paying late rent when really the check was just lost in the pile of mail on his cluttered coffee table? Maybe old Mrs. H. had come to ask him if he wanted some of her cookies, or the young couple from Maine had stopped by to ask if he could babysit again. But no...

It was Sylph. Brody didn't even have a chance to fully recognize her before she squeezed in around him, setting a greasy bag and a tray with two coffees on the counter.

"Sorry, had to knock with my shoe," she said, "My mom always hated when I did that. Some people are so anal."

"Do come in." Brody grinned, closing the door behind her. "How did you find where I lived?"

"You told me last night."

Had he? Brody watched her set her purse on his beaten-up armchair and then hover over his essay. He was seized by a sudden impulse to clean, and began dashing and collecting papers, biology books, study cards he had made for himself, and unwashed dishes, stuffing them in their proper places.

Sylph didn't comment on it but she said, "I think you misspelled arraignment,'" tapping his essay on her way over to the window, where she stood observing the street outside like a soldier studying an unfavorable battlefield.

"*What?*" Brody rushed over to check. He didn't feel up to rewriting a whole page of his ten-page essay. It was true. He had missed an "r."

"You had a long night," Sylph said sympathetically but with a roguish smirk. Then, in a more business-like tone, she spread her hands and declared, "Hence, the coffee and donuts. A peace offering. And a reward for trying to do the cabbage-patch, that was pretty rad."

Brody's smile became pained. He hadn't been doing the cabbage-patch, but rather trying to avoid stepping on anyone's feet or bumping into them. He didn't correct her.

"Come on." Sylph swept past him, whiffing her perfume in his face like a rain-rich breeze coming down from the mountains to refresh a summer meadow. She snatched up the donuts, took a coffee, and waited for him by the door. "Let's walk and talk. We can do all the sitting we want in class."

Brody hesitated, looking at his botched essay, but then the sun peeked through a cloud and the brilliance of it gleaming through his window nearly stole his breath away and inflated his sense of defiance. He was a hard worker. A goal-oriented student. There was a time once, when he had been younger and free, when he would've loved to gambol outside, wild and curious and full of a zest for life. He massaged the scar on his neck. Was he going to give all of that up so easily?

Without a word, he took his coffee cup, opened the door for Sylph, and led her downstairs where he held open the lobby door for her. A pleasant gust sent her hair up into his face as she slipped by and he was reminded awkwardly of his dream.

"Um, someone should tell you that that's not a thing anymore," Sylph teased, nodding at the door as Brody let it shut slowly behind them. "Chivalry's dead, dude."

"Ah-ah, don't you start," Brody argued with a roll of the eyes. "If it's dead, it was murdered."

They bickered playfully all the way to the park in the center of the city. As far as parks went, it wasn't much: a few acres of green grass with some benches and a central fountain in the form of a bugling elk standing on a rock. They chose a bench under a cherry tree with tiny pink blossoms just beginning to spread their petals and ate their donuts in companionable silence.

Sylph finished first, and, licking the glaze from her fingers while rummaging for a napkin in the bag, she said, “Penny for your thoughts.”

Brody considered... He’d been thinking of his dream. After making a few edits in his mind, he related it to her sans bed-scene, skipping from standing in a moonless field to confronting the giant griffin. Sylph appeared amused. She sipped her coffee, looking at the elk statue, a child romping by, the cars on the street, as if they were all hers. Brody noticed her smile to herself enigmatically and then she gave him a friendly look.

“I can help you look it up?”

Brody was taken aback. “Look what up?”

“The dream. Maybe it means something.” She caught his skeptical look and added, “Hey, dreaming about giving a presentation naked or cramming for a test are one thing, but mythical monsters with glowing eyes? Dude, that’s just trippy.”

For his major, Brody had taken a couple of psychology classes, which taught that dreams were the brain’s way of dealing with the day’s issues, tossing in a few of the more lingering sights and sensations it had picked up while awake. Dreaming about his father, he understood, leaving his parents, his home, to get an education had been difficult for him and the parting still stung. Dreaming about Sylph, well, that was pretty self-explanatory. But the beast? Where did *it* come from? Then he thought of what Sylph had said–giving a presentation...cramming for a test...school.

Brody leaped up, pushing up his sleeve and looking, aghast, at his watch. His first class started in six minutes!

"I'm gonna be late!" He looked helplessly at Sylph, who appeared unconcerned.

"Oh no, the sky's falling," she said emotionlessly, gathering up their garbage with no sign of haste. "Cool it, Speed Racer, it isn't the end of the world."

Brody got ready to make a sharp retort but she interrupted him. "How many classes have you ever missed?"

At Brody's meek silence Sylph nodded and said, "We will walk to campus nice and easy, I'll walk you to your class, and you'll go in with your head high and your chest out. Everyone'll think you were just held up by your girl."

Brody felt a slight warmth in his cheeks. If his fellow classmates, let alone his professor, assumed that *Sylph* was his girl, they'd probably be too busy staring at him in wonder to resume the lesson. But really it *was* Sylph's fault he was late...she owed him this favor.

They left the park at a bustling gait, Brody pacing like an athlete training for a speed-walking marathon at every crosswalk barred by traffic. In his agitation, he forgot to cut through "C" street and take the longer but safer path to school, instead darting through alleyways along a little-known shortcut.

Here, car alarms blared, people could be heard shouting aggressively at one another from inside apartments much shabbier than Brody's own. Old, hunched women pushed shopping carts full of knick-knacks, and youths in ill-fitting clothes stared with mocking, and at the same time, wounded, sneers.

Brody had learned to ignore them. Apart from the occasional idle shouted threat meant to make the aggressor look tough for anyone listening nearby, Brody had met with no trouble. But halfway along his route, in the middle of a sun-bathed alley between a laundromat and a decrepit credit union, he stopped short, remembering that Sylph was with him. Why had he brought her here? Though she didn't look at all frightened, Brody felt angry at himself for dragging her into an environment that the lack of police presence alone classified as dangerous.

"What's up?" Sylph asked. "What put the fire out?"

"We shouldn't have gone this way," Brody replied, torn. Should he take her back the way they'd come? Or just hurry on through? They *were* almost there...

Seeming to guess at his motives, Sylph looked ready to snap something at him, but then she perked up, looking at something behind him, tense, like a hare spotting a distant predator. He followed her gaze, immediately alert. There across the street, a confrontation had arisen. A small boy, whip-thin, wearing a backpack, probably a student hurrying to school like Brody, had been accosted by two unruly-looking characters loitering by a dumpster in an alley thick with shadow.

The boy hesitated, lingering, and that was all it took. The pair of criminals grabbed the boy and dragged him, squalling and clawing for a handhold, into the darkness. Great sounds of struggle ensued and Brody could just see two silhouettes tearing at a third struggling on the ground, attempting to remove his backpack while at the same time beating him to keep him silent and still.

"We should–" Sylph cut off, surprised when Brody sprinted across the pothole-laden asphalt to the opposite sidewalk and stood glaring into the alley. Anger, disgust, and concern all churned within him like winds in a vortex along with a question: *why?* Why was humanity so venomous? Why was Man so cruel?

Taking a quick breath, his eyes slowly adjusting to the inner-alley brawl, Brody fixed an aggressive stare on the larger of the two bullies–a man maybe ten years Brody's senior.

"Leave, now," Brody said firmly. His mind flashed briefly to the woods behind his house many years ago...to the deranged man he had foolishly ordered to stop.

The other thug, looking up with one foot hovering in the air mid-kick, sized Brody up, snapped, "Get lost, man, this don't concern you," and drove his boot into the shoulder of the boy rolling about on the ground.

Brody took a step into the alley and the older thug tensed, reevaluating him warily.

"What is it that you want?" Brody asked civilly. "Tell me and maybe I can give it to you."

Both of the thugs eyed him greedily. The older nodded at the younger. While the older returned his focus to the boy, bending to riffle through the backpack's contents, the younger thug approached Brody, drawing something–a knife–from the back pocket of his pants.

A sickly wave of melancholy washed over Brody. *Why?* But then his anger and dismay transformed into that old, powerful feeling from that time, years ago, in the woods. Hatred and fury coursed through him like fire billowing through his veins; writhing in his insides. His awareness of the moment, and his place in it, dulled and faded like it had when he'd smashed his baseball into the drug-addled madman's skull.

Brody's temper broke, and as if watching, detached, from someone else's body, he strode forward and struck the man hard in the throat. Taking the man's knife, he continued moving, locking the other thug with a dangerous, intent stare. Brody slashed once with the blade and the man jumped, dropped the backpack, and ran from the alley, dragging his companion along.

Sylph rolled around the wall from where she had moved out of their way, something fierce on her face. It was a passionate but brutal expression. Seeing her instantly caused Brody's blood to cool and he deflated, his clenched muscles relaxing. The vitriolic combination of emotions that had just left him now brought him shame, and the look on Sylph's face didn't help. That light in her eyes was almost crocodilian; sharp like the points of holly leaves, sparkling like the tip of an obsidian arrowhead. He shook his head irritably.

"You can fight?" she asked.

Brody, shivering with adrenaline, looked the boy over with a well-trained eye. The poor kid was beyond tears and in that worrisome stage post-trauma where he could only moan uncomfortably, gazing at nothing from pouchy, swelling eyes.

"My father always stressed the importance of being able to take care of yourself," Brody said, speaking with forced cheer for the boy's benefit. "He would say that it's important to 'talk smart, think quick, and fight well.'" He finished up his assessment and carefully guided the boy's head down, facing his knees. "I don't care what experts say.

You don't want to tilt your head back with a bloody nose. Too much blood in your stomach'll make you sick. Spit it all out."

To Sylph, Brody said, "He needs a hospital. They kicked his head really good." He sighed. "And I should probably get a hold of my professors. I don't think I'll be making it to school today."

At the hospital, Brody waited anxiously in the ER lobby to hear about the boy's condition. His stomach growled with hunger, but he barely noticed. Sylph sat down beside him, holding out a sheaf of papers: graded assignments and homework. She had gone to school to collect the day's work and explain to their professors what happened.

Brody accepted the papers but didn't look at them. Sylph spoke quietly. "Pretty cool how you rescued that kid. Your teachers were all impressed."

He didn't say anything.

"What's eating you, champ?" Sylph pressed.

Brody lifted his head, meeting her cool, crystalline eyes.

"I… This…" He breathed out heavily, depressed. "This world is a miserable place." His heart ached. Pain, poverty, selfishness…he had seen it all that day.

"Hey," Sylph moved as if to touch his arm, then drew her hand back and said, "What happened to having ideals? Something to die for?"

"It's a bit harder to believe in, sometimes," Brody said glumly, thinking of the ugly wrath that had surged within him when the thugs attacked.

"Well don't give up! Because of you that boy has hope! Faith in humanity–"

"Because of me that boy has medical attention," Brody snarled. "Any faith in humanity he might've had was taken from him today, along with his dignity." Then Brody softened. This girl, who had more right to bitterness than himself, was trying to cheer him up. Maybe she had found something worth fighting for. Perhaps *he* had helped her to find it. The thought warmed him a bit.

"Sorry," he said. "Maybe you're right."

"'Course I am!" Sylph cuffed his knee. "I know what'll cheer you up. I'm gonna head on home and see what I can find out about that dream you had. You take a load off. Watch some *Survivor.* Smoke some pot."

Brody raised his eyebrows.

She shrugged. "Or not. See ya."

Filled with gratitude, Brody watched her leave. He had just settled back in his chair and began reading over his pre-law homework when a nurse came out of the ER, a sweet smile on her tired face. Brody stood up and the woman held up her hands in a calming gesture.

"Todd's fine," she said. "A minor concussion and some deep muscle contusions but that boy's going to be alright. He's resting now. His parents are on their way."

Relieved, Brody thanked her and departed. He treaded wearily towards his apartment, considering squeezing in a nap before work. When he checked for mail at the front desk, he was handed two letters by the landlord's wife before she promptly returned to the book she was reading.

One of the letters was political junk, but the other was from his parents. Stamps were cheaper than a phone bill, and with tuition and living expenses costing what they did, Brody had had to make some sacrifices. At times these letters were the only things that kept him going; kept his chin up. Tearing it open while tripping up the stairs, Brody read hungrily by the wan hallway lights, remembering to step over the toys the child from Maine always left outside on the rug.

There wasn't too much in the long letter other than encouragement and love and a few updates. His father's cancer was in remission–*What a blessing!*–some new houses were being built in town–*Like we need more houses*–his mother had spotted a doe with a leucistic fawn and sent him a sketch of it with the letter.

Brody's mother was a talented woman. The fawn's normal, speckled pelt, mixed with patches of pure-white, made the baby deer look as if it were half-finished. Making it into his room, Brody sat on his bed, wondering if his mother could identify the creature from his dream if he sent her a drawing.

The letter ended with his father reminding Brody of the bright future he had. He was so proud of his son. He knew how difficult living in the city was, far from home and hearth, but he reminded Brody that great sacrifices often yielded great rewards in the end; that by giving something up, something was gained in return; that the higher the mountain, the more beautiful the view at the top, and the more mountains there were on one's journey, the stronger one was by the end of it.

As usual, the letter from his parents heartened Brody, and the words were like a blanket that warmed him as he drifted off to sleep.

Chapter Four:

Discoveries

"Snatch from the ashes of your Sires / The embers of their former fires;"

–Lord Byron, "The Giaour"

That night, deep in the silent, dark hours after his work shift and before dawn, Brody dreamed again.

He walked between fourteen lamps, seven on either side of him. Each was tall, with a plate of fine-smelling oil at the top of the thin iron post, but though the seven on his right burned brightly, flames turning the oil into sweet-scented smoke, the seven on his left were deep in shadow. The darkness clung to them in tendrils, syrupy and sickly like cobwebs of tar.

When Brody moved closer to one to examine it, strange feelings crowded in upon him: fury and anger, belligerence. Hatred. He wanted to lash out; to seize something and tear it to bits.

Alarmed, he staggered back and into the proximity of the lamp burning directly across from the one he'd investigated. This time a warm, judicious feeling embraced him. It was clarity and patience. Nothing could bother him because he could deal with whatever problems arose with level-headedness and wisdom.

Brody stepped away and stood with bemusement almost in between the lamps where he'd first started (though a bit nearer the lit ones). Some awareness of the dream came upon him, and he looked about with a more detached air, wondering lethargically what was to happen next.

All of a sudden, the seven bright lamps flared up even brighter, as if encouraged by a gust of wind. A large pane of glass was illuminated at the end of the aisle of lamps, standing of its own accord. Brody saw himself reflected in it–and behind him loomed a great, pale beast, the same monster from his previous dream, giant on its claws, towering at a height of more than seven feet.

Brody gasped and spun around. Two orbs of sun-brightness, the creature's eyes, dazzled him, blinded him, above his head. He threw up an arm to block that stinging light, that stabbing beak.

In that instant, Brody awoke. The arm he had put up to protect his face in the dream now tossed the pillow from his bed. It struck the keys to his apartment from his bedside table, which clattered against the wall, and he sat upright, hair askew, nerves frayed.

In the time he spent getting ready for school, Brody came to a definitive conclusion: he could not keep this up. His schedule was already busy and stressful *without* dreams that disturbed what little sleep he got. Though he didn't believe in dream interpretation as Sylph had intimated that *she* did, he really did wonder if finding out what the big creature represented would help to ease his dreams.

When he entered his first class of the day, Brody sensed that he was the object of a more intense scrutiny than usual. Having heard that the previous day ever-prudent Brody was late to class because he had rescued someone from a mugging, they didn't know what to make of him. A few eyed him as if hopeful of catching his attention and conversing, but he ignored them and went directly to Sylph at their usual private row.

"Looks like you're big man on campus," Sylph said in greeting.

"No longer just a face in the crowd," Brody agreed dryly. He rubbed at his scars. Sylph noticed. She squinted at his face.

Her eyelids were shaded a glittering plum today. Something about the lighter tone made her look friendlier, like the long-haired cat that had wandered into their house one day and claimed his mother as its human. Though it did little more than tolerate Brody and his father most of the time, there were days when it would curl up in Brody's lap and purr away like a tiny Harley.

"You sleep okay?" Sylph asked.

Brody filled her in on the new dream and all she said before the professor called the class to order was, "Let's go to the library after school. I think I have some idea of what we're looking for."

And so, after his final class, Brody could be seen stepping over the fine, oak threshold into the college's old and many-shelved library.

Here, books–mainly heavy, drab textbooks meant to provide supplementary research for projects–tightly packed the multitude of bookshelves and cubbies, heavily perused by students and faculty for many, many years.

Slipping around tables crowded with sleepy schoolmates turning book pages with about as much interest and forced effort as if they turned over blocks of cement, Brody found Sylph at a small, private window-table, its surface laden with not-oft-used tomes.

"What'd you find?" he asked, sitting across from Sylph in a patch of sunlight.

"See for yourself," she replied cryptically, turning one of the books toward him, her thumb holding a place in the pages. With a flourish she parted the covers to reveal a griffin, standing on two legs as if dancing. Here in print it looked almost as fierce as the behemoth that haunted his sleeping hours: its tongue lolled from its wicked beak, its front-half was shaggy with feathers, its hind-half lean and short-furred. Talons sliced on the front bird-legs, claws were shot on the back leonine paws. Wings were spread on its back. Apart from a few small details, it resembled the monster from his dream exactly.

"Yep, that's it! W–I mean the one in my dream's more muscley, and white, and it had ears, but this... Man, it looks scary..." At the last, Brody remembered to lower his voice in the sanctimonious quiet of the library.

Relishing the effect her efforts had had on him, Sylph watched him scan the text with a pleased smirk.

Brody touched the image. He could almost hear it crying out. What would it sound like? Would it shriek like a bird? Roar like a lion? He looked up, puzzled. "But why would I be dreaming about griffins of all things?"

Sylph shrugged and said, "Maybe you saw one in a painting or on a poster somewhere recently and just forgot. I found it in this mythology book," she tapped one of the spines in a pile of books, "and it had references to other books. There's a griffin in *Alice in Wonderland*," she tapped another book, "And here, in this book about popular heraldic symbols," she indicated the one open before him. "Honestly, I didn't know where to start looking at first until one of the librarians gave me some suggestions. There's not what I would call a *wealth of information* about them."

"But what *is* it?" Brody pressed, taking up the mythology book and opening it to a folded page, laying it atop the other book. "What does a griffin *mean*?" Now he looked upon an illustration of drably-hued griffins diving down from cliffside aeries to attack men on horseback. Each paint-stroke bespoke the violence of the assault, every sweep of color blending into a hectic myriad that unsettled Brody if he looked too closely.

"Well, it originated in the east, but there's so much lore on it that it's hard to get a clear picture." Sylph spread yet another book atop the first two, showing him a black and white image of a pair of griffin-head earrings on display in a museum. "It's right up there with dragons and unicorns. Pretty trippy."

When she reached across him to indicate the image, her hair brushed his cheek and her hand brushed lingeringly against his arm in returning to her side.

Brody's skin tingled where she'd touched him and heat crept up his collar–a very different kind of heat from the sort that he'd felt in that alleyway. Her face was very near his, her red lips close enough that the heat of her breath stroked his chin. Flustered, he had to take a few seconds to regather his scrambling thoughts.

"And *why* would griffins be haunting my subconscious, little-miss dream-speaker?"

Sylph picked up a tome, opened it, and said in a bracing and punctilious way, "Let's find out."

Time ticked by while the two friends sat there, researching in silence except for occasionally pointing out a picture or a snippet of information that particularly interested them. The more absorbed he became in the research, the less Brody noticed Sylph's nearness; the patchouli scent of her hair; the pressure of her leg against his; the curve of her lips.

Fascinated, Brody drank in pictures of a Greek tomb-painting showing skinny striped and speckled griffins; a cheek-piece of an ancient horse's bit that displayed two griffins rearing up and seeming to attack a central, horned, bull-man; a griffin drinking from a fountain on a Frankish belt buckle. And there were more: Egyptian friezes of griffin-headed men, Roman architecture panels showing griffins with flowering tails, Persian jewelry with horned griffins standing tail to beak.

The lore was, indeed, varied. They were guardians of a Minoan goddess, chariot-pullers for Egyptian deities, they pulled Apollo across the sky with the sun, they jealously guarded the Scythian treasure.

Brody had been raised acknowledging the dual nature of Man. Of life. In all mortal, transient things, there was both good and evil. Children, so sweet and innocent, often said the most hurtful and malicious things. The rose, with its sultry, waxen petals, bore sharp thorns. To Brody, things were black and white, right or wrong. He never saw in shades of gray. Sometimes, things that were normally wrong might be right–if a man had to steal food for his starving family, for example–but, to Brody, things were never iffy. Well, he began to see some of this same duality reflected before him in the griffin. It was a guardian, a companion to heathen gods, a stone sentinel atop cathedrals, Christ-like in its kingly form and divine splendor. But it could also be rapacious, greedy and wrathful. It hovered over ships to feast on sailors. It abducted people for the devil's whims.

Was that why Brody had dreamt of this creature? Because it symbolized his hunt for an ideal? Represented what he believed in? Was this monster a subconscious extension of himself? Maybe a physical manifestation of the wrath that seemed to consume him at times? He shivered at the idea.

A couple of hours later, they were no closer to an exact answer as to what Brody's dreams signified, if anything. That was not to say that Brody didn't discover other things that were just as interesting, however. About forty minutes before he would have to start worrying about leaving for work, Brody pressed his finger to a rice-paper-thin page in a heavy anthology of essays and said, "Listen to this,

"'Man has mastered his greatest gift over the years: words. He has given sight with poetry, given life with prose, founded nations with declarations, and started wars with speeches. Yet, over the centuries, Man has determinedly clung to something more prosaic: the symbol.

"'The symbol, that grandfather of letters and language, is more than just a sign on a wall. It is meaning that has been compacted into an image. People of all nations have rallied behind the symbol on a flag. Superheroes have displayed a symbol on their chests and vigilantes have worn symbols over their faces in the form of masks. So is it too much to study the relevance of the mythological for to understand Man's nature? To understand the subtler currents of meaning and identity that words, alone, fail to express?

"'Look at the vampire and his sadistic lust. Do we not all have an insatiable hunger? A passion that drives us to madness? And, like the werewolf, who has not succumbed, at times, to a bestial nature of uncontrollable rage or hatred? Yet even in Man's darkest times, he finds an anchor; something, some spark to snatch hold of in order to retain his humanity and remember his goal. Maybe that anchor, that symbol, is his family crest. Maybe it is a scar, a wedding band, a tattoo.

"'The griffin is such a symbol. The griffin *is* Man; all of Man's complexities, all of Man's sins and virtues are reflected in this binary being: the dark animal nature, and the noble, lofty idealism that makes philosophers and dreamers gaze in awe at figures of history painted astride their snorting steeds and gasp in wonderment at the general's words of inspiration to his steely-eyed troops. This is the creature that represents one of our most precious aspects: our *potential*, which causes even the most lackluster heart to be stirred, to shine, and to proclaim, "this...*this* is truly Man, made in the very image of the Almighty God."

"'The griffin is the symbol to keep fighting–to encourage those afore-mentioned dualities to come to terms with each other and to channel the combined might of their immortality into protecting all that is just, righteous, and moral.'"

Brody looked up at Sylph, his broad smile full of cheer, just in time to see her wipe a startlingly condescending expression from her face. She looked as if she had been warring with the urge to roll her eyes in disgust. Brody couldn't understand it–the essay had spoken to him in the same way his father's lectures spoke to him. His spirits were lifted–he felt that he was glowing with a rare kind of eager energy–the kind that moved people to sudden exhibits of wild vivacity, like a free-spirited sprint down a hill or a throwing open of the arms in speechless euphoria to bask in an especially beautiful sunrise.

Before Brody could raise a question, Sylph glanced at the clock on the wall over the exit and said, "You'd better get goin' for work," her tone as mellow as usual.

It was getting late. Brody stood quickly, gazing helplessly down at the mound of books. Sylph waved him away, joining him on his feet and resting a few books on her hip. "I'll take care of these. Go on–we'll talk tomorrow."

Brody gave in, but as Sylph moved away to re-shelve, he grabbed the book he had read aloud from, and went to find the checkout desk.

Chapter Five:

Devastation

"Where there is no imagination, there is no horror."

–Sir Arthur Conan Doyle

Sylph did not show up at Brody's work. He was a bit bemused; he'd thought she would be just as excited to discuss what they'd learned as he was. But eventually his own thoughts distracted him and when he returned to his apartment, he fixed himself a late dinner of warm porridge and ate while reading the anthology he'd checked out.

Curled up in his chair, time progressed without his being aware of it; the nighttime traffic beyond his window dwindled and was soon overtaken by the thick silence of a city asleep.

Part two of the essay he had read earlier aroused Brody's sense of accord just as the first part had. "There is great evil in the world," the author had written, "Some will say that the prevalence of crime has statistically decreased, but if this is true, what does a decrease in crime matter if the crime has become more repugnant? Or maybe criminals have become better at hiding their crimes? Or, most concerning of all, in light of the rising opinions that good and evil are subjective concepts, perhaps what was once foul, unwholesome, and corrosive to one's well-being is now considered harmless, innocent, and humane."

Thinking of the debate with his professor, Brody snorted in agreement.

"We need more griffins as our symbol, our sigils," concluded the author, "We need a reawakening of that mighty creature from times of knighthood and warrior's-tale, for the vampires and werewolves are closing in. And they are hungry."

Brody turned the page and saw a brief bio of the work's author, including a badly-saturated black and white photo. She was a pretty woman with light, wavy hair and a welcoming smile. In her life she had been a grief counselor, a famed essayist, an advocate and speaker for military veterans, neglected children, victims of terrorism. She had passed away about five years ago, leaving behind a husband and son.

Brody's spirit soured. This woman, so persistent in her search for modern-day heroes and "never-say-die" fighters, had vanished from the earth in the same way her griffin symbols had. He touched the essayist's name, in bold, above her biography.

"Esther He'klarr... You will be missed..."

The days passed sluggishly. Brody wrote back to his parents, and resumed his dull routine of work, sleep, and school. His only reprieve from this schedule were the times he spent in Sylph's company. She didn't bring up the essay Brody had read and neither did he, remembering her reaction and not wishing to cause her discomfort. But they did discuss what they had learned about the griffin and half-jokingly tried to apply their new knowledge towards deciphering Brody's dreams.

In the following days, Brody had no more bizarre visions of the terrible, giant, white griffin, and the whole thing began to fade into memory. It had been weird and random, yes, but maybe (most likely) Sylph had been right and the griffin was nothing more than a subconscious ghost stirring in response to his rekindled efforts to come to terms with an ideal. Though homework remained tedious, work so-so, there was one addition to Brody's normal schedule: he began paying closer attention to the world.

Brody bought a newspaper every day and scanned the headlines and leading stories. He turned on the radio in the mornings and evenings and listened to the reports. He found a television station that he liked and tuned in regularly to the broadcasts. Brody had to side with Esther: crime seemed to be just as booming a business as ever. In fact, there seemed to be a lot of it–more than he would've expected, *much* more. Robberies, brutal confrontations, murders, coups and uprisings, and corruption the world over seemed to take worse and worse turns the longer Brody paid attention.

When he brought it up to Sylph, she only said, "Blood sells. It's not like they're going to write stories about which puppy was adopted from the pound or who got promotions at work."

But Brody disagreed. There was something more than just a morbid fascination with the grim and grotesque on the part of journalists and news anchors. There was an *ambience*...a tension in the air, like a foul scent on a wind or a bad taste in the mouth. Something foreboding and oppressive day by day crept up Brody's spine until at times he felt as if he could barely leave his bed. But leave it he did. Midterms were coming up and it was vital that he maintain participation points and take copious amounts of notes to prepare for testing.

Sylph provided welcome distractions from the mounting stress. Her lack of concern for the issues of the world bothered him, but brought him release as well. There was peace in ignorance, and simple joy in shrugging away the burdens of life to dance or talk about nonsense with a witty, pretty woman. And Sylph was a very pretty woman.

The more time they spent in each other's company, the more comfortable Brody felt. When she drew near, he didn't shy away. When they walked the streets together, she slung her arm around his waist and he draped his across her shoulders, and it was as natural as if they'd grown up together.

Sometimes she came by in the evening to pry him away from his studying and watch a movie on his small television set, and sometimes she stayed the night. She usually fell asleep before the end credits, her faint snores buzzing like a bumblebee, and he would cover her up with a frayed quilt and shuffle off to his own bed. Oftentimes he lay there, clutching at his own blankets, watching his door, waiting...maybe hoping...for it to open, and that Sylph would come in and join him.

When he left his apartment one morning, Brody brought the anthology of essays with him to turn back in. He had checked it out twice more since first reading it and now almost had it memorized. He had plans to meet with Sylph after school to study...maybe he would finally bring up Esther and her inspirational words. Maybe it would actually bring Sylph a little cheer to hear more about the heroic griffin–a noble fairytale to replace the melancholy story told to her in her childhood.

Preoccupied with such thoughts, Brody made his way to campus.

The day had been long and busy, but not without its merits. Sylph had been good company as usual, and had appeared very interested in what Esther had to say. Perhaps he had only imagined her first, adverse reaction. She had even joined him for more drinks at work and before he knew it, his shift was over and it was time to go home.

But Brody didn't leave. He and Sylph spent the next few hours immersed in casual conversation, discussing their classes, laughing about things their classmates had said, joking about their professors. Sylph shared her drinks with him, and, without really realizing when it happened, Brody's mind became fuzzy and detached. Laughter came easier, and the latent attraction he'd been harboring for Sylph began to float to the forefront of his thoughts.

Midterms? Ideals? Crime and strange happenings and dreams? What did any of it matter? All that mattered was the carmine of Sylph's lips; her sparkling teeth; her twinkling eyes. She had been a friend to him; shown him the kind of respect and affection that he hadn't felt since leaving home. And he wanted nothing more than to kiss her, right then, if his vision would only stop swimming and if he could focus enough to follow through with the desire.

Eventually, it grew too loud to converse as the late-night crowd filed in and the DJ set up his turntables. Sylph declared it was time to take him home. Brody's boss, amused at Brody's tipsy, uncoordinated gait, bade him goodnight, and Sylph, hooking her arm in his, began escorting him along the drowsy streets toward his apartment.

"You're like a sieve," Sylph teased him after a while. "Can't hold your liquor."

"I think that phrase only qualifies if I throw it all back up," Brody slurred, thinking that there was a strong possibility of him doing just that. He had consumed more alcohol on this night alone than ever before in his entire life. And how? He had just been having a dapper conversation with Sylph and the drinks had kept on coming, and now he could hardly see straight.

"Well, excuse me," Sylph said with exaggerated offense and laughed lightly at his expense. Brody tried to focus on her. In the streetlights that illuminated the sidewalk, and the darkness in between, Sylph herself seemed split in half, one side of her bathed in light, the other half seeped in shadow. He blinked hard, forcing back his creative mind's eye. For a second, it was as if Brody could hear the heartbeat of the world and see the individual threads in his jacket, then the dizzying sensations passed. With the hand not trapped 'round Sylph's arm, Brody massaged his scars absently.

"You ever going to tell me the story behind those?" Sylph asked.

Brody considered...then decided that there was no better time than now, in his intoxicated state. So he told her everything. The dead hiker, the mutilated and dying derelict, the anger that had burned away his fear and drove him to savagely attack the man. Old memories floated back up into his mind like rotten things in water. The whole time Sylph remained silent; even when Brody had finished, she didn't speak.

"So that's how," Brody said. "Throwing myself at a maniac. A lot of good it did." A loud truck came up the road behind them, its headlights reflecting painfully off of the closed storefront windows. Brody grimaced, suddenly nauseated. “But my father would tell you there are worse scars,” he mumbled, trying to control his stomach, “Deeper scars.”

“Well...” Sylph said, as softly as if she were miles distant–or was she? Brody wasn’t certain of his location on the material plane anymore. “Well...he would know.”

Then Brody toppled and spun away as if the earth had moved. Those headlights filled him with knives of fire. He tried to right himself, arms flopping. The screeching of tires made him turn his chin into his chest.

An odor of rubber.

A flash of silvery-blonde hair.

His name screamed out.

Then something struck his lower body so forcefully that he spun into the air, tumbling up along an unyielding surface that crackled beneath him. He hit again–his face this time–and then he was flying, fragmented, numb, fading to a place where there was no reason for thought. No room for pain.

Chapter Six:

Pebble Embark

"Dead men don't fight back."

–Tolmezzo

As he drifted, the babble of raised voices quieted until silence pressed upon Brody's ears. The refreshing, night breeze chasing away the stink of the city became chill and dank, like the air in a cave.

Brody floated, intangible, between dreams and deep sleep. A red moon arose from an invisible horizon. It hovered, round and malevolent, over a sea of bubbling tar. As he watched, his mind muddled and his thoughts disjointed like a jumbled-up jigsaw puzzle, two people appeared out of the darkness.

A man and a woman walked hand-in-hand across the top of the tar. Where they stepped, the oozing liquid solidified and became opalescent puddles of crystal. Brody didn't recognize the couple–he only saw them from behind–but they stood tall and unafraid and beautiful.

Then something happened. The woman stumbled, and the man immediately after. The tar began to crawl up their legs, sucking them down, stretching across their bodies until they were smothered and their cries were muffled. In a few quick minutes, their struggles ceased and they were pulled under. Gone.

Though still only half-aware, Brody's heart twinged as if some deep part of him knew that he'd just seen something tragic, something that had complex, profound repercussions for the whole world and not just two random strangers.

The tar began seething and boiling madly. Arms and hands reached up from its depths, and then hideous, malformed faces emerged, jaws stretched wide to moan their first, foul breaths. Hundreds of these creatures crawled up out of the ooze. Many were downright monstrous, with narrow, dog-like skulls, thorny bear claws, or stretching, bat-like wings, but most common among them were figures that resembled malformed humans. They stood, skeletal, mutilated, some with extra, multi-jointed limbs, some with horns, and tar dripped off of them in gooey strands. But when the tar had finished running off of them, every figure in the vast multitude was revealed to be a human as plain as any Brody had ever seen.

Unassuming and unremarkable, each one of them wore a long, black cloak. Their faces were blank, placid, as if listening for instructions, and did not at all betray the monstrosities of the true forms beneath their fleshy costumes. In unison, each head turned up to look at where Brody hovered. As Brody drifted away into nothingness, millions of eyes flickered red all around him like a universe of stars, ever-watching and patiently waiting...

In the way of many heroes before him, and many after, Brody awoke on Pebble Embark's golden shores.

It was a gentle awakening, like the slow emergence from a nap on a breezy, summer day. The sun beat down hot on the side of his body and face exposed to it, but this heat was exquisitely balanced by the rhythmic lapping of cool water kindly washing over his flank.

It was a good while before Brody felt encouraged to leave his position and emerge fully from his stupor. The sun had moved far to the west and the water receded to just touch his toes and the temperature was obtaining the haunt of a chill before Brody's mind snapped-to.

In a burst of energy, he pushed himself up–or tried to.

Brody's body felt oddly-jointed and unresponsive. Even as he cycled through his memories, struggling to remember how he had arrived on this beautiful beach, the sea hushing behind him, a verdant jungle before him, Brody felt that something was wrong.

Gulls, flapping around their nests in the grand, arching cliffside curving down into the sea to his right, seemed unusually wary of him. One circled over his head, reluctantly diving twice to just above him, before shrieking half-heartedly and leaving him alone.

Appealing scents wafted to him from the jungle, rich with the promise of ripe fruits and growing things. The sun painted the sparse line of clouds on the horizon royal-violet, hot-pink, and molten-amber. Even the water sparkled with an other-worldly marvelousness that stole Brody's breath away. It was only when he firmly planted his hands in the sand that a stab of terror unsettled him.

Brody's hands were huge. Scaly, black, and monstrous, each elongated "finger" was tipped with a hooked claw. The sun shone on those keen edges, on the rough, pebble skin. Beginning at his wrists, ebony feathers with an iridescent, midnight-blue sheen, shifted in the slight wind. These feathers traveled up his arms where they were slashed with white bars at the elbows before continuing, dark again, up his shoulders. What he could see of his neck was yellow-on-white, deepening to crimson on his chest, which bled into a white underside. Brody's self-examination became more frantic. Wings–*wings!*–were folded on his back. A long tail, arched like an angry cat's, protruded behind him, tufted with orange-tipped feathers. The rest of his hind-half was not feathered, but furred–the contrast noticeable at about his rib cage where the wing-joints appeared to begin. Long quills with brilliant-yellow feathers at the ends sprang from his body: the longest pair stuck out near his tail, two more extended along his flanks, poking out from beneath his wings, and on his back right in between the wings themselves extended ten more of varying lengths.

Awkwardly lifting one talon, Brody felt his face, mindful of the claws. He felt four more quills set between a pair of large ears which, he realized sickeningly, he could move independently. Most prominently, however, was the charcoal-gray beak poking out beneath his eyes like an unfortunately protuberant nose.

Brody's reaction to the bizarre shape he found himself in was to promptly and heavily sit down. He was a griffin. Somehow, he was a griffin on a beach. The possibility of this being a vivid dream never crossed his mind–nor did the why, or really, the how. He could feel it all the way down in his hollow bird bones: this was real. Everything around him, all of his superhuman senses now told him, was part of a tangible world, perhaps an alternate reality of sorts, as undoubtedly as if he were in one of his college classrooms sitting at a desk.

His fear mounted and the sunlight suddenly seemed too hot, scalding to his dark feathers and pelt. First his tail-tip started twitching, then his hackles slowly lifted in a spikey ridge down his spine, and then he leaped to his feet, his every cell super-charged.

Gasping panicked breaths, he stumbled into the tide and plunged his face down into the lapping water. His beak smashed painfully into the sand and some of it trickled into his mouth, but he ignored it, holding his face under until the next wave rolled in and washed over his talons.

When his skull began to pound and his lungs to ache for fresh air, he pulled his head back, shaking it so that droplets of seawater sprayed everywhere in sparkling, diamond drops. Nothing had changed. He was still a griffin on a tropical beach.

Brody sat again, tilting his head toward the sky so that he didn't have to look at his new body and could pretend that he was still... himself. His eyes stung, but not because of the saltwater and gritty sand. Tears threatened to join the rivulets trickling through his feathers and dripping off his gray beak. Helplessness almost overcame him, almost broke him.

Why was this happening? Why was he here, alone? Where was Sylph? Had something happened to her, too? And what, exactly, had happened to *him*?

The smell of burnt rubber, the screech of brakes, the sensation of flying through the air a split second before his body registered unbelievable pain, flickered in his mind. He clenched his beak against a sob and dug his claws into the sand as if to tear apart the panic and anguish ebbing in his blood like the ceaseless tide.

What would my father do if he were here? He grasped at the question as it floated through his thoughts and let it anchor him. He couldn't really begin to imagine how *anyone* would act in this kind of bizarre situation. But if anyone would've taken it in stride, adapted, and concocted a plan, it would've been his wise father.

Brody took several long, slow, deep breaths–the kind his father had taught him when he was eleven, after he'd started having night terrors about the incident in the woods. Bit by bit, reason returned to him, and he lowered his gaze from the sky and back to the beautiful environs.

Of one thing Brody was certain, besides the fact that he was now in a fantastical realm as true as a heartbeat: this was linked to the visions he'd so recently had of the white griffin. Though he burned for answers, Brody had the good sense to take into account the settling twilight. He had no idea of the region's nocturnal beasts, nor how far it was to the closest civilization. It would be best and wisest for him to create a shelter for the night and then strike out questing at first light. Besides, he needed time to try and settle down and recall what he last remembered. Maybe he could answer some of his own questions.

Rising onto four mismatched feet, Brody hobbled and limped to the tree line. He spent most of the remaining sunlit time scouring the jungle's fringe for something that would leap out at him as useful for making a shelter: fallen trees whose roots would form a den like the one back home used by coyotes; some tree with plentiful boughs that he could climb up and recline on... But all he saw were tall, tropical trees with straight trunks, and a barrier of foliage that grew so close and dense, it would be difficult even for a griffin to muscle through.

At one point Brody passed a trail, and he made note of where it was so that he could investigate it in the morning. Finally accepting defeat, he returned to the shoreline and studied the cliffside for niches or ledges. His vision took some getting used to–if he strained his eyes on something his vision zoomed in on it, causing it to swell in size. He could literally *feel* the powerful flexing of his lenses as they adjusted for his eagle-vision.

There was no room for him, it appeared, up among the seagulls, and he knew that he'd be a very unwelcome neighbor anyway. He was just beginning to give in to the likelihood that he would have to spend the night exposed on this thin strip of beach, trapped between the sea and a potentially hostile jungle, when an irregular shape caught his eye. To the beach's most western edge, a rocky outcropping of vine-and-moss choked stone poked out just over the trees, like a tongue sticking out from between teeth and descending into the throat of the forest.

Just as the moon appeared in the sky, Brody made it to the top of the stone outcrop, a great chunk of time having been spent climbing and jumping up its craggy surface. Though he now had wings, Brody didn't feel brave enough to give them a try. He just wanted to rest up, wake up, and get home–preferably in a *human* body.

Laying himself down at the very tip of the rock, Brody faced the jungle, a shadow in the light of the stars. The cliff would not make for a very defensible position should jungle predators come stalking up while he slept, but at least he wouldn't be surrounded–and he would have the high ground. On all fours he stood at about the same six-foot-two-height of his human form, which probably wouldn't intimidate many big predators, but now he had talons to claw with, his excellent hearing should forewarn him of approaches, and he had wings. If push came to shove, Brody supposed he could survive the fall, though he was hesitant to try. He had to admit that, deep in his heart, the idea of flight enamored him, but he was too tired and bemused to try at the moment. He would rather return home, find Sylph, and tell her how he felt about her.

Despite all of his fretting and precautions, Brody's senses and instincts told him that he was safe. The beach felt to him like a neutral zone, a gateway of sorts, beyond which would be adventures good or ill, depending on how the die fell. And the hundreds of chirping crickets and the susurrations of the waves and the gulls in their nests cooing to their mates were anything but ominous. So Brody finally allowed his mind to wander and his thoughts to spin, his head resting back, chin on his chest.

He and Sylph had been walking and talking... He had had too many drinks. He distinctly remembered descending through the stages of drunkenness: becoming pleasantly buzzed, unpleasantly concerned at how slippery his focus was becoming, and finally carelessly *un*concerned as the world swam around him and his body became tingly and charged. And then walking to the apartment. The headlights. The sensation of his limbs flapping grotesquely like a rag doll in a dryer and his bones shattering like peanut shells under a shoe. Misery and, finally, true fear, not panic, began to worm their way into Brody's heart. Had he been hurt badly enough that he had... died? Was this Heaven? It didn't seem right, though. Where were the angels? Was there a sun and a moon in Heaven?

Brody looked up and his mounting worries were washed away at the sight of the night sky.

"Wow," he gasped, and so great was his wonder that the sound of his own human voice coming from an eagle-beak escaped his notice.

The stars were so many that it was difficult to tell whether the sky was white with indigo speckles or indigo with white speckles. Great, nebulous stellar clouds made mountainous, ethereal formations in muted, dreamy colors, glittering at their fringes with solar dust of gold and silver. A comet suddenly bisected the sky; a brilliant, white-hot streak as fast as a flash. After he'd blinked the image of it away, Brody made an unintentional cat-like mewling sound.

The constellations were *dancing.*

As if awakened by the comet, stars coalesced into obvious forms yawning across the heavens. A centaur kicked up his heels, a dragon twined its neck around a tree. Orion fired an arrow that exploded into meteoric fragments which then rained down on the Gemini twins who capered with starry maidens.

The longer he gazed, the more Brody saw–until it seemed that *he* floated up among the astrons, frolicking in moonlit clouds as soft as down, causing the constellations to laugh with amusement as he rolled among the planets and joined their mysterious dance in their infinite realm...

Brody was unaware that he had fallen asleep until he opened his eyes to brazen sunlight and the roguish nip of dawn. He was only partially dismayed to see the beach below him instead of the floor of his apartment–the indescribable experience of the night before still lingered. But it was time to seek out answers and then make a game plan. Wherever he was, despite its tantalizing beauty and impossible magic, he had people at home who cared about him and who would worry at his absence.

Standing, Brody stretched, his back arching fluidly. There was much to be said about his new form; he could feel its raw power, and his super-senses made him feel quite impressive, like an apex predator among ants. Being a griffin wasn't like being stuffed into a bulky, four-legged costume. It was a complete transformation. Though it would take some time to adjust to his new abilities, it would be more like a child's transition from crawling to walking, and not like a struggle to completely re-learn simple actions. Like any predatory creature, Brody had a sense of his capabilities and he was just as much at home in this body as his own human one.

Newfound power aside, he hadn't accounted for his hunger. A grumbling pain in his gut and a demanding burn in his esophagus immediately caught his attention. He could ignore it, forage for fruit in the jungle, or (his gaze drew towards the seagull colony) he could try hunting. Did griffins eat meat raw? He hoped not, though something told him that his raptor beak wasn't there for chewing a cud. Well, he could worry about preparation later. His safest option was probably to try his hand, or talon, as it were, at fishing.

As a cat has difficulty descending a tree it has climbed, so Brody faced the same predicament on his high, stony perch. He paced back and forth, glaring down the steep rock wall, much more intimidating looking down than it had been the previous night looking up. A frustrated growl vibrated in his throat and he was distracted for a time when he discovered that he could spread the long feathers at his tail-end into a fan and close them again into a bright bushel. Finally, when his claws had scored countless hash marks into the rock, sending strips of moss floating to the sand to be picked at in a cursory way by bold seagulls, Brody spread his wings.

Their size astounded him. The interiors, white and eggshell with some faint, gray patches, dazzled in the sun. When he stretched them as far as they could go until the muscles trembled delightfully, the tips were so far distant from his body that he couldn't believe that they belonged to him. They were lightweight, and the tiny inner feathers twitched in the salty sea-breeze.

Brody paused a moment, then slowly moved his wings in what his new instincts told him were a natural motion. With a majestic rustle, they revolved forward, down, back, and up in the circuit of an oval, or maybe a figure eight. The pinions brushed the ground, sending pebbles skittering. He tried again, and again a little faster, his fore-half suddenly rising up.

"Whoa!" Brody laughed, exhilarated, his hind legs tensing to push his weight back forward. This could work. He stretched his neck over the cliff. Should he jump off, like a hang-glider from a hilltop? The hawks back home seemed to fly best when they left their tree branches, diving headlong instead of power-flapping from the ground.

He braced himself, large ears nervously twitching toward a sound. This went against everything he had ever been taught about gravity and human beings' submission to it.

In the periphery of his field of vision a brilliant-white dot suddenly spread and shut wings of its own. The rational part of

Brody's mind rang alarm bells–it was way too large to be a seagull–and his head snapped up, thick, feathery neck-ruff hackling, to the cliffs across the beach from him.

There at the top, above a funnel-cloud of gulls shrieking piercingly and leaving their nests to flee before it, stood a griffin much larger than Brody. But it was not just any griffin...it was the great, hulking beast from Brody's dreams. As white as a cloud that had fallen from the sky and snagged on the narrow plateau, it stood taller than a Clydesdale. The distance was too great for even Brody's untrained griffin vision to distinguish minor details, but the monster's eyes seemed to be glowing yellow like flames and there seemed to be a black net over its face. A war mask?

For moments they stared, Brody feeling like a scrawny kitten discovered on the turf of an aggressive tomcat. He frantically tried to remember what a lion did to look humble and harmless. He hunkered low in a crouched position, eyes slightly averted and half-shut. Maybe it would go away. But wait. Griffins were also part eagle. What did *birds* do to look non-threatening? The giant griffin screamed a violent cry punctuated by a terrible lion's roar, its own vast wings thrown wide.

Idiot! Brody thought, talons clenching, *They fly away!*

And the white griffin folded its wings and dropped over the cliff, sending gulls wheeling and dodging. Halfway down it spread its wings again, longer than a small airplane's, and glided straight at him.

Brody balked, stumbling back, terrified at the behemoth's swift, unfriendly approach. He half-fell-half-lunged off of the outcrop, crazed with self-preservation. The sea exploded to dominate his vision. Warm wind thundered around him. He heard a sound behind and above him as of something immense striking rock. With a minute lean to the left, keeping his wings rigid, Brody curved gracefully around his outcrop. The beach slid into view, and out of the corner of his eye he saw the white griffin right behind him.

Brody flapped hard and with each wing beat he scooted up and ahead, gaining speed. Flapping exhausted his energy, though, so he stuck to using his smaller size to his advantage, curvetting and diving and once, even rolling. He had no time to admire the view that flight offered him. He folded his wings briefly to shoot under the arch of rock that plunged into the sea and heard his pursuer swoop over it.

They followed the land, keeping it to their left. Now Brody faced a minefield of jagged stones stabbing up from the sea like teeth through a blue pelt. The water was choppier here, agitated by the strange columns interrupting the tides. There was no beach here either; the land rose steadily to tree-lined cliffside. Brody stuck close, hoping to find a break he could dart into. For good measure he dodged side to side to keep the white griffin on its toes, maybe tire it out. It was alarming to think that the only way Brody could know if he was going too slow would be if–when–he felt its talons in his spine.

A great tree, larger than his whole university campus, loomed out over the sea ahead, its roots climbing down towards the water and anchoring it in place. Brody angled his wings and rose higher–higher–until the jungle was a lumpy green mass below and in the distance he could see mountains. He found himself on a level with the highest branches of the enormous tree. He reached out with all fours and hit a bough so hard that his momentum almost sent him over it. Impact thudded up into his joints where it was absorbed indignantly by his muscles. Bark split and burst into flakes over his claws and his wings tore leaves loose. Panting heavily, he looked over his shoulder.

The white griffin filled his vision.

With a yowling squawk, Brody pitched forward into a somersault so that he was clinging, back-down, to the branch, his forelimbs wrapped around it. The other griffin sailed overhead, bringing a shower of scents with it: gunpowder, smoke, rain, the pages of an old book, ink, and a myriad of others. Brody blinked the disorienting crowd of scents away, scrambling back onto the tree limb proper. His pursuer wheeled around back towards him to try again, white as angel's wings, blindingly pristine. Brody began to despair.

"Hey!" A distant voice–a *human* voice! Brody's ears and head spun and revolved, seeking out the welcome herald.

"Hey! Down here!" A crimson speck of color appeared between two jagged leaves. Far down below him, in a cave formed from the tree's roots and the cliffside, waved a man in a brilliantly-colored shirt.

Swift as a starling, Brody leapt beak-first from the branch. The white griffin turned to follow, now as silent as a puma ready to spring. With an aerobic feat that surprised even himself, Brody calculated his distance from the cave mouth, positioned his wings, and flitted right in. The man had pressed against the wall to allow him room. Grabbing at the sandy cavern floor, Brody skidded and fumbled to stop. The cave widened in the back, and he was aided in his efforts when he hit the rear wall face-first; which stopped him very fast indeed.

Ignoring his own weariness, Brody turned, speaking into the darkness that rapidly resolved into clarity as his vision adjusted.

"Hurry–hide! It followed me!"

The man had followed him back, his stride indicating nothing close to concern. His clothes were wild: a spicy-red cotton shirt with deep-green embroidery and a violet vine motif, beige trousers and indestructible-looking workman's boots. He had a pointed face, longish black hair, and expressive, sparkling, calico eyes that were at once steely gray, sky-blue, pale green like the Caribbean Sea, and unusual, shining-gold. Close up, Brody could see that the man was not much older than he was–maybe in his mid-twenties or early-thirties. He had a critter on his shoulder like a weasel or a rabbit. It squeaked at Brody in a cheerful way.

A peculiar sensation washed over him suddenly, like a skin of cool air sliding off of him, and Brody found himself small, trembling with fatigue, and very much human. Instead of relief, he felt hopelessness. He was now much weaker and more vulnerable–a mouse against a raptor. He held his hands up, staring dejectedly at the long, talon-less digits now only good for holding a weapon that he didn't have. A pale light shone on them, from his face it seemed, but he had no time to consider this new puzzlement.

The white griffin appeared in the cave mouth, entering gracefully, its hulking frame filling it up and blocking the light.

I thought griffins were supposed to be good! Brody thought. He moved to stand protectively in front of the human stranger, reminded unpleasantly of his useless efforts years ago to shield the hiker from the deranged man. The griffin came forward slowly, talons clicking and paws thudding, massive shoulder blades shifting as it approached.

"Stop!" Brody commanded, voice breaking, wrenching his mind away from unhappy memory. "You get back!"

The monster's eyes changed from a quite-literally-glowing yellow to a muted black and flax. The sclera were as jet as nothingness. Slitted pupils, wide in the cave shadows, studied him intelligently from the midst of the golden irises. Now that it was so close, Brody saw that it didn't wear a mask; intricate black markings like fine henna-tattoos twined around its beak, eyes, and short, cat-like ears.

To his astonishment, the beast *did* stop, sitting docilely on its haunches, still watching him from a good three-or-so feet over his head. And then, to Brody's even greater shock, it spoke in a voice like slow thunder.

"You fly well."

Brody straightened and startled when the man said loudly and jovially at his shoulder, "That was a neat trick on the tree branch! Don't think I've ever seen it done before!"

A person can only be pushed so far before his limits are reached and he must either act, speak, or give in to the pressure. His residual tension, mounting anger, and adrenaline obliged Brody to the second of these options.

“What–what? What just happened?” His tone was dark.

“You were tested,” said the griffin. “You passed.”

“Chasing me around was a test?” Brody’s tone quivered with wrath.

“Israel wrestled with God,” the griffin said curtly, in a manner that suggested Brody should consider himself lucky.

Brody stammered nonsensically and the man took the opportunity to say, “Congrats! You’ve earned your title for sure.”

The weasel added, “For sure!”

Brody was too overwhelmed to acknowledge that the rodent could speak except to swat at the air in its direction. “Title?” he repeated.

In a grand voice that somehow warmed Brody to his bones and cleared some of the cobwebs from his mind, the griffin declared, “Welcome to the Land of Dreams, Great Griffin Prince.”

Chapter Seven:

Royal Destiny

"...Let the man we are seeking be exceedingly fierce, harsh, and always among the first wherever the enemy is, and in every other place, humane, modest, reserved."
–Castiglione, *The Book of the Courtier*

Though the griffin's greeting had stirred within him some strange elation, as though he had just been told that he'd won an all-expenses-paid trip to all of the best places in the world, Brody's tone was still frosty.

"Who are you? Where is the Land of Dreams? And why did you call me a prince?"

With a loud, good-humored sigh, the man began bustling about, removing small pots and mugs from a pack. The scent of food wafted up to Brody, almost making his knees weak. The weasel helped to set up. The *talking rodent* parsed out placemats. Brody focused on the white griffin, to whom the task of answering his questions had apparently fallen. A *griffin*. And he, himself, had flown on actual wings! Just where exactly *was* he?

"You are of the royal griffin lineage," the griffin began.

Brody frowned. "But my father wasn't–he never mentioned–"

"It is not that sort of lineage," the beast interrupted, not unkindly. "Yours is a rule not determined by heredity, but by destiny.

As you were being knit together in the womb, you were chosen. The throne, the crown, the scepter, are your inheritance."

"And where does the griffin part fit in? How is it that I can transform? Or you can speak English? None of this is possible." But it was obviously real. What explanation could there be? He was crazy? On drugs? Maybe someone had slipped something into one of his drinks? A powerful bit of memory resurfaced as he wrung his mind, seeking an explanation: headlights, a flashing curtain of hair, the fragmentation of his thoughts like butterflies one by one lifting into flight.

"Here, possibilities are limitless," said the griffin. "The only boundaries are what the human mind is incapable of conceiving—which is sometimes quite little. The Land of Dreams is what it is: a beautiful place beyond reality and comprehension, above mortality. It is the manifestation of all dreams past, present, and future. Every human has been here, every human has contributed at least a thread to the tapestry of wonder that is the dreamworld. Few, however, have the gift to fully appreciate its magnitude. You are one who does. As such, you are capable of ruling and protecting it.

"As to your transformation and my language, understand that there is little to understand here. What spare rules there are upon which this realm turns are not the same that keep your reality from collapsing into chaos, but they *are* set into place by minds far superior to any man's. What you must understand, you will. What must remain enigmatic, shall.

"Here, the body is capable of reflecting the soul. The protectors of this land are blessed with a form of majesty and power. Thus, you are a griffin. Once you have fully adjusted to your...transition from reality to fantasy, you will be able to transform at will. The griffin form is as wielding a fine sword or wearing a cape of fine cloth; it is no costume with which to play. Practice grace and respect, for it is a symbol of the power and nobility with which you have been entrusted."

It was difficult for Brody, especially as shell-shocked as he was at the moment, to understand the griffin's aloof way of speech and riddle-like turns of phrase. He felt like laughing; giggling madly. It was all just so absurd! Yet...what other explanation was there?

The griffin intruded upon his musings, the feline ears focused his way. Muscles like plates of steel shifted beneath that white pelt as the griffin moved its talons. "The human mind is beautiful, terrible, fragile, corruptible, unstable. It requires protection. Your protection. Your guidance."

"Why me?" Brody asked.

The black and yellow eyes flickered. "Why did the potter make his vase? Why did the carpenter carve his table? What right have the vase or the table to ask?"

I am not just some tool! Brody thought angrily, but immediately cooled. *Humility. That's what it meant. There's something going on that's a lot bigger than me and somehow, I'm meant to help.*

"What do dreams need protection from?"

"Nightmares," the griffin replied bluntly, and when Brody thought of the blinded madman from his past, the dead hiker, the beast seemed to have read his mind. "Yes, the most crippling fears in your heart. Dreams are hope, inspiration, challenges, the strong foundation of a wise man's soul. Nightmares corrode this foundation, drown the mind, and eventually, unchecked, *claim* the soul. These nightmares, if not vanquished or overcome, become Rankers." It looked away, out the mouth of the cave, and Brody saw that its hackles had lifted on its spine and all the way up its neck, fur and feathers as jagged as a snowy mountain-range.

"The nightmare-shepherds," murmured the griffin. "The stewards of fear and the children of evil."

Brody suddenly recalled the strange dream he'd had as he drifted through the place between sleep and waking up in the dreamworld. Had those awful creatures been Rankers?

"What do they want?" he asked quietly.

As if it hadn't heard, the griffin said, "They are amassing. We know not how, or what ultimate goal drives them on. They stir in the deep reaches, in the shadows. Like vermin they squirm in the cold and the murk."

Finally, the creature looked back down at Brody, and something in the young man's eyes seemed to soften the terrible majesty of that eagle brow.

"*You* bar their way. *You* are their greatest threat. With your armies gathered behind you, you shall strike fear into their black hearts."

A strangled laugh threatened to escape Brody, but it died in his throat and became a tiny whimper. *No one* feared him. He was no one, nobody. A hick-kid with a lame job, a cheap apartment, and a big mouth with foolish notions of idealism. But then a startling thought came to him.

"Can they hurt my family?"

"Not now, weak as they are," the griffin said.

"But if they become stronger...?"

"Then yes, even reality would be in peril."

"Can I send them a message? My parents? To let them know that I'm okay?"

The griffin's ears flattened momentarily, as a cat's will when it hears a loud sound. For the first time since it had started speaking, the beast was at a loss for words.

"It shall be as it is willed..." the creature began solemnly, then in a precise and rather apathetic way, continued, "You were struck by a vehicle going approximately forty-five miles per hour. Around half of the bones in your body were broken on impact, and upon striking the ground. You were taken to a hospital, Prince, and there you rest, comatose, until the die ceases rolling."

Brody felt as if his lungs had been squeezed and held tight in a vice. Taking deep, loud breaths, he bent over, trying to calm down. The back of the cave helped to support him–he leaned against it and slid down into a squat. His bones felt like paste and, according to the griffin, many of them literally were. He wasn't sure if he felt like vomiting or bursting into tears.

"Will I wake up?" Brody's voice tremored.

"All shall be as all shall be. The sun rises and sets, the seed becomes a tree, but not all eyes witness such changes. Yet, whether you see them or not, the cycles still turn until the race is finished by all. You are but one shining star among millions, Prince. With bravery and faith, you shall burn brightly until the day you are welcomed into the bosom of eternity and are gifted a very different kind of crown."

Though some of the words were still bizarrely perplexing, they helped to comfort Brody a little. They meant that he was but a small part of a grand plan, and whatever happened to him in the end, death would be just the first step in an awesome journey. It reminded him of something his father might say to him. Yes. He could be brave, and faithful.

Brody managed to control his breathing and the nausea went away, leaving him feeling weak, but cleansed. He *hoped* he would see his parents, and Sylph, and all of his old hometown friends again, but for now, he had a big job ahead of him, and who knew what sort of adventures were in store? As the griffin had said, what happened, happened.

Studying him, the griffin nodded, lifting its head, and smiled. It turned its head to the man now smearing some intoxicating-smelling condiment over round pieces of flatbread and said, "I shall return by dawn." That said, it then clicked-and-thudded its way to the cave entrance, long tail outstretched behind, and ducked out. Brody heard the enormous wings flapping open a moment later. He stood and went to watch, but in the short time it took him to stand uneasily at the lip of the cave, the mysterious white griffin was gone.

"Forgive Michael," said the man, now handing the weasel the flatbread so that it could add pieces of meat to the spread, using its forepaws daintily, "Answering questions is above him. And I'm not being facetious."

Brody was taken-aback that the griffin had a name, and that the man had referred to it as a "he," rather than an "it," though it made sense. The creature was obviously intelligent, and its voice had been quite clearly masculine.

"Is he a prince too? Or a king?" Brody asked, returning to where he had been sitting and watching his two remaining cave-mates work.

"No, he's a Celestial. An angelic being."

Brody decided not to comment on that at the moment, his head still fit to explode with all that he had learned. But he thought of the brilliant, glowing eyes and suddenly felt very small.

"He's here for me?" Brody tried to wrap his mind around the concept that an angelic being had deigned him important enough to converse with.

"All three of us are." The man folded the flatbread over. "We're going to escort you to the throne. There are a few things you need to do before you're qualified enough to become king. You have to learn a bit, get trained up, let the council fill you in on the nitty-gritty of what's been happening. Then, when you're ready, there'll be a few ceremonies and *voilà*. You'll be king. That'll grant you the office to rule without having to seek advice or permission from a higher council.

"Here," the man twisted where he sat cross-legged and held a plate piled with food up to Brody, who tried not to look too eager in taking it.

"What is it?" Brody thought to ask, before taking a famished bite. He didn't care if it was poison–whatever it was, it was perfect.

"A quesadilla." The man grinned at him. Recognizing the tastes of guacamole, chicken, cheese, and black beans, Brody grinned back. He sat beside the man, who extended his hand and said, "I'm Josiah."

He looked about, spotted the weasel timidly crouched among some canvas-type bags and added, "That's Rexus. He's a charlatan."

When Brody looked at Rexus, the creature flinched so that all Brody could see were the charlatan's eyes. "It's a pleasure to meet you," he said kindly, and Rexus perked up and squeaked so loudly that his long ears trembled.

As they ate, Brody and Josiah talked. Josiah shared stories of his own travels in the dreamworld, describing sights he had seen, things he had learned, people he had met. He explained that he was one of a few dreamers who could recognize and control their dreams. He was Spanish on his mother's side, which had been a big part of his growing up. He also explained that some things, some people, were not real, but dream-created–like Rexus.

"The older his creator grows," Josiah said, stroking the Charlatan's speckled back, "the more experiences she has and people she meets, the stronger Rexus will become. He'll become an independent, created being...a conglomeration of all of the personalities and events that have profoundly affected his creator until he's as unique as you or I." He heaved a sigh. "It's remarkable."

Brody remembered his more recent dreams, blushing in embarrassment at the idea of Sylph and he in bed together, and hoping that, in the cave's shadows, Josiah couldn't see. "Was that Michael in my dreams? Um...watching me?"

"Protecting you," countered Josiah, now cleaning their plates with a cloth wetted from a waterskin, "and whatever else it is he does. Sometimes he sends messages, but they aren't always clear."

"Messages from whom?"

"Who do you think?"

Brody was silent, suffering that small feeling again, and Josiah said, "Michael told me that yours is the clearest mind he's seen in a long time… I have to say, you don't seem as concerned as I expected you to be."

Brody was thoughtful, choosing his words. "My father was a soldier. He fought in Vietnam. He always taught me to have an ideal–to find something worth fighting for and stick to it because that's what keeps you going. I don't know, I guess I'm still searching for it… maybe I'll find it here." He chuckled. "Fighting to protect the Land of Dreams sounds noble enough… When 9-11 happened, I wanted to enlist. I thought I'd found my ideal. Father didn't approve. He never said, but I could tell. He knows what war does to you better than anyone. I don't think he wanted that happening to me. So I promised him I'd go to school first, get a degree, and then I wanted to enlist as a medic, or a chaplain. Save lives. Help the wounded soldiers like they helped my Dad when he got shot…" He hesitated, then sighed and gazed out of the mouth of the cave. "Looks like I'll be doing some fighting anyway."

Brody wrapped his arms around his legs and after a courteous pause, Josiah said, "Sometimes battles have a healing effect too. Wildfires cleanse the forest. A virus purifies the body."

Brody smiled thinly. "You sound like Michael."

Josiah let his head drop back and barked a laugh. "*You* travel with him for three weeks and see what it does to you!"

The very thought chilled Brody. Spending that much time with Michael would doubtlessly affect *anyone* in a great way.

As the rest of the day passed, Brody chatted amicably with Josiah, accepting rare interjections from the shy charlatan with an obliging nod. When the temperature began to drop and the moon to rise, they all sat at the cave mouth wrapped in thick blankets, sipping hot cocoa heated with a few drops of what Josiah said were an elf potion. It was supremely cozy.

"Did you arrive here last night?" Josiah asked drowsily.

"Mm-hmm."

"We saw the comet. Michael said it was an omen. It's how he knew you were here."

Brody's eyelids became heavy. The sound of the waves, the rustle of wind through the leaves of the giant tree somewhere above, were a lullaby of sweet promises. Earlier, Josiah had told him that, after he was ready to be crowned king, they would journey to the fortresses to reinforce and resupply them, paying attention to any reports of suspicious Ranker-type activity along the way. Though his chest started to ache when he dwelled on how grief-stricken Sylph and his other friends and family in reality had to be, Brody was charged with excitement: griffins! Elves! Castles! Flying! A sleepy smile twitched his lips and he snuggled deeper into the blanket.

"Oh...before I forget..." Josiah lazily reached out for one of the packs. Rexus, a spiral of tail, spine, and ears curled between them, stretched and retrieved something from within the pack, returning and handing it to Josiah.

"Thanks... Here," Josiah leaned forward and gave Brody a long violet feather with pale yellow chevrons. A griffin's feather. "It was your predecessor's. King Uriah. He's the one who ruled before you.

It's tradition for griffin kings and queens to pass a feather or a talon down to the next in line. A symbol of trust and faith."

Brody held the feather against his body under the blanket. "What happened to him?" he mumbled.

"He died," Josiah's voice was far away...a gentle jumble of sounds that vaguely made sense but didn't really matter. "So now it's your turn to rule. The Rankers killed him, and he died at the same time in reality. That's how things work here..."

How what works? What killed who? Brody's focus was slipping. But before he could grab it, sleep overcame him and the questions went unasked.

Brody awoke with a deep breath of cool dawn air. The sky was still a dark, blue-gray with hints of green to prelude the sun. The seagulls were already up and about, circling the breakers, looking like small, white paper chains. Josiah and Rexus still snoozed deeper within the cave. Brody had remained near the entrance. He pulled the long purple feather from under the blanket and marveled at its length; the way it shone in the daylight. He wished he could try flying again...he hadn't been able to enjoy the previous day's hectic flight, but it was definitely something he would like to try again.

Michael arrived soon after, winging right past him into the cave with but a whisper. Standing, Brody slid the feather between the hem of his jeans and his belt. The griffin said nothing of where he had been but lay down and waited patiently for Josiah to awaken. The man soon did, mumbling a hoarse apology for sleeping in, and began to rummage around gathering the packs together. Brody offered to help and was given a pack to carry. Josiah shouldered another, and the rest were carefully laid over and strapped to Michael's back like saddlebags.

Brody was pleasantly surprised to discover that Josiah was also a griffin. The man transformed in a strange, blurred patchwork of shifting colors to become a griffin of brilliant crimson feathers and fur with sporty, black-tipped wings and a darker-red crest of spiky feathers along his head.

Noticing Brody's stare, Josiah gave a chuckle punctuated by a purr and said, "I'm from reality, just like you, just like every griffin you'll meet here. When I fall asleep here, I'll wake up in reality, and when I fall asleep in reality, I'll wake up here."

"So...you aren't in a coma?" Brody forced down a surge of bitterness.

Josiah clicked his beak, sympathy in his slitted, cat's eyes. "No, I'm not, but I'm one of the few people from our world who can dream lucidly enough to comprehend what's going on. Most people just...float passively through their dreams and then wake up"

"Is it possible to... Could you explain all of this to my parents...?"

Josiah blinked, then looked at Michael.

The white griffin gave Brody a gentle look, the warm, yellow glow emanating from his eyes like fresh, spring sunlight. Brody already knew what his answer was going to be. His heart sank.

"They would not believe such an explanation, child. And even if they did, they would be helpless to interfere. As Josiah said, it is a rare dreamer who remains *compos mentis* in the dreamworld."

When Josiah stretched and unfurled one wing a little to preen it, Brody saw that the pack Josiah had been wearing had also transformed to fit around the long forelegs and the shoulder-joints of the wings.

Between beak-fulls of pinion Josiah said, "Hop on. It took us three weeks to get here and Michael has no intention of the return journey being any longer."

"It is unwise to leave the throne vacant for too long, especially in these times," Michael said sagely.

Josiah crouched, his wings spread enough to expose his spine. "Put your legs behind my wing-shoulders against my ribs and hold on to the bag."

Brody was worried that he would be too heavy–Josiah was a good three feet smaller than Michael in height, and also much leaner of muscle, built like a cheetah moreso than a lion. However, once he'd settled into place, Josiah stood effortlessly and closed his wings snugly, blanketing Brody's legs and hiding his hands.

The two griffins, Rexus, huddled within Josiah's pack, and Brody, took a preparatory moment to evaluate the sky beyond their cozy cave. Brody's heart thumped crazily. Then the griffins thrust themselves out and Brody could not have suppressed the wild, visceral cry that escaped him if his mouth had been taped shut. Josiah's long, curving wings spread to either side, and with a brief pang of envy, Brody remembered admiring his own lovely wings just a day ago. But the day was too glorious to leave him pouting and he exalted the God of his father for witnessing such splendor.

Brody's journey to the capital, to his throne, had begun.

Chapter Eight:

To Be a Griffin

"Once you have tasted flight, you will forever walk the earth with your eyes turned skyward, for there you have been, and there you will always long to return."

–Leonardo da Vinci

Brody felt that he had reached his limit on happiness. If he'd felt any more joyous, safe, and peaceful during that three-week journey, he would have believed that his head would explode. The fact that he faced an imminent future as a king, warrior, and leader of a nation didn't distract him at all. They followed the ridge, flying over the ocean and resting at night among the trees or in cliffside caves when they could.

On the first afternoon of travel, when they had found a glade of flowers to rest in, surrounded by holly and yew, Brody startled at seeing a flash of amber-and-white in the trees, there and then gone.

"'S'okay," Josiah said. He used a quill to write a letter in the waning light of day. "It was a unicorn. They're attracted to purity."

Brody pinkened, remembering the fables growing up–stories about unicorns going to the aid of young virgin women. Josiah said, "Contrary to popular belief, a unicorn will approach most anyone. It's like, if you smell like blood, some animals will not want your company and some will tolerate it. If you're impure, a unicorn'll still approach, but it'll be skittish." He squinted into the trees as if to get one last look at the creature. "The darker ones tend to like males more than the lighter-colored ones for some reason. The one you saw probably just wanted to get a look at you."

The man gave Brody a brotherly smile. "You know, I once heard that when Adam and Eve dreamed the first dreams, they created the very first dream-beings. Adam made a griffin: pride, strength, bravery. Eve made a unicorn: beauty, purity, compassion. These two creatures then roamed the dreamland, settling it, tending to it. Whether or not it's just a Land of Dreams bedtime story, none can deny that the griffin and the unicorn are linked by a strange and special bond."

Brody peered into the shadows, hoping for another glimpse at the unicorn, then focused instead on the small fire Josiah kindled. The fire made him think of his old dream about the fourteen lamps, seven dark and seven light. Then his most recent dream came to mind–the horrible sight of the monsters emerging from the tar and taking on human disguises.

"If this is the Land of Dreams, how can I have dreams while being here?"

"There you go," Josiah beamed at him, fetching a small teapot and some food from his pack. "Now you're getting it."

"Getting what?"

"That there's not much to get!"

Brody frowned and Josiah laughed at the irritation on his face. "Michael, you want to take this one?"

Michael blinked slowly and said, "Humans are dreamers. It is what you do. While you are here and lucid, dreams within dreams can manifest physically, but not always in expected ways."

"If you dream about a bear, you might wake up with a teddy bear in your arms," Josiah added. "But that doesn't usually happen unless you have an incredibly strong imagination. It's usually only children that can spontaneously dream-create."

"When you are merely asleep in reality, your dreams often reflect an adventure that is happening to you in the dreamworld," Michael went on. "But here... Dreams that are formed while *in* the dreamworld carry special weight and depth. They are often the dreamer's way of revisiting memories or simply processing the magic that has touched them throughout the day. Or they are not dreams, but visions."

"Visions?"

Michael's yellow eyes drilled into Brody's with an intensity that implied he somehow knew why Brody was asking–knew about the eerie nightmare he'd had.

"Yes, visions that are meant to communicate a message or a truth to the dreamer from the world beyond."

"From...*your* world?" Brody asked tentatively.

Michael blinked again, but didn't answer.

If that were the case, if it had been a vision that Brody had seen and not a dream, then he had a suspicion that he needed to confirm. "What do Rankers look like?"

Michael's pointed back-feathers instantly lifted along his spine, though he didn't otherwise react to the question. Josiah glanced uneasily at the white griffin before setting up the teapot and folding his hands in his lap.

"Like me." Josiah said, and Brody felt as if a chunk of ice had dropped into his stomach. "Like you. They can disguise themselves as easily as sin can, and they'll often mimic their creators or take on their traits in some way, just like Rexus and other dream-creations do."

Rexus, passing Brody a clay teacup, bared his fangs at Josiah and hissed as if insulted.

Josiah snorted an amused laugh before elaborating. "But Rankers are the *bad* parts of their creator. They're the embodiment of their creator's deepest fears; the manifestation of the worst things their creator has seen, done, and experienced, and so their *true* form tends to resemble that in some way. Each one is unique, but when they aren't in human form they like to hide themselves under long, hooded robes."

"They may seem harmless," Michael added. "They may appear weak. But it is not so. Do not be fooled, child, when you meet a Ranker. They may *look* like men. They may *act* like men. But they are monsters of the vilest kind."

On the second day, more questions about the mechanics of the dreamworld trickled into Brody's mind.

"How did you and Michael know to come collect me at the beach?" Brody asked, picturing some sort of giant siren going off somewhere as if his arrival had tripped a security alarm.

"Pebble Embark is where *all* new rulers wash up," Josiah said. The pair of them, and Rexus, investigated a small, stone ruin, collecting mushrooms and herbs for the night's supper.

"Why?" Brody pressed. He stumbled a little over a rock mostly buried beneath the grass, and Rexus stuck out a paw as if the little creature would have caught him had he fallen.

Josiah shrugged, grumbling at a stubborn toadstool that didn't want to leave the earth. "It's the way it's always been. Michael said once that being a griffin king or queen is just as much about the journey *to* the throne as it is about what comes after. I think he means it's important for the next ruler to start at the beach so that they can pass through their kingdom on the way to the capital; get acquainted with some of the citizenry; get in touch with the way things work around here; develop a respect for the beauty of the place, you know?"

"Mmm..." Brody chewed on Josiah's words, and mostly what Michael had said, for he suspected that the journey *to* the throne also encompassed one's life before they made it to the dreamworld. Had his life really been so remarkable as to warrant his becoming the protector of dreams? He thought of the fury buried deep inside of him that clawed its way to the surface in times of despair and bitterness. Though the fact that Michael seemed to believe in him gave Brody hope, it also placed a heavy burden on his shoulders, as if he were clamped in a vice. He had a lot to learn, and a lot to prove... maybe especially to himself.

Brody tugged a sprig of mint out from near the base of the remains of a fireplace. Something glinted near the hearth, and he pawed away some low-growing creepers and revealed a small, segmented piece of metal, perhaps once one of the fingers on an armored gauntlet.

"And why is everything here medieval?" Brody asked.

"It isn't," Josiah said. He shifted into his bright-red griffin form and lifted his wings to let Rexus scurry up onto his back. "You just haven't seen much of this world. But if you're referring to a lack of technology...?"

Brody considered, then nodded. He hadn't seen any hint of an airplane, phone lines, or even a glass-and-metal skyscraper. Josiah nodded. The black feathers framing his eyes in sharp streaks made him look fiercer than Brody knew him to be.

"I've asked Michael that, too. When you hear the word 'fantasy,' what do you think of?"

"Dragons, knights...griffins." Brody grinned.

Josiah nodded again, the corners of his beak pulling up into a smile. "Right. Fantasy is the realm of possibility and magic, where anything can happen. Well, so are dreams. They're the part of us that long for something else and hope for better things. The closest mankind has gotten to realizing fantasy as a reality was in medieval times, when virtuous knights walked the earth, protecting villages from bandits and swearing oaths of chivalry. Or, at least, that's how storybooks tell it. I mean, even today, a selfless hero is called a 'knight in shining armor.' Many label the medieval era the 'dark ages,' because of the lack of proof of any cultural and scientific developments. But that isn't really so. Peoples' minds were *alive* in the dark ages, hoping and dreaming and creating–and much of what you see in the dreamworld is evidence of the wonder and curiosity of that time, even if there's nothing tangible to show for it in reality. The cars and batteries and computers and things like that that are so common today? Those *kill* imagination, dull creativity, and...bottle-neck dreams."

"So technology is, like, the anti-dream?"

"Not necessarily. There are pockets in the dreamworld where you might see a robot or a steam-powered engine, or a gun, and there are some more modern-esque commodities in big cities like the capital, but they're rare. Things like magic are much more common, and if the dreamworld existed without that magic...well, then it would just be reality."

"And what a shame that would be," Brody said solemnly as Rexus started humming a jaunty tune and patting the fluffy feathers at the base of Josiah's neck.

On the third night, Brody saw beautifully colored balls of light darting in a cluster far above the treetops, piercing the shadows and making the lantern he read by appear dim. He lowered *The Book of Adages,* a compendium of the complex social phrases passed between griffins that Josiah had packed, to stare upward.

"Are those fairies?"

Both Josiah and Rexus followed his gaze–Michael was gone on one of his random errands at the moment.

"Pixies," Josiah said, with the air of someone who'd heard the wrong assumption many times before. "Same family though. They teach children a rhyme here to help them remember: 'Fairies ring and glitter, pixies make pretty lights, and sprites are playful devils that prank like poltergeists.'"

With a delighted chuckle Brody leaned forward. "And elves?"

With a smirk, Josiah composed a rhyme on the spot: "Elegant and noble, wiser than is man, but do not dare insult one with weapons near at hand!"

On the fourth day, just as they prepared to depart their camp and move on, Brody transformed back into a griffin. He quickly discovered that this meant an end to enjoying the simplicity of alternately riding on Josiah's back and camping out. It was time for training. And Michael was to be his mentor.

First, they tackled flying. Brody picked it up quickly. Each of them was different at it, and Brody appreciated those differences. Michael, though gigantic, had no problem at all with flight, as if he could bend the winds to his will, rather than having to cater to the fickle whims of the sky. Josiah was fast; a bolt of red cutting remarkable turns through the air between Brody and the multi-colored patches of land, dizzying him. Brody himself, he came to discover, was gifted with endurance and strength. Should he face a strong headwind, one mighty flap of his wings sent him powering through. He even adopted a way to take off from the ground, a feat difficult for griffins, especially surrounded by obstacles blocking wind currents. He thrust his forelimbs beneath him, his chest out, shoving against the earth with his hind paws and focusing all of his considerable power into the rock-hard wing muscles in his back, neck and shoulders. Michael and Josiah were both impressed, which pleased him to no end.

Then they taught Brody griffin-combat techniques. He quickly learned not to go easy, because he himself was shown no such mercy, and threw all of his energy into wrestling Josiah down when they grappled. Michael had a useful parable for every situation.

"When a warrior handles a sword for the first time, he learns not to exert himself with wild swings," Michael commented one session when Brody was straining to flatten Josiah against the ground. "Calculate. Think of cold, not heat."

Josiah made a sudden movement and sharply pinched Brody's elbow with his beak, drawing blood. With an involuntary hiss, Brody withdrew.

"See?" Michael said. "Move swift, cutting like steel, cold as ice and fluid as water. Save your heat for your blood."

When trying to get the hang of using his talons, scratching at a tree like a cat, Michael said, "One does not strike only with his fingertips, nor does he wet only the edge of his blade. Use your whole talon to rend flesh and the claws alone for a warning." He demonstrated by swiping at the tree and gouging a divot that oozed sap into the feeble stripes that Brody had left behind.

As the woods became more deciduous with a few evergreens, replacing the jungle of tropical plants and trees as the third week began, Michael began to duel Brody directly. Brody felt like a kitten trying to fight a bear. Though he knew Michael was going easy on him, he could not make the white griffin yield and always ended up pinned beneath those giant claws or with his neck grasped delicately in the deadly beak.

“When a runner sees a rock in his path,” Michael said one day, letting go of Brody, who sat back and fluffed his neck feathers to try and get them to settle properly, “He does not trip over it, nor does he leave the trail to avoid it. Challenge what you perceive are your limits, but do not tempt your opponent.”

“I’m not meaning to,” Brody protested. He let Rexus scurry up his back to inspect his throat for injury. “But it’s difficult to adapt. You’re so much bigger than me! And if Rankers are so unique, then how can I expect to settle into a comfortable fighting style when I might be up against something that spits poison one day and...something with six legs the next?”

“Your greatest weapon, your greatest *gift,* is not blade or bow, might or muscle,” Michael’s pupils almost vanished as his glowing yellow irises flashed laser-bright, “It is your mind. Be clever and wise. The mind of man in the body of a beast can be quite potent indeed.”

“Did you tell him about powers yet?” Josiah came from the bushes of huckleberry and rhododendron around the stream they had camped beside, dragging a young stag in his beak. Transforming into a human, he settled to the grisly task of gutting their night’s meal.

“Alright! Venison!” Brody’s spirits lifted.

“Makes a nice change from wild fowl, huh? We’re pretty close to the capital.” Michael must have given Josiah consent via the unspoken communication they shared because he began to explain griffin-powers as he worked.

“Every griffin has them. Sometimes you develop yours on your own, sometimes a dream-creation bestows it upon you in the form of a gift: King Khafra had a harp and King Medici had a necklace of coins. It varies."

"Will my power help me fight?" Brody went to cool his head in the stream.

Michael curled up, shining like a white diamond. "Undoubtedly. That is why they exist."

They reached the capital right on schedule, in the wee hours of Wednesday morning. They stood just in the trees, staring up a rather thin, windy trail flanked by a steep rocky descent to the sea on one side and a thickly-treed gorge obscuring the base of a small mountain range on the other. The trail ended at a thick iron portcullis steeped in shadow by the high, pale stone walls above and on either side of it.

Brody, in human form, felt that his breathing sounded absurdly loud. And he couldn't seem to stop moving his hands–right now they worried a loose thread on the tunic he wore–one of a bundle that Josiah had brought for him.

The clothes were very fine–nicer than anything he owned in Reality–of bright, bold colors with gold-thread stitching, silver patterns of celestial bodies, embroidered motifs of heraldic griffins, stags, vines, apple trees, grapes, and clover. Each tunic, and the vest or sash accompanying it, was of velvet or silk. His new belt was genuine leather stamped with talon-prints. He had also been given a sort of floppy, feathered beret that he was fond of, and some soft, comfy, leather boots.

For this day, the day he would enter the kingdom, Josiah had also fastened a long, glittering gold cape to two buttons at his shoulders. Everything was a little baggy, because the outfits had belonged to his predecessor, but Josiah said that once the royal tailor had his measurements, new clothes would be made.

Brody knew how regal he looked. That didn't stop the jitters.

"We ready to go in?" Josiah asked at Brody's side.

Michael, on the other side, griffin eyes piercing the pre-dawn shadows, replied, "I would rather we avoid crowds."

"You're not saying we take him through the aqueducts, are you? I think the people *should* see him. They need to know that King Uriah's been succeeded."

"Have them ring the bells in the chapel. We must get Brody situated and prepare the council."

Josiah, defeated, sighed wistfully and began to lead the way up the trail, Rexus on his shoulder and Brody hastening to follow. A pushy gust from behind and the whisper of wing-beats indicated Michael's exit.

A good hundred yards or more from the portcullis, Brody and Josiah were hallooed by who must have been a guard. A husky voice rasped down from the armor-clad figure silhouetted against the sky atop the crenellations of the wall overhead.

"*Who goes there?*"

"Josiah Fairbanx!" Josiah still sounded put-out that Michael had denied him a grand celebratory announcement. But Brody was grateful for the anonymity. Rather than identify Brody at all, Josiah hesitated and said in a significant tone, "Change the guard."

The husky voice replied gleefully, "Right away, sir! Lord be praised!"

The portcullis cranked open and Brody heard men rushing about and whispering to one another from behind the arrow slits in the walls beyond.

Though it still slept for the most part, like a great, drowsy anthill, the city set Brody's heart to pounding and his mind to spinning. It even resembled an anthill–far off and high up, he could see the turrets and towers of a good-sized castle nestled close to the dark-stone mountains curving around the kingdom. The city ascended in tiers, beautiful, gilded, pristine. The houses and architecture seemed derived from all sorts of historical periods in reality from Victorian manors to modern villas. He saw a Gothic cathedral, a Romanesque bath house, a bank with somber, Baroque-era elements, and a squat, medieval-style apothecary of heavy cut stone. There was too much to take in, especially at the speed with which Josiah towed Brody along.

What few people there were out and about, yawning widely and crossing their arms against the nip in the air, hardly spared them a glance. Soon, Brody passed beneath a crumbling arch into a derelict courtyard and through a small door in a covered walkway. For the first time since they'd entered the kingdom, Josiah spoke, closing the palace door behind them and shrouding them in darkness.

"Why don't you go on up to your chambers, have a bath, take a nap while we get everything ready? You'll start lessons tomorrow, but we'll have you meet your council and heads of staff this afternoon before dinner."

Brody's knee connected with the wooden handle of a broom or a mop in the dark and he almost fell. "Wh-where are my chambers?"

Josiah caught his elbow and opened another door, shedding light over racks and shelves of feather-dusters, clean rags, candle-sticks, lavender-scented bricks of soap and other supplies in their storage-room.

"Take a right out here, then a left into the Grand Hall. Go all the way down to the staircase, up the stairs to North Tower, and your rooms will be on the left through the door between the suits of armor." Josiah guided Brody out, held his shoulders, and looked into his face. He smiled, nodded, clapped him on the arm, and departed in the opposite direction he'd instructed Brody to go.

Brody stood alone in the middle of the hall, the reality of where he was beginning to creep in. He gazed at the vaulted ceiling and half-columns against the paneled walls, all of rich, handsome wood. Paintings, bisected into two halves, were evenly spaced between the columns, each above a small vase with flowers on a pedestal.

Approaching one as he began to stride down the hall, Brody saw a person painted on one half, in ermine-trimmed robes, wearing a crown, a solemn, regal expression on his face, and a griffin of yellow and black glaring out on the other half. The paintings stretched to the hall's end, with empty spaces for future rulers. Brody paused to study King Uriah, an older and wiser-looking man with a short beard, his griffin form a bizarre violet with yellow markings like gold gilt, and then he looked at the empty space beside it. For him.

His hands clammy, Brody moved on, repeating Josiah's directions under his breath. He turned into the Grand Hall, a long and broad avenue of alabaster, treading along a rug trimmed with gold tassels and patterned red, violet and yellow. He climbed the staircase, peeking out of Tudor-style, leaded-glass windows of diamond-shaped panes at gardens and courtyards. He passed landings, now of brown marble, climbing higher and higher past more halls and doors until finally he saw a pair of dark-wood doors flanked by suits of armor made of electrum, gleaming like the sun and moon united. Pulling wide the doors, Brody's jaw dropped.

An exceptionally rare few in Reality can claim to have seen the same level of finery and opulence as that which embellished the Griffin-King's chambers: rugs of fur, of fine-stitching and a master's weave; fabulous glossy curtains long enough to robe a giraffe; a chandelier that could make ten families rich; a fireplace decorated with coats of arms, its mantlepiece populated with all sorts of intriguing bits and bobs... Expert portraits and landscape paintings shared the walls with tapestries, and a crucifix sat humbly over a bed that was so big, Brody could get lost in it. Everywhere he turned, there was something to ogle at: the suits of armor, the writing desk in an adjoining room that looked like an office, covered in shelves and drawers holding quills, wax for making seals, heavy reference tomes and more. Across the room from his four-poster were two glass-paned doors hidden by curtains that led out onto a balcony. He could look out over the whole city and beyond. Just when he thought his mind couldn't be boggled any further, Brody found the bathroom.

A good two hours after having entered his room, Brody left the bathroom bathed, content, and pleasantly sleepy, having strained what was left of his excitement in experimenting with different bath-bombs in the in-ground, Olympic-sized bathtub. Now he had finally reached sensory overload. Dragging his feet over to the more-than-king-sized bed, Brody smoothed the quilted covers smelling of lilac and honeysuckle, and lay face-down atop them. His arms tucked beneath his chin, legs dangling off the side of the bed, he listened to the sound of giant bells ringing merrily somewhere nearby but muted by stone walls. Then a great crashing cry rose up from somewhere much further away–joyous cries, triumphant yells from an entire city full of people. And then Brody drifted, dreaming of bath bombs that turned into fluffy pink birds before becoming flower petals that spun and danced above bubbles and pastel-colored bath water.

Josiah came for Brody at around two in the afternoon, knocking gently at his doors. Disturbed from his deep sleep, Brody stirred and sat up, mumbling something in the way of an invitation to enter.

Josiah came in swiftly, found Brody rubbing sleep from his eyes, and went to help him stand up, smoothing creases in his clothing and trying to settle his still-damp curls.

As he worked, ignoring Brody's embarrassed, half-hearted attempts to shrug him off, Josiah said, "Your council is waiting. I left Rexus to keep an eye on them and make sure they don't start without you."

Brody's heart lurched like it was full of grasshoppers. "Would they?"

"They're not supposed to. The king begins the session–or prince, as the case may be. But you know, politics being what they are... It's been a month and a half since these windbags have had to answer to someone and I think they like how power fits...especially old Isa... You'll love him..." He gave Brody a final once-over and nodded, satisfied. "Okay. Follow me."

They went back downstairs to the third floor, and wended around the landing until they were at the last room before the next staircase down. Josiah stopped and murmured, "You go in before me. A leader leads. They'll be looking for that."

Brody felt more like a contestant in a pageant than the monarch of a kingdom. But he had faced judgment every day from his professors and peers, walking into his classrooms as the noted pariah. So, with more confidence than a different man could claim in the same position, Brody threw the door open and strode in. Having not yet had the chance to acquaint himself with this room, Brody was disoriented, seeing only faces, furniture, and a row of arching, mullioned windows. But he forced himself to keep moving, bee-lining as he did so for the high-backed chair at the head of a long, dark, birch-wood table.

There were five men and women there, seated, and Brody was mollified at their expressions of uncertainty at his abruptness as they hurriedly stood and re-seated themselves once Brody sat. Even Josiah, closing the door behind him and smiling at the two stoic guards on either side of it, looked impressed. He took the seat vacant at Brody's right. Rexus, who had been clinging to the chandelier over the table glaring beadily at the council, dropped down to recline by Josiah's arm.

"Your highness," Josiah said with formality, "Allow me to introduce your council, bestowed with powers of influence, with the authority to enact the King's will, proclaim his word, and move as his right hand wills. Each has served long and truthfully, upholding the duties of the griffin-hearted."

He gestured to the nearest council member, a portly older woman with a pink apron and silvery hair in a bun. "Councilwoman Persimmon, matron of agriculture and farming." She bowed her head, blushing a little. As he returned the nod of greeting, Brody found himself gauging each person there at the table, trying to read them, and images floated in his mind's eye. Persimmon reminded him of a bucket of ripe and ready apples, or a clicking pair of knitting needles making socks for a grandchild.

Councilman Argo, patron of finance, wore heavy black robes spangled with medallions, and had very slick, oiled hair smelling of spices. He made Brody think of a winking ferret and a firm handshake.

Councilwoman Serafine, matron of trade, was tall and elderly with a heavily-lined face but lovely, pale-gray eyes. She was like a glass figurine or dew shining in a sunrise.

Councilman Owf was patron of battle and as gruff and chiseled as a mountain face.

And finally, Councilman Isa, speaker for the people and patron of services, dipped his head expressionlessly at Brody. A tall, gaunt, and bony man, Isa was balding but had a short gray beard around a thin-lipped mouth. His eyes were cold and he reminded Brody of a spider or a snare. He didn't seem...evil, but Brody sensed that it was as Josiah had said: this man enjoyed his power and would enjoy having more. Of everyone there, Isa made Brody feel like a student back in a classroom the most.

"He is young," Isa said to Josiah, who made a "thanks for stating the obvious" face and then gave Brody a covert, beseeching look.

Scrambling, Brody asked, "What is the plan? It is a true pleasure and an honor to meet you all, but Michael has informed me time and again how short we are on time, and I should like to proceed with this meeting quickly."

"Yes, to business!" Councilman Argo proclaimed approvingly.

"Such courtesy! The people will like him," Persimmon said to Isa, who only blinked slowly, stretched sideways in his chair with his cheek resting on his fist.

"Tomorrow you will begin your courses," Serafine said. "How to manage foreign affairs, how to battle and ride, and there will be some remedial courses on history, geography, and etiquette. When you are ready, you shall be crowned king, and entitled to make your first proclamations."

"This sounds like it will take a while," Brody said apprehensively. What would these mysterious Rankers get up to while he was away learning how to differentiate between a soup spoon and a dessert spoon?

"Our kings, unfortunately," said Isa, "Are oft not long in their thrones. The land must adjust and readjust to the constant cycling through of its rulers. Perhaps showing caution and restraint will prove beneficial to a longer reign, sire."

Josiah's eyes flickered red but only Brody saw. "Our kings are out on the battlefield risking their necks for the people, Councilman. Perhaps you should show more respect and be grateful that your own cavernous gullet is nice and safe from the chopping block."

Ignoring Josiah's last, Isa said calmly, "I meant no *dis*respect."

The other council members watched the exchange like attendees at a ping-pong game.

"What of the Rankers?" Brody asked.

"In due time, sir," Isa stood and bowed stiffly at the waist. "As you said, time is of the essence. If you will excuse us, we have tasks to attend to."

The other council members began to follow suit, mumbling meek tidings to Brody as they shambled out of their chairs.

A hot flash went down Brody's spine as if he were in griffin form and his wings had flared open. His hands spread on the table, fingers clawing at the wood, and he shouted, "No!" in a voice that rang around the room, snapping off the walls. Persimmon jumped and blushed again. The others whirled about with varying degrees of surprise. At his tone, the guards at the door moved to stand in front of it, blocking the council members from leaving. Isa looked furious.

"I *will* be kept informed." Brody's eyes were round and terrible, the irises rings of glowing red.

Though perhaps a fool, Isa was at least a bold one. He drew up his bony frame. "You are still but a prince! As such, we–"

"Will have records of accounts sent up to your room," interrupted Councilman Owf, with a look of loathing in Isa's direction. "They shall inform you of firsthand experiences, battles won and lost, eyewitness reports and known Ranker identities, though I warn you, it is not for reading before bed, in the dead of night."

"Thank you," Brody said.

Owf bowed deeply. "Your highness."

Brody stood and Josiah followed him to the door where the guards moved aside. Brody could've sworn that one of them was grinning on the other side of the visor on his decorative helmet.

When they were in the corridor and Brody began walking he-knew-not-where except that it was downstairs, Josiah laughed loudly and said with glee, "Well, old Isa's gonna be eatin' some humble pie for dinner!"

Now that he was away from his council, Brody felt much more relaxed and welcome. "I didn't intend to become impolite."

"Oh yes you did!" Josiah's laughter slackened into a happy sigh. "But at least you were *politely* impolite."

"'No!'" Rexus squeaked, mimicking Brody's frown and baring his little teeth.

Josiah started laughing again. He thumped Brody's back. "Ohhhh... Oh, you'll do just fine."

Chapter Nine:

To Be a Prince

"Hardship often prepares an ordinary person for an extraordinary destiny."

–C.S. Lewis

Brody's palace was so large that by the time he went to bed that night he still hadn't seen even half of it. True to his word, Councilman Owf sent a box full of scrolls up to Brody's room for him to peruse and as one of his manservants helped him to remove his cape and tunic and turned down his blankets, another offered to read the scrolls aloud to him.

Brody wasn't sure if this was allowed, or whether or not the scrolls were top secret, but after scanning each, none seemed to be so. As he pulled on a night shirt, he listened to an eyewitness account taken by a villager while his other manservant saw to lighting the fireplace.

Brody learned the hard way what Owf had meant by the reports making unsuitable nighttime reading. The reports told of utter decimation. Rankers and their monstrous allies raided villages, pillaging, slaughtering, torturing. They had invaded the eastern and central cities, enslaved, killed, or chased out the citizens, and settled factions in place among the ruins before moving on.

Accounts from generals and ousted dukes, governors and minor kings and queens together shed no light on any possible rhyme, reason, or pattern to the attacks, but even if the Rankers' goals were unclear, their tactics and strategies were on-point. They had taken a smattering of fortresses manned by knights of the Griffin King; fortresses that had stood for hundreds of years and protected the numerous cities in the land. They goaded troops to their doom and left behind such carnage that entire rivers ran red with gore.

Brody, now tucked into his bed and frowning thoughtfully as he listened, heard the aggrieved waver in his manservant's voice, and so had him switch from reading grisly reports to scanty dossiers. Though seeming to lack governance, the Rankers *did* abide by a strict chain of martial command. The dossiers referred to "lieutenants": the rank Brody's generals had assigned to those Rankers that exhibited the most signs of leadership and control in the actively-fighting forces. To the Ranker heads left behind in conquered cities the higher rank of "lord" had been assigned, but little to no information was available on them. One Ranker in particular was receiving a lot of attention: it was moving fast in the direction of the capital and the troops were having difficulty keeping an eye on it.

The last thing the manservant read before Brody dismissed him with gratitude was a brief that detailed councilman Owf's broad plan of attack: to kill the lords, extract information, and have the kingdom's most intellectual strategists attempt to root out a sign of the Ranker's intentions in the long run.

Councilman Owf had elaborated further on these plans in a private letter he'd addressed to Brody, tucked neatly in amongst the documents. While smaller workings–like intelligence-gathering–could occur without the king's direction, the larger actions, like amassing allies and shoring up distant fortresses, would require a king's authority.

Our very first step, his letter read, *is for you to receive the training you will need to survive and navigate your role as Griffin King. Then we'll send you out to battle when we're sure you know enough to avoid a sword in the gut. As a griffin, you possess powers over the Rankers that the rest of us don't have. The griffin-hearted are among the only beings capable of putting fear in a Ranker's heart. It'll be up to you to take down those lords that've been roving around causing so much trouble.*

In the meantime, while you're being educated, we're waiting for some final pieces of intel to come in from our spies. They've been investigating some odd activity nearby and we want to see if it's Ranker-related. And it would be best if, before we send you out, we could gain a better idea of why the Rankers have gotten so bold and whether or not they have a plan, or are causing mayhem for the hell of it.

Brody made a fist, crinkling the letter in his hand. He hated feeling so trapped. He was no soldier, not like his father had been, but he desperately wanted to help...he could transform into a flying beast with talons for crying out loud! However, as Owf had pointed out in his letter, Brody wasn't prepared yet for any martial action. At this point he would likely trip over his own feet and fall onto a Ranker weapon.

Needless to say, Brody's dreams were quite turbulent that night, filled with screams and sulfur, rivers hot and red with blood, and earth white with corpses.

Brody's classes were on the fourth floor, in a large tower off of what his manservant called "the corridor of windows." As Brody sidled toward the door leading into the tower, finishing up the crumpets with jam that he had been brought for breakfast, he reveled in the sensation of warm sunlight beaming at him through the famous windows. Horses grazed in the royal pasture beyond and the glass skylights glinted in the distant ballroom.

The first class of the day was etiquette, taught by an austere, long-nosed man with a thin face like he had pressed his hands against the sides of it too often. If Brody was to win hearts and influence minds, then he needed to understand the world of politics and high-society. Brody was taught how to walk with his head up, chin high, and habits like waving and bowing the right way. He learned "King's Speech," the more formal manner of talking reserved for important guests and speeches.

"I am the ambassador from Grechus," his teacher said, taking a step, crossing his leg, and bowing low and elegantly. "Such a great honor, your highness. May your wings always touch the sky."

Brody obligingly bowed back, trying to remember how to respond to a griffin adage given by a non-griffin, but was spared the struggle by a knock on the head from his teacher's hickory stick.

"Am I a woman?" the man chided. "Unless I was *Lady* Ambassador and you were bending to kiss my hand, your head should be no lower than mine! The king bows to no one–just lower your head slightly, like this."

After 45 minutes filled with more rituals, scoldings, pretend scenarios, and thwacks from the hickory stick, Brody was allowed to break for brunch. He dined in the minor dining room a floor below, lit by the crystalline daylight that filtered through ivy-clad balcony doors beside him. Josiah and Rexus were there waiting for him, Josiah enjoying a salad and Rexus a hunk of cheese.

"Not good, huh?" Josiah remarked upon seeing Brody's sour expression. "Looks like you got a good-sized egg on your head."

Brody asked the cook's servant to bring him up some fruit and then groused, "Gol-*ly*! I thought it was just his walking stick until he started beating me with it!"

Rexus bounced over, bringing with him a cheddar-y scent, and balanced on Brody's shoulder, parting his hair as tenderly as if he examined an infant. Brody felt the charlatan touch his muzzle to the lump on his skull and heard him make a kissy sound: "Mwah! All better!"

"Thank you, Rexus," Brody said warmly, touched as always by the little creature's sweet demeanor. He asked Josiah, "Do *all* the kings have to go through this?"

"Some. Most. Depending on where the kingdom's at in terms of danger or crisis, a few learn on the road or have their lessons delayed for a time. According to your council you've enough time for at least *some* lessons."

"Who are they? My council? Where did they come from?"

"Michael chooses people from reality to council the kings and queens. Each is gifted with the ability to control their sleeping minds so that they appear here when they dream. They are sworn to secrecy–should they tell anyone in reality about the true nature of the dreamworld, they would be stripped of their gift and forget everything about you, your kingdom, and the Rankers." He lifted his silver goblet, muttering into it, "No need to reveal *that* nightmare to the world just yet."

To Brody's pleasure, the royal dresser came in soon after that and took his measurements, which he would send with some suggestions to the kingdom's most esteemed seamstress: a gypsy woman named Maricella.

After the dresser departed with his roll of measuring tape and panels of cloth, prattling to his retinue about how blue and gold suited Brody best, Brody departed for geography lessons. His instructor took him to the glass greenhouse and aviary on the ground floor and pointed out various plants and their properties, also describing some of the animal species native to the dreamworld. Brody tried to take profuse notes on the scroll he'd been given–it was rather difficult to do with a quill.

The last lesson of the day was riding. Even though Brody could fly as a griffin, there would be times where ground travel would be necessary; if leading troops for example. He had ridden before–one of his childhood friends had owned horses–and he was fond of the beasts. The palace stables boasted a variety of fine stock from humble, noble Friesian war horses to clever, nimble Lipizzaners. There were proud, swift Arabians and even a sweet, friendly palomino-Morgan. The stable master paired Brody with an obedient, older dapple-gray, and though the lesson went well, with Brody even learning how to stay in the saddle if his horse rolled, he didn't feel as if riding suited him.

He slept deeply that night and began history and combat the next day. He learned of Great King David the First and Foremost, who had wielded the mighty Word, a sword that had been lost to darkness during the short, ill-fated reign of Prince Achilles the Thief. Brody learned of the architectural feats of King Demetrius, when the palace transitioned from a medieval-gray color to its current golden-white, and he learned of past battles such as that which destroyed the Mad Usurper, who was said to have first empowered the Rankers.

Brody's pulse beat a rapid tattoo through his veins when he entered the castle's rumpus room for combat training. To make matters worse, Michael was there, smiling at something a tall, beefy man was saying, ears perked forward and head slightly tilted.

When the man, whose grin revealed silver canines, noticed Brody, he bowed deeply and said, "Your Highness," in a booming voice. Josiah had told him that the shining teeth were an enchantment gifted to the man by the elves from the Misty Pass; they allowed him to project his voice over the whole of the king's assembled army–for this was Amos, the highest-ranking general in the royal military.

Brody had met Amos already, after the council meeting when he had been introduced to all of the staff, but he was unable to greet Amos at the moment...his jaw was clenched too tightly.

There were others there: a few battle-hardened-warrior-looking types, a servant with a tray of refreshments in crystal goblets, Josiah, and Rexus laying across Josiah's shoulders under his hair like a furry boa. Was Brody to have an audience?

"You're gonna wanna strip to your skivvies, sir." Amos stood by a rack of swords of varying lengths and widths of blade and style. "Wouldn't want to soil them nice new duds o' yours."

Brody wore the first of a set of fine new tunics. In the promised color scheme of blue and gold, it was patterned around the hem and ties with white trim and little yellow suns. Of extremely fine silk with an over-cloak of fur, Brody had to admit that it was not an outfit for exercising in. His primary manservant hustled over and helped him to dress down until he wore only his simple white under-tunic and leggings.

Amos looked him over critically. "Lean 'n lanky, eh? Is it too much to ask for a little more brawn? Give me a man like ol' King Antony–now *there* was a fighter! Oh well..."

Brody, affronted, said nothing, but something his father would say crossed his mind: *It isn't the size of the dog in a fight that matters; it's the size of the fight in the dog...*

Amos handed Brody a long, thin, needle-like sword, lifting one himself. The big man put one hand behind his back and settled so that his knees were bent. Brody emulated the pose and asked somewhat derisively, "Fencing?"

"For poise," Amos explained. "We'll focus on your footwork and reflexes so I can get an idea of your style and hopefully by the end of today's lesson we'll have settled you with a weapon."

They began, poking and thrusting at each other, with their audience laughing, jeering, or making sounds of approval and delight in response to the match. Brody felt a fool, hopping and darting about to avoid the sword, adjusting and accommodating where advised.

His griffin senses aided him just enough, but still, Amos's foil-tip managed to find Brody's body again and again.

Both duelists became cranky and frustrated.

"No! Your ripostes need to be quicker! Don't just stand there after you parry like a farmer in the city! Consonnit, boy, don't you know *anything?*" Even those watching were quieter now, as if bored, but too polite to sneak away.

There were no breaks–only Amos's consternation and insults and the two flicking foils. Brody thought it should be quite obvious by now that he was no swordsman, and his consternation began to turn into anger. As he attempted to control it, his irises flickered red, but at another sharp jab from Amos's sword, followed by an equally-sharp comment, that anger rushed forth and before he knew it, Brody had punched Amos on the cleft of his chin.

Amos grunted and retreated a ways, massaging his jaw. He peered at Brody appraisingly. Brody gazed back with defiance. Amos grinned and said, "*Now* we're talking!" He took two giant bounds, just enough for Brody's eyes to widen and for him to begin a futile escape, and then tackled him to the ground.

Brody's molars rattled as his head struck the floor. An involuntary sound of pain escaped his lips as the shock of impact became an ache that traveled along the crest of his skull all the way to the bridge of his nose as if he'd been strafed by Lilliputian warplanes. Immediately and without conscious thought, Brody threw up his arms and closed them over his face; a wall to hide behind until the mist in his mind could dissipate. The men watching exchanged looks;

this was how Amos tested all new recruits, and it was often a brutal test.

Amos's meaty fists thumped down on Brody's arms now, smooshing them against his nose, sending vibrations shuddering through to his spine. His little flesh-and-bone fortress was being broken in. One of Amos's strikes came in from the side and glanced off an ear, bringing with it a sharp, tear-jerking sting. Pain, confusion, humiliation...Brody was losing himself to those faceless demons, ebbing away, as helpless as the hiker he had witnessed beaten to death in the woods. Had that man felt like this in his last moments?

Brody's defense crumbled, the arms sliding apart just enough for Amos to force his hands through and wrap them around Brody's throat, squeezing, shouting insults or encouragement, Brody was too far gone to know.

Now panic became a fourth entity crowding Brody's mind. His tongue arched in a mouth that fought to allow air into his lungs. Alarm caused new sweat, *cold* sweat, to spring from his skin. He saw a leering, bruised face above him, but that didn't matter. The hands mattered. What had he been taught? Too late...he was departing...his being took shelter in the last stronghold it could find when the physical one failed, retreating deep into his mind.

Seizing on a scrap of knowledge floating amongst the disarray, Brody tapped one of the sinewy arms throttling him. He was tapping out. Giving up. But nothing happened. He slapped harder, tapped the floor, but the vice was unyielding. Amos either didn't know what the gesture meant, or didn't care.

Two new demons shoved into his brain, chasing the other ones out. Anger and fear. His oxygen was gone, but he would not submit. His father had not, when faced with cruel enemies, shattered bones, putrid, fire-blasted jungle. Wasn't Brody his son?

Brody's struggling began afresh. He hoped to perchance knock Amos off of him while grabbing at anything he could collect from his air-starved brain that would help him. Grasp something he did, but it wasn't how to break a chokehold–at least not in the normal sense.

In a flash of light and transformation, Amos found himself sitting on a griffin, his fists slipping in the sleek, fiery-colored feathers on the muscle-clad neck. Amos only glimpsed the red, cat-slit eyes before he threw himself aside. He avoided a stab from the beak, but was sent tumbling when Brody stood and opened his wings. They fanned above him like a great, feathery lapel beneath the vaulted ceiling.

Amos rolled over, saw the prince glaring wildly back, talons ripping at the air. A horrid shriek, as of some prehistoric raptor, forced most of those gathered to clap hands to ears, and as the rasping note faded, Brody pounced and Amos hollered, reaching for a weapon.

Watching closely, Michael made a soft whistle and Brody pulled up short, post-battle sanity returning to his avian features. His flanks heaved as he gasped in air and his pupils remained aggressively narrow. When Amos stood up, he saw the prince's tail lashing behind him. The situation sank in, and Amos chuckled.

"Good! Never forget that there are two sides to every coin, sire. You have advantages you can use. But your opponent will have an advantage of some sort as well. You'll need to find it and exploit it." When Brody shifted back into human form, sitting on his knees, still breathing heavily, Amos asked, "Have you been trained how to fight?"

"Bojutsu," Brody panted. "Some jiu-jitsu." His nostrils flared, his head rocked back and he shut his eyes a moment before pushing to his feet and approaching the weapons racks. "I should've... remembered how to...defend myself... Out of practice... *This,*" he lifted a long staff from the wall and twirled it, swinging it around his shoulders, "is what I used."

"That?" Amos looked from Josiah, to Michael, then back at Brody. "I don't know, Your Majesty, why it's–it would require pretty close-quarter combat and a claymore would cleave right through it."

"I could crush a man's skull with this," Brody said calmly. "Or rupture his spleen." He gave the staff one last twirl, letting it come to rest along the back of his arm.

"If I may speak boldly," Amos pressed, "You aren't fighting men, sire. You... You can't take out Rankers with a stick!"

"Then *this* will," said Brody, and he became the griffin, lunging playfully at Amos, who swore and automatically put his fists up. Laughter filled the room and after a few seconds of recovery, even Amos joined in.

Chapter Ten:

To Be a King

"We've done the impossible, and that makes us mighty."
—Malcolm Reynolds, *Firefly*

For four and a half months Brody trained and learned and read about the Ranker actions, thinking all the while that his silly lessons would only really matter if he didn't die within the next year. What councilman Isa had said about the short reign of the kings bothered him—it forced him to confront his own mortality; to ask at night as he struggled to fall asleep: *Am I going to die?*

Man is seldom wise enough to ask himself such a question until the tolling of the eleventh hour. But Brody had joined the select few driven to ponder such an alien and oft unwelcome personage as death. Unbeknownst to him, Brody's own father had asked that ringing question often when he was but a lad of eighteen, his hands wrapped tightly around a gun, the chopping helicopter blades overhead carrying him toward some smoking battlefield in Vietnam.

Brody fought to stave off that tireless question and its myriad threads—how, when, where—attached to it. His classes helped. He learned how to address and present himself to the many ambassadors from the many different cities and smaller kingdoms in the land. He memorized the monetary system, and learned how to sit, walk, move, and even eat like a king. He mastered King's Speech, how to ride a horse with such skill that he could direct one of the beasts with just a touch. He impressed general Amos with his jiu-jitsu and bojutsu, the old lessons reemerging from memory the more he practiced, and he even came to learn how to manage a blade. It was often a habit of the guards, servants, and bashful handmaidens with a little freetime, to slip into the rumpus room and watch Brody train. No longer unsettled by the staring eyes, Brody whirled and leaped, his spinning staff or swinging sword accompanied by kicks, leg-sweeps, punches, and, if his audience was lucky and his opponent *un*lucky, a takedown involving grappling, holds, maybe even chokes.

Jiu-jitsu was new to the palace, Brody being the first to introduce it, but General Amos and councilman Owf swiftly moved to incorporate what they could into the troops' adaptive style of combat.

According to gossip, Brody's coronation ceremony would take place by the end of the month, and then he would have the power to address the Ranker issue on his own and make his own declarations.

One day, when Brody was on a "field trip" in the palace treasury as a treat for his knowledge-retention in class, Josiah came bursting in looking thoroughly stressed. Brody's instructor, in the middle of describing the history behind a pearl drinking horn, lifted his head sharply. Out of habit, Brody shrugged back his cloak and extended his right hand, welcoming Josiah, but Josiah, who usually encouraged the observance of royal rituals, did not bow.

"There's a war meeting downstairs. Michael wants you to attend!"

"Go on," Brody's instructor said quickly. "Make haste, sire!"

Brody accompanied Josiah at a swift walk, brushing past obsequious serving staff and cleaning maidens who were obviously a tad anxious at the demeanor of their prince. Trying to erase the concern from his features, sweeping his robes around him as he descended the great staircase so that they wouldn't get caught, Brody said, "I have never been invited to a war meeting. Why now?"

"You haven't been invited to one 'cause there hasn't *been* one since you got here. Council meetings are different–they're the prerogative of the council members and as long as you approve of the agenda and are allowed access to the notes you don't have to attend. But this–" Josiah's hand squeaked on the railing as he jogged along the fourth-floor landing. Brody was forced to escalate his pace to a feline-like lope. "This is a meeting with your council, your leading generals...and whomever it is that comes bearing news important enough to *warrant* a war meeting. It's mandatory that you attend these."

"Of course," Brody replied, but he still didn't quite get why. As a prince, he didn't have a lot of authority to *do* much of anything. But then he recalled Owf's letter to him. It had stated that while Brody had been training, the council had also been waiting for spies to return from their missions, hopefully with more information on the Rankers' goals. His pulse quickened with a mixture of anxiety and eagerness. That *had* to be what this was about!

They reached the ground floor, shining in the light beaming in through the windows, and proceeded down the East Great Hall past the greenhouses and aviary. At the hall's end was the main guard-room and the armory. The men within, lovingly polishing the racks of gleaming plate armor, laughing at the ribald stories of their comrades or readying for their shifts on the battlements, snapped to attention when Brody entered. Brody waved at them with a distracted and meager smile, trotting down the stairs in the corner of the room.

The passage was narrow and cold. Behind and above him on the stairs, Josiah blocked the light from the guardroom so that only the glow of fire burning in a sill around the room below lit the way. They emerged on a landing with three doors that led to the aqueducts, dungeons, and the Lower Hall, which they entered. Much better-lit than the stairs had been, the Hall was still chilly and gloomy. The War Room entrance was a deep-set door with a heavy steel knob, flanked on either side by a pair of giant stone wolves.

Brody automatically entered first, remembering to hold his chin high and to keep his face blank. The shadowy figures within, around a table speckled with little braziers of scented fire, arose, mumbling respectfully. They sat when Brody took his place at the end of the table, their chair legs scuffing along the flagged stone floor.

Brody's council was there, Michael sat on his hindquarters in the shadows behind him, glowing like a ghost, and select members of the King's Army were present as well. Everyone kept looking at the semi-transparent ball on a three-legged iron stand at the center of the table. The only men Brody didn't recognize were the pair at the table's end opposite his own: a broadly-built man with dark stubble and a round nose wearing the red sash of a general, and a young man with fly-away brown hair and shocking gray eyes.

Councilwoman Persimmon, her ruddy cheeks dimpling in a matronly smile, said, "Thank you for joining us so swiftly on such short notice, your highness." Brody dipped his head.

Councilman Argo motioned toward the two strangers, heavy rings sparkling on his fingers. "That is General Jara. He has been away on a campaign in the south-central cities to attempt to track down our elusive Ranker."

The Ranker approaching the capital. Brody felt his pulse quicken. What news did this man bring?

Argo indicated the man beside the tired-looking general.

"And this is Pylgrim, the Eyes attached to General Jara's company."

Brody looked more closely at the pale, unassuming youth with interest. The King's Eyes were scouts and assassins; masters of disguise who could change their identity with some dirt and a limp. When in public and not working they often wore low-brimmed hats or scarves to help conceal their true appearance. Though Pylgrim's face was exposed now, Brody saw that he wore a gaiter around his neck that could be pulled up to cover his lower face.

Councilman Isa, snippish as always, said airily, "Perhaps we should explain the proceedings to his majesty before we carry on. This is his first war meeting after all."

An irritated look lingered on General Jara's lined face—Brody had the feeling that he, himself, was not alone in viewing his inexperience as a hindrance. But the man pointed at the ball on the table and said, "This is an elf-sphere, my prince. Your Eye has used it to record his recent endeavors to track down the missing Ranker and what vileness it has wrought upon your lands."

Pylgrim stood up and when he did, the elf-sphere flashed and projected moving images into the air above it like a hologram. Brody saw a city of sweeping vistas, twinkling lights, cobblestone paths, and grandiose, dignified architecture that had elements mimicking parapets and towers as well as colonnades and balconies.

"Syranade," he murmured, pleased to see the satisfaction on Jara's face, "*That's* where the Ranker is?" Syranade was dangerously near the capital city–a week's horseback ride and no more. The others in the room grumbled uneasily.

Standing beyond the hologram now panning down into the city, his unimpressive features lit white in the sphere's glow, Pylgrim said, "And about a hundred or so minions."

Councilman Owf sounded like his lungs had shrunk when he coughed out, "Hardly an army!"

"But it explains how it stayed hidden for so long," said one of the other generals. "Go on, Pylgrim, what did you find?"

The images in the sphere settled on the crowded doorway of a ritzy restaurant called *Sonnets*. No Rankers were in sight, and the people in line laughed raucously and chatted restively. Pylgrim said, "This is where it's rooted itself." The hologram changed to show a Ranker in mid-stride, hidden as they always were beneath its robes. Unlike the average Ranker-black, however, these robes were adorned with all manner of oddities: tiny lacquered boxes, vials of liquid, and phials of dried herbs.

"This is their lord," Pylgrim said, his tone vacant, as if he were trying to dissociate from the situation.

"Why were all of those people smiling?" Councilwoman Serafine asked, sounding as shaken as Pylgrim looked.

The sphere flickered to reveal a scene of soundless battle. Soldiers wearing the king's crest and Syranadian guards mingled in a choked city street, pushed back further and further by a mass of Rankers.

"At first, we couldn't pin down their methods. We arrived at the city just after the Rankers and helped the civic units to hold the Rankers back so that the civilians could evacuate. But there were too many–more than had originally been reported–and they fought us like wrathful demons. We were all separated. The general and I, and about a fourth of our unit, were forced to the eastern outskirts of the city and we holed up in an old winery, but they left us. The Rankers pulled back."

Brody watched his men in the hologram, some pulled down by the Rankers, some chased to positions further and further back. Then the images changed again to show the inside of a building with fine wood paneling carved with silver musical notes.

"By the following morning, we heard no more sounds of combat. I was sent out to Watch. Most of the Rankers were gone, and bodies had been left where they had fallen. The civilians I spied wandered the streets, weeping. None of them had escaped. My comrades had died for nothing…

"We remained in hiding for three days to see to one another's injuries and in that time, I found what remained of our unit and led them to the winery. I found out that only a hundred Rankers lingered still in the city and that their "lord" nested in *Sonnets*. After that came changes…"

A collective murmur arose: the hologram had changed once more to show a group of the king's halberdiers using their weapons to punch holes in one of the giant wine casks in the winery's main room, thrusting their faces under the gushing founts with expressions of rapture.

"Syranadians were behaving similarly, that I could see, gorging themselves on rancid food in the market, prostituting themselves in broad daylight, brawling until death or debilitation."

Brody winced at the images he now beheld. Pylgrim's voice was flat.

"And it got worse."

Gasps filled the room: the hologram showed men chasing a woman, grabbing her hair, pulling her down and tearing at her. She had a young child with her–one of the men lifted her and threw her aside out of the way–

"We had to leave some of our own behind," Pylgrim said, looking over the hologram at the wall above Brody's head. "They were too far gone."–

A man sat on the steps of a fine house, holding a knife. He drew the blade along his arm and blood ran from the wound. He laughed and his eyes rolled up into his head–

"They're coming and we need to push them back..."

Corpses began to putrefy in the streets, some with bite marks in their flesh–*human* bite marks.

"We need the Griffin King."

Brody slumped over the table, feeling sick. What Ranker sorcery was this? What had happened to those people? *What was their plan?*

"Perhaps we should stop it there," Isa said.

Pylgrim stared at him as if he had just made a joke. The elf-sphere froze on the image of a child in rags eating something bloody behind the crumbled statue of a man playing a violin.

"Keep it going," Brody said.

Isa spoke over him, not even looking at him. "His Highness is unaccustomed to such sights of–"

Brody pounded the table hard with his fists. "*Keep it going, damn you!*" A lion's growl gurgled in his chest.

His council shrank away, shocked. Josiah's shock looked more like the surprise-birthday-party variety. For the next few silent minutes, Brody absorbed the terrible, obscene images the sphere had recorded, soaking them in, trying to understand. In some corner of his mind, he went over the reports he'd been reading for the past weeks. Was there a pattern? It wasn't until he thought of his lessons that he started to puzzle things out.

Centuries ago, one of the former Griffin Rulers, King Khafra, had also faced trouble in Syranade. Everyone in the room watched him and waited.

"Am I correct when I say that each city the Rankers have claimed was at one time visited by one of my predecessors?" he asked.

"...You know, I think...I think that's right!" said councilman Owf.

"It is," said General Amos. "Crystalia...Goodwind... In the past, griffin kings and queens had to step in and rescue these places from some villain or other. He's right."

The generals began to converse, thinking along Brody's lines with the martial leadership and tacticians' minds that had guided them through their long military careers.

"Why?" Brody turned in his seat to face Michael and the conversations paused. "Why these places? What are they doing to the people?"

Michael blinked slowly, his yellow irises smoldering beneath his eagle brow. "There is power in those places. The Rankers have learned to tap into it."

"Do you mean that...the Rankers have learned to use *good,* griffin-hearted power? They're able to tap into the *positive* energy that has been blessing these places since the last time they were rescued by griffin rulers?" Councilwoman Persimmon fidgeted with a loose thread at her lacey cuff, her eyes round.

Michael was silent for a few moments before answering. "They cannot use it without corrupting it first. So they have built nests. And they wait."

"They had to've known we'd do something about it, though," Josiah blurted, frowning to himself and tapping a finger against the tabletop. "Why are they being so bold?"

Brody wondered that as well. Clearly the Rankers weren't doing all of this to indulge in simple pleasures. They had a plan, and if even the King's Eyes couldn't uncover their intentions, perhaps it was time to take matters into his own hands.

As if reading Brody's mind, Michael tilted his head down, his fierce, eagle gaze focused on Brody. "They seek to test you as the old kings were tested. Should they break you, it would take too long to find your successor and they would close in on the Jewelled Kingdom and claim the Seat of Griffins. Will you answer their challenge?"

Brody wondered if Michael had known the Ranker plans all along. What was it like to watch humans formulate their plans and chase their ideals, knowing what would pass and what would fail? Was it like watching ants about their hill? Did Michael know what was coming?

Brody turned back around, looking down the table. "I will answer." His insides squirmed excitedly. Now he would meet the Rankers. Now he would know what he was dealing with. And they would know, too.

"His Majesty has not completed his lessons!" Councilman Isa protested over the babble that had arisen at Brody's words. "A prince cannot go charging off to battle!"

"No..." Michael's ears swiveled thoughtfully. One of his formidable talons scraped the stone. "The man before you came to you on the eve of the Dream-Comet. The heavens danced to celebrate his destiny. The path of the griffin kings is not marred by trifles. To obstruct them is to hinder God's chosen."

Isa flinched.

"It is time. This very eve I shall crown Prince Brody King, for he must depart at once."

Chapter Eleven:

The King's Six

"Ole bull he comes for me, wi's head down. But I didn't flinch...I went for he. 'Twas him as did th' flinchin'."
–Flora Thompson, *Lark Rise*

Josiah tugged the mail tunic down to Brody's thighs, the silver and gold links twinkling like tiny diamonds. "Your job is to fix it, okay?" He watched Brody pull on a red over-tunic splashed with a rearing griffin in gold, a white crown hovering over its head. "Fix it, find out why the Rankers are doing it, and don't be an idiot about it."

The two of them, and Rexus, stood in Brody's chambers before a mirror. It was the dawn after his coronation. It had been a quick and somber ceremony attended by his council, Josiah, and Michael, who had placed a ceremonial crown of gems, feathers, and velvet upon his head. For campaigning and battle, however, Brody had been given a more modest circlet of gold and rubies along with the armor now heaped at his feet.

In proper warfare, Brody would wear a full suit of heavy plate armor. But this was a mission of stealth and speed. His great-helm, engraved with griffin-winged knights in combat, topped by a cross and a fan of pheasant feathers dyed white, would be packed into an easily-accessible saddlebag along with his gauntlets, pauldrons, and greaves. For the ride to Syranade and–he hoped–most of his venture, Brody's attire would consist of a hauberk, boots, tunics, maybe his crown. Plate armor, even just singular parts of it, were too clunky and uncomfortable; especially for someone trained to brawl with a bo staff instead of a broadsword.

Rexus tightened the belt that held the tunic snug against Brody's body, his little tongue poking from between his teeth, and Josiah, who was beginning to sound uncannily like Brody's doting grandmother, said, "They've taken six cities that we know of, and four fortresses. We've managed to keep them contained, but it's been tough without the leadership and abilities of a ruler. Now that you've been educated somewhat in monarchical methods and combat stratagems, you're a credible threat. They're probably high on success right now. Shouldn't see us coming."

Brody slid his staff, the violet feathers of King Uriah tied around the shaft, into the strap on his back and gave Josiah a look through his eyebrows, one that expressed bemusement at his friend's fretting.

On their way out to the stables, his mingled excitement and dread mounted so as to become nearly palpable. Josiah threw a thick riding cloak into Brody's arms. "You let your men do the fighting. It's what they're trained for. The king stays out of the way. You give orders, give guidance. Michael chose you for a reason. Just trust your heart and your mind. Your griffin nature will take over."

Oh, what fun it is to prepare for an adventure! How sweet smells the air, how promising the sunlit path! Even the shadows have a compelling charm. The booming shut of the castle doors, the walk through the crumbling courtyard, held less gravity than usual. Everything seemed to be urging Brody on–that's how *he* felt–and finally, for the first time in his life, Brody felt powerful.

This was a moment that history had forgotten: the King in all of his blessed majesty, departing the kingdom for battle; his armor shining, his steed tossing its wild mane, its every sinew trembling; his knights arrayed behind him. A Guardian of the Land of Dreams. The Bane of Rankers.

Brody's eyes flashed gold. Josiah tskd. "Sweet slap of a harlot, you haven't been listening to a word I've said."

Brody chuckled.

Yet...for all of the grandeur of the moment, even though it conjured boyhood daydreams of the chivalric knights of Camelot riding out to do good deeds, it was marred by the dread that sat heavy in his chest. His fear for what was to come gnawed at Brody's heart and sent random chills creeping down his back. The images from Pylgrim's elf-sphere crawled past his mind's eye in greater frequency than they had even the previous night, when he'd tossed and turned trying to force them from his thoughts long enough to squeeze in a few hours of sleep.

Brody's objective frightened him more than the thought of confronting these wicked monsters and seeing first-hand the carnage they had wrought in Syranade. He had the weighty obligation of finding out what the Rankers were plotting, and he doubted they would be forthcoming with the information. The road that waited ahead was likely to be violent, dangerous, and messy.

He lifted his head, Josiah's grumpy natterings a backdrop that plucked at his already fraying nerves. No matter the danger, leaving the Rankers to their own devices was much worse. The dreamworld needed him to step up and be its guardian. *If my father were in my position, he wouldn't hesitate to dive into danger and fight something as evil as the Rankers.* Thinking of his father gave Brody the strength to square his shoulders and lift his head for the remainder of the distance to their destination.

Six horses stood awaiting them on the path from the royal stables, already saddled and having their saddlebags and packs seen to by their riders. A patient, old stablehand with whiskers and a droopy face held the reins of two vacant horses. One of the horses, brown with a white stripe down its face and a basket on its croup, belonged to Josiah and Rexus. The other, a dun, was Brody's–it had been the most tolerant of him in his lessons, besides the old veteran he had started out on.

Brody went to the dun and began filling its packs with the spare armor Josiah had helped him to try on, laying the helmet fondly atop the pile last. He climbed into the saddle, throwing the traveling cloak around himself and fastening it, exchanging curious looks with his companions as he did so. He had never met them before–they had been chosen by Michael for their skills, from across the land. But Brody had read the dossiers that had described them and explained what they had to offer to a journey such as the king's.

Khogar was a snow leopard tribal. Though Brody had read about the large, humanoid cats, it was still jarring to actually see one. Khogar's white whiskers were long and curving, like her tail–around which were tied colorful bands. She was lithe, her fur silvery with darker rosettes, her eyes the color of an arctic sky. Her packs smelled strongly of leather and when she sprang into the saddle without even using the stirrups, Brody heard the muted slosh of several containers of liquid as her shaggy, dappled pony pranced in place.

Domine was a young titan, already seated atop his black stallion and just finishing up a pipe. Burly and intimidating, he wore his shoulder-length, dark, wavy hair bound into a loose sort of bob, exposing his mighty neck and the necklace of sharp teeth around it.

Aydran reminded Brody of a dancing fox in a jester's hat. He was bright-eyed and fair-haired and there was an unhinged sort of grin on his face. He couldn't seem to keep still and kept twisting around on his pinto to look around at them all affectionately, whistling snatches of tunes at random. Brody saw a viol strapped to Aydran's bedroll, and a thick scar on his lower lip, and found that, for whatever reason, he really liked this man.

Lastly, farthest down the line on a white mare, was a man that Brody recognized by sight alone, having seen him in the palace cathedral from time to time: Abram, a minister and a griffin, which meant that he came from reality just like Josiah and Brody did. Lanky and scrawny, he was the oldest one there aside from the stablehand and had a fatherly smile that he directed at anyone who made eye contact with him.

"Your most esteemed, affluent, bird-beaked majesty." Aydran leaned over in his saddle, doffed his poofy bard's beret, and kissed the back of Brody's hand before Brody could suspect that he wasn't getting a simple handshake.

On Brody's other side Josiah said dryly, "Count your rings."

Aydran put his hands to his chest as if wounded. "The audacity!" He shook his head in such an enthusiastic parody of indignation that his cheeks flapped.

Brody waited until Rexus was safe in his basket before encouraging his dun into a walk and then a canter. Horseshoes clattered on stone and tile. They began their descent into the tiers, passing the griffin lift-off platform, the sea inlet, the first of the farms that dotted the hills around his kingdom within the mountains.

Brody heard the others close behind him falling into a sort of diamond-shaped riding formation. He looked over his shoulder, bidding a silent farewell to the towers, turrets, and chambers that had been his home for the past four and a half months. His gaze dropped to the rider at his ten o'clock and he saw Aydran beaming at him.

"You know, another king would have your head for showing him such disrespect," Brody said, trying to sound stern.

The manic smile didn't waver, but Aydran shrugged. "It's been said, by kings much your inferior. But–" he wagged his eyebrows "–think of what an annoying ghost I'd make!"

The people had arisen early to watch the departure of their king. They packed the sides of the streets and children sat on their parents' shoulders to see. Interspersed among the human faces were other dreamworld denizens: tusked Angkaboores, fairies, elves, talking beasts, bizarre things dreamt up by ultra-creative minds. They all looked solemn, maybe doubtful. Brody saw some of their gravity on the faces of his own companions following in his wake–even Aydran, in spite of the man's earlier teasing. After all, their king was but a young man, untested. As the women waved white handkerchiefs from their windows or threw roses into their path, Brody felt himself overcome with a passionate protectiveness. Each of these citizens had a story—a creator. He *would* prove himself to them.

Close to the city gates, a spot of white on a rooftop caught Brody's eye. It was Michael. The White Griffin's wings were spread, tilting toward Brody. Time seemed to slow to a crawl. Michael's voice spoke in Brody's head—or maybe his heart. He couldn't tell.

Seek virtue, and you shall have your answers. Take hope, Griffin King. Your journey begins. And in those wings, Brody saw images—childhood memories, his desires given form, beautiful, sweet things that flew right past his eyes and settled into some warm, special part of his being. He saw, but could not recognize or remember later, things that brought him sorrow, joy, and peace. Then he had ridden past, the wings were shut, and Michael's black and gold eyes followed Brody out the portcullis. Just like that, Brody and his companions were alone on the dusty trail beyond the capital.

His heart thudded, his blood raced, and he gasped as if he'd almost drowned. Trying to overcome the shock of *whatever* had just happened, Brody blinked hard and rubbed at the scars on his chest beneath his tunics and hauberk. The others hadn't seen anything peculiar.

Aydran, whose familiarity with the land as a traveling bard would take them along the swiftest path possible to Syranade, shouted over the drumming of their hooves, "We'll cut across the Plains of Season and into the woods! I know a shortcut—it'll carve our ride in half!"

They had to slow to a trot when they entered the trees and forced their way along an overgrown trail to the plains. When they emerged onto the great, rolling, sweeps of grass however, Brody kicked his steed into a gallop. The dun's stride lengthened and soon the thunder of their speed made speech useless. They rode in silence, spreading out into a line, their cloaks flapping behind them. Though they wrestled with their own trepidation for the future, and though they glimpsed their own fear mirrored in Brody's eyes, not a person there, glancing occasionally at Brody, doubted the greatness of their king; his posture, fluid and at ease in the saddle, his dark curls tossed in the wind of their run, his crown sparkling in the sun, all spoke to the sovereign confidence of a man whose destiny it was to fight, to protect, to rule.

When making camp that night in the pine forest that separated the Plains of Season from the main thoroughfare and the King River preceding the lands near Syranade, everyone was preoccupied individually for a time.

Brody sat propped up against his packs, trying to recall what-all he had seen in Michael's wings and why it had comforted him so. He mindlessly ran his thumb and forefinger along the edges of the violet feathers tied around his stave, sometimes rising from his reverie long enough to see what the others were doing.

Domine was intensely focused on the gameboard he had brought, moving figurines about according to rules similar to those in Risk, but with a bit of gambling involved. His opponent, Khogar, kept passing square-shaped coins into his hand with frustrated growls.

Josiah read a book with an old but finely-embossed, green, leather cover. Rexus snoozed in his lap, one mule-like ear trained on Aydran. The bard softly strummed his viol and sang a song that must have had some lewd strains because he occasionally fell to muted humming with guilty looks at the minister.

Abram cooked the evening meal, which smelled divine, turning chunks of jerky garnished with brown sugar and a thick sauce smelling of teriyaki on a spit over their campfire. Cold beakers of cider waited nearby–their first meal on the trail would be a lively one.

As the scent of the food wafted out, attention became drawn to Abram, who now cut into a loaf of bread and paired the slices with generous amounts of cheese and grapes. Domine folded up his game, pocketing his newly-gained money, Aydran set aside his viol, even Khogar looked eager despite her lightened money-pouch.

When food and drink were finally passed out to all, conversations were struck up and Brody listened raptly to the stories of his companions.

The titan, Domine, hailed from the reclusive villages of the east where the majority of the land's titans dwelled. Each titan was sent away at a young age to settle a new community with the rest of their generation, a test that not all survived. Eventually, each young titan, through mysterious ceremonies, discovered their animal totem.

Domine proudly displayed his necklace of teeth. "I am as the mountain bear," he said, his rough accent causing each word to fall heavy and precise from his mouth. "None of you has seen one. I know, because you would not be alive. He is ten feet tall on his legs with claws like the crescent of the moon and hair like a woman's–long, and all over. His might is my own–should I call him, I am as a..." he searched for the word and then snapped his fingers, "juggernaut."

Khogar was an experienced veteran of former territorial wars between her people and the snow beasts of the high mountains. She had lost many friends, and tied a ribbon around her tail in memory of each. A talented tanner, she modestly showed them her own hand-made saddle, stamped and painted with the colorful, jagged motifs of her clan, her whiskers twitching at their compliments.

Aydran regaled them with fantastic tales of his journeys, bar fights, songs he'd picked up and the stranger-than-strangers he'd picked them up from. His was an elf-name, he said, given him by his mother whose mother had been an elf. He hadn't yet discovered what the name meant, for apparently no one was left from his elvish ancestry who spoke that particular dialect, though he liked to think it meant "amazing singer" or "great lover."

Abram spoke humbly of King Uriah and what achievements he'd made, what battles he'd fought. He had been one of the few kings to marry and Abram had officiated the ceremony. Once Uriah had passed, no one saw his queen ever again. Whether or not she had died, or her grief had been such that her dreams were now too fragmented to allow her focus, was anyone's guess. As for himself, Abram admitted that, like Josiah, he would awaken to reality when he fell asleep in the dreamworld. This caused a painful pang of envy to prick at Brody's heart, but he didn't remark on it.

Josiah was unusually quiet. Brody kept waiting for him to speak up, to relate some adventure of his own–as a semi-confidante of

Michael he had to have many–but he was mum, and though he was the recipient of a few polite, encouraging looks during pauses, he didn't respond and no one else pressed except for Abram, who only asked what he was reading.

Finally attention fell on Brody. Though it was clear that he was a topic everyone had saved for last, no one seemed to know what to say first or how to say it, clearly viewing him like a powerful celebrity. Uncomfortable, Brody slowly finished his grapes, one at a time, rubbing at his scars.

"Tell me how you got yours, I'll tell you how I got mine," Aydran said, his cocky smile pulling the scar on his lip into a thin, white line.

Brody considered. Everyone was so happy and content, full of laughter and good food. He didn't want to disrupt that. But he didn't want to remain an enigma either. These men needed to understand him, as much as the mission required that he have their loyalty. And in his opinion, loyalty was much stronger when given out of friendship than fear or respect.

So, Brody told them about the manic vagabond who had murdered the hiker, torn Brody's flesh, and then taken his own life. He saw their smiles fade, slip right off their faces as disturbed frowns took their place. He told them of his father's illness and remissions, attempting to intersperse these dark moments with fond memories of his father's life-lessons, his mother's silly doodles on his lunchbox napkins, the visits from passing hikers. Then he told them about college, about Sylph and their conversations...and now his own mood darkened as he finished up with the truck accident.

No one there except for Josiah and Rexus had known the circumstances that had brought Brody to the Land of Dreams. Although most of them were clueless as to what a "truck" was, they understood enough. Mingled horror, glumness, and melancholy had turned their faces down. Rexus added an armful of twigs to the dying fire and dusted his paws with a heavy sigh.

Yet, seeing the sadness of their king brought out a sort of fraternity in these men, and by an unspoken, unanimous decision, they worked to cheer him up.

"So tell me more about this Sylph," Aydran said with a professional air. "On a scale of *blech* to–" he wolf-whistled–"Where is she?"

"She sounds too troubled to me," Josiah said mildly.

"But strong," said Domine. "She has not shown her demons her back. Always they have seen her eyes."

"Or is she right in the middle?" Aydran pressed. "An 'eh,' is she an 'eh?'"

Astonished at their interest and already feeling his mood improve, Brody said, "Her hair was silvery like...like a comet's tail. And her eyes were like...if winter could embrace you."

"Yeah, okay," Aydran said dismissively, leaning forward and holding his hands apart, "but how big were her–"

"Aydran!" Josiah snapped, exasperated.

Aydran very slowly and comically turned his head to face Josiah, his hands still holding open air, and he said, affronted, "Dreams. I was going to say dreams."

"This jiu-jitsu you speak of," Khogar remarked, stroking her long, drooping whiskers like she was twirling a lock of hair, "We have a similar style of combat among my people. Does it address all situations? Back-to-ground? Throat-in-hand?"

"I-I think so," Brody replied, taken aback.

"Show us!" Aydran exclaimed. "Fold Josiah into a little box!"

Josiah looked like Abram's presence was the only thing keeping him from making a rude hand gesture.

"I, too, would benefit from an exhibition," Khogar said hopefully. Domine beside her looked like Christmas had come early.

Abram said, "If any of you break our king it shall be on your shoulders if the world ends."

"Yeah, Domine, I don't trust you not to channel your bear spirit in the middle of a spar and take off his Highness's head," Josiah said dryly.

"A mountain bear and a griffin," Domine said, as thrilled as a child shaking their first present, "Now *that* would be a battle to behold!"

Brody was apprehensive; wrestling about did not seem a very kingly thing to do, and he had reservations about tussling with Khogar, whose retractable claws and muscle-clad legs he would have to contend with. But machismo won out and Brody unfastened his cape, letting it fall from 'round his shoulders. He rose to his feet.

"One round," he said, "no holds barred, no rules."

Aydran jumped spryly to his feet, removing his rings, fingerpick, and hat, which he threw at Josiah. "I won't hold back!" he warned cheerfully.

"Good," Brody said with confidence. In his experience, jiu-jitsu was a means of preparing oneself for the sorts of attacks that were most likely to occur in the real world: ambushes by criminals, street-fights with thugs, that sort of thing. Versatile and deadly, it had fostered in Brody techniques and tricks for most any situation, including this one, when Aydran charged him and dragged him to the ground.

The ground was the worst place to be for an inexperienced fighter, but for Brody, it would be a tool with which to teach a lesson. Aydran scrambled up over Brody, grasping at his tunic, plainly bewildered that he had made it so far and wondering what to do next.

Brody, flat on his back, with a fluid, graceful, practiced manner as if he were doing something mundane like tying shoelaces, wreathed his right arm beneath Aydran's chest and fastened his hand around the man's right elbow, taking the wrist of the same arm in his other hand. Then, before Aydran even gathered what sort of situation he was in, Brody had pushed off of Aydran's hip to spin sideways, twisting Aydran with him, wrapped his leg around Aydran's body, and pressed down while stretching the arm he still had trapped at his chest.

Aydran yelped in pain, "I yield! I yield!" and Brody released him. "Ow..." the bard sat on his heels, rubbing his neck and rotating his shoulder. "I thought you were just gonna get out of it, not turn my arm into a noodle! Wounding a musician's arm..."

Brody wrapped his arms around his legs, looking pious. "Sometimes you have to hurt your opponent–make them respect you."

"*Yeeesss*!" Domine agreed emphatically.

“It is the law of the wild.” Khogar nodded her speckled head sagely. “When a low tail does not prevent a quarrel, you must bare your teeth.”

Seeing that he would get no sympathy, Aydran made a sullen face at Brody, said, “I take my leave of you, sah,” and returned to his viol, flapping his arm limply behind him as if all of the bones had been liquefied, to the amusement of his audience.

Chapter Twelve:

Syranade

"When you eat too much chocolate, you get sick of it. When you drink too much champagne, you get sick of it. Gorge yourself on fear."

–Khang Kijarro Nguyen

Syranade was renowned for its fine lyricists, instruments, and wine. The latter two they exported in trade and even Brody's palace boasted their high-quality work, be it a flute so sweet that birds came to listen to it, or an oaky bottle of *Velvet Requiem*. The buildings were of a sort of Tudor style, with half-timbers, patterned brick-wall cladding, arched doorways, leaded oriel windows, and massive chimneys. The wineries, concert halls, restaurants, and other public places, had a more "fairytale" theme, with heavy, carved, wooden beams, quaintly-arranged sections of plant life, and masonwork of stones in differing, pearly hues.

Even with parts of houses missing, cobblestones upheaved, carriages knocked asunder, and here and there corpses exhibiting signs of cannibalism, Syranade was still a beautiful place. Strings of twinkling lights connected flowering trees and lampposts and pagodas. The sun lit the paths and trees and streams surrounding the city so that leaves looked made of stained glass and the grass of softest silk.

As there was no wall but what birch and beech could provide, Brody and his team rode in on the outskirts near the winery Pylgrim had sheltered in, dismounting once within city limits. Brody had cobbled together a plan of action on the journey. Step one involved finding a base of operations, somewhere to safely stow the horses, and the winery seemed as good a place as any. Picking their way in careful silence, their mounts' hooves wrapped in cloth, the group met no resistance and no signs of life, though sound could be heard echoing from the city-center. The stench of putrefaction had the horses pinning their ears and Khogar wrinkling her muzzle.

Remembering what he could of landmarks seen in Pylgrim's elf-sphere, Brody soon found their winery, recognizing the silver music notes carved into its timbers. Now that the moment of action had arrived, Brody felt a bold euphoria tempered by caution and terror. He had seen death before, been traumatized by it. But this was something else entirely. Now, he warred with monsters.

"Okay, get it open," Brody whispered urgently, patting his dun's pale neck to soothe it. Josiah passed his reins to Abram and slipped up to the winery doors, Rexus teetering on his shoulder. He pushed open the doors and everyone hurried in, feeling much safer out of the open. There were the giant wine casks, almost all gouged open, their contents sticky and long-dried in shining patches on the floor.

Competing with the scent of so much wine was the foul odor of decay. Two men in the light armor and red and gold of king's knights lay dead near the casks. One of them had a halberd through his chest. The other had taken a few steps before succumbing to a similar injury.

"Drag them out," Brody ordered softly. "We'll settle upstairs if…" *if there are no more dead bodies,* he thought, "…if we can."

Khogar and Domine obeyed after tying their horses to two pillars reaching to the upper-story balcony that looked out over the main room.

Abram, after finishing a hushed prayer for the two men, tied his own mare and joined Brody in removing the horses' tack and seeing to their feed. "They died fighting each other," he said. "Brothers-in-arms…"

"Pylgrim said that something came over them. That they changed."

"And some of the company had to be left behind to their gluttony, their madness, yes. But his report indicated more than two. Where are the rest?"

Brody straightened one of the strands in his horse's dark mane, listening to the homey sound of it munching oats in its feedbag. "Out there, most likely. With the rest of them."

"Then one must wonder: why hasn't the whole city killed itself off?"

"Maybe it affects others worse," Josiah said, coming to join them. "But it doesn't seem to be a contagion or Michael wouldn't have sent us all here."

"Ranker sorcery," Abram nodded.

Aydran stuck his head over the balcony above. "All clear, sir! Just an office and some storage rooms."

They picked up their supplies and Brody said direly, "Well, we need to know what kind of sorcery we're dealing with. I'll take a team this evening to do some reconnaissance on the restaurant Pylgrim mentioned. *Sonnets*. Once we find out *how* they're absorbing the power left behind by Griffin King Khafra, we can put a stop to it here and anywhere else they've nested."

Josiah looked like he wanted to object, but something in the somewhat wizened way that Brody removed his crown and studied it before tucking it in with his armor made him hold his tongue.

There was a room upstairs maybe once used for meetings or events with a chandelier like silver lace and flowers in pots on the walls. A large fireplace would keep them warm at night, and a row of windows facing the city would assist them in making their observations. The table and chairs occupying the room's center were pushed out of the way, replaced by their bags and sleeping rolls.

Brody waited until nightfall, his griffin vision casting the world in shades of whitish or blackish gray, sitting on his roll and massaging his scars until Abram looked at him in an empathetic way and he stopped. He chose Josiah, Rexus, and Aydran to go with him, knowing that a barbaric titan, a tribal, and a griffin could hold the fort until they returned. Rexus' small size could come in useful out and about, as well as Josiah's griffin form in a fight, and Aydran's skills of picking up on gossip and blending with a crowd; skills his file had attested to. Brody had yet to see these skills in action.

Josiah, who did not approve of Brody putting himself in danger, was pacified at having been invited along. Everyone shivered in their upstairs room, lit by Khogar's funny little oil lamp that smelled of jasmine. The party staying behind watched those preparing to leave, making sure that they had all the supplies they needed: cloaks for the chill, snacks in case they had to hole up elsewhere for a bit, and Abram had given them a scrap of parchment for taking notes.

Brody waited by the window. It was drawn, with deep-blue curtains stitched with treble clefs and bass clefs. He wondered if it was an actual song, not just decoration, and what it sounded like. He sighed through his nose and looked down at himself. They all wore black tunics and trousers so as to work, inconspicuous, from the shadows. Not for the first time, he wondered how sensible it might be for him to just transform into a griffin and do a fly-over on his own, saving the others time and effort, sparing them danger.

This was the moment that many have faced; when plotting a course and the way is suddenly clear, there is that moment of hesitation: *should I marry this person? Should I choose this career? Should I lead my men into battle this day with these plans I have made?* And then there is that plunge forward into victory or defeat, carried along in a rush, unstoppable, building momentum until all of the long days of preparation come to fruition.

When he tried to get a sense of his feelings, to picture them, give them a physical form, Brody visualized a broad valley misted with heavy rain, the steel-gray quilt of clouds perforated in sections by promising little beams of chilly sunlight. His confidence waxed. When Aydran came over to him, holding out a small satchel filled with supplies, Brody took up his staff and asked, "How did you get that scar? You never told me."

Aydran grinned, hiding his fair hair beneath his beret. "I was seeing a woman, *gorgeous* she was, just beautiful, in...Wilkerson Shire, I think, or near it. Well there was another man jealous for her attention and as you can imagine he did *not* like me. One evening this peach and I are getting to know one another, right? And this fool storms in and sees us together and pulls a knife. He comes in fast to cut my throat." Aydran was laughing now. Brody's smile had become stiff, as if he had suddenly discovered that he was in the presence of someone a little unhinged. "And I tuck in my chin–gut reaction–and, just by luck, I catch the blade in my teeth!" He threw back his head, his laughter lapsing into silent, heaving breaths. "Cut my lip pretty bad, but he let go of the knife, looking at me like I's a circus animal. Got away without a problem that night..." He sobered up a bit. "Let's hope my luck lingers, eh?"

"Let's hope it's contagious," Brody said.

The company parted ways, padding downstairs, past their resting horses, and out the front doors. As they passed abandoned houses and dark side streets lined with apple and plum trees whose leaves rustled ominously in the shadows and wind, Josiah whispered to Brody, "Are you wearing your mail under your tunic?"

"Yes," he replied. Josiah nodded approvingly. It was the only exchange of words among them until the gradual increase in sounds of life drove them all closer together and against the last houses between them and Syranade's main street. One by one they climbed from the lower-floor oriole window of a house, to the cross-beam of the upper half timbers, to the steeply pitched roof. There they lay, side by side, peering down at the goings-on that were so unbelievably at odds with the carnage and destruction left behind by the recent battle.

Syranade's city center consisted of the innermost rings of streets and buildings in the middle of the city, which had been built in a circular sort of shape. It boasted the most popular restaurants, wineries, artisans, and music halls, all arranged around the city's centerpiece: a great, bronze fountain with an elevated stage in the center for musicians to perform upon.

Here, Syranade's Tudor style meshed most with its more fanciful, storybook elements: ivy-shrouded towers with gilded roofs that looked like wedding cakes or piles of artfully arranged lace; broad verandas sheltering harps shaped like angelic women or other instruments that Brody didn't recognize; front yard topiary gardens with shrubs clipped to resemble men and women waltzing.

"That's a bay!" Aydran spoke very fast, pointing at a horn-like instrument in the window of the Museum of Music. "A *bay*! They only exist in legend! And that's a twins fiddle! And a dragon's-head trumpet! Why have I never stayed here before?"

"Women too picky?" Josiah muttered and Aydran looked as if he'd remembered something unpleasant.

"Picky, that's right. Not fond of folktales here. They like their stories pretty and their music rich. Like I like my women." He glanced over at Brody. "Does that make *me* picky?"

"Shush!" Rexus hissed, bushy tail lashing. In the crowds packing the avenues below there was an unsettling ripple of movement. The people packed the bakeries and cafes and eateries, even spilling out of doors. Their clothes were filthy with stains and whomever was not eating ravenously as if famished, or drinking deeply from wine bottles or pints of beer, was smoking pipes filled with a pungent substance, jockeying for a place in line to get *more* food, or chatting easily. Now, however, heads began to lift in the direction of the main street to the south. People began to make a plaintive, feeble sound of collective hunger.

"Shall I see what's going on?" Aydran asked, uncharacteristically grave.

"Yes, but stay nearby," Brody replied, staring fixedly at the main street.

No sooner had Aydran slipped away than the source of the Syranadian focus ambled into view: a troop of around twenty Rankers. Brody was eager to see how they compared to the figures in the vision he'd had before waking up on Pebble Embark. He scooted a little higher up the roof, his chainmail dragging unpleasantly against the under-tunic he wore between it and his skin.

Standing tall and straight, every bit of them hidden within their black robes and hoods, the Rankers emanated vileness that Brody could feel even across the distance between them. It was an unsettling sensation that made him want to squirm as if to scrub spiderwebs off his skin, but it was tolerable. These twenty Rankers however, surrounded another, who laughed jovially at the crowds of people now pressing in and trying to get to him.

This Ranker, Brody knew, was the Ranker lord they sought. He resembled a very large man, with a girth like a hippopotamus on two legs, and several chins. Beneath his bald pate, his tiny eyes were mirthless. Dark veins ran down his cheeks from the sockets–just the sight of them put a chill shiver in Brody's guts. Where the other, lesser Rankers made him feel unclean and slightly sickened, this one struck true fear into his heart. As Michael had once told him, though this important Ranker resembled a man, there was a monster hidden within the human shell. It was something very old, and very clever. Though he couldn't explain how he knew it, Brody *sensed* that this Ranker had visited and shaped the nightmares of hundreds, thousands, perhaps many *millions* of people. And Brody was supposed to defeat him. He slid back down the roof a little, his muscles weak.

The Syranadians moaned, reached out to the human-looking Ranker, sprang back up when shouldered hard enough by the other Rankers to send them sprawling. The corpulent Ranker just laughed his benevolent laugh, a jolly, Santa-esque figure with Krampus eyes. Reaching into the tiny boxes and drawstring bags attached to his robes, he threw pills or tablets of some sort into the crowd and the men, women, and children fell upon them with abandon.

Watching them for a moment, like a man watching pigeons pick at breadcrumbs, the fat Ranker went on his way, stepping through the doorway of a multi-story building with an iron archway over the footpath that displayed curvy, looping words.

Sonnets: Fine Dining.

"There." Brody pointed with his forehead at the opulent eatery. "That's where Pylgrim said the Ranker lord has nested."

"Wow, look at them!" Josiah's voice was strained with morbid fascination as the people, having finished gathering up whatever it was that had been thrown to them, rushed to line up and file into *Sonnets*, rocking the wrought-iron arch as they squeezed beneath it.

Brody took a scrap of parchment from the pouch at his belt and began to sketch the layout of the square, noting how many Rankers he had seen and drawing from memory what he had seen of the fat Ranker, however brief.

With the addition of new, loud sounds of carousing coming from *Sonnets*, things returned to normal–however abnormal that was. Brody had rolled up the parchment, put it away, and was wondering where Aydran was when the bard suddenly crept up and stretched out beside him. Brody jumped, sliding down the roof a ways until his boots found purchase.

"Sorry." Aydran held one end of Brody's staff so that Brody could pull himself up with the other end and resituate himself. "Didn't find out too much. People are about as chatty as woodlice."

"How did they seem? Functional?" Josiah asked.

"That part's a little iffy. They can talk, but they aren't talking about battle. They're all about what sort of fun they're having. No one spoke to me unless I engaged them first, no one recognized that I'm not from these parts. In fact, when that Ranker threw his candy into the crowd, I got in a fellow's way picking some up and he growled at me."

"*Growled* at you?" Brody repeated.

Articulating each word, Aydran said, "Growled like my mother's cat when I first started learning the viol. I kid you not, there is something fishy going on here." He shook his head helplessly and pulled from his pocket a pill that resembled a semi-transparent purple-black stone, smooth, the size of a grape.

"They were calling him the 'Fat Man.' These are all different colors and shapes. I can't figure it out. No one was eating them–" he gasped.

The pill had, in the blink of an eye, become a bottle of spirits. Aydran almost dropped it–it followed Brody's earlier example and went rolling down the roof, sloshing as it bumped over the shingles, picking up speed. This time Rexus snatched it, grabbing it in his fangs by the cork. The Charlatan muscled back up to them, acknowledging their thanks with squeaks.

Aydran frowned down at the label on the bottle. Brody observed the crowd lit by the streetlamps. Their own pills had transformed into a cornucopia of various foodstuffs, drinks, drugs, each of superb quality. A man gnawed on a turkey leg thick with meat in one hand and a great fistful of mutton in the other, the juices running down his arms. A woman chugged a bottle of wine, eyes closed contentedly. A young boy squatted to strike a match against the cobblestones, lighting a large pipe with trembling fingers. For a while conversations became bestial noises of consumption.

"This is a bottle of liquor from the coast of Tidewater, how is it..." With grudging admiration Aydran slowly crawled up to perch on the summit of the roof, speaking as he went. "Fine little fishing town if you can stand the stench of seafood. This stuff is strong enough, you'll forget your own name by the third shot and your mortality by the fourth... Where's the guy what growled at me...?" He dangled the bottle over the edge of the roof like a man waiting outside a mouse-hole with a sledgehammer.

Brody thought fast. People who were always hungry. A fat Ranker constantly feeding them the best they could hope for. Something that Abram had said came back to him...then the dream he had had of the seven burning lamps and the seven dark, tarry ones. A possibility, an explanation, came to him both startling and terrible.

"We need to get back," Brody said, drumming his fingers against his staff. "I have suspicions about what's going on and if I'm right then we have to move right away."

"Oh, okay..." Aydran said disappointedly. To someone below he said, "Hey! Both hands," dropped the spirits, and slid down the roof with the others.

"So...what? The Rankers are fattening people up? They don't eat humans, do they?"

"Some do." Josiah jumped over some crumbled bricks. "But Brody's right, this isn't just about Rankers leading Syranadians to slaughter."

"Since when have a full stomach and a nightcap or six ever really hurt anyone?" Aydran said grumpily.

Brody suspected that the bard was upset at giving up what would, in any market, have been an expensive bottle of alcohol. His voice was sharp when he said, "Corpses are being eaten, Aydran. Dead people." Aydran blanched, looking guilty, and Brody added, "What if they reach the capital? It seems to have affected some more strongly than others, but what if that's just because it takes longer to work on some? That guy who growled at you? How long before he's trying to take a bite out of you? How long before *you* start changing? Or *me*? What happens if the Griffin King caves in to a Ranker that can...zombify you?"

"Okay, I get it," Aydran mumbled.

Brody rounded on Josiah. "The other captured cities didn't report this sort of behavior."

"No, but no one's set foot in any of them in weeks. Who knows what conditions are like now?"

Josiah looked over Brody's head down the dark sidestreet they passed. His eyes flashed white and he shouted, "Look out!" shoving Brody ahead.

Brody stumbled forward. A rock hurtled through the air where his head had been. His eyes snapped up, focusing on a pack of humans hurtling from the darkness, shrieking like banshees. Their clothes were filthy and ragged, their skin pale. Dried blood clotted their lips and teeth, and their eyes were black with swollen veins that also ran down from the sockets.

In the breath before combat, Brody counted about forty people, all holding knives, broken bottles, and nooses made from strings taken out of instruments. Then he held his staff horizontal in both hands and thrust it up just in time to prevent a man's hands from wrapping around his throat. He twisted the staff, breaking the man's grip, and then hit him upside the skull. The man fell back, clutching the side of his head, and roared at Brody, gnashing rotted teeth.

The taste of vomit arose in the back of Brody's throat. Were these Syranadians too far gone? He quickly closed with another adversary, this time a young woman, and easily sent her tumbling into the grass. The pack fought fiercely, desperately, saliva oozing over their chins. And they were clever, surrounding the foursome, brandishing their weapons, jabbing at any bit of flesh they could reach as if to carve off a piece to eat then and there.

There was no breath for talk. The whole confrontation had happened in seconds. Then, from the same street down which the pack had charged, came another guttural, more commanding shout. The pack cowered, now moving to put Brody, Josiah, and Aydran between themselves and this new threat.

It was another pack. This one was smaller, but each member wore the blue of the Syranadian city guards, or the red of the king's knights. They held true weapons, swords and halberds, and were quite imposing with their capes flapping behind them, their armor still gleaming in places, walking in formation.

Slowly, they stalked toward Brody and his friends. Brody could hear their teeth grinding together.

"Go griffin!" Aydran cried.

"Brody?"

"Hold," Brody said, straightening from his combative stance and pausing, wondering. There was something different about this pack. Though under the same spell as their whimpering counterparts, they weren't displaying starving aggression so much as...territorial protectiveness.

Brody deliberated...his father had always told him: once a soldier, always a soldier. Perhaps these men could prove it.

"By order of the Griffin King you will stop your advance," Brody said in formal King's Speech, stepping forward. Josiah started to say something, but Brody threw out his hand, silencing him.

The knights fell out of sync, some slowing, bumping into each other, then resuming their predatory approach.

Brody raised his voice. "You do not know me, but you soon will! I am your new king and you *will* heed my command! Stand down!"

One of the knights stopped on the spot. The rest parted around him, and he trailed behind like a fish in a school.

Brody took one more step forward and a lion's roar boiled in his lungs behind his words: "*Stop in the name of Great Griffin King Brody*!"

The griffin's call drew a reaction from both packs. The first pack jumped, babbling incoherently. The second, for the briefest of moments, stood at attention as if Brody's words had galvanized them back to their true selves. The man who had stopped before grunted something, and a haze lifted from his eyes long enough for him to focus on Brody's.

Then the first pack broke and ran and the intelligence, the moment, was gone as the knights gave chase like cats drawn to movement. They veered around Brody, Josiah, and Aydran in pursuit of the other pack, their armor clanking, slobber dripping from their jaws, their hungry, hunting roars echoing back to Brody's ears.

Chapter Thirteen:

Gluttony

"We each day dig our graves with our teeth."

–Samuel Smiles

When the others heard the story they were aghast. That fifty-something human beings had almost made a meal of their king, that their king had temporarily *stopped* them with words alone, dumbfounded them all–even Brody. As a student of medicine, biology, a lot of psychology, Brody knew what the long-term effects of cannibalism were: impaired motor coordination, depression, malnutrition, and dementia, among others. *His* main concern was that, even if they did manage to save these people and return their sanity, how would they react upon realizing their atrocities? What would his knights do when they learned that they had turned on each other over wine? The psychological trauma would be severe. Maybe *that* was the Ranker goal. Even if they lost, they would win, in a way.

Exhaustion sank in now. Brody tried to tune back in to the conversation the others were having as they pored over his notes. Was this how his father had felt in war? What advice would he give Brody at this moment?

"And the...tablets turned into food and drink?" Abram asked, looking puzzled, as if he'd just heard of a bogeyman handing out flowers. "Then what?"

"Well, it wasn't exactly nourishing food and drink," said Josiah, Rexus on the step beside him shaking his head. "It was rich; like something on a nobleman's banquet table. People were falling over each other fighting to grab something." He scowled.

"I do not get this fat man," Domine grumbled, snatching the sketch Brody had made from Abram's hands and slapping it with the back of his hand. "I thought the Rankers were monsters and nightmares. This, *this* does not scare me. Only if he were to *sit* on me, then I would be afraid." He and Aydran shared a snicker.

"And the knights listened to you?" Abram asked Brody.

Hiding his impatience at having to repeat himself *again* that night, Brody said, "*Yes.* They were fighting against the Fat Man's spell as soon as I started talking to them. And when I made a griffin call they totally ignored us and went after the other pack."

"Presumably to eat them?" Khogar asked, showing her teeth and spitting like a cat that smelled something revolting.

"Mm-hmm." Brody rubbed at his eyelids. He *had* to stay awake for a bit longer; *had* to share his earlier insight with them.

"You said you had an idea of what's going on," Josiah said, scratching behind the charlatan's ears so that one of his little hind paws started thumping. "Care to elaborate?"

"Something you said earlier came to mind when I was watching everyone in the square, Abram. You said that some of the knights had to be abandoned to their gluttony." He considered telling them about his possibly prophetic dream featuring the fourteen lampstands but decided that that would remain private. Everyone was looking at him now with enough skepticism as it was.

"I can't remember, but I believe you..." Abram's eyes went round as he made the same connection that Brody had.

"Yes." Brody nodded and met the perplexed frown of each of the others, saying meaningfully, "Gluttony."

"One of the seven deadly sins..." Abram breathed.

"You think that Ranker is one of the big seven?" Aydran asked. "How can that be? A sin is a sin, not a...being?"

"We need more proof," Brody admitted, "but it fits that the Fat Man is at least *tempting* people to gluttony. It would also explain why some are affected differently–some are more prone to gluttony than others."

"And our troops were already probably hungry and thirsty from the battle, so they gave in quicker," Abram added.

Aydran gestured around them. "And what better place for it than the city of wine. Right."

"The best way I can see of battling sin is with virtue," continued Brody. "Gluttony versus diligence."

"So, what, we all fast?" Aydran complained.

"We'll figure it out." Josiah stood and went to pet his brown horse. "But examine this on a larger scale. This Ranker embodies a sin. That's more powerful than any Ranker we yet know of. Up until now, our greatest advantage has been Michael. Now we have demonic powers to contend with."

"Demonic?" Khogar's claws shot out and her silver fur fluffed up on her neck. "Rankers are not demons!"

"We still know so little about them," Josiah said. "They might not be demons, but they're getting power from somewhere."

"Fear not, brothers." Abram's calm, tender voice made everyone look at him, seeking the comfort that his tone provided. "All is happening as it should. Our steps do not fall without them being carefully guided to the proper path. And the powers of light will ever overcome those of darkness, for, though rare amongst man, they are mighty."

Brody remembered Michael saying something similar months previously when he was just a frightened newcomer to the land. They warmed him, those words. He stood tall, fists clenched. This was a world that thrived on the very principles that his father had instilled upon him. This was a world whose heartbeat was in sync with Brody's own; rich with the ideals that he so desperately sought to find and understand–if only he fought for them like he had been taught to do.

"They will see whose power is greater. They will see that ours is a force not to reckon with. If it's a challenge they seek, we will answer it. If they dare to fight us in our own lands, we will vanquish them. They are foolish not to fear the king!"

The men grinned toothily at him, but they were not the sort of smiles one sees among loved ones, or out of humor; these were wolfish smiles, feral smiles, smiles worn by the warrior even in the face of carnage and horror. They were hungry smiles that would cause even a Ranker that incited gluttony to shy away, for these grins came from an appetite that could never be satisfied with food or drink–only vengeance, blood, victory, and death.

Brody awoke the next day well-rested and ready to act. He felt similar to the way he always had before a test: the farther away it was, the more time he spent worrying about it. The longer they procrastinated here, the more paranoid and anxious they would all become. It was time to move.

Brody was satisfied with the time at which he had stirred himself: it was early, judging by the milky quality of the sunlight squeezing through the part in the drapes, just gaining the buttery tones of true dawn. He wasn't the only one up: Abram read his Bible under the window by a beam of sunlight, Josiah had just entered the room from downstairs, and Khogar examined a scrap of leather she'd brought, occasionally licking a hand-like paw and smoothing the cow-lick atop her head.

"The horses were getting noisy," Josiah said to Brody, seeing him awake. "They're hungry. We can't keep giving them feedbags to tide them over, they need grass or hay."

"Did you water them?" Brody asked, hiding a yawn in his arm.

"With what?" Josiah asked testily. "Water I carried all the way from the fountain in the square?"

They couldn't just let the horses loose to graze in the treeline around the city for fear that they would raise suspicions or be captured and eaten.

"I'll send out a team to find them something. There are a lot of breweries around here, so we're bound to find some grain if not grass," Brody said.

"I volunteer," Aydran said sleepily, dragging himself out of his sleeping roll. "I'm still tuckered out from our near-death experience yesterday."

"Aydran and Abram, you both get food for the horses. Khogar, you stay here with Rexus and send him out to find us if anything happens."

"And what will you, me, and Domine be doing?" Josiah asked.

Brody fought the impulse to rub self-consciously at his scars. His voice may have given the cannibal packs pause the previous night, but he felt that he had not yet proven himself to the company as a leader, warrior, decision maker, or even griffin. So it was discomfiting to have his every little word valued so much, his every choice weighed against the wisdom of his station and his forebears.

"We have a good idea of what we're up against," he began, "so we can defend against it. But we still need to stop the Fat Man, and cut off his power, the power left behind by the kings that Michael said the Rankers are learning to use."

"Michael also said that they want to test you as the past kings were tested," Josiah added, as if Brody might have forgotten.

"Where is the source of this power?" Brody mused aloud. "Is it in the air? Does it come from memory?"

"What if," Aydran said slowly, "it's more physical? Like something the king touched?"

"In that case the Fat Man probably has it protected somewhere," said Abram.

"If you found it, maybe you could imbue whatever it is with your *own* power!" Aydran said excitedly.

"I haven't discovered my power yet." Brody frowned.

"That's...not what I really meant." Aydran exchanged a tolerant look with Josiah.

"Not your griffin power." Khogar pointed at Brody's heart with the flap of leather in her paw. "If the Rankers wish to use sin as a weapon, then we shall use virtue, as you said last eve. The same virtue that King Khafra left here in the first place, when he rescued Syranade before."

"Any idea how I...transfer virtue?" Brody asked.

Aydran shrugged. "I don't think it's something that happens intentionally. I think it just happens by your presence alone. Maybe *you* just have to touch whatever-it-is, sneeze on it, roll around on it, I don't know."

"'Think,' 'maybe,' and 'I don't know' are not words that inspire confidence," Domine said, shambling over to join them and sporting outrageous bed-head.

"Oh, nobody asked you," Aydran snapped.

"It's as good a place to start as any," Brody said. "So that's what Domine, Josiah, and I will do: look for whatever is giving the Fat Man power."

Dusk had fallen and Aydran and Abram already departed to find horse feed by the time Brody was ready to leave the winery. They had spent the day closely studying their maps and pointing out likely areas in which to hide an important object, narrowing down their options to three buildings on the main streets, and the cemetery about a mile distant. All but one were places that King Khafra had once been.

"Rankers in a graveyard just seems poetic," Josiah had said wryly, "and the church there could have all sorts of places to hide an item. It's where I'd look for power."

Brody had disagreed on the grounds that Rankers feared churches and the power within them, but it wouldn't be out of the way to at least stop by and peek.

The last thing they had mulled over was what, particularly, they might be looking for.

"I know nothing of past kings," Domine had said a little defiantly. "My people live in the present and plan for the future. Why was King Khafra here in this place?"

King Khafra had been a member of the capital's musicians guild, which bore the Syranadian flag. He had, during his reign, been called to Syranade to put an end to the...singular tastes of a nobleman who would hire dancers from the city's temple of music to entertain him privately. While there, Khafra had discovered his harp, which would awaken within him his griffin power, and befriended a youth who would eventually come to be known as the Mad Usurper, the first man to see Rankers in the land and the first to ally himself with them.

The temple, the place where Khafra had found his harp—an abandoned cathedral and now the Museum of Music that Brody had seen previously—and *Sonnets* were the other three places marked on their map to examine.

After he'd finished describing Khafra's adventures in Syranade, Brody led the way out into the balmy evening, striking out toward the cemetery with the trees that fringed the city on one side for cover and the newer, more spacious houses and estates of the city on their other side. They were unmolested, and arrived at the graveyard with ample time before true night set in.

Here, what houses there were, sharing space with exposed earth, tufts of weeds, and long-imploded structures, were shabby and derelict. Even in the dreamworld many were reluctant to live too near a cemetery, and so the poor, who perhaps understood death better than most, took advantage of what empty spaces they could find and had created their own little neighborhood, shunned from the more welcoming areas of the city.

Now, however, the little homes appeared deserted. Perhaps the residents had fled once the battle had began; even here there were signs of warfare: puddles of blood turned black and crusty between the cobblestones; claw marks in the side of a house; the pink bones of a dead warhorse picked clean by scavenging animals, cannibal packs, and the advantageous poor. Or maybe, drawn out by the sudden lull in the fighting and the sounds of frivolity coming from the city center, they had gone to investigate and been caught up in the spell of gluttony. Of course...the answer could be worse...

In the narrow space between two houses they passed, they saw a pair of children, hunkered down, their eyes blackened and veiny. One snarled hungrily, rising, a bone in one hand sharpened to a lethal point. Josiah flashed his eyes red at them and they withdrew, whining.

As if he hadn't noticed the incident, Domine sourly nudged a pile of discarded refuse with his foot and said, "My people do not have such hovels. We do not have 'poor.' If any titan was treated with such disrespect, he would rise up and take."

"Every place has its poor," Brody countered, "but sometimes it isn't money that they lack."

"Well-said," Josiah remarked. "Now be careful up here...graveyards can be sheltering zones for nightmares, even if those nightmares *aren't* Rankers."

The cemetery crept subtly upon them as they walked, showing itself first as tombstones rising even in the midst of the houses before the ground dipped into a broad, bowl-like valley where they appeared en masse, an abundance of stone markers with the church on a slight hill in the center. Marble mausoleums, the final resting places of the more well-to-do Syranadians, were grouped almost artistically on either side of the crooked path winding to the church doors, along lanes and roundabouts. It was like a city of its own. A necropolis.

"We burn our dead," Domine said in a small voice, looking out over the misty scene like he was confronted with a great, solemn work of art.

Nothing moved below as far as they could see, but they still navigated the path down into the hollow with caution. To prevent rainwater from running down the slope to collect at the bottom and erode the soil, a deep ditch had been dug and lined with bricks. The trio crossed this ditch over a plank bridge and then proceeded in the direction of the church.

As planned, Josiah slipped away to investigate the church, and Brody and Domine stuck together to search the older mausoleums for an artifact once touched by King Khafra. They split when they reached the first lane, each to look in a different building.

Brody tried to remain respectful as he opened the cabinets and chests and rummaged through the trinkets that had once been a significant part of someone's life. Most items, he knew, were protected with cantrips–the wealthy could afford the services of magicians–that would cause them to vanish once taken through the doorway and reappear where they belonged, but Brody hoped to tackle that issue when and if it became necessary.

When he went downstairs to browse the alcoves in the wall surrounding the casket, Brody found that he couldn't prevent his gaze from wandering to the polished coffin. For the first time in weeks his thoughts turned to reality. Where was his *own* body? Was it mending, or was it losing its fight with survival? Would he, too, soon be stuffed into a wooden box, nothing more than an exsanguinated heap of skin and bone? Would his spirit linger a while, to watch his parents and friends cry over his body as if he were some sort of heinous bit of decoration on display?

Brody tamped down his mounting panic, that fear that mortal man has of the ultimate unknown. He replaced the goblet he had been squeezing in his hands, looking from the mesmerizing splendor of the agate-and-opal stones in the cup to the shiny sarcophagus.

What use had those bones for such finery? Like the bodies disintegrating under simple grass and stone outside, so, too, was this corpse destined for the ethereum. How strange is death. How disinterested in the fragile trappings and transient belongings of the soul still trapped in its flawed, fleshy shell. How hungrily and indecently it ripped the bright, shining, special soul from the breast and transported it to the marvelous beyond where it truly belonged, free from strife, pain, and other earthly limitations.

Somehow, that comforted Brody. Death was nothing to fear. Death was but a step on a journey. He finished his search and moved on to the next mausoleum.

Brody and Domine both had excellent nocturnal vision. When night fell and the stars emerged, they had progressed to the final mausoleum nearest the church and were losing hope of finding what they were looking for in the graveyard. Josiah had joined them earlier on after thoroughly searching the church and finding nothing.

When they had done, they departed back along the path with the intention of a brief rest in the winery to check on the others before investigating the temple in the city center. About halfway along, however, they were stopped by a dry, rasping voice.

"Feast and be merry."

From behind the tombstones to their right came a Ranker. Its sibilant voice hissed again. "Feast and be merry! What reveling is there to be found here?"

Brody saw with disgust that, clinging to the Ranker's robes with long, spidery limbs were humanoid creatures the size of cats with bat wings, scraggly hair, sharp teeth, and greenish skin. As the Ranker strode out to flank them, the creatures made complaining sounds, dangling like insects on a leaf.

"Go to the sounds of life," the Ranker continued, pointing a clawed hand up the path. "Eat and drink, for you look hungry and thirsty. This is not a time for dwelling here among the silence and the solitude."

"We seek the temple of music," Josiah said forcibly. Brody detected how tense he was; his jaw muscles shifting and flexing, focused straight ahead. But his eyes didn't even flicker white...he wasn't afraid.

"Make merry." The Ranker pointed again. "Follow the sounds, and what you seek, you will find. Music, food, and wine. The Fat Man has all–" The Ranker silenced and then cried, "You!"

Brody looked over just in time to see the Ranker turn its hooded head from Josiah to him. The creatures on its robes shrieked in unison, also twisting to stare.

"Ah, you have come!" The Ranker dropped its placating tones for something more sinister. "I have found you!"

The gremlins sprang from off the Ranker's body. Two latched onto Domine's head, two flew at Josiah, and four, their extended wings filling his vision, darted at Brody. He hit one with his staff, heard its tiny bones crackle, and the other three changed direction, sliding past him. Right behind them was the Ranker. Its hands grasped Brody's tunic and pushed him off the path and against the side of a mausoleum.

Expecting the impact, Brody didn't lose his breath, but then one of the gremlins came back and barrelled right into the side of his face, slicing a thin rent in his cheek with its one hind claw. He shouted, more to channel his adrenaline than out of pain, and ripped it away from his head.

Another gremlin sank its teeth into his hand and he dropped his staff. The Ranker wrapped its hand around Brody's throat, squeezing, while the three gremlins continued harassing him, pulling at his hair.

"You will come with me, your Highness," the Ranker growled. "No merriment for you, I fear–" and then he was gone; crushed beneath the forepaws of a gargantuan bear. Brody, still staring at where the Ranker's hood had been, now faced a wall of shaggy fur. He blinked and squinted up, uncomprehending, at a great, wide face and a long, dog-like snout full of teeth snapping at the remaining gremlins.

Brody's shaking legs gave out, and he slid down the wall onto his rump, picking up his staff and coughing into his shoulder–the Ranker's hand had really been squishing his throat.

Finally, the gremlins were dead, and the bear settled back onto all four paws, studying Brody with a pair of small, pale blue eyes.

"Domine?" Brody rasped.

Josiah, his head up to Domine's shoulder, came over and knelt to examine Brody's scrapes. His voice trembled when he asked, "How did it recognize you? We've kept your identity secret."

Brody didn't answer. He supposed Rankers had their ways of getting information. What concerned him more was the new issue of hiding his identity. He would need a disguise...

Chapter Fourteen:

Sinister Sights

"I may be running out of options, but running out isn't an option."
—Mark Lawrence, *Prince of Thorns*

They first returned to the winery to gather more supplies and tell the others what had happened. They gathered in the main room downstairs, the horses let loose to wander the building and stretch their legs, munching happily on the great pile of grass and grain that Aydran and Abram had spent all day collecting.

Brody left Domine and Josiah to tell the story. He stood over beside his dun, brushing its coat, mentally berating himself. He had been so close...*so close* to failure; to dooming the Land of Dreams to collapse, chaos, tyranny, a throne without a king, a world without a protector...

When he started on his horse's hindquarters, Josiah and Rexus moved silently over to him. Rexus scampered along the dun's back to sit at its withers and braid its mane with his nimble, little paws.

"The others were wondering if the Ranker said anything to you," Josiah said.

"Just that he was going to take me somewhere," Brody said noncommittally.

"Ah. Well, we figured as much. All of the Ranker lords are probably racing to be the first to claim your head as a trophy."

Brody grunted.

"Hey." Josiah leaned against the dun's flank. "What's wrong?"

Brody's hand tightened around his curry comb, causing pain to blister from the thickly bandaged bite mark. Before he could fabricate a response, Josiah said, "No one thinks you're weak, you know. No one is saying that–it hasn't crossed anyone's minds."

"If it hasn't crossed anyone's minds then how come it crossed yours that it could be crossing mine?"

Josiah looked stunned, as if seeing a part of Brody that he'd never expected to see, and Brody hated himself for it.

"Stop that," Josiah said darkly, moving closer. "No self-pity. We can't have that now, okay? We need to act quickly before that dead Ranker draws attention. Now somehow, it recognized you. Can you imagine what would have happened if that had been the Fat Man instead of some footsoldier? This was a blessing in disguise."

Brody, feeling his neck grow warm, turned the comb over in his hands. Josiah leaned away again and though his voice wasn't as sharp, it was still stiff.

"When you're ready, Aydran will disguise you."

Brody nodded and Josiah departed. When he looked up, Brody saw Rexus watching him as if he wanted to speak.

"What?" Brody asked, a little hostile.

"All afraid," Rexus said, hopping closer, "but king can't show it." He twitched one ear, then made a pair of squirrel-like leaps from Brody's shoulder, to a windowsill, and to Josiah's retreating back.

Brody had decided that they should collectively move into one of the buildings in the square. The Ranker that Domine had killed had been proof that newcomers wandering about weren't regarded with suspicion. However, the Rankers *were* on their guard, clearly expecting the Griffin King's arrival. So Aydran, with the skill of one of the King's Eyes, used a mixture of charcoal and Khogar's tanning oil to smudge up the contours of Brody's face, making it seem thinner. He gave Brody his beret to wear and told him to avoid shaving. Looking in the mirror that Domine had in his mess kit, Brody thought he looked a good five years older.

They would have to leave the horses behind. Abram opted to stay with them and watch the graveyard for any signs that the Rankers had discovered the body of their comrade. His griffin ability to slow time and even stop it briefly in a bubble around himself would be a great asset. Rexus would stay behind as well, acting once more as a messenger.

They moved out in the deep of the night, around the witching hour, when Josiah warned that the Rankers would be most lively. But they couldn't afford to wait. They found the remains of someone too slow for the packs, but otherwise they made it to the well-lit city square, still noisy even at this hour, without an issue.

After choosing the upper-floor of a pianist's shop for their new base of operations, Domine stayed behind, face pressed to a window overlooking the street, his pipe in his hand, and the others took the plunge, risking everything and joining the crowds without.

It felt obscenely wrong to Brody to be in the midst of a great many people whose pleasant conversations mixed into a babble, when just beyond them were roving packs of cannibals and, overseeing all, the Rankers. However, he did relish this opportunity to examine the Syranadians up close.

They were certainly sleep-deprived. Their skin had an unhealthy pallor and was bloodless beneath the eyes where their sockets showed through. They were grubby, with unbrushed teeth and filthy, frumpy clothes that reeked of unwashed skin. Disorderly grizzle sprouted on the mens' faces and the womens' hair was falling out of their flowery, Syranadian braids in lank strands. Soon, that hair would fall out, and their nails, Brody knew, if they didn't get sleep or adequate nutrition. But a lack of rest and cleanliness were not the only maladies.

The Syranadians' pupils were dilated as if by some drug. Veins of varying shades of black and varying thicknesses depending on the person appeared under every eye, mirroring the ones Brody had seen on the Fat Man's face. A diet of non-stop rich foods and alcohol had caused weight gain in many. A dependency on powerful drugs had caused excessive weight loss in others. Though young children still walked beside their parents, clinging to their clothes so as not to be swept away in the crowd, they were treated like parasites. An adult might tolerate the little hand grasping their robe, but the children were roughly nudged aside if they got in the way when their parents hustled to investigate a bottle or a wrapper for something palatable.

The Temple of Music was a fantastic coliseum-like building, easily the largest in Syranade, created to accommodate the great dancers and musicians of the city. Of brick set into sweeping aesthetic patterns, in places obscured by climbing roses, the building had five entrances for each of the five main Syranadian orchestral sections: strings, woodwind, brass, percussion, and *sui generis*, which was composed of the more singular instruments that Syranade boasted.

Each entrance opened onto a different hall lined with private alcoves where people could play the instruments, and, through a pair of oak doors at the hall's end, was the theater itself: rows of seats in tiers surrounding a broad platform, itself circled by jets of water spurting into the air and floating globes of giant water-lilies and pretty, elegant fish.

Before entering, Brody stopped and studied the crowds of sickly Syranadians once more, this time focusing his hearing. What he had been mistaking for conversation these past few days was really just chanting: he caught a few people murmuring, "Hunger...I hunger..." over and over again while others said, "Fat Man come, Fat Man come," and still others kept up a mantra warning others to keep away from them as if the little path they rambled in their search for food was theirs alone. It was a fascinating but frightening pack mentality, a mimicry of animal behavior, the ultimate sign that under the Fat Man's curse, they were less-than-human; more than mere victims of a sin too-much indulged. They were a message to him, the Griffin King, of what powers the Rankers possessed, what they could do, and that he would be made to face the same fate.

It took Brody and his men three hectic, harried days to completely search the temple. It was here where Khafra had gone to speak with the dancers being picked off to privately entertain, and he could have touched anything that now served as a power receptacle.

Sometimes, when he was shifting around trumpets and piccolos and lyres, hoping that some object would leap out at him as particularly powerful, Brody came upon a Syranadian picking, desultory, at an instrument, as if somewhere in their muddied minds they remembered that they were a people moved by music; masters of song.

They would look up slowly when Brody entered their nook, watch him vacantly as he stood stiff and ready to bolt, then tilt their heads once more to hover just above the exposed soundboard of a grand piano and pluck eerily away while he rummaged around them.

During those three days they all took turns staying in their room. They even convinced Brody to stay once–Josiah had to threaten him–and he paced about, haunted by his thoughts and the sight of the shambling masses in the square outside.

Were they dreamers? Or dream creations? What did it mean if either of them had succumbed to this gluttony? What was happening to the dreamers or dream creators in reality? What about the other taken cities, who had been under the control of Ranker lords for longer than Syranade?

Each evening the Fat Man threw his pills into the eager crowd before shambling into *Sonnets* with the same line of Syranadians filing in each time. Khogar once beckoned everyone to the window to watch a Ranker chase a Syranadian into the vacant back streets surrounding the city center. The man, eyes and cheeks black, snarled and snapped and tore at the Ranker's robes, but was eventually evicted and had no choice but to limp away when four other Rankers joined the first to ensure his departure. He wasn't seen again.

Brody witnessed this act of banishment seven more times. Each day it occurred more and more often and sometimes entire clusters of people were forced out at a time, shrieking like coyotes. Brody felt that the solution to this puzzle lay inside *Sonnets*, but entering the lair of the beast was a last resort. Two griffins, a tribal, a titan, and a bard, though all noteworthy, would face quite an uphill slope in winning a battle against one hundred Rankers.

Sometimes they had to subsist on what vittles they could snag when the Fat Man showered the square with his tablets. Brody felt no adverse effects yet, but faintly swollen veins began to rise beneath Aydran's eyes. No one blamed him–after all, man was not perfect–but the bard became hard on himself, refusing to eat even when necessary, no matter how much his companions tried to press upon him a crust of eclair or a slice of good steak.

When they were done with the temple, they turned to the Museum of Music across the street. By now, people were literally dropping dead from exhaustion; first the children, and then the unfortunates too weak to muscle through their brethren to get adequate sustenance from the Fat Man. Abram had sent Rexus to check in on them once, and in that time still more Syranadians had been banished to join a pack or be eaten by one.

Stress had started to disturb Brody's sleep. Brody had developed a fine growth of stubble, which would help to disguise him, but he felt himself weakening...flaking away like old vellum, breaking down like a rusted machine. Tension made knots of his muscles and put aches in his bones. The drive to save these poor people filled him with savage anger like the kind he'd felt in reality, protecting the boy from the thugs in the alley. Once again he witnessed the suffering of innocents, but this time he was helpless to intercede. And then, a glimmer of hope.

Their second day of searching the museum, Aydran gave a great holler and, grabbing Brody–who was nearest–by the arm, dragged him to a glass-fronted alcove in a wall. The exhibit, one of many in this room commemorating Syranade's "romantic era," displayed a long, peacock-like griffin's tail feather. A plaque beneath it read, *One of King Khafra's own feathers; all that remains of his visit to our humble city.*

Brody felt like a star had just burst behind his eyes; he had a sudden boost in energy; everything looked a lot brighter. "Okay–" he felt around the alcove, pressing against the oak paneling framing it while Aydran tapped a vigorous rhythm on his back, bouncing on the balls of his feet.

"Okay, I can't–" Brody struck the wall with the flats of his hands– "There's no way to open it! How do we open it?"

"Like this." Domine came up behind them, they moved to either side, and he struck the glass with his fist. The moment that air rustled the feather on display, the instant that the glass shattered into flakes around it, a terrible whistle went up. They covered their ears, groaning in pain.

Josiah came skidding in from the "contemplative era" room, alarm on his pointed features. He grimaced when the whistle came again, gave them a lethal look, and pointed to the narrow transom bar above them where a red-eyed bird had appeared, made of dust. It glared beadily down at them all and shrieked–a whistle that pierced through their heads like needles.

"A minor golem!" Josiah shouted. "The exhibits are all protected by them! You didn't see the signs?"

"There weren't any signs!" Brody argued loudly.

Josiah pointed. "Beneath the 'keep your hands to yourself' signs there's the golem insignia!"

"That's not a sign!" Aydran roared. "*That's not a sign, Josiah*!"

"Come on!" Brody said before the two could start arguing. He led them at an awkward trot–hands still over ears–out into the hall where he ran into a posse of Rankers coming to investigate the racket.

The one in front grabbed Brody by the tunic-front and growled, "What is going on?"

Brody heard the others stop behind him, too startled to act. He said the first thing that popped into his head.

"I hunger."

The Ranker hissed from within its hood. It snapped at one of its fellows, "Go shut that thing up!" and then resumed staring at Brody, who felt the weight of its eyes like a suffocating void.

Cleverly picking up on Brody's idea, Domine grunted, "Hunger..."

"Silence!" The Ranker turned around, still holding onto Brody like he was dirty laundry, and said to the four other silently observing Rankers, "We will take them to the Fat Man."

Chapter Fifteen:

The Fat Man

"A bone to the dog is not charity. Charity is the bone shared with the dog, when you are just as hungry as the dog."

–Jack London

This could either be really good, or really bad. Brody felt like a wrung-out sponge or a newborn fawn trying to escape the teeth of wolves. Should he fight off the Rankers? Let them take him to the Fat Man? What did the Rankers know of their plans, if anything?

For the moment, he let the Ranker pull him along, trying not to show any resistance lest it arouse even more suspicions.

Out in the square, Brody looked up toward the window of their lodgings and saw Khogar watching from the near-impenetrable darkness beyond the glass. The tribal appeared frantic, her pink nose twitching and her tongue protruding slightly from between her long canines. Brody shook his head and Khogar's ears went back, her pupils contracting to small dots in their fields of blue.

The Rankers took them through the ceaseless, sluggish crowd with no qualms about knocking aside any Syranadians who were too slow. *Sonnets* loomed nearer and nearer, larger and larger. The line had already started to develop outside its doors, which were manned by two more Rankers. The amount of intelligent curiosity these Syranadians leveled at them surprised Brody, as did the hush that fell as the Rankers dragged them inside.

Brody tripped over the threshold and was forced to tear his gaze away from the alert Syranadians–the first that Brody had seen in the city since his arrival–to maneuver through his new environment.

Sonnets was both an inn and an exclusive restaurant where the city showcased its finest wines. The entrance hall epitomized this bounty with gold incense boxes dangling from the ceiling like fancy birdhouses and filling the area with the aroma of saffron. Paintings in great, square frames depicted scenes of merriment: dances, hunts, and leisurely outdoor concerts. Even the benches were luxurious. Through a wide doorway to his right Brody saw an assortment of tables and chairs, antlers on the walls, and a piano on patterned tile before a high, leaded window looking out on an orchard behind the building.

A fat little bard sat on the piano bench tuning his lute. A crowd of robed and cowled Rankers, probably the majority of the Rankers in Syranade, lined up along the walls as if waiting for something, their arms at their sides. A few early guests, vast, pompous men, sat on stools around the corner bar, jiggling in their ruffles and tails, laughing uproariously at a joke one of them had told.

One of the men looked up at Brody and the others, leaning back to see them properly around his rotund neighbor, and said, "Oh, lookee there! Dinner and a show!" to an outburst of cackling from his pouchy faced friends, already red-faced with drink.

The Ranker manhandled Brody up a staircase. He caught a glimpse of a side room, where a silvery flag hung on the wall, before being dragged into a study. Perhaps it had been a meeting room in another life for the businessmen staying at the inn. Bookcases and leather-backed chairs took up much of the space inside so that Brody stumbled and bumped into several pieces of furniture. Silhouetted before the tall casement windows at the room's end, looking out at a sunset the color of honey, stood a giant creature with rounded, musclebound shoulders.

At the sound of their intrusion, the creature snorted gustily and shifted out of the window, where it became the short, hugely overweight Fat Man, smiling warmly, his veined eyes glistening like oil. Though the Ranker lord had somehow instantly disguised himself, Brody's heart still pounded as the Fat Man bustled toward them; pounded so hard that he could hear it in his ears and almost couldn't breathe.

The boxes, pouches, and bottles on the Fat Man's robes rattled as he came close, glancing up inquiringly into the shrouded face of the Ranker holding Brody. "Who are these?" His voice was high and weak. His chins wobbled when he spoke.

"They were in the museum, breaking into a case," the Ranker explained. "They set off alarms."

"What was in the case?" The Fat Man looked playfully flabbergasted, as if Brody was just a harmless young rascal.

"A griffin's feather, sir..." the Ranker growled.

"Really?" Now the Fat Man was interested. He looked at Brody again, more closely, lifting one pudgy hand to hover near Brody's eyes as if to feel for the swollen veins that should have been there but weren't. Brody mentally kicked himself. How could they have forgotten to apply some with makeup? The absence of black veins made them suspect–it indicated that they hadn't been there long enough to be influenced by the Fat Man's corruption. Brody hoped that the faint veins appearing under Aydran's eyes would serve to assuage any suspicion. But then, the Ranker lord's oozy eyes fixed on Brody's midsection and he said, "What's that?"

Brody's tunic had ridden up in the fist of the Ranker holding him to expose his chain-mail shirt. He had to battle with himself not to shoot Josiah an accusatory look.

"Chainmail armor." The Fat Man sounded thoughtful, rubbing his lower lip.

"...Hunger..." said Aydran feebly.

Brody tried to keep his expression slack; disinterested.

Seconds that felt like minutes lagged by. Then the Fat Man broke into a jovial grin and waved the Ranker off Brody, throwing an arm around Brody's neck like they were reunited frat brothers.

"Well, if you kids are hungry you've come to the right place! Whatever you crave, I can provide!" He stopped at the window, which looked over the smaller buildings beside them and the south end of the main street which led to the Temple of Music. The Fat Man stood, imperious, over all like a king over his empire, and beamed at what could be seen of the aimlessly milling Syranadians.

"Look at them. Everyone has an appetite. Sometimes it just takes a little extra time to find out what gets the mouth watering... I've seen you and your friends wandering around out there. You're looking for something. And you-all are a lot more together than most, which means that you crave a little somethin' more'n good tuck." He laughed, showing small, even teeth.

Brody was clammy now. He couldn't seem to wet his eyes no matter how hard he blinked, or settle the queasiness in his stomach no matter how often he swallowed. Images swam across his mind: a dead whale bloated on the sand, about to burst; a cadaver on the mortician's table, its heart choked by adipose. If he didn't get away from the Fat Man soon, he felt he would be sick.

The Fat Man turned and spread his arms. "Well, tonight you're my guests! Join the others and see what I have to offer!" Brody, now facing the other Rankers and his friends, saw that Josiah, Domine, and Aydran let their gazes drift around the room laconically, but kept him in their sights, waiting to follow his lead.

The Fat Man clapped Brody across the stomach, eliciting from him a sound like a mouse being poked with a stick, and said cheerily, "You-all are too skinny, eh? Go eat and drink, at my own invitation." He gave Brody a little push and Brody slouched over to the others, letting the Rankers shunt them back out of the room, being a lot more gracious than they had on the way in.

Over his shoulder, Brody heard the Fat Man say, "Enjoy yourselves! The party's just beginning and this one'll be a doozy!"

The Rankers left them in the lobby, departing for the entrance doors, conversing in a strange, dark language–Brody suspected they were discussing what had just transpired.

He wondered about that too. They had been dismissed too easily; invited to be a few of the many who crowded into *Sonnets* each night for what, he didn't know, but was soon to find out. Had the Fat Man assumed he was a stubborn knight not yet taken by gluttony?

The early guests at the bar were obviously surprised to see Brody and his friends intact and none the worse for wear but were soon too wrapped up in their conversation to be interested. What about them, and the people Brody heard lined up outside? Why were they unaffected by the Rankers' evil when they had so obviously fallen to gluttony?

When the Rankers were out of earshot Aydran groused, "Good idea, forcing his Majesty to wear mail, Josiah, that didn't raise suspicions at all."

Bristling, Josiah retorted, "Nice touch not adding veins to his Majesty's face when you painted it, Aydran, that didn't raise suspicions at all."

Aydran held his hand at about head-height and hissed in a forced whisper, "I am up to my *eyes* in shit here, I don't need *yours* on top of my head."

"Of us all, you are marked," Domine said placidly to Aydran. "Perhaps you helped to protect the rest of us just now."

"Oh, can it, you giant bugbear," Aydran mumbled.

Domine, who had not understood the insult, looked at Brody, nonplussed.

"Calm down," Brody murmured, sounding a lot more nonchalant than he thought possible. "We can't leave or it would be abnormal behavior and that would bring them down on us for sure. Let's go take a seat. We need to talk."

They entered the restaurant part of *Sonnets*. Each table was covered with a snow-white cloth shaped like a lily. Gold-and-crystal wine glasses stood empty, placed perfectly among their silverware around a centerpiece composed of fake apples and fat grapes surrounding a wicker basket full of moldy bread sticks cut to resemble flutes.

Choosing a table far from the Rankers and hiccuping patrons and placed in an alcove between two ficuses, Brody sat facing out so as to keep an eye on the main room. Pushing all of his concerns into the perimeter of his brain, he looked meaningfully at each of his friends.

"We can't eat. We can't escape at the moment. Right now our main objective is to blend in without giving in." He smiled at Aydran. "We'll keep an eye on each other."

"What about the power source?" Josiah asked. "It wasn't in any of the other places, so it has to be here."

"Where? I thought *Sonnets* did not exist when King Khafra was here?" Domine looked lost, one hand buried in his thick, tumbling waves of hair as if his head hurt.

"It didn't," Brody said, "but the object must be near the Fat Man. Maybe on his person, because nothing's leaped out at me yet that I've seen."

"Or maybe it's not even an item at all," Aydran said glumly. "Maybe it's like you said, Josiah; they're getting their power from something else…from…demons."

"How can we fight evil?" Domine asked despairingly.

"With good," said Brody simply.

Aydran scoffed. "How? We aren't good–*I'm* not good. You see my eyes, right? I'm as weak-willed as any of these putzes."

"Maybe we aren't good enough to overcome all this evil, all this temptation, but what we fight for is."

"And what's that?"

"An ideal. Peace. Dreams. Truth."

Aydran looked up at Brody and saw a young man besmirched with dirt and wearing his hat. But beneath that dirt and that hat he saw a king sitting tall and fearless and ready to keep fighting. Even if everyone else gave up, everyone in the world, Aydran knew that Brody would raise the standard himself and charge into battle alone.

"So what shall we look for?" Brody asked Josiah. "What first comes to mind when you think of King Khafra?"

"Music. Dance." Josiah shrugged.

"He was in the musician's guild," added Aydran.

"We search now?" Domine looked ready to jump out of his chair.

"No." Brody held up one hand to stop him. "Let's wait until they let the Syranadians in. Then we'll sneak away."

He sat back and began tucking his tunic back into his belt while the others lapsed into edgy silence, flinching whenever the bard by the piano struck a raw note on his lute, watching the row of Rankers behind them from between the leaves of the ficus trees.

Chapter Sixteen:

Diligence

"By perseverance the snail reached the ark."
–Charles Spurgeon

While they waited for the Fat Man's so-called "party" to start, the group entertained themselves by watching the drunk men sway on their stools like reluctant bowling pins.

"Maybe we'll get to see their livers fail," Aydran said darkly. At a look from Josiah he added defensively, "Hey, even *I'm* not that bad." He inclined his chin primly. "Shameful behavior, just shameful."

"My people," Domine snorted proudly, "we do not wave to and fro like a sapling against a gale. We drink without fear of such things as a weak liver."

"Yeah, but how long is the lifespan of your average bear?" Aydran asked.

The pair began arguing about which of the two of them could hold more liquor and Brody hoped that their good spirits would see them through the evening. Rexus would be ideal for a search-and-retrieve, but if they wanted to survive the night, Brody had the feeling that they would have to act soon, because the Rankers would soon see their diligence in the face of gluttony and realize who Brody truly was.

As soon as it became dark, after the Rankers had lit the candles in the wall brackets and lowered the chandelier hanging from the broad-beamed ceiling to light it, Brody heard the people clamoring outside. The Fat Man, right on schedule, had to have been tossing his pills like confetti into the bewildered crowd, which meant that the doors to *Sonnets* were soon to open and the line of lucid Syranadians waiting without would come pouring in.

"Brace yourselves," Brody said quietly with a steady look at each of his friends. "Don't eat or drink anything."

Aydran clenched his jaw and nodded.

Domine shook his dark head vigorously like a dog shaking off sleep.

Josiah's pointed face was paler than usual, but he swallowed loudly and gave Brody a weak half-smile.

Brody just had time to wonder what Khogar was doing at that moment when the lobby doors above them in the hall opened, preceding a sudden volume of noise. People came flooding into the restaurant, eagerly seating themselves, carrying on conversations they must have been having outside about such normal things as their families, finances, and recent trips or music compositions, to Brody's astonishment. Their eyes were as black and tarry as those of the cannibals prowling Syranade's back streets, but their wits were sharper than any of the rest of their fellow cityfolk. It didn't make sense.

When everyone had come in and the doors had been shut once more, the Fat Man appeared at the top of the steps from the hall. The people cheered riotously and he held up his meaty hands to acknowledge the praise, black eyes like a shark's.

"Nothing but the best for you, my friends!" the Fat Man said grandly, to more applause. "I know you all, and I know what you desire–short speeches!" The people chuckled. Aydran pretended to be doubled over in a fit of uncontrollable laughter, hidden from the Rankers' sight behind the ficus nearest him.

"So without further ado, feast! Fill yourselves! Let your cups runneth over!"

Brody heard an ominous growl beneath the Fat Man's passionate words, but if any of the Syranadians heard, they didn't care. Identical men in white suits embroidered with musical notes in shiny, white and pastel threads–Rankers in disguise?–filed down the stairs in two lines around the Fat Man, carrying trays heaped with all sorts of delicacies.

When the scent of fresh, hot, fine food reached his nose, Brody's stomach gurgled. This could be harder than he'd anticipated. Each person's meal was unique, catering to their own appetite.

The waiter carrying an overburdened tray to Brody's table as if it were no heavier than a tea set, met Brody's eyes and didn't break eye contact the whole time he served out their plates. Brody felt a dark scrutiny, as from a predator watching man around his fire from the safety of the untamed wilds. Just as that predator might wonder at man's power and intellect, so this Ranker wondered what made Brody so special.

After the "waiter" traipsed away, Brody examined his food wistfully: a brilliant-red lobster, homemade applesauce just like his mother made it, steamed pork buns like the ones he loved from the Chinese-food place down the street from his apartment...all of his favorite foods were arranged before him, and his goblet full of chocolate milk, which stirred up painful memories from his childhood–his parents, his home, the security and peace of a child with his loving family.

"No!" Aydran had been left a pale-blue bottle glazed with a sort of cloud motif. He lifted it by the neck as sounds of comfortable chatter and clinking cutlery swelled up from the other patrons. "This is a Nimbus vintage! I've only ever had a sip of it at a wealthy woman's estate before her husband chased me out. It's like drinking mist; it just...evaporates on your tongue and it tastes oh-so-sweet!" Looking extremely pained he set it back down and crossed his arms.

Domine poked disconsolately at the cigar beside his plate, which was loaded with his own cultural, titan food. Josiah, who only had a large cheeseburger and some steak fries, looked like he was trying to withstand agonizing torture.

Somehow they managed to pass one hour without touching their food or drawing Ranker attention. Brody had covered his plate partially with his cloth napkin in the hopes that it would take the edge off his temptation to feast and also make it look like he'd at least eaten something.

Whenever someone finished their plate, another was brought, and another. Smoke from peoples' cigars and pipes drifted on the air, creating a thin haze that tempered the smell of food with tobacco and other, stranger spices. The fat little bard had begun strumming his lute and the music, coupled with the smoke, made Brody feel groggy. He soon found that chunks of time were slipping past without his being aware of it. One moment his hands were on his lap, the next they were stabbing his lobster through the napkin with a butterknife and he had no recollection of the time between. He felt strange... numb...his vision was blurry; he was seeing things–or was he? What was real and what was fake?

The bard's music became erratic–he was drinking deeply of something he'd poured into his lute while still trying to strum its neck. The Syranadians now tore at their food like rats. One man had climbed up onto a table to chew on a luau pig like an animal. A woman tried to drink from two pints of ale at once.

Brody felt sick. Visions overlapped in his head. He saw the Fat Man wending around the tables toward him, followed by a Ranker that resembled a stone gargoyle. "The Bowl of Bemusement," the Fat Man grinned, passing the gargoyle a slip of parchment, "my own little recipe." Then he was gone. Brody squeezed his eyes shut. When he opened them he saw the Rankers giving the Syranadians black cloaks. Aydran stood among them, the veins on his face now thick and dark like ink spilled on cracked vellum. *Corrupting dream creations corrupts the dreamer,* Brody's own voice thundered overhead, like his thoughts were being broadcasted through a megaphone, making him wince. *Corrupting the dreamer makes more Rankers...* The Syranadians began lethargically slipping into the robes, but when he blinked everyone was still busy gorging themselves, the Rankers still by the wall. Nothing made sense. They had to move–had to leave.

He tried to stand up but lost his balance and ended up sort of lunging to the side, out of his chair. The top of his head collided with the wall and he cricked his neck. He was looking at the ceiling. All of the colors were melting together and dissipating like gas. Where was he? He turned his head. Sylph stood behind Domine's chair, watching him. Brody attempted to say her name, but it was remarkably difficult.

"He was in a guild," Sylph said. Her voice was very far away. "What do all guilds have in common?" She knelt over him. Her hair touched his face. A truck horn blasted in his ear; a pair of headlights blinded him. He cried out, and turned his head.

There at his other side sat Michael. The White Griffin spread his wings as he had the day Brody had departed from the capital and Brody saw one image; one image that he suddenly recalled flashing through the soft white feathers: a silver flag stitched with the image of a white harp. The same flag he had seen earlier in an upstairs room. The flag of Syranade. The flag of the capital's musician's guild.

And Brody's sight dimmed until he saw nothing and knew nothing.

Brody woke up disoriented, but clear-headed. His ribs were sore because he was lying prone on the cool tiles by the piano. When he lifted his head, he saw out the leaded window very pale, gray light permeating the orchard beyond as dawn approached. A great weight pressed against the small of his back. Craning his neck, Brody saw that it was Ayrdan's head. The bard snored gently, cradling a lute.

"Aydran." Brody's voice came thick. He cleared his throat. "*Ahem*, Aydran!" The man didn't stir, but made a very grumpy, belligerent noise.

Brody rolled onto his back, took Aydran's head, and scooted out from under it, laying it gently on the floor. For a moment, he sat on his legs and surveyed the room. The Rankers were gone. The Syranadians, scattered around the room, were just beginning to wake up. Some stood uncomfortably, stretched, and began slouching toward the door out, smacking their lips and rubbing their eyes. There was no sign of the previous night's refuse; no chicken bones, oyster shells, peach pits, or dirty dishes.

Brody stood up, twisting side to side, grimacing at his own aches. What had happened? Had he maybe seen the window when befuddled by last night's fumes and been drawn to it as if to escape? The chubby bard sprawled under the piano with his rump in the air. Aydran's beret was perched on top of it.

Domine seemed to have pulled the ficuses in their alcove together to make a fortress and was curled up behind them asleep. Josiah snoozed nearby, using their tablecloth as a blanket.

Brody looked down at himself. Nothing seemed amiss, except that his bo staff was propped up in one of the pairs of antlers on the wall. He retrieved it, checking it over, and heard a familiar squeak of relief.

"Rexus?" He turned. The charlatan came hopping toward him, low to the ground, like an excited ferret. Springing off someone's head, making them grumble in their sleep, Rexus landed on the piano bench and then jumped from there onto Brody's chest, snuggling him under the chin and purring.

Brody half-held the creature, stroking his fur and ears fondly. "I'm very glad to see you, too."

"Go! Go! Khogar and Abram worry!" Rexus cried.

"Not yet. I know what we're looking for." Last night's weird visions emerged from his memories where they'd been camouflaged by confusion. He looked seriously down into Rexus's big, brown eyes. "I need you to find a Syranadian flag somewhere in this building and then direct me to it. I'll try to wake the others, but hurry!"

Rexus, though clearly confounded, departed obediently and Brody tried to rouse Aydran again. The veins under Aydran's eyes were no darker than usual, and Brody wondered if they had all managed to pass the night without partaking of the feast.

Aydran stirred and rubbed his face when Brody slapped him lightly on the cheek. Brody left him and hurried to Domine, who shifted onto his hands and knees at Brody's voice, and then to Josiah, who jolted and began feverishly kicking the tablecloth off of himself as if snared. In the time it took to tend to them, Aydran had fallen asleep again. Brody growled in frustration.

Rexus returned and squeaked, "Upstairs, in room, on wall."

"Guarded?"

"One Ranker," Rexus said grimly.

"Make sure the others stay awake, and then take them to Khogar and Abram. Tell them I've found the power source."

Rexus's eyes widened and his tail swished side to side. Without a question he scampered over to Aydran and began pawing at him, chirping loudly like a car alarm.

Moving around the recumbent Syranadians, Brody ascended the staircase at the end of the hall, every griffin-sense straining. His every cell felt charged with electricity. He was the speck in the eye's blindspot; an owl passing unseen and unheard overhead beneath the moon.

A Ranker stood as still as statuary outside a closed door directly opposite the room Brody had met the Fat Man in. Pausing slightly behind the wall, Brody took a few deep breaths. What sort of Ranker was this? What were its weaknesses? He counted to three, then rounded the wall and stood in the center of the hallway, his stance loose and accommodating.

The Ranker's head turned sharply; the dark recess of its hood faced him and from within it came a strange clicking sound. It rushed at him, lifting its arms and revealing hands with three claws and bristles. Planting his feet and leaning slightly forward, Brody caught the Ranker and gripped its elbow in one hand, using his staff in the other to pull its hood back.

Its head was like that of an enormous flea, with dead eyes and a long, stabbing mouth-piece. It clicked loudly, trying to upset Brody's balance and throw him down, pulling him this way and that. Brody fitted the arm holding his staff around behind the monster's back, clutching its waist and feeling a hard, smooth, shell-like carapace beneath the robes. With a graceful twist and pivot, he had flipped the Ranker over his hip. It hit the floor hard and Brody smashed the staff down with all his might into the monster's delicate-looking mouthparts. It would never move again.

Brody stood over the carcass, panting, exhilarated. He felt like he could do cartwheels down the hallway, or jump up and touch the ceiling. He had defeated his first Ranker–if only Domine and the others could have seen him. Adrenaline carried him into the room the Ranker had been guarding; it looked like a living space for one of the inn's guests. On the wall behind an ugly-patterned sofa and a heavy table with a chessboard built into its surface, the sparkling, silver flag of Syranade shifted in the breeze created by his entrance.

Approaching cautiously, Brody felt a force emanating from the flag the nearer he moved. It was like walking against a strong, arctic wind; at once breath-taking and refreshing. The fabric seemed to glow as he stepped toward it. He rounded the coffee table and thought that he saw black flecks falling from the flag like dust. He stepped up onto the couch and reached up to where the corners of the flag were pinned to the wall with nails. Where his fingers touched it, he felt tiny vibrations, as from hundreds of bee wings. Where his breath hit it, he saw a patch of gold appear and then fade like steam on a cold window. Something seemed to be flowing out of him; transferring into the cloth. He held still, letting the transference happen, wondering how long it would take to finish.

"Gotcha!" the Fat Man's voice exclaimed behind him.

Brody half-turned before he was gripped around the chest in a powerful bear hug, his arms prevented from touching the flag. In a panic, he kicked off the wall, shoving back into the Fat Man, transforming as he went. By the time the Fat Man had fallen against the table, his grip had broken, and Brody had rolled backward to hit the floor on his feet in griffin form.

His hind paws kicked at the rug like a bull about to charge and his tail swung like a pendulum. A spiky ridge of feathers and fur traced his neck and spine and though he couldn't spread his wings in the confined space, he held them out from his body like arms cocked to fight.

The Fat Man arose from the table. He glanced at the flag to ascertain its safety, and then grinned at the large griffin now filling a fourth of the room.

"Well, I'll be. The Griffin King. I believe I owe you a formality." He dipped down into an exaggerated, mocking curtsy. "Now if we're gonna do this on even ground..."

The Ranker began to swell in size. Shadows gathered from every crevice and crack in the room to obscure him in a swirling orb. Brody's head swayed side to side and he clicked his beak loudly, a gurgling growl rolling in his throat.

The Fat Man gave a loud, huffing snort and the shadows retreated to reveal a monstrosity with four eyes, a heavy muzzle full of overlapping tusks, jagged and broken, and gray, saggy skin. Drool ran down its chest and it stretched out four, fat limbs, each holding a small mace.

Bloodlust filled Brody like boiling fire. Never in his life had he felt such an awful, amazing, inhuman desire to rend and end. This was like the anger he had felt in the woods as a child or the anger he had felt in the alley toward the thugs, but *magnified*. Fear was only a word–this was above fear...this was anger tempered into something dark and lethal...something that had, for centuries, made a warrior out of man and an animal out of the warrior.

"I will be rewarded for what little work I've accomplished, for what little I've contributed!" the Fat Man shouted.

"Contributed to what?" Brody snarled.

"You will fall as every griffin before you has! Today, tomorrow, it matters not. How can you best us when you don't understand us? When you can't fathom the depths we will plumb to succeed? My life will be one of glory and feasting!"

"No! Your life is *forfeit*!" With a rich, lion's roar in tandem with a hawk's scream, Brody pounced, each talon spread.

The pair of them burst through the wall in a shower of splintered wood and pulverized plaster. Glass and dust sprinkled onto the streets and upturned faces below. His talons locked in the Ranker's upper arms, Brody spread his wings to lessen their impact into the roof of the building next door. Still, they hit hard, skidding across the shingles and fetching up in the valley between two rooms.

Their battle became a whirlwind and a thunderstorm. Gusts from Brody's wings ripped leaves from their branches. The Fat Man's footsteps shook the earth. The Syranadians could only duck and dart to avoid debris tossed up by a talon or fist.

Khogar and Abram were doing damage control, trying to clear the area. They looked up and dove aside just in time; the Fat Man smashed into the cobblestones beneath Brody right where they had been standing. Their growls, hisses, the sounds of their strikes making contact, were deafening. Feathers and blood and torn shreds of black cloak and scattered pills flew from around them like flies.

Brody closed his beak around the Ranker's neck. Four maces thudded against his shoulders and ribs. They rolled into the wartorn rubble of a house and Brody lifted the Fat Man in his claws, carrying him along with mighty sweeps of his wings and dumping him onto another rooftop. The Fat man's foamy tusks spread for Brody's throat, but Brody warded him away with a few cat-like swats of the talons.

Countless bruises and lacerations and possibly even fractures were, for the moment, mere twinges of discomfort, insulated away beneath Brody's energy. But he had given as bad as he'd got. The Fat Man was now down to two maces, one of his eyes had been reduced to a pulpy mess, and a bad gash on his neck bled profusely.

"Did you know who I was?" Brody asked. "When you saw me yesterday?"

Even with his face brutish and malignant, the Ranker was able to give Brody a very human *are-you-serious* expression and said, "Your eyes are not marked. You wear fresh chainmail and carry a staff with griffin feathers tied to it. Of course I knew. But to kill you with allies whose powers I could not know at your back would be foolish. I had to isolate you. Weaken you."

"*Am I weak*?" Brody interrupted, lifting his head high. The Ranker kept speaking, ignoring him.

"So I penned you in with my prize sheep. Tempted you with fine feed. I hoped you would gorge on my feast, but nevermind. This is enough." He roared, spittle flying, and attacked.

With a flit of the tail-fan, Brody dodged around behind the Fat Man and donkey-kicked him in the back. The Ranker stumbled, almost toppling off the roof, his two free hands grabbing at shingles.

"What of your prize Syranadians?" Brody asked. "In *Sonnets*? Why aren't they under your spell?"

"'Under my spell,'" the Fat Man chuckled wheezily. "How cute. Do you think Rankers are the only wicked things out there? The only 'bad guys?' What a pretty little world that would be."

"Answer me!" Brody commanded, stomping one talon so hard that he dented the shingles.

"Look at the big picture!" The Fat man sneered, his saliva tinged pink. "Whatever your kind thinks about Rankers we don't just invite war for the fun of it! What drives us?"

"Evil."

"Bigger!"

Brody considered. "The darkness in the people who created you?"

The Fat Man grinned, exposing all of his tusks. "Better, much better, but it goes even further than that... This," he gestured broadly, "this is destiny."

Brody scowled, his eyes flashing bright red.

The Ranker laughed. "You think I jest!" His smile faded. "But I don't. Ask your people about the prophecy."

"Prophecy? There's a prophecy...about me?"

"Every human plays a part in some prophecy or other, but this..." The Fat Man came closer, his tone conversational, mystifying, his maces lowered, his three eyes intent on the griffin. "This is a big one. It's not often that they divulge their prophecies for regular folks to hear."

"What do you mean?" Brody looked pleadingly up at the Ranker. Was there more to his appearance in the Land of Dreams than being its king? "What's the prophecy say? What are your plans?"

Those eyes came closer. "'*Eclipsed the sun, corrupted all, a King shall rise, a King shall fall,*' et cetera, et cetera… It's our time, boy; a time of darkness, when the dreamworld will fall into shadow. You will fall, too. Everyone is corruptible." The Ranker's voice was soft. "Everyone has an appetite. Even you." The lower arms shot out to grab hold of Brody. The upper arms raised to bring the maces down on his skull. But Brody had expected it.

He knocked the lower arms wide with his wings, staid the upper pair with his claws, leaped up, and spun around to land behind the Ranker. With one talon and a push from his hind legs, he pinned the Fat Man down. He sank his beak into the monster's upper back and with a savage twist from his other talon, broke the Ranker's neck.

Limping back away from the twitching corpse, Brody tried to ignore the pain accompanying his weariness as his adrenaline faded. His griffin instincts urged him to crow over this noble kill–to roar at the justice of it. Instead, he backed to the edge of the roof and lay down, his brain buzzing. Corrupted dreamers…a prophecy…

"No way!" an amazed voice came from somewhere distant. On a rooftop across from him stood his friends. Aydran, the one who had shouted, had his hands on either side of his face as if he had just seen something spectacular. Domine pumped his fists. Their voices all overlapped, but Brody knew that they were congratulating him.

He purred happily. That was one problem solved: it was quite apparent that Brody had proven himself to his companions. Syranade belonged to the Griffin King once more.

Chapter Seventeen:

The Magic of Dreams

"Friendship is unnecessary, like philosophy, like art... It has no survival value; rather it is one of those things that give value to survival."

–C.S. Lewis

After the Fat Man perished, Josiah told Brody later, the Syranadians stirred from his trance and the other Rankers fled. Brody transformed once he swooped over to join his comrades on the nearby roof. Though the Ranker blood staining his beak and claws now ran down his staff and hands, his aches and wounds remained the same.

Abram directed him to sit propped against the chimney and Aydran's comic reenactments of the fight and Domine's litany of praise were interspersed with the minister's gentle words: "does this hurt?" and "this might sting a little."

As Abram applied bandages and poultices, Brody observed the Syranadians with a kingly stare. He was tired to his marrow, so weak that his every movement trembled, but his people fared far worse. Most collapsed where they stood into exhausted faints; some were busy retching first. Children began wailing for their parents to comfort them or take away their pains as only parents can, then adults began to cry out desperately for missing loved ones. The Syranadians that Brody could remember from *Sonnets* looked around themselves at their decrepit city with misery, guilt, uncertainty, and disgust. Were they Judases to be cast out, Brody wondered, or prodigal sons to be welcomed back into the fold?

Rexus clambered up onto the roof dragging the flag in his teeth. The heavy fabric looked no different than it had before, but for the lack of black flakes drifting from it. However, when he touched it, Brody could feel an indescribable warmth and strength running through its threads. The transfer of power had worked, and the flag would serve to safeguard the city from further Ranker intrusion. At least, that was the hope.

Brody held the cloth in his fingers. Now that the adrenaline had left his body and he had time to think again, the Ranker's taunting words crawled through his tumultuous thoughts. If there *was* a prophecy unfolding, what was his place in it? Were the Rankers seeking to stop it from happening, or actively working to *make* it happen? If, as the Fat Man had claimed, the Rankers were destined to win and conquer the dreamworld, then would all of Brody's efforts to repel them prove fruitless?

When Khogar appeared below, cautiously leading their horses around the prone Syranadians, Brody took Abram's hand and let himself be pulled up.

"Hey," Aydran said with concern, "let him rest! He's not a battle-virgin anymore–he just made his first kill! Come on..."

"No," Brody said. "I'm fine. Abram, take care of the Syranadians. Maybe there are some doctors down there who can help you. There are a few people I need to speak with."

He transformed into a griffin to dive from the roof, though it felt more like falling because of how slack his sore muscles were.

Becoming human once more, Brody watched a few still-conscious Syranadians approach him apprehensively. They reached out and touched his clothes as if by doing so they could be healed, or as if to prove to themselves that he was real. They whispered benedictions and sighed their relief and began to weep like they were in the presence of a great comforter; a counselor; someone who could erase the nightmare they'd been living. Compassion for these people stirred in Brody's chest, and steely determination began to fill him like hot lead, giving weight to his steps, pulling him back down from his wandering thoughts to the present moment. They *needed* him. They *needed* some prophetic hero to rescue them, soothe their hurts, and put things right.

Brody didn't know much about prophecies, but, mulling over the verse the Fat Man had recited to him, it sounded as if he had a chance to stop the Rankers before they gained much more traction. If his predecessor, Uriah, had been the king 'to fall,' then he, Brody, *would* be the king 'to rise.' Yes, and he would rise like the sun, cleansing this beautiful land tainted by the Rankers' corruption, starting here in Syranade.

As Brody continued walking along the street, new strength continued to flow into him as if from some external reservoir. He moved among the people, embracing them, gripping their shoulders, but silent. He would not allow sympathy to goad him into making false reassurances. When he found the crowd of Syranadians who had frequented *Sonnets*, his eyes became focused and flickered red as if with static. They watched him fearfully.

"Who am I?" he asked.

After a long pause, a woman said, "The...High King... The G-Griffin King..."

"Who am I?" Brody demanded, more loudly.

"The Griffin King!" more people replied.

He asked again and again until everyone responded, and each of their affirmations pounded through him like a hammer ringing against an anvil. *Yes,* he thought, *I am the Griffin King, and I was chosen for a purpose. If that purpose is to fulfill a role in some prophecy then I need to convince my people as much as myself.* He took a steadying breath and said, "I have been given terrible responsibilities and the divine authority to perform them. I am no heifer to chew cud whilst wrongdoing poisons this land and my people. I am no slug to lie useless in the shade. My talons bring reckoning and my staff, retribution." He raised his voice further, speaking now to every Syranadian who could hear and listen. "See to your own. See to others. Practice diligence. For if your sole focus is on satisfying your hunger, then others will starve around you, and I will return to separate the wheat from the chaff, as is my duty."

Brody's gaze scraped over the Fat Man's prize sheep one more time, and then he strode purposefully toward Khogar and the bronze fountain in the center of the square.

"Well-said," Josiah commented, as he and the others merged into Brody's wake. Brody made a sound of thanks.

When he reached the tribal, Brody climbed onto his dun, which pranced eagerly in place, ready to stretch out its legs in a good run. Khogar and the rest of their companions except Abram, who was still checking on the Syranadians, looked up at him, at a loss as to what to do with themselves. But in a few minutes, it became clear who Brody waited for.

From the alleys and backstreets came the roving packs. Though healthier-looking than their inner-city brethren, the gauntness of their cheeks, the hollowness of their eyes, were proof that with the Fat Man's death, they had become aware of the atrocities they had committed. Brody was pleased to see the outcasts embraced by other Syranadians; led toward Abram and the healers he'd found to be examined; greeted warmly by friends, family, and neighbors on whose shoulders they broke down and wept their shame and sorrow.

One pack, larger than the rest by now, shepherding the others before it, tramped wearily to Brody when its members saw him sitting above the crowd, his crown removed from his saddlebags and shining on his head. These men, their beards filthy and matted, wore tattered, bloodstained uniforms of blue or red, and rusting armor. They, too, showed the trauma of their realized cannibalism, and looked as if the presence of a superior was the only thing keeping them from falling on their own swords.

They saluted Brody weakly, clumsily.

"Do you remember saving my life?" Brody asked quietly of one of the men that he recognized from that night when they had confronted the packs. "Do you remember sparing us?" The man shook his head, looking as if he saw a glimmer of redemption.

"That is because your hearts are true, even if your minds were deceiving you. My men and I may very well be alive because of you." He looked at the men in blue. "See to your city. Set up patrols to bring any stragglers still in the outskirts back into the fold. Reinstate a mayor and recruit to bulk up your numbers if need be, then position guards to watch your borders. Take only what food and supplies you need. Leave the rest for the people."

To the men in red swaying on the spot, Brody said, "You will join us. We will travel to the Fortress of Ice to send aid back here..." he looked over at Josiah, who absently petted his horse's stripe, adding, "And to get an idea of what's next."

They spent the rest of that day and the next resting but busy. The only horses in Syranade that were still alive had fled into the woods around it. Josiah flew out and fetched a small herd of them for the Syranadian guards and king's knights to use. They all helped to bury the dead, tend to injuries and reunite families. Because of the Fat Man's gluttony, there was almost no food at all left in Syranade, but what gardens and orchards remained unspoiled were just beginning to divulge their bounty. With careful moderation, the people would survive until extra supplies came.

When the day of departure arrived, Josiah bade them farewell. It was a two-month journey to the fortress with injured knights amongst them, and he would cut the journey in half, if not more, on griffin wings. The rest of the company would meet him there, and hopefully pass a support train on its way to Syranade along the journey. Brody watched him arc into the heavens like a crimson arrow, wrestling with dismay. With all of the commotion and everyone at their own tasks helping Syranade back onto its feet, he had missed the opportunity to ask Josiah about the prophecy.

He took one last look at the city and its people before urging his dun into a gallop. With a roar like thunder, Domine, Aydran, Khogar, Abram, and eleven knights kicked their horses into movement. Soon, trees had swallowed them up and they left the oppression of the devastated city behind. Brody gratefully breathed in the scent of pine and raspberries and lavender. His first adventure was behind him. Whatever lay ahead would be much more challenging–battling Rankers who had had more time to sink their claws into the territories they'd claimed, rescuing people who had suffered longer under dark spells. But now...Brody was ready.

The Fat Man had all but confirmed that Brody's mind-muddled realization in *Sonnets* had been correct; the Rankers were corrupting the positive energies left behind by past griffin rulers so as to corrupt dream-creations, which in turn would corrupt dream-creators–people from reality like Brody, Abram, and Josiah–and make more Rankers. The Fat Man had even revealed a little bit of the 'why': they felt that they were fulfilling some mysterious prophecy. But which Ranker had decided that *now* was the time to act on the so-called prophecy, and *why* had they decided it? What was their ultimate goal?

There were still a lot of answers to find, and Brody expected to find them at the Fortress of Ice. If anyone had information about any prophecies, it would be Josiah, the confidant of the White Griffin. Not only that, but the fortress overlooked the next-nearest city overtaken by a Ranker lord, and the fortress-keeper would likely have vital information to share about his observations by the time they arrived...

For a few days, Brody worried that they wouldn't ever make it to the fortress. The knights were in very poor spirits–though physically healthy, or at least uninjured, their appetites had been satisfied of late with human flesh. Some of the men randomly broke down and wept, claiming that they couldn't get the taste out of their mouths. Their captain, slipping back into his role nicely no matter his own grief, berated these moping knights; challenged them; drove them on. Brody, whose sympathy had been roused at the sorry state of the warriors rather than any ire, knew not to interfere. It wasn't his place. And, to his surprise, after about a week, the tough love seemed to have paid off. He saw no more tears, heard no more sorrow.

He was recovering as well. Brody had sustained badly bruised ribs and some severe scrapes in the battle with the Fat Man, and his face had become tender and swollen on one side, the sight from one eye reduced to a slit until it healed. Still, he caught the looks of impressed awe that his knights gave him in passing, accompanied by respectful salutes.

In the next two months, Brody tried to get to know each knight personally. He respected and admired these men more than they knew, and even the youngest among them, a boy of fourteen, had amazing stories to tell about life in the dreamworld. Evenings around their campfires became enjoyable affairs, with laughter and contented sighs issuing from the bedrolls spread beneath the stars and tree boughs. Food was plentiful, the weather was mild, and Brody recovered swiftly from his wounds. He felt as if they were all suspended in limbo; allowed a brief sanctuary before the next trial, granted a respite to think things over. And think, Brody did.

The young king was often to be found sitting a little separate from his companions, taking stock of his newfound knowledge; he hadn't asked anyone about the prophecy yet, but he turned over and over in his head the memory of the corrupt Syranadians feasting among the Rankers.

He dissected the battle with the Fat man, whose sin had been his downfall; his ample weight had made him slow and easy to predict. As Michael had once said: the mind of a man in the body of a beast was a force to reckon with. That went for Rankers as much as it did for griffins. He thought of how it had felt touching the flag of Syranade as King Khafra had once touched it. He'd had the sensation of looking out over glittering Egyptian sands, feeling the Nile cool on his legs as he took in the splendor of ancient palaces, and hearing the beautiful melody of a harp playing an ode to a dreamworld-sunset. These and other sensations once experienced by Khafra had been transferred to Brody. It had bolstered his spirits knowing that he was part of such a legacy and he confessed himself eager to experience such memories again.

Each evening Brody transformed and flew up to check their surroundings, if only to admire the view and maybe spy some dinner worth hunting down. Indescribable beauty surrounded him: waterfalls surrounded by mossy willows, ancient paths of round stones wending through trees of white blossoms, mile markers in the form of statutes resembling mythical beasts, and every now and then a glimpse out over distant cities sparkling with life, or rich palaces holding mysterious secrets. Brody marveled, speechless. What fantastical stories were playing out in those glens and sunlit glades?

What princesses were meeting their princes? What starry-eyed youth was discovering their strength on some harrowing adventure?

And the nights seemed almost sacred. He would soar up by the moon, above a silvery landscape of clouds, with the stars shining in their billions. He returned to earth feeling a little more changed each time.

About halfway along their trek, they passed the supply train sent to aid Syranade. The men driving the oxen bearing carts loaded with foodstuffs, medicine, blankets, building supplies, and even a few toys to cheer up Syranadian children, were greeted heartily by Brody and his men. There was no time to spare for idle chatter; a few pleasantries, bits of news, and laughs were exchanged before both parties moved on.

One day near the end of their journey, Brody drifted into a sort of doze in the saddle and had a half-dream. In the dream, though he was still aware of rocking in the saddle, and even opened his eyes once or twice to gaze around him, he beheld a young griffin walking alongside his horse. The griffin was male, still small, about the height of a large wolf, and had a fine growth of yellow feathers beginning to lengthen over each eye.

"I feel like I know you," Brody said in a slurred voice. The griffin ignored him, collecting twigs from the ground as they walked, pausing every now and then to weave them together into a crown.

Brody started fully awake, his hand flying up to his curls where a bug had gotten tangled in his hair. His hair was longer now, almost shaggy, and a short beard, hardly more than stubble, had sprouted on his face. Both brough irritating new sensations with them–he constantly felt like things were caught in them.

When he departed to hunt, Brody dwelled on the odd dream he'd had, and strained once more to remember what-all he'd seen back in Michael's wings. In the Land of Dreams, the smallest thing could bear great meaning.

Spotting a nice, plump boar hog in the bushes below, Brody circled once and dove like an arrow. It was a swift kill; any heavier and he would've been unable to carry it. As he wrapped his talons around its legs and prepared to lift off, a sound, as of a long, low breath, came from behind him. He whirled with a hiss.

But there was only an old, crumbling stone monument behind him. Mostly hidden beneath ivy and brambles, it had been carved into some sort of barbaric likeness. Brody carefully clawed some of the overgrowth away. The monolithic figure had wide, staring eyes, and its mouth was a round, gaping hole stained centuries past by what horribly resembled blood–gallon after gallon must have once been poured down its stone gullet. Two claw-like hands grasped either side of its face, two more were outstretched and also stained. Despite its fearsome appearance, Brody felt that any dark power it had once possessed had long since drained away. Carved into its face, with much finer tools than whatever had been used to make the figure itself, was a cross.

As if in a trance, Brody slowly rose up on his hind paws like a cat investigating a dangling string. Were sounds issuing from the mouth? His ears perked forward, the quills on his head lifted like whiskers... slowly, becoming louder as if the sounds were being increased by increments with a dial, Brody heard the flap of giant wings; marching feet, invisible, overhead; the crackle of flaming chariots; the wailing of terror as sudden darkness plunged a city into chaos; bone-shaking concussions of explosions as fire rained from the sky like bombs, demolishing the filth of evil, of sin...

Another noise, this one a snort, brought Brody back to himself. His beak almost touched the statue's face–he was straining upward with his talons braced between its arms. Blinking his third eyelids, Brody peeked around the monolith. Standing a stone's-throw behind it was a black unicorn with gold, cloven hooves, a spiraling golden horn, and a mane, tail-tassel, and beard of white and amber.

Taken by surprise and speechless in the presence of the beautiful, legendary creature, Brody froze. Though it knew he was there–indeed, it stared right at him–he didn't want to frighten it into running off.

For many minutes they studied each other, griffin-eyes with cat slits on unicorn-eyes as dark and round as a doe's. Then the stench of his kill and the silence of coming twilight drove Brody to reluctantly depart. As he power-flapped into the air, lugging the hog, Brody felt the unicorn, now a shadow beneath the evergreens, watching him fly away.

Chapter Eighteen:

The Fortress of Ice

"It's better to stand by someone's side than by yourself."
–Jack London

Accepting a thick slab of wild pork handed to him by a knight with an Elvis lip, Brody grinned and tapped his foot in time to Aydran's latest musical creation.

Strumming his viol in a bright, spunky way, the bard winked and nodded charmingly around at his rapt, cheering audience and sang,

"*The bigger you are, the harder you fall, goes the old, sermon-ly fundament.*

And that mean ol' Ranker, though a glutton he was, was really a glutton for punishment!"

As Aydran began everyone's favorite verses, about Brody's somewhat embellished, epic showdown with the Fat Man, Brody's eyes settled on the flames in their cheery fire pit, whose embers closely matched the scarlet of Josiah's feathers.

With Josiah, his closest confidante, gone, Brody could think of no one else he'd feel comfortable telling about the unicorn and the statue. One or two of the knights were confidential, but they didn't seem the type to believe in omens or much care about old, crumbly statues. Aydran would have a difficult time being serious. Domine saw discussions about anything other than the present and the known as pointless, and Khogar, like all felines, would be *too* curious and pester him with silly questions until Brody forgot what they were even talking about in the first place.

With a stab of shame, Brody looked suddenly at the man sitting propped against a tree-root, taking turns chewing on neatly cut bits of meat and sharpening the nib of a fluffy, green, tabby-striped wing feather quill–probably one of his own. Abram. Why hadn't he considered the pastor?

Brody took his food and joined Abram. "I don't know what's in the spices you use, but you continue to outdo yourself, minister."

"A good cook never tells, your Highness," Abram chortled, lifting his spectacles onto his head to afford Brody a fatherly smile. "To be honest, I can never remember what I throw together for supper or how I do it, but all I ever hear are compliments! Must be doing something right... What's on your mind?"

Brody told him about his outing as the man listened, as attentive as a doctor considering the symptoms described by a patient.

"What was it doing there? Can unicorns be...evil? Tainted?"

Abram, tapping the quill against his chin in thought, widened his eyes and shook his head.

"Never," he said emphatically. "Never-ever. Firstly, a unicorn would die before it let itself be corrupted. Secondly, they have their own brand of magic that negates any and all impurities of Dark Magick. No, any evil unicorn you see is just a puppet animated by a sorcerer doing the work of the devil. Trust me when I say, your Eminence, that had that creature been nothing more than a pseudo-unicorn...you would know."

Abram looked up and around them while Brody listened, mystified, absently running his finger around the sauces on his plate and licking them off. "No," he continued, "I imagine that the unicorn was only passing by and decided to get a look at you. I can't say much about the monolith; this land boasts many such secrets from bygone dreams."

Dreams...secrets... Brody pondered the half-dream he'd had about the young griffin with yellow brow-feathers. Had that, as Michael had once said, been a vision? Then the words of the prophecy the Fat Man had mentioned floated through his mind. *Speaking of secret things...*

Brody tilted his head a little closer to Abram and asked in a low voice, "Do you know about any prophecy? The Ranker mentioned one."

Abram paused in the middle of fiddling with an ink pot to blink at Brody as if perplexed. "Why, yes, a little. I can't remember all of the verses, but it's ancient... You say the Ranker quoted it?" Brody nodded and the pastor's brow furrowed. "Hmm. I find it concerning that those monsters even know about it, but I suppose word was bound to get out over several hundred years."

Brody continued staring at the man, waiting, and when Abram realized that the king's curiosity had not been sated, he gave him a fatherly smile. "Don't you let them get in your head, Your Majesty. Scholars have been puzzling over this onus for a very long time. From what I recall, it's quite vague. It would make sense for the Rankers to try and attribute their successes to destiny and their actions to fate. Villains have done so for millenia."

But Brody was not entirely convinced. He couldn't imagine the Rankers acting so boldly on the words of some dusty prophecy unless they knew for *certain* that its advent was nigh...

Their path soon took them higher and higher along treacherous, rocky back-tracks and cliffside trails that all but Khogar's shaggy pony found difficult. The air became thinner. Clouds gathered *below* them. Even the eagle chose her aerie at a lower elevation than the one they muscled through. Snow, deep, glittering drifts of it, appeared, defying what little heat from the sun could penetrate through the chilly ozone. At times Brody had to dismount and join the knights in scooping the icy powder, chest-deep in places, out of their way. Brody wondered how the supply train had managed the descent.

Right on time, on the last day of the second month, Brody's sharp eyes picked out the Fortress of Ice framed black against the watery blue sky. Also known as the Fortress of the Iron Teeth, King Cato had built it to guard the Howling Pass, from whence the snow-beasts made their cyclical marches on the villages spread across the mountains. It had stood firm for centuries, manned by knights in shifts of one or two year terms. And now, Brody hoped, its master would yield vital information for the next stage of his journey.

They reached the fortress after noon when the sun was just beginning to shift from directly overhead. Brody and his company mutely absorbed all that stretched below them down the mountain's slopes and beyond. Mountain ranges, some boasting peaks even higher than their own, cut jaggedly into the sky, cobalt streaked with white.

Pastures, plains, forests, and metropolises, all had blended together into tiny, insignificant patches glimpsed through gaps in the cloud layer. And nearer-at-hand, the terrain only yards from the treacherous trail to their summit plummeted into vast valleys of snow and waterfalls and outcrops of bare rock. Brody, with a heaving sigh of contentment, wondered with a thrill what it would feel like to drop from this height and dive all the way to the mountain's feet on griffin wings.

Brody nudged his dun onward, letting the reins drop and guiding the horse with his knees so that he could stretch his arms and return his staff to its straps on his back. It was amazing that the dreamland was an island, bigger than Hawaii, bigger even than the continent of Australia. Off to his right, to the north, Brody saw glittering ribbons of sunlight on ocean waves. Far over there somewhere was his kingdom. Josiah had once explained that time and space folded in on themselves in the dreamworld, much like a brain does to create more surface area in a confined sphere like the human skull, where both the Land of the Dreams and the brain creating it belonged.

Now Brody led the way across a flat-land of snow, along a stony road between two rows of steeply-roofed cottages. People clad in heavy furs shoveling snow from their steps, or standing in groups around communal braziers, watched them first with concern, hunkering low as if to bolt for weapons, but then one woman pointed at Brody's crown and soon the small hamlet rang with cheers. These were the families of the knights stationed in the fortress, which arose like the bristles on a boar's back about a half mile from the hamlet, anchored on a jutting pinnacle of rock like a bird of prey.

It was a hard life these people had: braving the elements, hunting elusive prey, keeping fires burning hot for warmth, and waiting perhaps days for aid-griffins to arrive with emergency rations in the leaner times. Those who volunteered for such a life were rewarded with their choice of living-place for their year's turn off. Not surprisingly, many of these families had more tropical climes to look forward to as the year's end approached.

The fortress itself was of an oily-black stone so as to soak up as much heat as possible and help counter snow-blindness. It was a tall, narrow, gothic sort of construction; all stairs and arches, pinnacles and hook-like crockets atop towers like spear-points. The towers themselves, if seen from a bird's-eye-view, were star-shaped to cut the winds. Layers of walls stood tall, meant to delay an enemy's intrusion. The horses' clopping hooves echoed sharply in the formidable killing grounds between gates as Brody noted the new sights around him.

Giant torches and empty pitch-cauldrons awaited their call to action on the crenelated wall-tops. Brody saw a flight-platform meant for guests with wings about midway up a tower that seemed to be an observatory. Silos full of grain and preservable foodstuffs nestled around a belltower. Bronze pipes wending about pumped water up into the romanesque bath house from deep hot springs. In the last yard before the inner court, Brody noted an abundance of empty carts lined up in a row.

A tall man wearing a heavy fur cape and followed at a polite distance by two burly guards had just left the innermost court to meet them. In a soft voice tinged with an accent that made his every word somehow pointed, like a silver dagger-tip, the man said, "You are lucky–you have just beaten the snows."

When he'd drawn close enough that he didn't have to raise his voice, he indicated the carts with a hand and added, "Our emergency supplies from the capital. Your councilman Isa is always..." the man rolled his head side to side, searching for a word, "...punctual."

He reminded Brody of a shadow in a blizzard, a keen ax edge, a drop of blood sizzling in the snow, a man raised by wolves. This was Skâlger, master of the fortress, a man who wasted no breath on petty formalities. His eyes were the color of a fish's: a silvery bluish-white. His hair, pale blond, was much longer atop his head than on the sides and braided in loose rows. His beard was similarly braided. Beneath the fur cape, he wore the scaled armor of a warrior of the ice fortress, the sword of a north-islander belted around his waist, and the hip-sash of a captain. At his feet just under the cape, watching Brody impassively as if it were an emperor borne on a palanquin, sat a black, fox-like creature with gold markings.

"Come," Skâlger said, moving buoyantly like a child, though he was a man in his thirties and had the mien of one much older. "I want to show you something."

They left their horses with the guards and followed Skâlger and his...pet?...into the inner courtyard. They passed the broad steps and reinforced double doors of the entrance, rounding the fortress and the knights milling around it who stared at Brody expressionlessly.

Behind the complex they went, until Brody began to wonder if they would walk in a complete circle. But then he heard the rhythmic sound of shouting, as of a great many men doing a drill.

In a vast, open section of ground spreading between the fortress dormitories and the inner wall, over which Brody glimpsed a fine view of the lands below the mountain, around eight hundred knights practiced fighting straw dummies in time to a co-captain's command.

Skâlger threw an arm around Brody's shoulders and said, "For your campaign in Crystalia."

Brody felt some of the color leave his face. This fighting force was his? He was to lead an *army*?

Skâlger chuckled and patted Brody's chest and the young king felt all the color return to his cheeks when the man said flippantly, "Let's take a bath."

Chapter Nineteen:

Illusions

"The Devil can cite the Scripture for his purpose."

–Shakespeare, *The Merchant of Venice*

The heated baths were the size of swimming pools and situated in dimly lit chambers that looked hewn straight from the stone. What was at first unseemly, craggy facets, however, resolved into a prosaic sort of beauty, like ancient paintings on a cave wall, as light from luminous yellow crystals on plinths shone off of the myriad and various-sized planes. It looked like a twinkling night sky. Smaller pink and green crystals flickered at times so that it seemed that the aurora borealis–or the dreamland equivalent–danced overhead.

Skâlger led Brody through the fortress and down to one chamber; the others were led elsewhere to another. Brody only had time to see the entrance hall–practical, broad, with arched bays to either side and a distant, vaulted ceiling painted with two stylized wolves–then he came into a close compartment and went down some stairs, the air becoming increasingly steamy.

The bath took up most of the center of the room. A few warriors already lounged at one end, strangely colored foxes of their own in various poses of sleep on the tiles above them. At the other end, Josiah leaned against the steps, eating what looked like a brilliant-magenta flower in loud, crunchy bites.

He looked up, saw Brody, and immediately stroked across the pool toward him. "Your Highness! I didn't recognize you with those bristles sproutin' on your chin!"

The warriors had all stopped talking to stare. An elderly servant came over bearing a silver platter and watching Brody with watery eyes as if he were just another regular returned to the baths.

Though his stomach rumbled with hunger, Brody hesitated. Colorful items littered the plate, looking like toys made of plastic. Here was a blue fish, there, an orange dragon-ship.

Skâlger, unabashedly pulling off his pants with one hand, plucked up a green bear with the other. Mouth full, he indicated the platter to Brody as if he hadn't seen it and said, "Eat. Good for you." His breath smelled of mint and something sweet.

Brody chose a purple ax and nibbled off a corner. It had the texture of dried frosting, and tasted like grape jelly–quite delicious, and the closest he'd had to a cookie since the last time his mother had sent him some at school.

"They are 'heilendi,'" Skâlger said, now shrugging out of his cape. "My people make them. Full of vitamins–all of the things you need. There are terrible winters where I was born. These help us to survive." He stuffed the rest of his heilendi in his mouth so as to use both hands to untie the laces of his kyrtill.

The servant set the platter down beside the pool, where Josiah paddled to hover over it, clicking his tongue in a choosey way. With a few elderly grunts that were maybe for Skâlger's benefit, the servant began picking up his discarded garments.

Not wanting to be last in the pool, Brody tried to ignore his self-consciousness and removed his own cloak, surcoat, tunic, and such, handing them to the servant who looked much obliged. Brody had always made sure to eat healthy and take care of himself, but training and travel had toned the young man into a bracket of physical fitness that he had never before belonged to. He couldn't help but feel a spurt of pride when he sank down into the pool, his muscles flexing and shifting as he did so. He even thought the warriors down at the other end, themselves bound with muscles like armor plates, looked impressed.

Skâlger bent and hopped gracefully down into the pool with an exultant sigh. His pet fox, its little paws clinking on the tiles like the pads were made of glass, looked down at the water, made a strange sound like the creaking mast of a ship, and then curled into a ball.

The hot water sucked the cold and tension out of Brody's body, penetrating all the way to his bones so that he felt he could drift right then into the sweetest of slumbers. The heilendi was also working its magic; vitality bubbled into his limbs, as if he could brave a snowstorm naked, dive beneath the water and hold his breath for hours, wrestle a giant! The north-islanders had to be a formidable folk indeed.

Skâlger watched the effect of the treat on Brody with a troublemaker's smirk, and Brody had the sense that he shared bathwater with a very dangerous man. Something in Skâlger's demeanor hinted at a storied past hidden beneath a dark cloak in a shadowy corner. He had the wit of a raven and the tenacity of a pit-fighter. Brody met the man's pale eyes, combing water through his curls, and felt a great rush of relief that the north-islander was on his side.

"So," Skâlger looked away, as if unnerved by Brody's much milder eyes. "What have you seen and heard?"

"Much," Brody answered softly. As master of the fortress, Skâlger's status was just beneath that of the king's council. It would be nice to puzzle out strategies with someone so experienced; so hardened. "Despite the best efforts of the council, the Rankers know my identity, which, as I'm sure you're aware, carries grim implications, in addition to the difficulties we now face in exercising stealth."

Skâlger nodded once. "Either you are betrayed, or the Rankers have eyes in the capital."

"I've been going over it again and again," Josiah said, his sharp eyes pensive, focused on the middle-distance, "and neither of those make sense. The people of the capital city don't know Brody from Adam–they could give a Ranker a vague description and a name, but they know nothing definitive about him as a person. The guards are on strict schedules, so we'd have noticed a missing man. And each of the council members, for all their flaws, are griffin-hearted. Even invisible Rankers couldn't have entered the city without drawing at least a dog to their stench."

Skâlger played with the water, cupping it into his hands and letting it trickle through his fingers. Then he said, "What of Syranade? Josiah has mentioned that you have composed addendums to the reports we have?"

"Hastily so, I'm afraid. I was hoping that I could send them from here to the Seat of Griffins where General Amos could analyze them.

Not every civilian seems completely susceptible to the Ranker lords' power." He described the Fat Man, the guards reacting to his own voice, and the Fat Man's prize Syranadians who had been both cognizant of, and unconcerned with, the destruction of their city and the suffering of its people.

"This is good information," Skâlger said brightly. His fox thumped its tail twice in its sleep. "Yes, we can use this..."

"What of the Ranker's chosen?" Brody asked. "What do you make of it? They're corrupting dream-creations and trying to make more Rankers. However, I believe that deliberately eschewing whatever sin the Ranker lord seems to personify by focusing on a contrasting virtue aids in developing some resistance, some... immunity."

Skâlger slowly smiled. "Immunity..." He looked up as the artificial northern lights danced across the ceiling and his face became wistful, tired.

"When King Cato the Icewing ordered this fortress built, it was only after a village's children were all killed. An entire generation–" he swept out his hand– "gone. Because he saw the snowbeasts going back and forth, coming and leaving, he assumed they were dragging the children to their dens to be eaten. Easy prey."

Although he didn't know where this was going, Brody listened attentively. He hadn't heard the story told this way in his lessons.

"But then he noticed the pattern, did King Cato the Eighth. The snowbeasts came at the same time every night. And one night, by the fire of a torch, he saw, around the beasts' necks, *collars*.

"He followed them up the mountain, losing men to hypothermia, until he found the pass and through it, their masters, the ice-nomads. They were draining the children of their blood, and drinking it to thaw. Even after the battle was waged and won, Cato found more ice-men frozen deep within the ice of the pass's walls. No matter the heat of their fire or the keenness of their weapons, the men could not break through to wipe out the rest of the monsters. So the king took precautions. He had the Fortress of the Iron Teeth built."

Skâlger looked at Brody significantly. "He had learned to see the whole forest–not just the trees. And we have since learned that every thirty years..." he looked up at the wall, in the direction of the Howling Pass, Brody knew, "they awaken."

Skâlger reached back to pet his fox, who yawned to reveal pearly, sharp little teeth, and closed its jaws again with its tongue stuck between them.

"Cato learned that sometimes things are not what they seem." The man rolled his head toward Brody. "The Rankers would have you believe they are taking your cities, weakening your rule, breeding, but there is more to it. Something grander. You mentioned immunity. They are behaving like a virus, yes, but what kind? They make your people sick, but how? They seek to multiply, but why? What is the ultimate purpose of this virus? To spread? Control? Overcome? Reshape? We need to first understand the symptoms if we are to understand the sickness. If we understand that we are surrounded by trees, *then* we can step back and see the forest."

"Well, we all have our theories," Josiah said, scrubbing at his neck with a musky-scented cloth, "but we need more proof."

"The proof is in Crystalia," Skâlger said with certainty.

"What do you know?" Brody asked. He studied his fingers, which had become distastefully pruny, and tried to recall the accounts and dossiers he'd read about the activity in Crystalia back at his palace. As the city was situated an easy two and a half week's ride to the west of the mountains, Brody also knew that Skâlger could see all the way to the city from his fortress on a clear day–and a griffin could probably pick out useful details in the city itself.

"The citizens evinced behavior similar to what you described in Syranade–at first, all was madness and carnage. We had seen the Rankers coming from up here, like a black stain moving across the earth, and so the crown council was able to dispatch warriors from Oceanview in time to meet them. But it was pointless. What men weren't killed or escaped fell under the spell just as the civilians did. After about a week, the Crystalians settled enough to begin showing symptoms leaning toward one sin in particular. Syranade was gluttony. After Josiah told me what you'd discovered about the Ranker lords inciting the seven deadly sins, the symptoms of the Crystalians came together to reveal the sickness: pride."

"Pride?"

"Pride. Before we knew this, we had requested the aid of non-griffin reconnaissance fliers when we deployed missives for the kingdoms to rally their troops for your cause against Crystalia." Before Brody could ask why they hadn't used griffins, the man spoke further. "Though many dreamers can take on the form of a griffin, only a special, valuable few are aware of it. Even fewer know exactly what the dreamworld is and the dire situation it is in and these are too few and priceless to expend on a dangerous fly-over.

"Within a day a pair of sapient falcons arrived from Syranade, and after they rested we sent one out, and then its mate the next day. Both described signs of civil habitation–of citizens going about their daily business even amongst the Rankers. The Rankers had cleared away the dead and were reportedly leaving the civilians alone, and the bulk of the horde moved on, to Syranade we now know, leaving behind a 'lord' and about a hundred lesser minions."

"Just like in Syranade," Brody mumbled thoughtfully. He looked up. "Then what?"

Skâlger smiled like a child with a secret and Brody wondered what sort of madness the man embraced.

They left the pool, throwing on some quilted robes over thick tunics and trousers. Beyond the steamy lower chambers, the frigid gloom of the gothic fortress penetrated the stone and fought to grip them with chilly fingers. It felt pleasant after the hot soak in the pool, and their clothes shielded them from most of the chill.

Skâlger's office was about midway up the central tower, full of bursting bookshelves, flowering plants, and tapestries to trap the heat from the fireplace. An assortment of heavy wooden chairs, and a large desk covered with neatly stacked documents and organized scroll cubbies, took up most of the space.

Using a torch from the hall to go around lighting candles, Skâlger said distractedly, "Make yourselves comfortable. If it pleases

Your Majesty, I would like to have a strategy prepared before we go to rest tonight."

The black and gold fox squeezed inside between Brody's and Josiah's legs where they still hovered in the doorway and Brody gave a small skip of surprise, then grimaced. His thighs burned from the long walk up the stairs and he missed the broader, shallower steps of his own castle.

His griffin eyes undeterred by the dark, Brody went to a small, round, thick-glass window in the wall behind the desk while Josiah grabbed another torch to help Skâlger. Beyond the glass now flickering from the dim little lights of candle flame, he saw, far below, opening onto a jutting shelf of stone, the entrance to the Howling Pass; a jagged rent in the mountain leading down into its depths, glowing an arctic blue-white from some ambient source. In the gathering veil of night, it stood a solemn, surreal witch-light to remind all who saw that monsters were nearer than they seemed.

Skâlger tossed the torch casually into the fireplace where the flames in its bracket migrated to consume the wood there with a sound like snapping bones. The smokey scent of pine began to permeate the room. Then the master opened a drawer in his desk and withdrew a heavy, dragon-skin journal with the silver, ice-wolf emblem of the fortress on its cover. He sat and said, "I've transcribed the information from all the reports we have into this book. All we know about the situation in Crystalia, every rumor, every account, every whisper, every bit of gossip exchanged between its blowflies is in here."

He turned the journal toward Brody and Josiah and the king opened it and scanned the pages with a finger. He read in silence, blindly reaching behind him for a chair and plopping down into the one Josiah nudged his way, massaging the stubble on his jaw.

Unlike in Syranade, perhaps simply because Crystalia had suffered a few months longer, the remaining citizens had retained their reason and intellect. There were no reports of extremes–where some of the gluttons had been driven to the outskirts to roam like zombies, most left to mill around waiting to be fed the Fat Man's pills, and a few taken in exclusively to join the Fat Man's "club," in Crystalia, pride had created a different, more troublesome dynamic.

Arrogance, conceit, had led to class warfare and a number of gangs representing various interests and factions and guilds–any available source of pride–fought for turf by means of treachery, wit, and poison. Worse still, each guild had built a quartz statue to represent it.

Renowned for its beautiful quartz mines, Crystalia was famous for the machines they built that ran on steam and performed tasks like serving the higher families as butlers or pulling heavy produce carts for outlying farmers. Now, however, these moving stone statues were idols of pride–and those who had created the most beautiful and powerful machines were also nearest to the Ranker lord in confidence.

The Ranker lord was a creature disguised as a tall, slender and aristocratic man in finery, his chest bedecked with badges and medallions reflecting perhaps past military achievements or his status among his kind. He carried a narrow, black cane topped with a rose-cut pink diamond and his fit physique was pronounced by the close cut of his silks and velvets. All of the gangs and rivals now booming in Crystalia answered to him and he cleverly pitted them against each other, whittling out the weak as the death toll climbed. Those who won–or rather, survived–his little games were rewarded with a place among his companions and whatever silly trifles they desired to feed their pride.

"Why aren't they marching out?" Brody vaguely heard Josiah say. "Why not take what they want, do their killing and pillaging and fear-mongering, make more Rankers, and then head for the capital?"

"You are thinking too small again," Skâlger said patiently. "You have assigned them a purpose and are trying to understand it. But what if their purpose is *not* to strike at the Seat of Griffins? Their *motives* are what we truly need to puzzle out–"

"Which means we need one alive," Brody said in a voice like rawhide–tough and unyielding. "We'll have to be covert. Sneak in, take a hostage, find out what we need to know, deploy forces." He shut the book, tapping its cover. "They'll recognize me... Are there any King's Eyes stationed here at the fortress?"

"A few came with the knights," Skâlger said.

"Good. They'll be able to turn me into someone else."

"There is another option..." Josiah said carefully, his eyes hard and flinty. "They recognize you. Let them. No more hiding. We take your new army, march in, and put the fear of God in them up-front, eye to eye."

Brody briefly considered it, then said, "No. To fight and conquer pride, we need humility. Not the boasts of a king," he extended both hands, one to Skâlger and one to Josiah, "but the might of his people. I would fight with your own soldiers, Skâlger. Let the army ready for war, while we prepare together for this small battle."

Skâlger looked like the only thing keeping him from clapping with glee was the desk over his lap. His fox, however, let out a few harsh, raspy barks like the metallic grate of metal on metal.

"Good," he growled, fish-pale eyes shining madly. "Very good. Yes, our axes thirst. We will fight, and gladly."

Brody twisted to give Josiah a wry look, thinking of the great army he'd seen drilling in the courtyard. "I didn't authorize the missives sent to take warriors from our cities and send them here. Send a letter of warning to my council, would you? They overstepped."

"No one authorized the missives," Skâlger interjected. "Belay your writ of insubordination, Sire. I merely took the initiative to seek volunteers from each kingdom who would be willing to ride behind you."

Josiah, who seemed to be hiding a laugh, said, "Every able-bodied male is required to be drafted into your armies when necessary, Sire, and train every other year at the capital from when they come of age to the age they retire. However, as we have not yet officially declared war, your armies have not publicly come together—though you can bet they're ready for it. The Rankers won't be expecting this shadow-army."

"Volunteers...?" Brody repeated weakly. His jaw seemed to want to hit the floor. He thought of the roaring mass he'd seen drilling earlier, imagined their steeds thundering behind him; a small sea of sun-bright metal and snapping pennants.

"Volunteers," Skâlger said, "from Feather Cliff to Starfall and the lands between. Mercenaries and rangers, wardens and elite veterans, all tested and proven and ready to follow you right into the heart of Ragnarok, your Highness."

Chapter Twenty:

The Prophecy

"Courage is not the absence of fear but rather the assessment that something else is more important than fear."
– Franklin D. Roosevelt

There was a pub in the hamlet whose casks contained but three kinds of brew. Each was strong enough to down an elephant and tasted a lot like how Brody imagined napalm might taste. It was a popular establishment among civilians *and* knights, and the cozy little main room was noisy with chatter, gut-laughter, and slow but sleepily happy music from a woman on a stool by the hearth, playing a lyre.

Brody sipped from his pint in thimble-fulls. Each forced swallow of the beer made his teeth feel like they were changing from a solid to a liquid, and he tried not to breathe in the general direction of any torches, but the alcohol helped him to cope with his stress. To work, his plans for infiltrating and reclaiming Crystalia would require precise timing and luck. And then what? The other Ranker-taken territories had to be circles of Hell by now.

He sat at the bar counter, his back to the main room and all its merriment, which, he considered numbly, probably reflected some deep schism in his own soul. He was bone-tired, and he didn't think all the sleep in the world would help him. He missed his family, his friends, the simplicity of life before...all this. It had been months since he'd thought about what he'd lost. But now, before their potentially suicidal mission, seemed as good a time as any to reminisce. He spun on his seat, leaning back against the bar, his legs hopping on the stool's bottom rung.

Some people danced before the fireplace–a northerner's jig involving swinging around each other's arms, kicking up heels, and occasionally shouting as the bard's lyre transformed into a sprightly tempo.

There were more foxes now; everybody had one, it seemed. The adults sat at the edges of the dance floor barking, wagging their tails. The kits entertained the hamlet's children, chasing corks, and wrestling. They were beautiful little creatures, Brody thought, as much foxes as a unicorn was a horse.

Aydran's viol suddenly added its voice to the music. He stood in the doorway, the moonlit snow-drifts on the street outside like a ghostly shroud framing his lean form. Everyone looked over at him, laughing and smiling, but the bard's stare was a playful challenge focused hotly on the woman and her lyre. His arm sawed, his foot kept a rhythm, and he began stalking across the room, wending around tables and chairs to the hoots and japes of his audience. Brody whooped, lifting his pint. This was art–not just the mastery of an instrument, but teasing the audience and captivating them, enthralling them with just a grand entrance and something new.

The woman's fingers hadn't faltered on the lyre, though her expression betrayed her surprise. Aydran stopped right in front of her, his lips crooking into a smirk, the scar a white line, and she flushed red, frowned, and joined him on her feet. People cheered, the jig resumed, two instruments now battled for supremacy.

Brody sought out the others in his party. Domine had attempted to start a good, non-hostile bar fight about an hour before and was now instead deeply immersed in a card game that some young men were teaching him. Over beneath a stuffed moose head, Khogar tried in vain to sketch an outline onto a scrap of leather, but a group of children played with the ribbons on her tail, patted her head, and talked over one another telling her silly stories as if she were a stuffed animal at a tea party. The minister was deep in group prayer with some anxious-looking pregnant women and their husbands and Rexus sat solemnly at his feet among the couples' foxes, his head bowed and a charlatan-sized wheel of cheese held in his paws.

Josiah and Skâlger came over, each bearing a pint and a plate of piping-hot meat and bread. They sat on either side of Brody wordlessly, watching the distance between the two competing bards shrink and their gazes turn into something that smoldered with sensuality.

"Rega has not yet had a man," Skâlger said. "Tonight will be good to her, it seems."

"I'm sure Aydran will tell her the same thing," Josiah said dryly.

Skâlger studied Aydran critically and shrugged. "Well. He is obviously very good with his hands."

Brody took a bold draught of his beer and, blinking tears out of his eyes, tried to speak with some clarity. "What's the prophecy?"

Josiah looked at him quick-like, but Skâlger said, "Which one?"

"The Fat Man said to mention 'the prophecy' to my people. I have a feeling he meant capital 'p.'"

"The Griffin King Prophecy," Josiah murmured. "I'm sure that's what he meant. Why are you only mentioning this now?"

"Why did a *Ranker* have to be the one to mention it to *me*?" Brody asked with some ire.

Josiah's tone mellowed into something less accusatory. "Right. Sorry... That prophecy's old–older than King David the First and Foremost. It was discovered centuries ago, carved into one of the foundation stones beneath the castle during structural evaluations. For a while it was news, but no one knew what it meant at the time and soon it just became a topic of gossip when conversation was particularly dry. It was only when King Uriah was crowned that Michael brought it up again. It says that the Griffin King will win a war; that darkspawn will be the foe."

Skâlger recited lowly,

"From darkest night, in dark, the light,
the Griffin King shall rise to fight.
Come nightmare shadows, darkest might,
the King shall prove himself a knight.
Eclipsed the sun, corrupted all,
a King shall rise, a King shall fall.
Millions rally to his call,
the bane of many, a King of all.
Foes from memory, heart, and mind,
he shall set free, and he shall bind.
To purge the world, to end the blight,
the King is coming with the night."

He took a very masculine swig of beer, even holding it in his cheeks a moment as if defying it to melt his teeth to putty. Then he swallowed and said, "Among my kin, the ancient voices still speak through our traditions and elders. We remember the prophecy still."

Josiah's voice was tight with sorrow, as if he were recalling a recent hurt that he still struggled to bury beneath scraps of denial and meager hope.

"The Rankers have been gaining strength and numbers for a while now. We'd assumed, when Michael brought it up, that King Uriah would... But then he died. Everyone had gotten their hopes up for nothing."

"Why would the Fat Man bring it up now, do you think?" Brody asked.

The song had ended and the dancers were catching their breath. Aydran played a few strings pizzicato, then caught the barkeep's attention, indicated himself and Rega the female bard, and tipped his hand back and forth as if drinking. The barkeep smiled so widely that his eyes almost seemed to shut and prepared two mugs.

"Prophecies are notoriously vague," said Josiah, scratching his head with the bottom of his mug. "A king shall rise to purge the world, but for whom? A king will rise, but a king will fall? 'He shall bind?' And 'bane of many, king of all' could mean we are to expect a cruel dictator who seeks to rule the world."

"History tells us of very rare cases where a griffin has been corrupted into a monster–one of the worst," said Skâlger. "A tool for evil; a powerful and dangerous weapon. Perhaps it is the Rankers' hope that you can be twisted to fulfill the prophecy in their favor."

"And, barring that, they'll keep killing the kings and queens until they achieve victory via chaos–the good, old-fashioned way."

"It all comes down to destiny," Skâlger said, and Brody looked up at him with a pang of remembrance. The Fat Man had assigned what he saw as the Rankers' inevitable victory to destiny. The master of the fortress raised his brows at Brody, firelight turning the pale irises almost white. "Do *you* feel you are destined for corruption?"

"No," Brody replied immediately, defiantly, and sneered down into his pint. No, he would never betray the helpless, the weak. He would not abandon his ideals, betray the blood of his father, shame his family. If the Rankers thought this prophecy was theirs, that it foretold their victory, then he would prove them wrong.

Skâlger gave a pleased stretch of the back, rolling his shoulders, and tapped his tankard against Brody's. "When I was a very young man," he said, "I was mocked for being a peasant. The son of a farmer. They did not care that the crops my family grew kept them alive to brag and mock, and I did not care about what sacrifices the nobles had to make for us. We each grumbled, unfortunate in our spheres. But I was..." he smiled slyly, coldly, at Brody, "different.

"There came an enemy from the seas: bandits–the Scions of the Sea, they were called. They lived on their ships, out on the water, and only came to land to raid when their floating colonies ran out of supplies. Our own ships rebuffed the initial questing parties, but then our bordermen were overwhelmed by the forces that came from east and west. They moved to the center of our land where the jarl sits. All men and shield-women united under the jarl and his sons and advisors. We knew they had to be ungainly because they had sea-legs for a life spent on moving waves. Now was the moment to move.

"I was a lad of eleven, under the jurisdiction of Frederick Jarlson, when my father and elder brother and I joined. No one had the tongue for mocking now. Thor raged in the sky, Loki played his tricks on us. Our enemy was one we did not understand and that sowed fear and discord. So one day I departed to find the Scions and study them and bring back my observations to the jarl's son."

He looked at Khogar. The snow leopard had raised her be-ribboned tail out of reach of the children, who seemed to see it as a game and were jumping up to try and touch them. Though she pretended to ignore them, Khogar's whiskers twitched and she bobbed and weaved her tail in time to the merry tune Aydran played. Brody recognized it as the new ballad Aydran had composed about the fight with the Fat Man and people hushed one another to listen. Rega listened as well, completely engrossed, memorizing the notes and lyrics so as to do her minstrel's duty and help carry the song onward into legend.

"Around their armor they wore tight scarves, so bright red as to hurt the eye. I saw their ways and learned. Their wounded, if pierced by our arrows, did not remove the shafts. They would instead unwind one of the scarves and wrap it around and around." He imitated the motion, stirring a finger in the air. "I learned of their plans, where they would strike, and so returned as swiftly as I could to warn my brothers-in-arms and shield-sisters.

"Victory was ours, eventually, but the price was high. The Scions fought with spheres full of glass that exploded and cut into us. I was wounded in the arm, but I wrapped the wound–I did not remove the glass. The others…they had not learned this trick, this gift of Loki's."

"Stabilizing the injury prevented blood-loss," Brody explained. "It was wise of you to adopt the technique."

"That wisdom was the result of my own odd curiosity and nonlinear way of thinking," Skâlger said professionally, as if repeating something his psychiatrist had told him. "I survived when more than three-fifths of the jarl's warriors did not, because it was my destiny. And now it is your destiny to show that you, too, are different; that what makes you different gives you power."

It was Brody's turn to tap his barely-emptied tankard to Skâlger's. He gazed down at the black fox with its jagged, gold markings reclined beneath the northerner's stool, its slitted yellow eyes on the twitching shadows by the fireplace.

"Did your fox fight beside you?"

The creature's nearest ear flicked and the animal turned upon Brody a distinctly miffed look.

"What's its name?"

The eyes narrowed to a squint of distaste, like the look an emperor might give a spot of dirt on his robes. Skâlger nudged the fox with the toe of his boot and it rolled onto its back with a squeak, paws splayed.

"The foxes appeared to us here on the mountain about five years ago. One night, to each adult in the village and the fortress, they just…manifested as weapons."

"Weapons?" Brody switched a puzzled look with Josiah, who said, "I'd assumed they were familiars."

"In a way they are," Skâlger said. He set his drink on the counter and slapped his thigh. The fox rolled back over and stood on its hind legs, stretching up its forelegs so that Skâlger could lean down and lift it up onto his lap. "Though we of the Iron Teeth are not witches. It is difficult to explain." He positioned his hands oddly, as if to hold the fox from suddenly leaping, and it shivered and melted into a needle-pointed, gleaming black sword with a golden hilt of jagged lines. Brody had never seen its like before. It was beautiful, and he *felt* its essence as if he sat beside a powerful magnet. The air around it seemed to warp, like the sword was a black hole into a dimension even the dreamworld couldn't accommodate.

"Whoa..." Josiah breathed.

"Since they first appeared, they have followed us everywhere. They mate, as living things do, bear kits who, when they come of age, choose partners from among our own children. Each one is a weapon of some kind, and they are loyal only to the partner they've chosen."

He patted the sword-hilt and it melted back into the fox, which cooed when Skâlger scratched its ears. "He is *me*. No one else can wield him, no one else understands him. He shares my sorrows, my pangs, my desires, like a reflection. He is my best friend."

"I don't quite understand," Brody admitted, looking around at all of the foxes.

With the mildest touch of exasperation Skâlger said, "You do not need to. I have met other dreamers from your reality before, and they have told me about your scientists–people who must understand all. The irony is that the only thing man truly understands is evil, because it calls to him; because every man is good at it. And he strives to either twist it to serve him, or to kill it."

He looked at the fireplace across the room.

"Some understand that. Therein lies their redemption."

The arduous trek up the mountain, the relaxing bath, the alcohol, the relief of safety, and the prospect of liberating Crystalia within the coming weeks all drove Brody to seek his guest bed early. He slogged through the snow back toward the fortress with a few knights whose turn it was to go on watch–an easy chore with the ice-nomads hibernating but treated seriously all the same. They passed a few of the volunteer-soldiers heading to the tavern and they were so transported by a story involving a gorgon told with dramatic flair by one of them that they didn't recognize Brody. He wondered where the rest of the volunteers were. Still training? Sleeping?

In the guest chamber reserved for nobility, an austere room with long, velvet drapes and a banner representing each of the low kings and one, set higher than the rest, bearing the crest of the Griffin King, Brody sat on his bed. He wore a tight, white, woolen undershirt and pants, and a heavy sapphire-blue night-robe belted shut at the waist. He sat against the windowsill, the drapes parted, a book he'd found on a shelf forgotten on the pillow. The snow outside glowed beneath the stars, a field spanning several miles, it seemed–much broader of an expanse than Brody could remember. Then he realized that what he observed was actually a landscape of clouds merged seamlessly with the snow-covered ledges of the summit.

Enchanted by the moonstruck world of cumulonimbus joining his own on the earthly plane, Brody sat thus until sleep came for him.

Chapter Twenty-One:

Pride

"I can't help it. I was born sneering."

–W.S. Gilbert

The clouds had a magical effect on Brody's dreams. He couldn't remember them when he stirred awake late the next morning, but they'd been peaceful. His mind, so troubled of late with worries, felt cleansed; ready to fill up with the next challenge. Last night's fire and the robe had kept him warm–he had keeled over onto his side, having gone without both blankets and pillows.

"Mornin' angel," said a husky, seductive, male voice.

Brody withdrew so sharply that he knocked his own breath out against the wall. Aydran reclined, spread-eagled, on the farther side of the bed, a spoon sticking out of his mouth, his hat resting on his stomach.

"What are you doing here?" Brody tried to sound composed.

"Well," Aydran knocked aside his hat and propped himself up. He leaned over a tray of food on the nightstand beside the bed, scooped up a spoonful of sugar from a dish beside a coffee pot, and returned the spoon to his mouth, trying to speak around it.

"I know I deserve to be hanged, drawn and quartered, and tossed in a gibbet for intruding upon your kingly repose, but folks were starting to think you'd be hungry so I volunteered to bring you up some brekkie." He placed the tray on the quilt next to Brody and then took the sugar. "Except this. This is mine."

Brody heard a soft melody pick its way over Aydran's voice and leaned to one side to see Rega, the minstrel from the night before, lounging on a sofa playing her lyre.

"*What is* she *doing here*?" Brody hissed.

"She wanted to play you awake," Aydran said innocently. "You should thank her, really. I had a hankering to satisfy my morbid curiosity about whether or not you're ticklish."

"'M not," Brody grumbled, flopping around until he stood on the floor and then padding over to his saddlebags for an outfit. He chose a pale-green tunic and a rogue's scarf, good for hiding the face on a covert operation and protecting it from cold, and then set the bag rattling with his armor on the bed for later.

"You know, I like these foxes," said another familiar voice by the fireplace. Domine squatted on the hearth rug stroking the minstrel's pink and white, shaggy-furred vixen. "They are cute, but dangerous–as should all things be."

"He's here 'cause he was bored," Aydran said when he felt Brody's astounded look, tossing a fruit of some kind up in the air.

"Yes," Domine said. "I want a good fight. Aydran would not indulge me. Rankers will have to do."

"He actually asked me, all polite, on my way to the loo this morning. 'Care to grapple, bard,' he asks me. My nose is right where I like it, thank you. I'm not going to cudgel any Rankers like some mouth-breathing ape."

"I told him he did not need to use his hands. I know how much he needs them for his music," Domine sniffed, as if this were a great kindness on his part.

"The hell I'm gonna hit you with, then? My face?"

"Bedrooms are supposed to be private," Brody said from behind his dressing screen, slinging his nightclothes up over it and pulling on his woolen trousers lined with caribou fur.

"If you'd been rolling around with a woman I'd have knocked first," Aydran said.

"For shame, bard," said Abram from the vicinity of the door. "Painting the king licentious? You should add branding to your list of punishments."

"He's here because I'm here," Aydran said.

"And I'm here because I was exploring," Khogar added, also near the door. "A tribal cannot be confined to one tiny room. She must be familiar with her entire territory."

Brody sighed loudly and when his head popped through the neckline of his tunic he started at seeing Rexus perched atop the dressing screen eating a heilendi, watching Brody with his big, friendly, brown eyes. Moving out from behind the screen, Brody looped the excess length of the belt around his waist into a sort of casual but efficient knot just as Josiah entered the room.

"What's taking so long?"

Lacing his boots Brody said, "The circus is in town and I wasn't informed." Then he yelped and almost fell over when something poked his ribs and Aydran burst into laughter behind him, helping him to regain his balance.

"I *knew* you were ticklish!"

Brody wondered forbearingly whether *all* of the griffin kings had had to suffer the sportive disrespect of their friends as he entered the fortress's banquet room. In lieu of breaking his fast in the crowded confines of his guest room, Brody had decided to eat with the other knights of the fortress. However, there was hardly elbow room here, either.

A tall man on a crowded bench at an overburdened trestle table waved Brody over. As he approached, Brody saw that all of the men seated there, and at five of the other eight long tables in the room, wore a uniform: red and gold with a rampant griffin on the chest. These, then, were the volunteers–his knights– interspersed with the much fewer and more-disgruntled looking guardians of the fortress. He squeezed in next to the tall man, tucking his staff beneath the bench between his boots where a quick maneuver of the feet would return it to hand's reach if needed.

The man who had summoned Brody had large, docile eyes, a long face, and a broad forehead–all of which made him look so particularly equine that Brody wanted to pat him between the eyes and give him a carrot. Under his volunteer's tunic, the man wore a long, red silk coat patterned with darker-red roses and a black cravat. He had a curly, bushy mustache, and, neatly strapped into place on his belt, were delicate-looking instruments like a watchmaker's tools. Though he had shaved and wore his crown and sparse bits of light armor, Brody felt underdressed by comparison.

"An honor to meet you, sah! Completely chuffed and all, wot?" The man seized Brody's hand and shook it so hard that Brody felt it in his cheeks. "Blinding good show in Syranade, sah, the rest of us are completely knees-up over what stunt you'll pull next!"

Brody looked at the others eating calmly at the table, and then back at the friendly stranger with a limp smile. The man slapped his own forehead as if remembering something.

"Ah, tosh. I've gone noggin over arse, 'm afraid, sah, what with Crystalia in her kerfuffle." He shoved his hand out at Brody to shake. "Puddle, sah. Lord Daghart C. Puddle."

"Greetings, Lord Puddle," Brody greeted, still a little put off and unbalanced by the man's extravagant speech and pattern of behavior. "You have my deepest gratitude and respect for volunteering–as do all of the men here." He glanced at the other knights around him, who acknowledged his thanks with humble mumbles or an incline of the head. One man lifted his cup and said, in an accent similar to Puddle's, "Cheers, your 'ighness."

"Well what the bally-well else were we supposed to do, wot? Those Ranker-wankers come tearing up our land? I tell you, no red-blooded male would stand for it, eh?"

Brody suddenly placed Puddle's accent and dress.

"You're Crystalian if I'm not mistaken, Lord Puddle?"

"Ah, spot-on, Your Majesty." Puddle's face fell, revealing the true pain beneath his hearty facade. "A fortunate escapee of the Ranker blight."

"We left our people," a man on the other side of Lord Puddle said bitterly to his grits.

"Bollocks, old boy," Lord Puddle said to him sternly. "We didn't run, did we? We came here, for help! A few good man-jacks couldn't chase off a great horde of Rankers without it all going to pot." He turned back to Brody, a shade glummer than before.

"I am the elected leader of the Crystalian volunteers, sah, the highest-ranking chap of the lucky few wot escaped and survived to be ashamed by it. I was a sapper and a thumpin' good un'. I can tell you wot you need t' know."

The Crystalians, not a very robust people, had to rely on means other than physical prowess in battle. They were famed for employing doctors, engineers, and scientists into their military and though they could boast no shining-armored knights on chargers they produced some of the most brilliant warriors in the dream-world. Sappers like Puddle, for example, could cobble together a device that would detonate on a timer out of items that Brody would normally overlook as useless and mundane. Behind Lord Daghart Puddle's gentle eyes danced a dangerous intellect. If he tried to put an image to that mind, Brody saw a bear trap hidden by leaves and a pit of spikes covered by a golden net.

"How many Crystalians are here?" Brody dragged his gaze away from Puddle's to look around.

"Only about fifty, sah, and all of us in collywobbles over this whole deal, wot? We're ready to reclaim our home and help you put down these Ranker buggers for good and all–" He leaned forward confidentially and Brody turned an ear– "And I do believe our mates here at the fortress will be pleased to see the back of us. They've been so kind as to share their winter supplies with us but soon we'll eat them out of house and stock. A movin' army has a whopping-great many mouths to feed. 'S why they move, sah. Will we act soon? 'Scuse the impertinence of the question?"

"We'll leave tonight," Brody said. "Master Skâlger will call a formal meeting later. But I need to know what you can tell me about Griffin Prince Faolan's visit to Crystalia."

Puddle looked blank. He fiddled with his cravat and said, "Well...not much more than what your own lessons've told you, I'm sure. 'Twas a long time ago, wot? Long before my great-great-greats and such-forth were a twinkle in any eye. But..." He tapped the tabletop thoughtfully.

"Well, he was young–only thirteen... It seems we were in a spot of bother when he came along. A bogeyman-problem or some such."

"Yes, that I remember learning."

"Well, he's only the bloody Saint of Crystalia! We call him Faolan the Black, owing to his sorcerous powers, don't ya know? You ever heard that old chant, 'Blackdog?' 'Cauldrons flew at Faolan's cough; a black cat told him 'knock it off'?"

"No."

"Well, it originated in Crystalia. Anywho, the bogeyman–the same sod what eventually killed the prince–had overtaken our machines and made a lair for itself beneath the city. Faolan cast it out."

"How do you access the area beneath the city?"

"The canal house, I s'pose. It's still a ruin down there from what I hear."

"Can it be reached through the canals?"

Puddle fussed with his cravat again, agitated by Brody's unusual questions and the fact that it was not his place to ask what they were about.

He must have had some idea, however, for he said, "Yes, but not en masse–perhaps in a trading skiff, but those can only fit one fellow each. No, a large force would have to gain entry through one of the compass gates. The west gate is the most secretive; it's right up against Crown Hill. But you can bet the Rankers have still got it sorted."

Brody smiled warmly, which unsettled Lord Puddle even further, and gripped the man's arm. "We'll get in, my friend," he said, taking up a slice of toast, "and we'll get your city back." He dusted crumbs off his lap, basking in the sun bursting radiantly through the high, mullioned windows.

A plan had come to him.

Chapter Twenty-Two:

The Paragon

"Pride goeth before destruction."

–Proverbs 16:18

Brody found something hauntingly majestic about war-meets, whether they were held in some grand room warmed by a fire and furs on the floor, or in a tent pitched somewhere cold and muddy. They made him think of cruelty and loss, but also of virtue and courage. To his mind came the image of a soldier's last sight before he died. A man fading, nestled into the roots of a tree where he'd pulled himself to die, the leaves a panorama of glorious autumn above him. The knight, numb and gasping under a distant sky magical with billions of stars. That distance unbreached between man, who waged his wars, and uncaring Creation, whose soil drank his blood and embraced his bones. That distance only passed with death, when man abandoned his broken, bloodied body for whatever mysterious form the immortal soul took.

These meets were where fates were shaped; where the foundations were placed to bridge that cosmic distance between noble warriors with their righteous cause, and the waiting Other. The best leaders knew that they were sending some to their deaths as surely as the headsman waiting by the guillotine. This was a matter of determining how many. How many good young men with families and sweethearts and extravagant dreams needed to be sacrificed for the greater good.

That was one of the reasons Brody decided to send the main force ahead to the next fortress nearest the next claimed city. Let his volunteers prove themselves elsewhere against some greater foe. For this, for pride, he needed only a few good men.

The war meet was somber, presided over by Brody himself. He made his plans, distributed instructions, ordered supplies readied and horses saddled, composed coded letters and had one sent to his council and the other to Storm Breath; the fortress nearest the next site of Ranker-blight.

They departed that night: Brody, his close comrades, Lord Puddle and the other Crystalian escapees, and Skâlger with a handful of knights from the fortress. Brody let his dun set the pace, a nice, steady canter, somewhat comforted by the now-familiar sounds of hooves drumming on earth and the clacking of armor plates rubbing together.

When they reached the base of the mountain, after the sun had set and painted the lowland fell a rusty orange, the dun suddenly stretched out its long legs. It gave a shrill whinny and Brody gave it its head. In seconds they flew over the grass toward the sun, the breeze scented with heather and mud from a river somewhere nearby.

Puddle and his fifty men rode an assortment of strange beasts, and many had to double up as some of their steeds had been killed in their escape and a few of the men had fled Crystalia on foot without a mount. There were horses, of a long-limbed brindled breed perfect for a swift ride across flatlands. But there were also glistening machines that steamed and whirred and resembled everything from insects to ostriches.

Puddle himself rode comically gallant high on the back of a mechanical Irish elk with antlers vast enough to make it anathema to most doorways Brody had seen. Its eyes were two yellow lights, and though all of its joints and sockets were finely greased amber quartz, it moved with lifelike grace and even bugled joyfully when it lengthened its stride to match the dun's.

That night, sitting beside one of their campfires, Brody scoured the black mountain behind them with his griffin's vision. It stood a behemoth against a clear, chilly sky and at the tippy-top, he faintly saw a few pinheads of light from the fortress. He would not be returning to it after Crystalia, but he hoped to see it again someday.

The two and a half week journey was an easy one. The horses did not want for food and drink and the Crystalians' mechanical beasts could somehow subsist on water and sunlight alone, both in abundance. Game and edible vegetation were also plentiful so that Brody didn't have to worry about supplies.

They passed the time singing songs and telling stories. Brody was pleased at how taken the men were with his renditions of the songs he liked from *Grease* and soon the lyrics to "Greased Lightning" could be heard rolling across the landscape from four-score throats singing it like a battle-chant.

The Land of Dreams did not miss the opportunity to show off either. One day, a large, violet-colored dragon flew overhead. Electricity flickered across the webbing of its dazzling, patterned wings. Its roar came down to them distantly, causing their mounts to shriek in alarm and zigzag erratically, but the beast flew on and Brody reclaimed control of his horse. Every day at sunrise, a strange city of sand-colored stone shimmered to the south at the base of the distant, scrubby foothills, wavering like a mirage and vanishing as soon as the sun had left the horizon. Once, inexplicably, clouds rolled in with the evening and white flowers smelling of absinthe fell from them, blanketing their campsite. Brody's dreams were particularly vivid that night.

These and other wonders Brody saw on that ride to Crystalia, his horse cutting a path through bounding herds of six-legged white antelope, leaping streams, his riding cloak a banner behind him. And on the ninth day of their ride, Josiah rode up on his brown horse, Rexus clinging to its neck, and pointed ahead of them and then at his eyes.

Crystalia's tallest towers twinkled over the curve of the fells against the rock-spires of Crown Hill. The city of quartz and canals; of golden monuments fashioned after heroes and heroines of legend, of living machines. This far away, it was a gem in the landscape, a welcoming beacon as the coming cold season frosted the grass each morning and tore the leaves from the occasional tree with howling winds. But then there came signs of carnage, of the fate that had befallen Crystalia and the plight of her people: a strewn skeleton, long-since picked clean by scavengers; the tattered scraps of cloth and shredded links of mail that had at one time been the vestments of a knight; large sections of bloodstained ground or abandoned supplies. Once, they passed a rotting human arm and Brody heard a man somewhere behind him mutter, “I was wondering where I left that.”

Other than that wry comment, none of the Crystalian escapees said anything about the signs of their flight from the city, other than to refer to them as a sort of trail-mark, an indicator of how much longer they had to reach the city. But Brody could see in their eyes that they recognized or remembered each of the mangled carcasses they passed.

When they finally reached the canal they sought, curving in from the mighty rivers to the south, they separated. Domine, Abram, Josiah, and Skâlger and his men remained with Brody. Puddle and his men, as well as Khogar and Aydran, began to set up camp. They had to practice the utmost caution now, so close to the city where there would doubtless be lookouts and sentries posted. Puddle would wait for dusk, when darkness would obscure his movement around behind the city to Crown Hill.

They were at a checkpoint; a cabin where incoming goods were examined and cataloged before being allowed to pass on. Inside, a number of small skiffs and repairing equipment were stacked by a desk dusty and cluttered with midlewy papers and toppled candles, as if someone had stumbled into it in their haste to leave. Brody and his team began hefting the skiffs outside in pairs.

When they’d done, Brody handed Aydran the reins of his horse and said, with a serious tilt of the head, “See you soon. Be careful.”

Aydran gave him a big, cheesy smile, and said through his teeth, “Let’s see those cuspids that make milkmaids swoon in their aprons.”

Brody looked at him sharply. His nerves jangled–he didn't have the patience for Aydran's humor at the moment. Then he remembered what Rexus had said in Syranade: everyone was afraid, but the king couldn't show it. He would have to work on that. After all, his father, who had soldiered through pits of Hell, only ever displayed a gentle, lamb-like kindness in public. Brody was sure that only his mother was truly privy to his father's demons.

So he smiled, shared one last steady look with Skâlger and Puddle, and climbed into the lead skiff, held steady in the current by a Crystalian wearing a pair of reinforced sapper's gloves.

Covering himself haphazardly with a dark blanket so as to break up his shape and make it less obvious that a human hid beneath, Brody evaluated himself, half-listening to the others clambering into their skiffs. He was completely healed from his injuries in Syranade, and a fresh vitality made his vision wink in the dark beneath the heavy burlap.

A King's Eyes had altered his appearance masterfully before he'd departed the fortress, which would afford him some freedom of maneuverability in the city: his curls were trimmed and styled into a looser wave, and dyed a temporary oaky brown. Powders and oils had been applied to his cheekbones to make them sharper and to his eyes to make them appear more sunken. His outfit was all heavy furs over a calf-length coat of hydra skin, which broke up his frame and made him appear smaller and ferrety. If all went as planned, he was confident that Crystalia would be cleansed in at least the same amount of time Syranade had been.

He felt it when his skiff was released to the current–a dizzying weightlessness and then the sensation of forward motion and the lull of rushing water. The sun soon warmed his burlap covering and then seeped through to his body and he fell into a peaceful doze. As dusk fell, a terrible stench pulled him rudely to alertness, speaking to some primal instinct in his mind.

Even over the rush of the current Brody heard the swarms of flies. The smell of rot increased sickeningly. Brody tried to hold his breath. The nose of the skiff, by his feet, caught on something and was dragged to a crawl. He shifted, wondering how near he was to the city, whether he should chance emerging to remove the blockade. Then the next skiff smashed into his and he swore in alarm and pain as his skull rattled against the wood. He popped free and resumed floating. The smell of death passed.

As the sun set, Brody saw two enormous shadows through his blanket and knew that they were statues, one pair of many around Crystalia, that marked the entrance to the inner-city canals. Now he tensed up, muscles straining. If he struck more debris now, it would cause a ruckus or even shatter his skiff and do him injury. The sound of a great many conversing people swelled up as his little skiff swept through the city toward its heart. He listened, trying to pick up sounds of agitation or a chant like that of the starving Syranadians, but this sounded like the usual casual blend of an active city. His stomach clenched uneasily.

The lights of the braziers vanished, darkness deeper than night fell, and his skiff struck something thick and rubbery–one of the sets of bumpers meant to slow skiffs as they entered the canal house. He kept moving, slower now, and hit another set of bumpers; he was reminded of the gradual, jarring application of roller coaster brakes. Eventually he came to a complete stop, tapping against a solid wall sounding of stone, and he waited. Another skiff fetched up against his. He heard the tap of the other eight skiffs settling in and relaxed slightly. All present and accounted for.

They waited a while, listening for someone come to investigate, but only the lapping of water against stone broke the stillness. Brody sat up, the burlap blanket falling off him, and grimaced at his stiffness. The only light in the circular room came from dim, blueish white crystals in spheres on the sections of wall between the many dark canal-tunnels. A few flickered. Some had burnt out. A small office took up the center of the room and a walkway around it formed a sort of dock with aisles separating the canals and mooring rings for the skiffs. Brody stepped out onto one of these stone aisles and looked up. There was no immediate ceiling; a ring of wood belied an upper level, and pulleys and tarps dangled like a torn spider's web in the open, empty middle space.

Their steps echoed in the confined space. Beyond the door out was a stairway going up and a corridor to either side. Following Daghart Puddle's directions in his mind, Brody wended along, leading the others, until he found a door with a shrine-like alcove on either side. A small statue of a man stood in each, their feet obscured by oft-used but now abandoned red and white candles. Each was carved from some soft, waxen stone with lifelike detail.

One statue showed a youth with elfin features and shoulder-length hair, one hand holding the royal scepter, the other reaching back to touch one of the wings sprouting from his back. On a banner-like carving of stone beneath the alcove an inscription read, *Great Prince Faolan: Saint of Crystalia.*

The other statue wore a set of Crystalian armor, all draping cloth and heavy plates, the helmet tucked beneath one arm to reveal the blocky features of a rugged, older man. He held a sprig of some sort of herb to his chest in his other hand. His inscription read, *To General Farrier and The Honored Fallen: We Remember You.*

"Puddle said this leads beneath the city," Brody whispered, touching the door.

"Where the Great Prince defeated the bogeyman long ago," said Abram. His face shone with academic interest.

Brody pulled on the door latch. It had to be down here where he would find the blessed item once touched by Faolan. He pressed the door open–its hinges shrieked. Everyone flinched. Brody saw the play of firelight on a sandy floor within, and then heard a voice say gruffly, "Who's that?" in a heavy Crystalian accent. Then came the sound of many people standing up.

"Back!" Brody snapped. They retreated hastily, taking the stairs up to a street busy even this time of night, framed by neat hedges and a generous swathe of unclipped grass. They weren't pursued.

Many people were gathered in small groups talking in loud, snobbish voices and chuckling on occasion, so Brody and the others didn't look out of place and weren't overheard. He let his gaze travel up and around, however, and saw that atop every high structure in the vicinity, Rankers perched, lazily observing the foot traffic.

"Well, this sets us back a bit," Skâlger said conversationally.

"No. We just have to switch a few steps around," Brody said, giving the area one last visual sweep and then meeting the man's pearly colored eyes. "If we can't access whatever power source the Rankers are corrupting right now, then we'll find the Ranker lord instead." He gripped his staff a little tighter, remembering to lean against it a bit like it was a walking stick and not a weapon. The King's Eyes who had instructed him to do so had also removed King Uriah's violet feathers from the shaft, attaching them instead to the belt around his tunic, hidden safely under his outer clothes. He twitched his hand at Domine. "Go. Tell them to remain but stay near the west gate and wait for the signal."

Domine was already moving eagerly, his upper body still at a weird angle to listen to what Brody was saying as if his feet had a mind of their own.

"Blend in," Brody said. "Mingle."

Domine set off at a speedy strut, his shaggy head high, and Brody couldn't help a small smile. He didn't give the titan enough credit. Skâlger started to follow, his five companions slipping away, their foxes in the forms of dazzling weapons glimpsed as a dull glitter under their furs.

"Three griffin calls?" Skâlger asked.

"Three griffin calls." Brody gave him a dark grin.

Skâlger returned the hungry expression and departed to the west, while Brody, Josiah, Abram, and Rexus turned south to see what they could see.

They called him "the Paragon," and his name was on almost every pair of lips. Much like the Ranker of gluttony, the Ranker of pride had garnered quite a following. But though the city and its people turned to the Paragon's tune, he wasn't the sole topic of conversation, and Brody was stunned at the normal yet alien atmosphere in the city. Shops were open, their doorways lit, and cheery faces could be seen within them through merchandise-laden windows.

In the hours the trio spent stalking past timepiece-shops, toolshops, clothing stores, and even a few stables where customers could custom-order their quartz servants and steeds, they finally pierced the facade to the troubled city within.

Whatever people had to say to each other, it was oftentimes spoken in a loud and challenging kind of way. One man asked another about the health of his daughter and the man responded ostentatiously, "She is well, thank you. Grew another three inches! She'll be taller than you, old boy," and the first man idly twirled his cane and said, "Not taller than *my* little girl. She can already reach the bloody cookie-shelf in the pantry!"

Everything was a competition–a verbal fight for petty bragging rights.

Sometimes these squabbles were neither verbal nor petty.

Brody and his friends had stopped along an avenue cutting between rows of higher-end homes to collect their bearings. The city was a sprawling mass that made Syranade look like a quaint suburb. It was organized, not with street signs, but by the figures in various colors of quartz atop the arches curving over the nearest canals. Letting the sound of the busy water comfort him, Brody glared sullenly at the starry, violet woman far above and tried to remember if he'd passed her already.

Josiah brushed his arm against Brody's and Brody followed his eyes to where he could pick out flashes of quick, violent movement through a curious ring of people beginning to gather.

"Looks like a fight," Abram said tensely. Rexus licked his teeth as if to emphasize their points to a rival charlatan. Apprehensive, Brody pressed in close to see what was happening.

Within the circle of onlookers two factions faced off. Both had the attention-hungry, hotheaded looks of the thugs and gangsters that Brody remembered from reality, but with slightly better fashion-sense.

One gang was composed of young adults in dirty overalls, red-tinted eye-protection goggles, heavy gloves and boots, and heavily-darned leggings or waistcoats. They were obviously laborers, with the pinched and defiant expressions of people struggling to stay above the poverty line.

The other gang was much better off, in top-hats, embroidered vests, frilly skirts, and poofy cravats like Lord Puddle's. Paler and smoother of complexion, their postures were supremely self-assured and they moved with a graceful frailty like folks who'd never known a hard day's manual work.

One of the youths from the worker's gang was being pulled to his feet by his friends, rubbing his cheek as if he'd been slapped. His eyes were fastened dangerously on one of the rich young men who was just slipping a clean, white, silk glove back onto one slender hand, his mouth hooked into a faint smile.

"'E jes called me a tool!" the stricken youth shouted. "A *tool*, eh? Bloody sod, I'll feed his bloomin' 'at up 'is bloomin' arse, I will!"

Brody assumed that "tool" was some sort of classist insult in Crystalia, for the whole of the working class to be taking such offense. The wealthy man who'd replaced his glove sneered.

"And your dirty little troglodyte shoved me to the bricks first," he said, speaking to the slightly older gentleman now dusting off the slapped boy's overalls and looking vindictive.

Neither of the two parties behaved as Brody thought they should–and neither did the audience for that matter. Everyone was flushed and excited and the mood was anticipatory. It was the posturing machismo that criminals from reality flaunted, but a drunken, exaggerated form of it.

"I challenge you." The boy in overalls spoke in little more than a hiss of breath. The onlookers gasped dramatically. He licked his lips, his face becoming oddly plaintive. "I challenge you."

"I accept," was the answer, to the crowd's pleasure. "Let us go to the Paragon and hear his reward."

Brody looked around him. An eerie, dreamy look had come over everyone's face at the Ranker's name. They began to shift and move away, following the two opposing gangs. Brody moved to follow as well, in his haste elbowing a man with a series of leather straps holding a toolbelt to his ribcage. The man scowled at Brody haughtily.

"Who do you think you are, guttersnipe?"

Forcing down the impulse to bark back at the man, Brody sketched a brief bow as he moved and said, "My apologies, sir, 'twas my mistake," in a Crystalian accent. The man blinked and stopped on the spot, frowning as if dizzy.

Brody almost held back himself, to observe the man further. Even despite having endured the Paragon's poisonous influence longer, the Crystalian exhibited the same symptoms as the befuddled soldiers in Syranade had when hearing their king's voice.

Here, even here...perhaps it was not too late.

Chapter Twenty-Three:

Humility

"True humility is not thinking less of yourself; it is thinking of yourself less."
–C.S. Lewis

The Paragon resided in a great coliseum meant to serve as a testing-ground for newly crafted quartz-beings. It was now the site of the most concentrated pride and vanity in Crystalia. People danced and sang with the same unrestrained, unabashed self-centeredness of children, but without the innocence. As he wound his way through them, the Crystalians jeered at Brody, darting at him as if in hopes of making him flinch. In fact, everyone treated everyone else this way: brusquely, rudely, haughtily, so that more than once Brody had to bite back his anger and remind himself of the Crystalian's plight. The *true* foe was within the coliseum.

The roaring of the audience within was enough to drive a wedge of pain into Brody's skull, bringing tears to his eyes. The tiered seats were so packed that they gave new depth to the word. Brody, Josiah, and Abram were forced to join the standing-room-only crowd plugging up any available pockets of space, and Brody was fortunate enough to find a small rise around one of the many poles holding up the colorful banners criss-crossing above the arena. He could see over everyones' heads now, and he began to absorb details.

A ring of open space separated the arena, a round area large enough to accommodate a battleship, from the audience. Turbulent water sloshed in the ring far below, no doubt pumped in from the city's countless canals. The arena was accessible only by four bronze gates that opened to four broad paths leading into the coliseum's bowels. Brody spotted a system of grates around the arena's rim, and two enormous portals hidden behind gold-and-red quartz doors lower-down around the coliseum's base that would open straight into the canal. Perhaps the Crystalians sometimes flooded the arena so as to test ships or aquatic machines. He would have to remember to ask Lord Puddle about it. What a sight that would be!

Then the Paragon captured Brody's interest in the second moment of his observations. The Ranker was just as he'd been described: lounging in his finery, a long and slender man in his prime with meticulous, close-trimmed sideburns following his jawline and a wavy swoop of stylish hair. His chest glittered with medallions, his fingers with rings. He sat on the impractically long train of his own cape, cupped in the hand of a silent stone statue the size of a skyscraper. A row of empty chairs far down between its feet probably once seated the city's leaders.

In the third, brief moment of his observations, Brody turned his attention to the center of the arena, where the Crystalians all directed their shouts and jeers. Two fantastic quartz machines battled fiercely on the tiles, sparks flying from the skids on their feet, their eyes shining, one pair yellow, one red, with an intelligent, desperate ferocity. Brody didn't know how long they'd been fighting, but he thought that he could tell the winner already: one, a purplish brute resembling a gorilla, had ripped gouges out of the decorative exterior plates forming its opponent's hide. The other, a pinkish-red creature somewhere between a rhinoceros and a huge hound, shuddered and occasionally locked up as it moved. Its back right leg made a harsh screeching sound with each step and steam came from a vent in one shoulder.

The gorilla pounded its rubbery chest, showed its teeth–as brilliant and sharp as sunlit icicles–and charged. The rhino attempted to escape to one side and let the ape's momentum carry it past, but it waited too long. Snatching the rhino by one leg and by the horn above its nose, the gorilla lifted it, cords straining and grinding in its back, and threw it down. The crowd screamed its approval. Silent, Brody turned his head. Two men stood on one of the paths connecting the arena to the rest of the coliseum. One shook his fists in the air, triumphant, the other had his face in his hands. Brody watched him with concern, then looked at the Paragon, who had stood up, and then at the mangled rhinoceros-hound.

The gorilla, its task done, rested on its knuckles, staring tamely out at the onlookers. Behind it, though, the defeated rhino craned its head up. The plates of its face slid back and overlapped, exposing a nozzle of some kind in its mouth. Whether it was the clicking of those plates or the screams of those in the audience who had caught on, the gorilla shifted around to return its attention to its foe. From the rhino's "tongue" came a liquid spurt of fire so dazzling to see that Brody had to throw his arms up and shield his eyes even from the great distance at which he stood.

The gorilla caught the fire right in its face and for a while groped blindly at where it knew the rhino to be before the damage became severe enough to cause it to malfunction. It spun around, took three quick steps, fell on its side, and made a series of clicking, chittering noises. Its limbs moved slower and slower, like those of a wind-up toy losing its juice, until finally it was over. Brody stared with a mixture of nausea and belated surprise into its melted face. The yellow eyes became dim, the convoluted metal and stone of its features still glowed with heat.

One of the two men who had been watching from the path ran to the rhino, patting it as its face returned to normal and it struggled to its feet, losing a few bolts and chips of quartz in the process. It was obvious why it had waited until the last to use the fire; it was completely drained now, and it would've needed to wait until the quick ape was close enough and unprepared.

When it had become clear that the rhino wasn't yet done, the Paragon had casually clasped his hands behind his back, remaining on his feet. Now he spoke, and everyone heard his voice. "An unexpected turn of events, but not unwelcome. Anything to break the tedium of this dry city, eh?"

The Crystalians all laughed like fools. Josiah gave the ones guffawing behind him a disgruntled look.

The Paragon gestured–a flit of the fingers–turning his face from his admirers to gaze steadily down into the arena. "By your leave, my champion."

The man by the rhino looked sharply at the man standing over the useless gorilla. At an unheard command from its creator, the rhino lunged with a terrible scream of scraping metal. The loser cried out and darted for the nearest path, but doing so put him directly in front of the rhino. With one powerful thrust of its horn and a sickening sound like that of a bird hitting a window, it sent the man flying. He cleared the canal, hit the wall across it with a meaty thump, and then dropped, limp and broken, down into the water.

While the audience went wild with renewed vigor, Brody stared at the canal. Were all of those who'd failed to win their way into the Paragon's good graces down there somewhere? In the split second before their tragic deaths were they released from the corruption of pride? Did they leave the dreamworld free?

The Paragon had dropped something down to the champion: one of his rings.

"Take this, that all of Crystalia may know of your success. Wear it proudly, for it is no small thing to be a champion of the Paragon! There are those who would wrest you from your new honors, your boy-king being one of them! He would come to you with pretty words and a tyrant's hand, just as he did in Syranade! I say let him sit and preen his down on his child's throne! Leave Crystalia be!"

As the onlookers shouted their agreement, Josiah leaned in and muttered, "Sounds like he's familiar with the Fat Man's demise." When Brody didn't reply, Josiah added, "Word travels fast," leaning back.

Brody knew that his disguise was more than adequate, but he couldn't help hunching his shoulders defensively as hundreds of voices bellowed their spite and scorn for him.

“Who now seeks my favor?” The Paragon raised his hands as if in benediction. “Let the next contestants bring forth their challenge!”

There was havoc in the tiers and Brody had to hug the flagpole before him or else become swept up in the frenzy as those with quarrels surged to be first down onto the arena platform. After a time, a few representatives from the trivial spat that Brody had witnessed on the street burst from the seething mass spilling onto one of the paths below. Their clothes were torn and they held themselves as if nursing fresh, tender wounds from their struggle through the coliseum’s brutal crowd and into the arena. They shouted up at the Paragon, voices lost in the cacophony of the still-rabid attendees, but the Ranker heard.

“Worthy,” he said smoothly–Josiah snorted– “Both of your guilds are excellent candidates for my inner circle. Inventiveness and wealth. Spunk and dignity. Yes, fine traits that would serve well.” He looked around at the audience and Brody sensed more so than saw the irritation that crossed the Ranker’s fine features at seeing his audience mostly too busy still trying to settle to pay his words mind. His cheeks hollowed, his eyes sank, the fancy clothes lay against a body that was stooped and bony. Then, as if a blink had wiped an illusory lens from the eye, he was back to as he had been.

“I declare a Gauntlet!”

The entire coliseum hushed at that. While the Paragon paused to enjoy the effect of his words the only sounds were those of the water lapping against the walls and, intermittently, the fritzing of the rhino-hound.

"Let every guild craft for me a machine worthy of their talents! Bring me beauty, bring me finesse, bring me originality! Three days hence, your creations shall all compete for my favor." He gazed down at the two men who had brought their case before him. "Then you will know the better."

As the Crystalians digested the cryptic statement, murmuring among themselves, a black-cloaked Ranker appeared from the shadowy doorway beside the chairs and below the Paragon. It looked up at him and he turned his face down in its direction attentively. He nodded and the Ranker departed.

"My friends, there is news of strangers in your city recently arrived and wandering your streets." A cold fist plunged down into Brody's guts from his throat–as if he'd swallowed a rock made of ice. "They know not our ways and no more belong here than a rat carrying plague." Brody felt the Paragon's eyes sweeping the seats, calculating, and would've sworn that he physically felt them pass over him.

"If these visitors are present, let them know that they are welcome to participate in the Gauntlet. In fact, it is their only chance of survival. Should they attempt to leave, they will be killed, for my captains are watching every entry, exit, nook, and niche as I speak!" The Crystalians were finding their voices again, growling threats and epithets with such spleen that Brody knew he'd be torn apart if he announced himself the stranger.

"If they are not currently in my presence and enlightened..." the Paragon sat down again, sprawling comfortably, "then let them know. Spread the word, friends! Any who brings me these interlopers alive shall be rewarded with treasures the likes of which this city has never seen! Now go! And remember, I beseech you, I wish to have them *alive*, or you shall serve instead as the victim of my ire."

"Well someone was bound to notice the skiffs," Josiah said reasonably. He looked at Brody, where he sat across the table massaging his neck scars, eyes vacant, then gave Abram a look that said, *help me out!*

The elderly minister blinked and said, "Oh! Y-yes. We're lucky we weren't snatched up as soon as we came up those stairs!" Josiah gave him the thumbs-up and a wink.

Brody made a very prolonged thinking sound. Josiah's trousers squeaked against the leather of the booth he and Abram shared as he fidgeted.

"'Hmmmmmm' what?" He waved his hand between himself and Abram. "We can't mind-read."

Brody focused on them. He took a sip from the sparkling cider he'd been turning in circles in his hands and studied the bar they currently occupied with a cozy armful of other patrons. In the Crystalian style, it was all warm colors and too large to be lit fully by the morose fireplace or even the candlelit brass tubes clustered over the tables. Everything seemed slow and sleepy, from the rosy glass rectangles decorating the otherwise drab brick, to the clock, all gears and cogs, ticking over by the assorted crystal decanters holding the various beverages behind the bar counter. What with the customers' abnormal tendency to challenge each other every time one of them was out-bragged, the place was also a little sinister.

"He reminds me of a leech," Brody said vaguely, his upper lip hitched in a distasteful expression. "Or a magpie seeking treasure when its nest is already too heavy with it."

Abram opened his mouth to ask a question, but Josiah spoke first. "Well, he reminds *me* of a Ranker with an ego big enough to sit on. Come on, we can just swoop in there right now! Shove him off that hand he's camped on and into the canal with the other poor souls he's killed."

Brody, tracing the reflection of candlelight on the table with a pinkie, screwed up his nose as if it itched.

"You'll answer that beast's Gauntlet?" Abram sounded appalled.

Josiah ran his hand roughly through his hair, leaving it brushed up and nesty on one side so that he looked as unhinged as he was starting to sound. "I don't know about either of you, but I can't make anything out of popsicle sticks let alone quartz. What, you want to make a machine in three days? It's madness."

"We'll bring the Paragon tribute, but it won't be what he expects." Brody showed his teeth.

Josiah drained the rest of his whiskey in a gulp as if hoping to liberate himself from Brody's insanity by relieving himself of sobriety.

The city criers, now belting out the Paragon's instructions on dealing with the strangers who'd stolen into the city, were as oblivious as the rest of the Crystalians. Brody, Josiah, and Abram, no more indiscreet than the city's civilians striding about, went undetected and unapprehended. There was no possible way that everyone knew everyone in the vast metropolis–people were dragging their fellow citizens aside to question them only to be challenged for daring to interrogate an indignant Crystalian. Pride had caused everyone to want to look no further than their own noses.

As such, all of the bustle allowed Brody to easily grab an inattentive young man strutting past a neglected storefront and pull him inside. Keeping one hand flat to his captive's mouth, flat so as not to provide loose flesh for him to bite if he had a mind to, Brody waited until Abram was positioned to guard the door and Josiah was beside him before letting the man go.

The man appeared ashen, unable to comprehend the odd turn of events. He trembled, making the glass knick-knacks on the shelf he cowered against tinkle, and pawed at his chest with fingerless gloves.

"What's your name?" Brody asked softly in a Crystalian accent.

At hearing the mundane, harmless question, a change came over the man. The fright slipped from his face, replaced by a spooky vacancy as if he were beyond caring about whatever happened next.

"I am Tobias Elias, you filth. What's it to you?" He fell back against the shelf when Josiah snarled and shoved him. One of the glass trinkets fell and broke heavily. Abram's head whipped around and he shushed them. Tobias looked, agape, at Josiah.

"You dare touch your filthy paws to my coat? You, who are no better than the dogs that eat my scraps?"

"I'll do more than that, you pasty little wart!" Josiah fought to keep his tone low, incensed at the manner in which the Crystalian spoke to his king, disguised though Brody was.

Stung by the sharp rejoinder, Tobias reddened. Black veins suddenly spidered out under the skin around his eyes, which themselves took on an ugly, oily-black sheen at the corners.

"You snakes! You swine! I'll have you licking my boots and begging for my mercy when I'm done teaching you respect!"

Josiah took a fistful of Tobias's red scarf, twisting it as if to throttle him, and Brody saw the skin under *his* eyes darken a little, too, as Aydran's had in Syranade. "*Respect?* You know not to whom you speak, you worm!"

Tobias screamed–a terrible, animal sound of embarrassment, fury, and frustration, thrashing in Josiah's clutches so that Brody had to lunge forward and grab two more glass baubles before they fell and shattered. As the man's screams pitched toward a bestial howl, something about him shifted. He couldn't tell if it was physical, or something in Tobias's demeanor, but a fear came over Brody of the sort he hadn't felt since many years ago when the crazed vagabond had clawed out his own eyes.

"Quiet him down! People are looking!" Abram hissed.

In one smooth movement, Brody nudged Josiah aside, took one of Tobias's hands, and dropped down onto one knee, pressing his forehead against Tobias's knuckles.

Josiah gasped as if stricken. "No! A king–"

"Is no better than his people," Brody murmured at the floor. "He is, in fact, their servant. Be silent." Keeping his gaze humbly lowered, Brody addressed Tobias.

"Tobias Elias. I ask you please, from my heart, to tell me what you know of Faolan's Vault, where the prince once defeated the monsters destroying your city."

A pause, and Brody felt Tobias gently retrieve his hand. Brody let him, finally meeting the man's eyes, but still kneeling. The veins had gone, as had the angry blush, but arrogance still warred with confusion. Brody could see the battle in the man's soul, plain on his furrowed features.

"Why...should I...help you?"

"You have heard of the Gauntlet, I am sure? Challenge me there. Meet me in the arena so all may see that you are better. But if others are to witness my abasement, then you must tell me what you can."

Tobias considered him. Then he stood from his slouch against the shelf, straightened his coat, and leaned back against it in an easy-going way. Brody could have cried with relief.

"The Vault is a shrine honoring the prince and the warriors who died beneath our city battling the bogeyman. It is also the entrance to one of our oldest mines. The artists have developed a practice dedicated to the prince in which we create black quartz. It is a very complex, one might even say sacred, task, and one of the components is snowflake obsidian, mined there in the deepest tunnels."

"Prince Faolan's token was a figurine made from snowflake obsidian, yes?"

"Hence the practice being dedicated to him," Tobias said a little tartly, and he reminded Brody so much of his tutor at the castle that he had to smile a little.

"It is there in the Vault, in the foyer before the mines, that we keep relics of the prince's time among us. Our most prized is the key our council had made, given ceremonially to the prince before he departed the city, returned to us when he passed."

Josiah made a sound like he had just connected a bunch of dots and now saw a clear picture.

Brody thanked Tobias profusely and let the man pass around him, looking dazed, and leave the shop. After making sure it was safe, Abram, Josiah, and Brody departed as well.

Chapter Twenty-Four:

The Secret Letter

"Those who stand for nothing fall for anything."

–Alexander Hamilton

Though the Rankers' presence seemed to upset the Crystalians' sleep-schedules, sleep they finally did, retiring when weary to their homes or whatever inns were nearby. The Paragon had given the city three days to prepare for the Gauntlet, and Brody, not wanting to pass up the opportunity to remain well-rested, led Abram and Josiah to an inn near where they'd entered the city.

Josiah apologized over and over again for his behavior, despite Brody having forgiven him at the first. His bitterness began to weigh on the king, however, so Brody sent Josiah and Abram both downstairs to fetch some food.

One benefit of the Paragon's presence in the city was that the cooks were all driven to try and outdo each other. The three friends feasted that night on drop-biscuits, spaghetti, peach preserves with sugared strudel, and a sumptuous pie filled with cinnamon, apples, and cream.

When Rexus came much later to relay a message from Skâlger wondering if they were okay, Brody packed some of their food into a bag for Rexus to bring back, along with some reassurances and a summary of the day's events. After a short rest and a snack of one of the larger meatballs in the spaghetti, Rexus scampered back out the window.

Brody awoke early the following day. By the time he had done sponging himself clean in the steamy washbasin of an adjoining room, the others had roused themselves. They departed as soon as they were able, jostled and bumped by Crystalians leaving or entering their own rooms who were too prideful to budge up and make way for others.

The streets were still empty, at least compared to the previous day, so that the Rankers stood out in their black cloaks, prowling like wild animals between buildings or along streets. Brody thought they behaved like creatures unused to being seen in daylight; like something vicious taken from its cave and only tamed just enough to walk among humans without tearing into them. Every small sound drew their attention so that they froze in place, all senses invisible beneath their hoods but clearly straining to identify what had made the noise and why. It was unnerving to Brody, but the Crystalians ignored the Rankers like they were shadows.

Cautiously, Brody returned to the entrance to the Vault and obsidian mines near the canal-hub. A lone Ranker, sinuous and tall beneath deep, black-green robes inscribed with a thorny pattern, stood still as a stick atop the stairs leading down to the two rooms. Brody looked questioningly at Abram, whose gaze became distant as he gauged his inner reservoirs of strength. Then he chewed on his lower lip and nodded.

The pastor lifted his hand, fingers spread and all pointing forward at the Ranker, and his eyes became penetrating. The outermost ring of his irises paled to a honey-brown. All of the ambient noises of the waking city silenced so that if Brody hadn't been expecting the manifestation of Abram's griffin-ability, he'd have thought he had fallen deaf.

Abram tore a loose thread from his sleeve and let it fall–it stayed frozen in place, hovering in the air. "Quickly now," he said.

They rushed around behind the Ranker, hopped down onto the stairs, and filed down the hall to the Vault before the thread had even dropped five centimeters and before the Ranker's hood had even begun to twitch in the direction they had been standing. All it would have seen would be a flicker of movement, like the passing of a hummingbird; and without having noticed them before, the Ranker would be none the wiser.

There were no sounds of movement near the door when they entered this time, and no sign of anyone in the foyer. Brody shut the door behind them and then moved to support Abram as the man slumped wearily, releasing his focus. Some griffin-powers were very great; the older the griffin, the more stressful the situation, and the more exacting the power, the more difficult it was to maintain focus.

With the withdrawal of Abram's ability, the clink of distant hammers, chisels, and pickaxes echoed from down some mining tunnels–there were many branching off the foyer. As time sped back up to normal, Brody felt the effects–the air warmed against his face as the normally unnoticed myriad breezes touched it. He felt heavier; locked in place and vulnerable.

Tapping a finger against his lips, Brody pointed at the far half of the room and Josiah went to search it, moving on the balls of his feet at a predatory stalk. Brody sat Abram down carefully near the door so that the pastor could catch his breath, only to have the man make a cross sound and then lever himself up and over to a nearby table where he started rifling through papers, taking long, slow breaths.

Brody smothered his amusement and admiration and crossed to a vacant area of the foyer, ears straining toward the sounds of labor down the nearest tunnels. Jitters jumped up and down his spine to coalesce at his extremities like tiny pins of ice. He wasn't relishing another fight. Though at the time he had been strengthened by anger and excitement, Brody's battle with the Fat Man had shown him how fragile he was–how easy it could be, with a simple lapse in judgment or one slow reflex, to fall and suffer a brutal death. His father had described battle this way–as constantly living on a knife's edge. A lapse in judgment, poor focus, one wrong step, could all lead to a fatal mistake, not just for one's self, but for their comrades as well. Brody envisioned a cloud of dread hovering above him, ready to sink down and wrap him in its apathetic embrace. What would he do if the Ranker lord of pride came charging into the foyer from those tunnels?

He took a pair of long, deep breaths and that cloud of anxiety dissipated. He couldn't misstep. He *wouldn't.* He would not let himself. As the prophecy had stated, the Griffin King would rise, not fall. *I will rise.*

The Vault was like a large shrine. Alcoves held more small statues with plaques commemorating the sacrifices of heroes who stood with Faolan. Glass-fronted cabinets displayed various items: cufflinks, torn cloth, a metal hand with articulated digits. The key he sought rested on a cushion in a case of clear green, red, and white glass sculpted so as to resemble a flower. It had the same black flecks drifting off of it that the flag in Syranade had had.

Josiah, nearby, spied the key moments after Brody and extended one arm hastily. "Careful. It might be warded."

Brody hesitated in place, drumming his fingers in the air, then touched the flower to lift it–but at the merest stroke of his skin, the glass fragmented into a glittering powder that settled atop the key on its pillow.

No alarms sounded, and the same power within him that had transferred to the corrupted Syranadian flag reached out to the key now. He pocketed it and braced himself against the rapid influx of sensations breaching the channel of cleansing connecting him to the key; sensations once belonging solely to the young Prince Faolan:

The lush, green artistry of a pristine river rushed in white ribbons over black stones. Rocks scraped roughly under his hands as he and his clansmen helped to secure the outer foundation of a cairn. The soul-stirring shrill of warpipes whined over the rainy curtain of wind.

Rocked by the heady visions, Brody leaned against the pedestal, blinking away the aftereffects. The movement upset the cushion the key had been resting on, exposing the tattered edges of three sheets of parchment. Brody pulled them out, giving them an initial glance.

It was a letter written in a neat and professional hand. Why had it been hidden?

Brody recognized the written dialect as the Ranker's quasi-pictograph style. An exhilarated flash of heat behind his breastbone made him laugh–a soft laugh punctuated by a griffin's happy cooing. His lessons had not been long enough for him to become a fluent translator of the Rankers' dark, secret tongue, but he wasn't going to pass up the opportunity to learn something important about the enemy for lack of trying! Leave it to the Ranker of pride to stash something so valuable in a trophy case.

There were entire paragraphs that Brody had to skip over, but he could interpret the majority of the letter. It read:

Fortunate lords of conquered lands,

I am sure that by now, news of–here, a complicated name that no doubt belonged to the Fat Man–*demise has reached you. Clearly, he was unprepared, as the rest of you cannot afford to be. Know this: it will not do to lose sight of our goal because we become drunk on power. The prophecy is fickle and must be handled with care if it is to be shaped in our favor.*

Brody skipped over a detailed description of his own identity and read,

Should the false king be sighted, restrain him, alive, until he can be dealt with by your superiors. Remember, the glory of slaying griffins goes to your lieutenants and generals. Should you deal the fatal blow, you will yourself receive the maximum punishment...

Continue recruiting. We are now beginning to see proof that your efforts are paying off. Dreamers are mirroring their corrupted creations and demonstrating aggression and disorientation. Soon, it will be time for the Crossing, and we may begin our work in earnest.

Keep us informed of the status of your contacts. They will not join us if they doubt our capabilities–we cannot afford more incidents like

the one that played out in Syranade. The moment everyone's assigned contact provides confirmation, we can distribute the pathmarkers for them to rendezvous with us here.

The only ones in our way are the griffins. Practice caution, give no quarter. Bring them fear that they may remember who and what we are.

Signed on the Half Moon Night,
High General Garrett

Chapter Twenty-Five:

Challenging Pride

"We can easily forgive a child who is afraid of the dark; the real tragedy of life is when men are afraid of the light."

–Plato

The crowd packing the streets outside the coliseum parted to make way for the three men being escorted toward the grand arena. Eyes stared, as if the men were exotic creatures and the Crystalians were wondering how dangerous they were. Mouths gossiped and jeered. Hands pointed, sometimes darted out to grab a shoulder or arm and clench it like the men being pushed and pulled through them were criminals that they wanted to savage.

And finally, one woman shrieked, "Tha's the King, it is! Lookit 'is 'air! It's dark an' curly as the Paragon described to us!"

"See him strut," a man crowed tauntingly. "Not so high and mighty now, is he!"

It was indeed Brody, and Abram and Josiah, being forced along through the tightly gathered bodies like a clot being shoved down a narrow pipe, although his stride couldn't properly be called a "strut."

Since reading the letter and sharing it with his companions Brody had decided to tweak his plans a fraction. The letter had raised two questions and provided a fantastic bounty of information that his council and generals could certainly make use of. First, what was the "Crossing?" And second, what was all that about the pathmarkers and contacts? It almost sounded as if this High General Garrett was trying to collect allies for an all-out war.

If the letter, and the essay Brody had read back home, were any indication, perhaps the Rankers had been meddling far longer than he–than anyone–had thought. Perhaps the essayist, Esther He'klarr, had seen the signs even as she'd put pen to paper.

The Ranker letter had disclosed one thing, though: only the Ranker elite had the privilege of killing griffins. Brody, Josiah, and Abram had only to fear the Paragon. And the Paragon could answer their questions. That didn't mean that the Rankers Brody had approached after leaving the Vault were treating them like precious cargo. The one in the thorny-patterned robes that they had all snuck past, incensed at their having done so, had at first reacted much the same as anyone could be expected to react when three people come from out of nowhere behind them.

The creature had squawked and swiped at them with four long and lethal fingers like sharp twigs, and when Brody had stood complacently before it long enough for it to get an eyeful, it had then warbled recognition and pounced, grabbing him by the hair atop his head. He had spent a decent length of time in the Vault removing his disguise and had to admit that it was refreshing being himself again. Thorns had punched through the earth to wrap around Josiah and Abram's legs, holding them in place and making them gasp in pain, drawing blood from small puncture wounds so that their pants were polka-dotted red. The Ranker had summoned reinforcements and now they were drawing near the proud usurper of Crystalia.

When it was clear that the three griffins were not resisting, the Rankers regarded them suspiciously and left their weapons bared, using them to prod Brody and the others, even if it was onto the heels or into the elbow of a Crystalian unable to squeeze out of the way in time. One man, haughty and supercilious, even slapped Josiah across the face in indignation after being stepped on before a combination of Josiah's angry, red eyes and a shove from a Ranker sent him wheeling away.

Finally, they burst free of the crowd and had only a few more yards to walk before they stood in the center of the arena, craning their necks to see the Paragon seated high above in the palm of the enormous statue. Fear oozed into Brody's heart when he made eye contact with the Ranker lord. As he'd sensed with the Fat Man, the Paragon was ancient. Being stared at so dispassionately by such a sinister, primeval being made Brody feel infantile and impotent. But his plan demanded that he keep a cool head and control his emotions carefully.

Now the seats between the statue's feet were also filled, with gaudily dressed men and women. Brody recognized one of the men, absently stroking the chin of the quartz rhino-hound and favoring Brody with a small smirk. These must be the Paragon's favored–those who had passed, or rather survived, his brutal challenges.

One of the women, an innocuous-looking, prismatic-green quartz-parrot on her shoulder, leaned forward. Brody could see the rings of white around her irises, her lips forming the words, "It's him!" Her top hat, adorned with a small timepiece and several small keys, slipped sideways off her head and knocked her parrot over.

"I suppose because I am the Ranker of pride you expect me to gloat over this unfortunate occasion." The Paragon's voice bounced off the walls, swollen in volume by the coliseum's clever acoustics. Brody could only see his pale face peeking down at them. "Well, you're right!" The people crowding into the tiers chortled appreciatively. Brody felt his lip start to lift with scorn but kept his head lowered meekly.

"You are either stupid to have been caught so easily, or you have something to say," the Paragon remarked shrewdly. "Out with it."

Brody looked up at him. He tried to keep his voice from shaking. "Where is your High General Garrett?"

An uncertain murmur flitted through the Crystalians perched in their seats and too far away to have heard Brody's question. But first shock and then panic crossed the Paragon's features at the abrupt revelation that the Griffin King had seen something very important that he was not meant to see. His speechlessness had an unsettling effect on the coliseum; people started to rise and speak in escalating volume and shift like an anthill slowly stirring from hibernation. The Ranker scrambled to save face.

"Fool. How like your kind, to interfere, to stick your beak where it doesn't belong and then whine when it gets blunted."

"Why are you corrupting dreams?"

"Be silent!" The Paragon's voice lost its luster, becoming shriller. The thorny Ranker beside Brody slapped him. He almost fell, his cheek aflame and his sight clouding. Josiah snarled.

"How pathetic, the vision before me," the Paragon said, in tones rich with malevolence. "Is this a new breed of griffin? Part chicken and part kitten? Now they sit children on a fancy chair and give them a pretty crown with which to play dress-up. You are no King David or Constantine, little chick. Your line is failing."

Brody was struck again, on the same spot, and he felt the blow all the way in the roots of his teeth. He had to focus on reorienting himself as his head spun. His formidable temper began to rise, flushing him with heat, burning away at the edges of his fear. His muscles tensed, his eyes flickered red as his instincts urged him to defend himself, as his body strained to fight. *Not yet*, he thought, the two steadying words becoming a mantra in his skull, an anchor.

"Look at you now," the Paragon taunted over the hoots and gibes of the tainted Crystalians. "You've not even the manhood to fight back. Uriah must have died of shame! Have I not dammed mighty rivers with the corpses of your people? Have I not caused the seas to run red or the skies to turn black with the flesh-eating, feathered scavengers? Hasn't my influence alone decimated *billions*?" Flecks of foam landed on the arena's tiles before Brody as the Paragon's ranting became more impassioned. The thorny Ranker slapped Brody again. His cheek was numb and raw. He could tell that it was swelling.

The Paragon's terrible words, the visions they brought to Brody's mind, caused fresh fear to stab at his heart, blending nauseatingly with his wrath. He had to remember that this was a being that had prowled the earth since the fall of Creation. Brody caught his balance and shook the fuzziness from his mind.

"What are you doing?" Josiah hissed.

"He's turning the other cheek," Abram said pointedly, to which Josiah made a small exclamation of understanding.

"Look upon the protector of your dreams, my children!" The Ranker lord addressed the cackling audience briefly before returning his cold stare to the Griffin King. "What do you have to say for yourself? Give me the satisfaction of some stirring speech directly from your self-righteous heart!"

Silence fell immediately, quivering with anticipation, heavy as a smothering snow. Brody felt the countless eyes aimed at his back like arrows ready to let fly. He chose his words as carefully as if they were the sharpest of weapons or the most finicky of medicines.

"I am the son of a laborer," he shouted, adding some of a griffin's lung-power–the same force that allowed a lion's roar to carry for several miles–so that at least some of the Crystalians could hear. "I come from a small town. I am no one...until you see who stands with me. What power is a king's decree or his signet ring without loyal subjects to enforce and obey? The power comes from you!"

An unsettled level of noise crept along the tiers. Clearly the people had not expected this. The thorny Ranker tried to grab hold of Brody but Brody shouldered it off.

"*You* make me king! I am here to fulfill my oaths to you. Like my father before me, like the kings and queens of the past, I am here to serve. Let me help you; let me care for you, not as a tyrant, not as a dictator, but as a shepherd tenderly looking after his flock."

Brody was aware of people in the coliseum cowering as others turned on them. He couldn't quite make out the details. The noise level exploded; the masses seethed. He spun around, looked beyond the stricken Rankers at the people seated at the Paragon's feet. They sagged, slack-jawed, watching the boiling cauldron of the city surge on the tiers. Rankers appeared to try and restore order. With a stab of hope, Brody saw one go down beneath a crowd of hysterical Crystalians.

"Brody of the Griffins," the Paragon called down venomously, "Meddlesome king. Face my challenge."

Brody flinched when a crackling report, like that of an arsenal of firecrackers, or a twenty-gun salute, sounded from high above him. He felt something like a vortex open in his chest, a dark and sucking hole pulling at his ribs, when he saw the giant hand holding the Paragon move. The figure was not just some artistic monolith of the arena, it was a one-hundred-foot-tall quartz statue!

Chapter Twenty-Six:

A Hostage

"I shut my eyes and all the world drops dead;

I lift my eyes and all is born again."

–Sylvia Plath, "Mad Girl's Love Song"

Steam pumped in clouds from vents in the humanoid machine's back. All along its body, seams of energy began to glow yellow, outlining joints and the turning gears that ticked softly beneath blue-black stone skin in the parody of a heartbeat. The head, fashioned after the plains-cats native to the wilds around Crystalia, worked its mighty jaws open and emitted an entirely mechanical but no-less-frightening metallic trumpet. Its eyes grew bright, like twin fires slowly coming to life; two round discs of hot-orange, baleful and somber.

It was as beautiful as a typhoon, as impressive as a thunderstorm, a mesmerizing work of human invention, the pride of some dreamer. And, like all else in Crystalia, it had been twisted into something dark and destructive.

The statue lifted one foot ponderously, causing an effusion of dust and pebbles that settled in a gritty cloud over the arena. The people at its heels threw themselves toward the exit ways, covering their heads and screaming. It was havoc in the audience where people wrestled with each other, charged the Rankers, stared, appalled, at the action below, or tried to flee.

The statue stomped its foot down at Brody, causing the ground to quake enough to upset his balance. He stumbled sideways and let himself fall into an over-shoulder roll that brought him directly up against the edge of the arena platform. He heard the statues' strides advancing toward him–there was no time to check on the others. The arena shook with the cannon-fire boom of giant, quartz feet.

Brody gasped, one sharp breath taking in all of his fear that he then held trapped in his lungs, and he rolled once, twice, right off the edge of the platform.

The wind generated from his fall forced his limbs into a spreadeagle position and scoured his eyeballs so that tears streamed back along his temples. Black water rushed up to meet him, a turbulent current marred in places by a pale, bloated corpse. The air fouled as he descended.

And in a blink, Brody became a griffin.

His tail feathers, and the long, quill-like feathers on his head and back, looked to have been dipped in a painted sunrise. The red patch of feathers on his chest was like a wound and his eyes burned with a wild light as savage instinct settled over his brain like a mesh net.

He flew back up, circling high out of the statue's reach, getting an eagle's eyeful of the Paragon. The Ranker had abandoned its fancy disguise for its true form, and now resembled a pitiful shadow of its former self: a hollow-cheeked husk of conceit with feverish eyes, dressed in clothes desperately drawing attention to silly, shiny knick-knacks.

The statue began to move gracefully toward the edge of the arena, purposefully.

“If I cannot have Crystalia,” the Paragon howled, “Then no one will!”

“Brody! He’ll destroy the city with that thing!” Josiah shouted, battling the thorny Ranker.

Brody looked out over the roofs of the city toward the west gate and Crown Hill. He gave a piercing griffin’s cry, and arrowed at the statue to pester its feline face in the way he’d seen crows pester squirrels back home. A flash of crimson–Josiah joined him, black-tipped wings beating about the statue’s eyes, and gave his own whistling call. Eight long seconds passed while the world spun like a mad carnival ride as Brody flipped and spun and strained his wings to their limits… Then Abram, a darkish-green color with tabby patterning, came streaming up to meet them, emitting a raspy screech.

“*He cannot escape!*” Brody shouted to the griffins, his voice almost breaking with the force of his scream. “*He has answers to our questions! Do NOT let him leave!*”

The statue, its quartz exterior impervious to their talons, moved on, only swatting at Josiah with irritation as the scarlet griffin thrust his hind paws at a warped gasket near the mouth. Stepping over the gilded barrier separating the arena platform from the seats, it advanced toward one of the exits.

“Do you think they heard us?” Josiah asked, shouting over the thunderous footfalls.

“We’ll know soon,” Brody replied on his way past. He dove at the Paragon, still kneeling in the palm of one of the statue’s hands, but as he did, the fingers curled up and with a growl Brody had to pull up, kicking off of the cool stone.

Fighting shamed Brody–made him feel out of control and savage and unclean, even if he knew that it was necessary. His wars were preferably fought with words and logic. But his regret would come later, after the carnage. For the moment, shame was but a small twinge in his heart, smothered by dark rage. Now, he thirsted for the sundering of flesh as if it were ambrosia. Now, his hatred filled him so that he thought he would burst, and he heard himself whimpering as his bloodlust went unquenched; as the statue denied him access to the Paragon again and again.

"*Coward*!" Brody raved, his words almost drowned by the lion's rumble in his throat. He latched on to the statue's fist and tried to dig his beak into the gaps between the digits' joints, hoping to tear something loose. He felt his hackles as a tight ridge down his spine, felt the flexing of his powerful muscles and knew he must look a sight. He scented the Paragon just out of reach and screamed his outrage at where the Ranker was hidden.

When the mobile monolith was perhaps five steps away from its exit, a white light flashed blindingly beyond it, followed by a noise so loud that it was felt more than heard: *CRACK-BOOM!*

The bricks and mortar of the coliseum archway before them exploded into red-gold dust, and the masonry above it imploded, blocking the way out with several tons of broken stone.

The statue came to a stop. As if confused, it hesitated and then turned around and made for another exit. Several more explosions came rapidly on the tail of the first. Several more clouds of debris betrayed the locations of more collapsed exits. The statue ground to another gradual halt. The griffins all landed on its head, panting, waiting.

From the final exit came Daghart Puddle with his sappers, and Skâlger with his men and Brody's, pursued by nearly eighty-five or ninety Rankers. Without a moment's consideration, Brody launched himself at the fresh, vulnerable targets, a black and white, winged omen of death that watched the hoods tilt up at him. He perforated a chest cavity with ten talons; left a throat in pithy ribbons with his beak; knocked a dozen down with his wings. Before they could recover, they were hit again by Josiah and then Abram. However, being surrounded and outnumbered was not a good place to linger.

Having created a sizable distance between the horde and the sappers, the griffins withdrew with a couple of fluid wing flaps. Puddle commanded his sappers as the men hurriedly placed charges in what appeared to Brody random spots on the arena floor. Nimble fingers connected wires, held others together with putty, and when finished lifted one hand in the thumbs-up gesture. When every sapper had a thumb up, Puddle said, "Well done, lads!"

Skâlger's warriors had each chosen a sapper and guarded his back, facing the Rankers, weapons an unearthly sparkle in their hands. Aydran, Khogar, and Domine, now a great bear, stood poised to protect the rest. The Rankers collected themselves for another charge. Those in the audience who had not fled the coliseum in time were now wailing in terror–it made Brody feel as if he were in Hell.

He landed lightly and in two bounds was beside Skâlger and Khogar. The statue had finally figured out that there was only one exit left, on the other side of the arena, and was advancing in long, slow strides.

"Your Highness!" Puddle called over to him in greeting.

"What do you need?" Brody asked. "How can I help?"

"Well, I'm not the sort of chap to order a bleedin' king about, am I, wot?" The mild-mannered gentleman barked. He was in combat-mode. "But getting rid of those Rankers would help!"

Wordlessly Brody spun and began to leap toward the approaching Rankers, springing with only minimal ungainliness on his mismatched feet. On his left were Josiah and Abram, on his right, Domine and Khogar on all fours. Domine's dark, shaggy fur rippled as his deadly, clawed paws slapped the tiles. A feral snarl twisted Khogar's lips up over her fangs. She made an incredible leap that carried her forward forty feet like a silver comet and into the midst of the nearest Rankers.

Then the fight was around Brody, and he lost himself to it. He heard the fortress folk engage behind him with primal yells. The griffins raked with talons, snapped with beaks. Domine sundered with spade-like paws. Khogar sliced with her saber, her tail ribbons flashing here, then there, misleading beacons that brought the Rankers flinching onto her steel.

But the Rankers powered through. One split a warrior's head in half with a hatchet. Another warrior was slain after slipping in his companion's brain matter. The two sappers they had been guarding went down with screams before Brody could back-flap, blind, using instinct to detect where to drop to plug the breach, and kill the Ranker he came face-to-face with.

"It's on us, chaps! Withdraw, and brace!"

Puddle's order was swiftly obeyed—the remaining Rankers were suddenly charged en masse as the warriors, sappers, griffins, a bard, a tribal, a titan, and a fierce little charlatan moved out of range of the explosives.

Fanning his facial feathers to circulate some cool air against the skin beneath, Brody looked back. The statue filled his vision, a tall, awesome, and terrible creation of stone and metal, bisecting what he could see of the world. It glared hideously down at them, one hand a claw at its side, the other still hiding the Paragon. It lifted a foot. Put it down. And then the foot was gone, reduced to shrapnel and crumbs in a flash of light. After the sight, a physical sound walloped them, assailed their ears, brought some to a pained crouch, clutching the sides of their heads.

With a shriek like tearing metal, the giant fell, landing on its free hand, knee, and the stump of the other leg. Its eyes smoldered hellishly over their heads. Yet, even as they watched, minute wires began to fray in the charred shreds and pulverized quartz. Extra bits fell loose until the stump was tidy...and then the frayed wires began to extend, twining together to form cables, like the roots of some freakish tree.

"Hold on, gents," Puddle cried in an interested tone of voice, as if he witnessed something no more alarming than a shot from a sand hazard in a game of golf. "She must've been built post-deficit!"

"Meaning?" Brody heard Skâlger ask. The north-islander watched the leg grow, picking at specks of bone stuck in the blood on his sword.

"Meaning she can repair herself. It was a program started a decade ago, meant to save the city money. Instead of having to fetch a new nut or bolt every time one goes wonky, our more costly machines can patch themselves up–least temporarily. We'll run out of pressure bombs long afore she's down and out." Puddle stood unafraid, studying the statue, with a dignified admiration rather than despair.

Skâlger puckered his lips and cocked his head at the statue kneeling over them, casting them in its shadow. He bent down, picked up two pressure bombs like they were bags of groceries, making the sappers nearest him cringe away, and then lobbed them both up at the monstrosity's open jaws in a mighty overhand. They landed in amongst the quartz teeth, the gums outlined with orange flumes of energy, clanging about.

Realizing some insult had been given, the machine began to rise. It clapped its mouth shut–and its head was pulverized into smithereens. Everyone below grunted in surprise.

The statue stumbled a little, raised both arms, then toppled stiffly sideways to hit the arena in a tremor of demolished tile. The remnants of the levers and ratchets that would've moved the head and mouth worked for a few moments then became still.

"Can't rebuild itself without a brain," Skâlger said mildly.

"Hmm, indeed. That must be taken into consideration for future schematics," Puddle replied, ever the scholar.

The remaining Rankers, weighing their options, saw that the tide of battle had changed and tried to retreat. They were hotly pursued and brought down.

The fingers of the fist holding the Paragon unwound and the Ranker poked his head out, looking as if he had just endured a rough tumble in a clothes dryer. Some sappers approached him boldly, daggers drawn, but Brody commanded, "Leave him. Fetch restraints and assign him a guard. We have questions he will answer."

Chapter Twenty-Seven:

Whispers of War

"If a guy like you can stand up and do what you did, then maybe everyone can. Maybe everyone can live beyond what they're capable of."

–Markus Zusak, *I Am the Messenger*

Seeing a griffin approach you after he has just drawn blood, his fur up along his spine, his neck feathers a bristly mane, his eyes crimson halved by narrow black slits; to watch him come closer until you hear the gurgling raptor's growl rolling in his beak; to then watch that griffin transform into a young man with glowing red eyes, a bo staff blackened with gore in one white-knuckled fist, sweaty hair all untidy curls, and loathing in every inch of him...to see such a vision would humble the stoutest of hearts, even if the countenance *wasn't* that of the Griffin King.

It had taken a lot of restraint on Brody's part not to give the Paragon at least a slap of rebuke as the Ranker watched him draw near with a wary sort of tension. But after Brody had seen the Paragon sequestered away in one of the nearest prison cells and guarded by Domine and a volunteer from the fortress wringing the haft of a glittering, mint-green mace, he could relax a little and focus on other matters.

First, he allowed Skâlger and Puddle to collect their dead. Though they were few, the sight of their disfigured remains tarnished their victory. Brody wasn't the only one shooting the Paragon murderous glares. Brody would allow the dead to be seen to in whatever manner dictated by Crystalian and north islander customs, but he asked that he be given a list of whatever compensation Puddle and Skâlger deemed justifiable for the families of the dead. He wanted to show that he appreciated their ultimate sacrifice; that they were more than just fodder. After all, he hoped that in reality others were supporting his parents in much the same way. And like his father, who would always remember the soldiers who had died around him in the jungles of war, so too would Brody remember. It seemed a most solemn and ceremonious curse.

Next, Brody ordered his own companions, the King's Six–minus Domine who took to guard duty with relish, as if hoping the Paragon would give him any reason to break his neck– to scan the city and see how people were reacting to the Paragon being captured.

While waiting for them to report, he quickly transcribed the letter he'd found from the Ranker general, intending to store the original in his saddlebags, and hastily wrote a detailed account of the events in Crystalia as well as a list of questions he had that he intended to ask the Paragon. Perhaps his council would uncover some useful information or some buried answers he'd overlooked.

He hadn't high hopes of there being any available messenger birds in the nearby rookery and sure enough they had long since fled. But just as he prepared to leave and seek out the next-closest roosts, a bird flitted down to him, having been sticking close and waiting for the city to be cleansed so that she could return home. She was a plains-hawk, a mottled brown and gray with yellow streaks, built for gliding long distances, perfect for his needs.

"I would be honored," she said, after Brody told her his intentions, and lifted her wings so he could have easy access to the ribbons around her legs. After he had bound the letter safe and snug, she dipped her head, blinked reverently, and flapped away.

On his way to the barracks, beneath which the Paragon was jailed and in which Brody had temporarily stationed himself, he saw that Abram and Josiah had returned. Both were in griffin form, having winged to the far reaches of Crystalia, beyond the little Brody had had a chance to see before challenging the Paragon.

The scarlet blot that was Josiah's pelt and feathers drew Brody's eyes upward. Josiah perched atop a narrow irrigation canal elevated high on slender columns that reminded Brody somewhat of bullet casings. Water, thin now, probably poison, choked somewhere along the source by the bodies of fleeing refugees, curtained down in spotty sheets onto a smooth stone slab hedged with flowers that identified the building across the street as the barracks. Though the aesthetic quality of the waterfall may have been somewhat diminished, the mid-sized silver dog statues in various hunting poses around the sign were not. Inert at the moment, like the Paragon's colossus had been, Brody knew they only needed a command or some switch flipped, probably by the barracks captain, to spring to duty.

Josiah preened his long, black-tipped pinions, his talons gripping the lip of the chute with a scraping sound like chalk on metal. Abram sat facing the other way, his tabby-striped wings half-opened to soak up the sun. Josiah twitched one curving, feathery ear and looked down at Brody, then free-fell to the earth, braking with his sharp falcon wings only at the last moment. When Abram joined them and the griffins had shifted into their human forms, they all entered the barracks, and Brody's makeshift "office" together.

Whoever the barracks captain had been, he had not returned to his post. Brody felt guilty about picking through his desk and making a mess of the formerly tidy place with the ink and several sheets of parchment that he'd found. He listened to Josiah's report while cleaning the room back up, and then Abram's while pacing behind the desk, his hands clasped behind him.

"It was much the same on my route," the minister said gravely. "They're scared. For whatever reason they're moving toward the walls as if...as if trying to squeeze as far from the Paragon as possible."

"But they've snapped out of the hex?" Brody asked, gazing out of the room's sole window into a neglected flower box.

"Well, kind of," Josiah said helplessly, "but it's like they're restarting. Or confused. They could've just been fleeing the battle. Last I saw Rexus he was trying to approach a few people so we'll know soon, but...Crystalia won't be cleansed until we get that Ranker out of here."

"I don't intend to stay long," Brody said, poking the soil in the flower box. He found a hardy little seed sprouting upside down and turned it over with a deep swoop of affection in his chest for the defiant flower. "In fact, I wanted to talk about that."

He moseyed over to a large map of the surrounding land and its cities; a chunk of the southeastern Land of Dreams that was more decorative than informative. He tapped a line of calligraphy labeling a large town some distance from Crystalia, a little less farther than Syranade was to the north.

"Goodwind is where we need to go next if I remember the reports."

"Frontier-town," Josiah said efficiently, as if reciting from a tourist's guide. "Arid, scrubby, dusty, but strategically placed between the desert kingdoms and the Anteroom. Wealthy enough, and the magic from the Anteroom is said to give some of the folks dreams or visions. They have seers who can supposedly direct you to whatever door in the Anteroom opens onto your alternate realities. In one, *I* might be Griffin King. In another, I might be a rich astronaut with a trophy wife, or a comic-book hero with superpowers." He sounded derisive, as if he thought the whole idea was bogus.

"What could the Rankers want with such a place?" Abram wondered aloud. "The Anteroom wouldn't reveal itself or open to the Rankers, if they're hoping to find a way in."

"No, but Queen Felicity the Nightingale once ended a large family feud that was tearing the whole town apart," Brody said.

"Ah. So it is a place of power."

"It was a bad feud," Josiah said seriously.

Brody circled a blank spot on the map with a finger, a few centimeters southwest of Goodwind. "The Fortress of Storm Breath should be right around here..." He drew back, a mixture of concern and relish churning a volatile, acidic burn into his stomach. "Where my volunteers will be waiting for us. And if my council can send me no word of what to expect, hopefully the fortress-keeper can."

"Things will be pretty bad," Josiah said softly, "by the time we get there. If Crystalia's any indication."

"But not unredeemable," Abram said, and Josiah's hopeless, sour look bittered a little further. He had doubts.

Brody ran the side of his thumb over the scars peeking above his tunic before stopping himself. He reached into a cubby on the desktop and removed the key from Faolan's shrine. It glowed slightly and warmed his entire hand to hold as if another hand enclosed his own. He could feel its energy pulsing out, warding away the Paragon's lingering taint.

"There may be something else. They've been tapping into the power the kings left behind, but this isn't like before. This isn't the Rankers just testing the next ruler. This is a strategic movement. They're setting things up for the main event. For the big shift." He took a deep breath, thinking of his father, of the corpses of those who had been too slow to flee Crystalia but who had been desperate enough to try.

"This could mean war."

Josiah nodded, resigned. He had been reading the signs and interpreting them the same way as Brody. But Abram was just short of scandalized.

"But it's been...eons since the last war!"

"The Rankers started that one too," Josiah reminded him.

The minister went silent, as if he'd stopped breathing, and ran his hands down his sides in a nervous gesture, like a man feeling his pockets for his glasses.

Josiah looked grimly at Brody. "We can't deny that everything seems to be pointing that way. They're conquering and corrupting locations strategically scattered in all corners of the land, they're fiddling with the minds of dreamers by their own admission; this reeks of a preparation for something bigger."

"I guess I've been in denial," Abram mumbled to the floor.

"The worst thing is that we still don't know their endgame or their ultimate plan." Brody put the key back and sat in the cushy leather chair tucked neatly under the desk, resisting the urge to massage his temples. As Aydran and Rexus had said, he could not show weakness, not even to his friends.

"Why send out a horde to traipse across the land just to stick a few in a city and have them poke and prod at dreams...unless it isn't just those cities that they really want to affect..." The thought had been swirling around in Brody's brain for a while now, just beyond his focus. But now that he'd voiced it, he felt a physical ache seep into his whole body like a bruise. His weariness almost got the better of him but then a bizarre idea came to him as suddenly and clearly as an image he had long-forgotten seeing in Michael's wings. Perhaps he had, once.

"Maybe their true target is the Winged Throne. Maybe they intend to weaken the dreamworld and topple the capital city itself." The Fat Man's words about destiny, the lines in the Ranker general's letter about something called "the Crossing," and the snatches of Esther He'klarr's essays he'd read in reality drifted, semi-substantial, in his thoughts. "Josiah, Abram, the next time you're in reality, see if you can compile some detailed information about anything amiss."

"'Amiss?'" Abram tilted his head and adjusted his spectacles.

"Yes. Anything that could indicate that what the Rankers are doing here is having a greater effect on reality. As for myself... If I don't wake up and return to reality soon, then I need to know how to identify dreamers from dream-creations. If I can find people with pull in reality, maybe I can influence their minds to keep an eye on and protect reality against Ranker influence. I can warn their subconscious."

Abram and Josiah both looked appalled at the idea and what Brody was implying.

"Do you honestly think it will come to that?" Josiah asked.

Brody considered Garrett's letter again; its overall tone of aggression, its sinister intimations of a grander plan. He gave a long, slow sigh through his nose.

"I think that if we move fast, if we crush the remaining five lords...we might prevent a catastrophe."

One week passed in a busy, bustling rush. Brody and his friends retrieved their horses and Khogar set to repairing their saddles, making sure they were ready for the next leg of their long journey. The others set about gathering provisions, saying farewell to the new friends they'd made. Brody's main task was observing the Crystalians as the days passed.

They seemed to be recovering–enough to start building a statue of him in sapphire and gold, at least. When one of Puddle's sappers led him to the work-in-progress where a group of artisans picked and chiseled the stone into masterful detail, Brody forced himself to smile pleasantly. He thought the chin a bit too square and the expression a little too misty, and the whole thing a little too dramatic, but he understood what the Crystalians meant by it and kept his criticisms to himself.

On a fly-over one day, the sun making his underwings shine blinding-white like beacons, Brody discovered what had become of the Paragon's "favored," those few men and women who had sat arrogantly at his feet and vanished mysteriously during the battle. The fresh stench of carrion guided him down to a pile of refuse yet to be crushed and incinerated in the city's huge, underground vats. The bodies were strewn, most hacked into pieces, leaving the remains in positions that indicated a violent frenzy of vigilante justice. The festering wounds and fear still apparent in the gray faces brought Brody pity. Clearly the city could take care of itself, and this was proof of its mending, of its citizens' minds clearing enough to identify their true foes, but Brody wished he could have saved them all.

Stepping over the crushed green quartz parrot, its head still twitching, stuck repeating, "No...stop! No–I command you...please stop," Brody crouched and pounced back into the sky.

One day, while Brody picked disinterestedly at the stringy meat of an antelope he had hunted down earlier and had Abram cook, a tapping came at the window behind him. The messenger-hawk had returned, a fat scroll rolled tight between her talons.

Brody made a happy sound of greeting and spun out of his chair to let her in. He let her eat his meat and left the window open so that she could leave again when ready, and then stood on the spot, reading the letter. He would have dearly preferred that someone other than Councilman Isa had composed the reply, but Brody overlooked the man's snarkiness, apparent even in writing.

More refugees sought asylum in the capital by the day, some half-dead from traveling by foot through the mountains or from places as far away as Raynarra to the very northeast. Others spoke woefully of whole villages destroyed, and Brody shuddered to think of what that did to dreamers' sleeping minds. Isa advised that Brody attempt to get the Ranker's goals and the location of their base, as well as more information about their High General Garrett, out of the Paragon asap. There was also some information on activity in Goodwind and a summary of Queen Felicity's time there, enough that Brody knew what to look for and expect.

Letting the parchment roll back up, Brody dazedly wandered to gaze out the window at the Crystalians milling around trying to cleanse and repair their city or still seeking lost loved ones. A mother ran by, calling out the names of her husband and children in a voice long-gone hoarse, and Brody winced. The Crystalians were recovering, yes, but they were listless, despondent, many were even physically ill, which explained the absence of the usual crowds packing the streets.

Letting the sounds of the hawk's talons clinking on his plate, her hungry chirps, comfort him, Brody lifted his saddlebags and gave the room a once-over for anything he had missed. Josiah and Abram had been right. The best thing for Crystalia right now was to get the Paragon out of it.

Still lugging his saddlebags and remembering to squat slightly going through doorways so his crown didn't get knocked off his head, Brody took the double staircase down to the barrack's cells. In typical Crystalian fashion, the area was lit by a dim, bronze glow, emanating from the bare bulbs sticking from a black pipe that circled the room. Four glass panels hung so as to make a broken square over the constable's iron-worked seat, showed four images representing the four Crystalian tenets of justice: manacles for accountability, scales for fairness, a sparrow for redemption, and a skull for penance.

He passed bell jars holding fantastic metal flowers that served to brighten up the room and probably had some other purpose he was unaware of, then stopped at the first cell. It was a gilt cage of welded gears and solid, copper bars set in a zany pattern of zig zags. Pretty, in its own way, on the outside looking in. The Paragon, however, sulking in a corner, did not look impressed. In fact, he looked maltreated. One side of his delicate-boned face was swollen and a nasty shade of purplish-yellow.

Dropping the saddlebags with a grunt of surprise, Brody took two steps and wrapped his hands around the cage bars, clinically studying the bad bruise while the Paragon moodily glared back. It wasn't lethal, but Brody was more than willing to bet it had rendered the Ranker unconscious for a while. He looked suspiciously at Domine to his left, who used one of the fangs on his necklace to pick unconcernedly at his teeth, then to his right, where Skâlger's man waited to give him an innocent smile.

"And how, prithee, did he come by that injury?" Brody asked in a terse way, hoping that the usage of King's Speech would properly convey his dire mood.

Domine, not even feigning shame, scratched at his scalp with another of the fangs and said readily, "He sneezed."

Brody floundered, wondering if a punch to the gut would perhaps *better* convey his dire mood; that it was treason to disobey the king's command for such a ridiculous offense, if it could be called that. His eyes brightened to a sullen, glowing red that finally forced Domine to look a tad more contrite and shift an inch or so away.

In a careful, hushed voice, the north-islander man, idly cradling his mace to his chest, said, "My best friend died in the arena, my King. We sailed the ocean together, grew up together, married each other's sisters. Visit upon me whatever judgment you deem fit, your Grace, for your companion prevented me from doing much greater harm."

Brody softened, sensing the sorrow in the man like it was a tactile thing: rainwater filling the muddy boot print of a dead soldier on the battlefield; a still silence where once there had been laughter. He looked again at the Ranker and saw that he wore a faint smirk.

Brody's anger swelled again but in a different direction. He grasped the bars of the cage, pressed his face to them, and, still using King's Speech, growled, "The only reason you are alive is because you have answers to my questions. You will tell me your secrets, even if it means opening your eyes to the definition of 'extreme duress.' Consider this our next challenge, Ranker of pride."

Chapter Twenty-Eight:

Seeing a Ghost

"To be able to forget means sanity."

–Jack London, *The Star Rover*

Most of the last day was spent on goodbyes. Aydran shared a private moment with the woman from the fortress. Domine finally got the tussle he wanted, wrestling with three young warriors at once, all of them laughing wildly, one of them even through his bloody nose. Rexus, Josiah, and Abram shook hands–and paws–with the sappers, exchanging promises of meeting for drinks the next time they came 'round. Khogar, one of her whiskers slick with what looked like a tear, tied a new ribbon to her tail, this one patterned with clockwork. Then she swooped up a gleeful child shyly approaching her and took the girl back to her parents on her shoulders while she played with Khogar's fluffy ears.

Brody had already finished most of his farewells. He had made some good friends over the past month, and though goodbyes were always bittersweet and left a sorrowful ache in his heart, he was glad to know that he would find them all safe should he ever stop by again.

Puddle and Skâlger were the only two left to say goodbye. They stood with Brody off to one side, sheltered from the crowd behind a quartz griffin holding a sundial in rose-pink, outstretched talons.

Daghart Puddle extended a large, velvety box to Brody and lifted the lid. Within, resting on a silk cushion, was a fabulous working of gold and bronze, a web of fine art resembling tree branches with tiny emeralds for leaves and tiny pairs of sapphire for the eyes of minute woodland creatures peeking around the boughs. Brody was speechless.

"This is *Fey*." Daghart lifted out the dazzling item, stuffing the box into Skâlger's hands so that he could turn it; let Brody figure out what it was. "She is one of our most priceless treasures, made with the materials from our first-ever mine, as old as Crystalia herself. May I?"

Brody nodded and let Daghart come forward, lifting the item to his face. It was an elaborate sort of ear-cuff that hooked around his pinnae and spread across his cheek, brow, and jaw like glistening arterioles.

Stunned, Brody reached up to touch the gift. "For me?"

"With our thanks, sah!" Daghart said, lively. Then, lower, "With...*my* thanks. You're a man of your word and, topping that, a buggerin' sight to see in combat, wot? This doesn't do my gratitude justice, but it is the best token I have to give."

Brody grasped the man's shoulder. "It's amazing. I...have no words."

Skâlger stepped forth, pushing the box back into Puddle's arms and patting the man's back. "You have stolen the words of a king, my friend. No one I know can claim such an honor." He transferred his pale eyes to Brody and their playful light became intense and stinging.

"I have no gift for you, your Highness, but an oath. Whichever way the wind blows, my people will be there. Whatever the tide brings, we will sail with it. My people do not fear battle. It is our..." he rolled his head, choosing his words, "...favorite sport." Skâlger bared his brilliant teeth. "If there is to be war, let there be war."

Aydran's maps guided them south from Crystalia, back across the plains. For a while they rode parallel to the distant mountains upon which the Fortress of Ice stood sentinel and Brody felt a connection to it like a rubber band around his chest. But as time wore on, so his sorrow at having left friends behind waned. It was the King and his Six again, and though evenings were a lot quieter, their joy was no less diminished.

Even the Paragon couldn't dim their high spirits, though Josiah made sure to give the Ranker a wide berth as he was most easily affected of all of them by the taint of pride. The creature sat, mute, his hands bound, on a lean palomino whose harness was attached to Domine's saddle horn with a rope. At night, they plopped him down between Domine and Brody around the campfire, like one of the company. Not a word he uttered. His expression was one of vacant expectation, like a man waiting for elevator doors to open. Not once did he struggle, and he bore Aydran's viol, their nighttime stargazing, Brody's stories of home, and Abram's infrequent sermonizing with as much attentiveness as a pinecone.

Eventually the plains became speckled with trees; evergreens that became denser and denser among grass that was steadily lusher and springier. This put the horses in fine moods. Brody took an afternoon flight and saw that ahead they faced a verdant forest. On the other side, many days away, Goodwind would be waiting.

The next morning, Brody's dun pulled toward a fresh streambed to drink and the others allowed their horses a respite also, remaining seated and languidly gazing around at the gorse, coneflowers, and wild indigo. Brody decided that there was no better time to begin interrogating the Paragon.

Despite their rough riding, the Paragon's hair was still slick, his lips still smooth and pink, not chapped, his complexion clean and clear. In his disguise, he was a specimen of the finest breeding; indeed, a paragon of the much-admired qualities that oft drove a person to become prideful. He was handsome, healthy, and confident...but Brody couldn't put his finger on what it was in the Ranker that exposed his inhumanity. It was something in the eyes, of course, those windows to the soul. They weren't dead or hollow, like most minor Rankers' were, reflecting the darkness in their creators' hearts and minds. They were actually quite bright and clear. No, it was something else; something dark, ancient, and foul.

The Paragon's eyes drifted up to lock on Brody's, pinning him like basilisk fangs. Indescribable images and sensations of suffering came to Brody's mind: wickedness the Paragon was in some way involved with, but that spanned centuries, *ages*, and Brody quailed to think that he had any hope of forcing answers out of such a being.

But something in the tightness of the Ranker's mouth or the twitch in one of his eyebrows exposed the Paragon's own tension. For whatever reason, Brody had the upper hand. For whatever reason, he intimidated this ageless monster.

Pulling on the reins, Brody guided his horse a little closer to the Ranker's.

"Our limits are what define us. What we can't and won't do defines us, not what we call ourselves or what we possess."

At his words, a soft challenge, an admonition, the Paragon's nostrils flared. The others' attention fell over them, a blanket of eyes. Thumping hooves and the slurp of the horses guzzling water were an odd, faintly annoying backdrop, but Brody wanted the Ranker to be annoyed–unsettled.

A note of steel arose in Brody's voice. His irises smoldered faintly red, framed by his crown and the ear cuff, *Fey*, making him regality personified. "Know this: there is nothing I won't do to protect my kingdom. My only limit is your sudden, useless death. Will you answer, or will you suffer?"

The Paragon's jaw worked. He glanced at Aydran, who looked unnerved by Brody's sinister words, then at Domine, who grinned madly, and back at Brody. He visibly gulped then said, "Ask."

Brody lifted his chin. "Where do Rankers come from?"

"From nightmares and fear. You know this."

"Yes, but where is your keep? Where is your high general stationed?"

"A keep? We have a keep, yes," the Paragon said evasively. He seemed to be fighting monumentally with himself, tortured by his treason, sickened at answering to a griffin. "In...in the ocean...a forsaken spit of rock."

"An island?" Brody's interest was piqued, but then his ear cuff suddenly grew warm–almost hot. He slapped his hand to it impulsively at the same time that an image, one of the most detailed he'd ever had, sprang to his thoughts like a vision.

A dark wolf with red pawprints loped at him through the snow, but the blood was not its own.

He leaned back, running the back of his hand across his eyes.

Rexus shrilled, branches snapped and hit the earth with tremendous quakes, brush crackled. The horses screamed in alarm. Brody's eyes flew open and he tried to make sense of what was happening. Out of nowhere, perhaps from above, six tall, slender Rankers in silvery robes like tissue-thin silk had appeared. They were beautiful, with skin like porcelain, faces like sad, marble angels', and immense, feathery wings folded behind them. Each expressionlessly reached out to take the reins of a horse.

One of the angelic Rankers landed directly in front of Brody. His dun reared and struck out with its forehooves, releasing a battle cry. Brody slid backward out of the saddle, only half intentionally, his crown rolling away. But before he could transform or reach for his bo staff the Paragon's palomino, sidling beside the dun, lashed out its hind legs in terror. One hoof caught him in the leg–he heard his fibula snap before the pain rushed through him like a thunderstorm of agony. The force of the kick threw him back onto the ground where he lay, dazed, sounds drifting in and out of his awareness without meaning.

Then a seventh Ranker stepped around him, looking down at his face. Tremors of fear made the pain in his leg go sharp and fine. This Ranker was a mockery of the female form. Long and sinuous, it was draped in a satiny blue robe and walked on four sinewy legs, each ending in hand-like talons with needle claws. Its neck was long and arched like a dragon's, its face hidden behind a white mask with purple-rimmed black eyes and a mouth of scarlet that pulled all the way up to where its ears should have been. It stretched its neck down, prehensile, so that its mask was less than a foot above him, and with one claw the length of a shortsword, pulled down his collar to see his scars. Somehow, that mask's painted lips lifted and Brody saw neat fangs like shark teeth bared in a savage, exultant grin.

"Do what you came for!" Brody heard the Paragon say somewhere to his right. The Ranker bending over him raised its head, gracefully lifting its serpentine neck. It moved away from him.

"Proud, even to the end," it said, its voice sultry, alien, but familiar.

Somewhere beyond Brody's line of vision there was a sound like a butcher's knife in raw steak, a wet grunt, a splatter of blood and a falling body. Sounds and sight faded again as Brody's leg throbbed. Then the Ranker was back at his feet. But it now wore its human guise: a young woman with white-blonde hair and blue eyes, an ear-length grin in the midst of melding into full, red lips.

Brody heard himself make an abject moan. Sylph stood before him, a monster wearing the flesh of one whom he had once counted as a friend; whom he had loved. At the sight of her, a memory fell into place in his mind, emerging from a drunken fog like something ugly crawling from a well. He recalled the sensation of her body shoving against his, driving him out onto the road. He had not *fallen* in front of the truck that had mangled his body and sent him to the dreamworld, Sylph had *pushed* him.

And this betrayal hurt more than any broken bone ever could.

Chapter Twenty-Nine:

Unmasked

"The prince of darkness is a gentleman."
–Shakespeare

Her hair fell in ringlets, her blue robe draped over her curvaceous figure in a way both flattering and obscene. Although the six other Rankers now towered above her, twice her height, she was the sight that captivated Brody's attention; beautiful as a fallen star, terrible as a fallen angel.

"Brody..." She sank onto her knees beside him. He was too weak to move away. Remaining supine, he blearily watched her hand extend and hover over his forehead, pass gropingly down his features, and then return to her lap.

"Forgive me, boy. Last I saw your face, I couldn't find it in the blood. You were in a bad way." She looked him over, getting reacquainted with seeing him whole and unravaged. "A very bad way."

Momentarily, maybe it was only in his mind, Brody saw the red, lunatic smile of her Ranker form as if her skin were translucent. He shut his eyes, gnashing his teeth. The pain in his calf had spread to his ankle and thigh.

Her voice was as he remembered it–silky, with a self-assured drawl–but it was older now; superior. She spoke as if she had lived centuries and he was but a newborn child crying for attention. Like the Fat Man and the Paragon, she was ancient, and her tone reflected that. *Is she one of the Deadly Seven?* Brody wondered, revolted at the sight of her, disgusted and ashamed that he had loved something so wicked. *Is she a Ranker lord?*

"Collateral damage," he heard Sylph say. Her unconcern was salt in his wound. She saw him as nothing but a nuisance; a piece on a chessboard to be swept aside to make her own path clear. Her indifference was worse than the hatred of mortal enemies. Hatred would at least imply that he was a considerable threat.

"Your leg, I mean. Collateral damage. I was sent to dispose of the Paragon before his tongue loosened.

"Collateral damage," she said again, and touched his cheekbone, "your face. The truck should have killed you. We suspected it wouldn't. It broke most of the bones in your body though. Ruptured your organs. Opened your face. Do you know the longest a human has been comatose?"

Brody felt tears well in his eyes and furiously strove to hold them in, trying to replace his anguish with a less impotent emotion. But anger, aggression, escaped him.

"Thirty-seven years, Brody. You will return an old man, if you return at all. Do you want that? Old and broken, never the same." Her voice lowered significantly. "But you haven't been the same, have you? Not since this..." Her fingers brushed his chest over the scars. "By the standards of many, you're already an old man. Inside, in your soul. That dry, withered husk."

He opened his eyes. The sky was blocked by evergreen branches, their sharp scent masked by blood and Sylph's perfume and his own sweat.

"Dry and withered. Like the old wheat fields by your home."

She remembered everything he'd told her, when he'd rambled like an idiot, a poor, misled idiot, yammering over drinks. A sob caught in his throat just to think of it: prattling on about ideals to a Ranker.

Sylph left him, pacing to the center of where her warriors held Brody's friends fast. "Get up. You know you can. You have a medical minor. It is not the compounded fibula that incapacitates you; it is the shock. Snap out of it, Brody."

Brody dragged himself up to sit against a tree. Sweat trickled down his ribs. There was nothing wrong to look at where his leg had been kicked, nothing that he could see above his clothes, at least. Good.

He saw a mound of torn flesh to his right, saturating the forest floor black, filling the air with the stench of blood and the foul odor of a dead Ranker. To his dismay, not only had the Paragon been killed, but the palomino he'd been riding, and Brody's own, brave dun that, even at the last, had readied to defend its rider as it had been trained to do.

His friends all seemed hypnotized, vacantly staring into the faces of the winged Rankers.

Now anger took him.

Helplessly he struck the dirt beside him with a fist and roared, "*What do you want?*"

Sylph looked perplexed, indicating the Paragon's body. "I have taken what I wanted, as all do. You expound virtue as well as a priest, Brody, but you would have convinced him to talk eventually." That smile-beneath-the-smile broadened. "Funny what you learn about yourself when left to your own mind long enough. Funny what you can turn into. After all, a griffin is, at its heart, a beast."

"You have what you came for," Brody growled. "Leave."

"You are in no place to give commands, boy. I am no vassal of yours."

"*Kiiiiillll himmmm...*" one of the beautiful Rankers whispered.

Sylph stomped one foot and it silenced. She watched Brody thoughtfully like a hunting cat, tail twitching, deciding whether or not to kill the rabbit hopping by. Her expression became sly.

"By all means, ask your questions. I will answer. *If*," she raised one finger meaningfully, "you answer mine in turn."

Pain, sorrow, and anger fogged Brody's mind and muddied his judgment. His kingdom needed answers. His own desire to understand why Sylph had manipulated him warred with his duty as king.

Be brave, he thought, or maybe it was the memory of a voice. Whichever it was, Brody managed to focus and ask his first question.

"Where is your High General Garrett?"

"Home. Where he is supposed to be."

"That's not an answer!"

"It is *an* answer." Her lips teased at a playful smirk, as if she was trying to remain professional in front of her underlings. "A king should choose his words carefully. For example, what is your special griffin ability?"

The question threw Brody. An answer might not be consequential enough to give Sylph any sort of advantage, and the Rankers would have discovered it eventually, but he answered as carefully as he could.

"I see images..." He almost touched the ear cuff, remembering how, just before they'd been ambushed, he'd seen the bloody wolf. Somehow his already unique way of considering things, of visualizing people and situations as tactile sensations, had become enhanced with Puddle's gift. "I don't always know what they mean, but they tell me more about...what I'm looking at."

Sylph inclined her head, satisfied. Brody gritted his teeth and asked, "Why are you corrupting dreams?"

"Because it corrupts the dreamer," Sylph replied. As if taking pity on him she added, "The dreamer, who corrupts reality."

Brody felt a little chill beneath his ribs. So it wasn't just about tainting dream-creators and making more Rankers–the Rankers were trying to affect reality as well. He almost missed her next question.

"Have you heard the prophecy?"

"Yes," Brody said challengingly, thinking of the first line that Skâlger had recited to him more than a month ago but that remained lodged in his memory all this time. *'The Griffin King shall rise to fight.' Keep talking, Sylph,* he thought, *and see me rise up. I have strength enough yet.*

It was true, his pain was fading, and his shock too. Endorphins were doing their job.

"What is the Crossing?"

Sylph went a little pale. She cast a disgusted look at the Paragon's body and then one of grudging respect at Brody. "You have seen what you should not have seen. I will not answer."

"Is a Ranker's honor so paltry that she would go back on her word?" He sat up a little straighter. If he could manage to get his good leg under him a little then he could stand and transform, ready for battle.

At his spiteful tone, Sylph suddenly came in close, her voice low and echoing as it had been in her Ranker form, as if she spoke from just beneath the water in a deep well.

"Do not speak to me of honor, boy. I know its every serrated edge." She backed away, but it took a while longer for her voice to get back under control. "Fine. I will tell you only this: we aim to be where we have not been, and rule where we have not ruled."

"Reality," Brody ventured. It wasn't a question.

One of the winged Rankers hissed loudly and Sylph made a shrill shriek in response. Brody's time was running out. *They're corrupting reality,* he thought, *so as to enter it...*

"Where are you going?" Sylph asked, still glaring at the Ranker who'd made the outburst.

"Goodwind..." Brody decided that Sylph didn't need to know he planned on stopping at Storm Breath Fortress first to pick up his volunteer army. "What are the pathmarkers Garrett plans on distributing for your 'contacts?'"

Sylph appeared distressed again, shifting her weight.

"They are varied; a means of conveying to allies the direction in which they should go."

Troop movements, Brody thought eagerly. *They want their allies to go somewhere. But where? What will the pathmarkers be?*

"I grow weary of our game," Sylph said. "We shall each have one more answer... Do you want to kill me, Brody?"

Brody bowed his head. On the grounds that she was a Ranker, it was his royal duty to end her, but that wasn't what she had meant. He hated her for her lies and manipulation, for getting him drunk and then pushing him out in front of that truck. He remembered the last words she'd spoken to him and found his last question.

"Yes. Yes, I want to kill you." He forced himself to look at her. When he saw the relish in her mad smile, rather than hurt or the bland detachment she'd shown him so far, he became bolstered.

"Before you...pushed me in front of that truck... I told you that my father says there are worse scars than those of the flesh and you said that 'he would know?' What did you mean?"

Still smiling to herself, Sylph became the long-limbed monster that was her true form, her neck curved like a swan's, her hellish mask ghostly as a barn owl's, painted like a harlequin. She started to walk away.

Brody, afraid that she wasn't going to answer, dug his fingers into the bark of the tree and pulled himself up. The lingering pain in his calf split through him like someone had taken an ax to the limb.

"You're my Ranker, aren't you? I created you."

Misery and loathing washed over him like magma, burning through him, melting him into something vulnerable and inept.

Sylph stopped. Her head turned to look at him over her back. There was bafflement on her face, as if she were astounded that he hadn't figured it out yet.

"No." She came back toward him. Her twenty stiletto-claws left pinholes in the earth. She loomed over him and said with the utmost gentleness, "I am your father's."

If Brody thought he could be brought no lower, Sylph had just proved him wrong. His father, his kind, wise, quiet father, carried *this* demon within him? It was impossible. A trick. A means of cowing him.

"No more lies!" Brody shouted. "No more mockery! My father is a hero! I won't let you sully that with falsehoods!"

Sylph looked amused, like a parent whose child had made a loud noise just to hear its own voice. She jabbed her face at him. He pressed back into the tree, scraping his head, losing his breath in fear. Her head, as big as his torso, swayed side to side slightly. Her voice rang with power.

"Oh, how it must sting, boy, this truth. There is more. Look upon me, the bane of men, she who leads sons to commit the sins of their fathers! I am the seventh of seven! The Ranker of many! I...am... lust!"

She rose up onto her hind legs like a grizzly bear but much taller, her neck twining and twisting like a pretzel, a sight of ruin and majesty.

"Lust?" Brody couldn't imagine his father lusting for anything. It was inconceivable.

"Bloodlust..." Sylph drew the word out luxuriously, savoring it, her violet-rimmed eyes closing. Understanding dawned on Brody. Sylph must have seen it on his features. She nodded.

"I knew him young, and I, too, was young in him. But in those bloody jungles I grew swiftly in his heart. A warrior, he was. Yes, a great warrior. I was drawn to him, drawn as I am, was, and ever will be, to lust. I saw it in his eyes, felt it in his mind. You think me a monster. *I* am no monster." She grinned again. "So where is your ideal now, boy? Name it! Name your virtue!"

Brody lunged at her, hands outstretched to wrap around her neck, to squeeze until he felt his fists close in her flesh. Casually, she lifted one hand and pinned him back against the tree, her claws wrapping around behind it.

"I see that you take after the sire more than the bitch." She met his outraged glare at eye-level. "You've the blood-sense. Rare among griffins, especially your kings and queens. Red eyes, irises *and* pupils, to forewarn of righteous wrath."

Brody struggled and she squeezed her hand so that her talons curled around to prick his side. "I should split you from breast to manhood. Then we would be done with you." She extended her head so it was beside his own. Brody tried to butt it but couldn't reach. "But I was not tasked with taking your life, boy. And unfortunately, you've a little friend who has been following you around and protecting you." Brody ceased squirming and frowned at her in confusion. *What is she talking about?* he thought.

"I must admit to some affection as well," Sylph continued. "After all, you are the son of him who summoned me."

Brody felt her lips on his forehead. They were warm and human, not the thin, cold lips over fangs that were Sylph's real ones.

He squeezed his eyes painfully tight, his every muscle tense, and didn't open them until he knew that the Rankers were gone.

Even then, when he did a head count and saw that his friends were all alive, blinking as if shaking off the effects of being mesmerized, he wasn't actually *seeing* anything. He was feverishly examining the glowing memories of his father, abandoning each halfway to rapidly latch onto another, turning them over and over until their pristine, gem-like quality fractured like kaleidoscope crystals and reformed. His father, a bedtime storyteller, his father, a bloodthirsty madman. His father's eyes going distant when Brody asked him about war, his father's eyes alight with ugly thirst. His father, helping him to create his school projects out of milk cartons and twigs, his father, summoning an ancient Ranker of uncontrollable, inhuman lust.

Brody's breath began to hitch and he dropped abruptly down onto his hip, his swollen leg delivering a thunderclap of pain that he barely felt. He couldn't breathe–his hands pressed against his own chest until it hurt, kneading the skin as if trying to dig through and massage air into his lungs. The others hurried over, their voices overlapping, frantic.

"I couldn't move! It was like watching a play; everything I saw was..."

"Separate. I knew a serpent titan, once. Her eyes, they were the same way. If I'd had my claws out..."

"Josiah, fly up, see if they're really leaving. I'm going to tend to His Majesty's leg."

There was a sound of flapping wings, a gust of refreshing wind on Brody's arms, then fingers picking at his trousers, tearing them where they'd become tight against his swollen leg.

"He was right," Khogar's voice, "about their plans. He suspected that they wanted reality."

Brody felt points of pressure on his leg and heard Abram's apologetic murmurs as he explored the extent of the damage done by the horse's kick. "Rexus, fetch me two long, straight branches and the rope from my saddlebags, then get Domine's aid kit."

He heard the charlatan scampering away with concerned chirps and lifted his head from his arms, his panic attack subsiding. Abram rubbed his shoulder comfortingly, quietly encouraging him to take deep breaths, that everything would be fine, they were safe.

"His eyes," Aydran said fearfully. "Is that normal?"

"It will fade," Abram said without concern, carefully straightening Brody's broken limb.

"So...that was Sylph," Aydran said, his voice shaking. It wasn't really a question, but Brody nodded.

"She's a Ranker," Aydran stated again. Brody clutched a fistful of fallen leaves beside him, crushing them in his hands, willing tears not to fall from his eyes. He nodded again, then said, "The Crossing. I was wrong. They aren't pushing for the capital city, they're moving on reality. Somehow they're manifesting in the waking world. *My* world."

"Maybe it's only Rankers like the Seven Deadly that can do it," Khogar said. The weak hope in her voice fell flat like a stone. "They're extra-powerful."

Now that his overwhelming anxiety leaked away, replaced with a hollow iciness, as if his chest were an arctic cavern of rock, Brody could focus enough to contribute his own strength to propping up the leg.

"Did you hear her? What she said about my dad?" he asked, his voice gravelly. Domine and Aydran switched uneasy looks. Abram adjusted his spectacles and gave Brody an evaluative, stern look that made Brody feel guilty for some reason.

"Pay her no mind. It is past. We will take this in stride, and we will move forward."

"I thought he was perfect." Brody laughed scornfully, taking his crown from Khogar and squeezing it. "I thought he could do no wrong; that he'd figured everything out. I know we all have demons and given what he's been through I could understand if he'd suffered wrath, maybe, but *bloodlust*?"

He made a mindless sound of fury and threw his crown over their heads. Khogar went to fetch it again.

"Was my father a *monster*?"

"Sire, *no one* is perfect," Abram said patiently, working now on cutting Brody's boot from his enlarged foot. "Each one of us has sinned and suffered for it. Each one of us has a limit beyond which we become someone or something else."

Khogar, placing the discarded crown reverently atop Brody's sweat-drenched curls, drew her tail across Brody's vision, displaying the many ribbons tied to it, each a splash of color, of carefully maintained fabrics in the silvery fur.

"Mine is greed," the tribal said. "Among my people, there are titles to be won for slaying wyverns. In my youth, I sought out the beasts in their nesting grounds, for it was the culling season; but such was my desire for recognition, that I strayed from the main hunting party in hopes of skinning a wyvern on my own–a feat worthy of the highest titles." Khogar squatted, fixing Brody with her ice-chip eyes, curving her tail around her boots and solemnly touching the ribbons with a paw.

"Lives were lost to save mine that day. My youthful greed became my eternal shame." She poked an old, faded green ribbon toward the fluffy white tip of her tail. "My first. To remind me of who I have lost. To honor them." She indicated the rest. "To honor them all. To remind myself that there are much better ways to earn respect than with greed."

Brody would not have expected the tribal to bear such a burden. Usually, the snow leopard was all smiles and patience, cutting away at some scrap or other of leather to add meaningful little designs to her saddle. Brody parted his lips to say something comforting but Domine spoke first in an awkward baritone.

"I was once a thief. Envy. Yes, that would be my sin. There were others among my kith who I believed possessed more power and respect than I: Judichal, the lightning fox; Karrigama, the stone bison. I was still a cub, freshly parted from my family as we all were, but I cared not for the loneliness of my fellows. I began to steal their possessions; the treasures they had taken from their homes. Powerful I felt, indeed, watching them mewl and pine for their trinkets.

"There was one; the sun lion Pieter, greatest of us all. He became our leader. I had stolen a silly little toy of his one day and then lost it in my apathy–but it had been his little sister's who had died in the cold winter of the former year." Domine's face twisted savagely. "And even after learning this...I did not care. I felt only pleasure, seeing his tears in the mud."

Domine made a disgusted sound and abruptly turned away, his hands on his head, fingers locked into fists in his shaggy hair.

"You already know my shortcomings," Aydran said with an empty laugh, looking over at his pinto rather than at Brody. "Gluttony; for wine, women, and song. If I stopped to think about it for too long, I'd probably realize how many marriages I've spoiled, what jest I've made out of the sacred bonds some girl made with her beau when they were young and hopeful and in love." A quick glance at Abram. "So I...don't think about it."

Rexus had returned with the branches, rope, and aid kit, and now curled up in Brody's ruined boot, blinking out at them with the same anxious, slightly feral expression of a cat at the vet's. Abram aligned the sticks close on either side of Brody's leg and began to apply a cold paste to the nasty bruise blackening his calf and shin. The pain began to numb to a sullen pulsation. When the pastor started to talk, Brody listened with a clearer mind.

"I'm afraid I've long sought penance for one of the worst sins of all. Cowardice. Many years ago, when I was a young man, I had a wife. Oh, we were madly in love, celebrating our one-year anniversary down in Florida. But there was a bad storm; a flash flood. The waters kept rising–they were sweeping people away. I remember holding her hand, hearing her prayers. Then the water was over my face. I couldn't see, I started choking, clawing over my head for anything I could grab onto and I...let her go."

Tears sparkled in Abram's eyes. One fell, warm, onto Brody's leg before the minister thumbed them away and began binding the sticks to either side of the broken limb. Brody wondered if Abram had ever told anyone else that story.

Then one final voice spoke. Aydran and Domine shifted to look over their shoulders at the source and between them Brody saw Josiah, freshly transformed from the scarlet griffin and lifting Rexus onto his shoulder. His pointed face was stoic, as if he were intent on not saying more than he should, his hands in fists as if he strained against chains.

"My pride almost cost me my life, once. Michael saved me, but at a cost. It is a price I still pay."

Everyone waited for him to say more, but when he didn't, Abram said, "Every man, including your father, your Highness, is an abundance of contradictions. Dark and light, sin and virtue, crime and redemption. Each of us has had to make sacrifices to set things right, and your father was a man prepared to make the greatest sacrifice: his own life, fighting for ideals that he cherished. Who are we, to judge your father, whose struggles were his own, whose nightmares were his own, and who, eventually, overcame them all?"

Josiah joined them, standing behind Abram. "Sylph mentioned your eyes. It's a phenomenon that sometimes manifests itself in royal griffins: bloodsense. A sort of righteous form of bloodlust borne out of a desire to visit the wrath of justice upon a wrongdoer. There's nothing wrong about that, Brody. Maybe *that's* what your father had."

Brody's spirits began to lift, his strength to return. Yes, he knew his father had been a warrior, had been imperfect, and was still a good man–and hadn't Brody's actions of late in fighting the Rankers been proof that good could come from the shedding of blood? Wasn't being a griffin, a primal beast, half lion and half raptor, two animals feared and revered for their ferocity, proof that bloodlust was justified if that thirst was slaked on the blood of wickedness?

"You want an ideal?" Aydran asked a little testily, seeing the color return some to Brody's cheeks. "How about 'keep fighting?'"

"We're all behind you, Brody," Josiah smiled. He turned, looking meaningfully toward the horses. "All of us and then some."

Almost invisible beside Domine's dark stallion stood a black unicorn with a mane of amber and white–the same unicorn that had spied on him during his boar hunt, the same that had been following him since day one with Michael and Josiah, the "little friend" Sylph had mentioned, protecting him with its ancient magic. It twitched its tasseled ears, watching him, its golden horn glittering in a stray sunbeam piercing the canopy. The purest steed–a creature of virtue that only ever chose a rider it wanted to befriend for life.

Honored, Brody intended to rise and greet the unicorn, but Abram stopped him, still finishing the knots on his makeshift splint.

"You are our king, Brody. If you seek an ideal, we will help you find it. But...I think if I had known you back when that flood swept my wife away...you would've made me braver...and I would've never let her go."

Chapter Thirty:

New Allies

"The ghosts I believe in are more earthly than that [...] They tell stories, and their stories tell me who I am."

–Michael Ian Black

It took Brody a long time to recuperate from his reunion with Sylph. Even six months later, after he had collected his volunteers from Storm Breath Fortress and proved them in battle against the Ranker of Goodwind, Jadine Green-Eye, lady of envy, even then he would awaken late at night, tormented by his thoughts. Wounds, even the invisible kind, take a while to heal.

But Brody was the Griffin King, and duty claimed more of his time than anguish. This was a mercy–he'd needed his wits about him for Goodwind. Aydran had really won the day, pitting the Lady of Envy against her own captains with a few clever phrases and rumors, but unfortunately the Rankers had also all killed each other off or died of their injuries soon after. They were no closer than before to puzzling out the answers to the riddles of Garrett, or what the pathmarkers were and where they led, or what made the Crossing possible.

However, each step *did* bring them closer to Sylph, and Brody's ever-larger army was already hard at work culling Ranker numbers, constantly evening the odds. Newcomers arrived all the time, sent to regions near Ranker activity so that they could join their king when he and his army marched in. There were dream-creations, like Marcus and a contingent of other gladiators from Grecchus, and some from reality–like Marine Sergeant Flaherty, made comatose from a grievous injury in combat in Iraq. Now, Brody's ranks were about to swell by two more recruits of a rarer but much-welcome sort.

In the Sky Above the City of Bells

Two griffins, new to the Land of Dreams, soared over the beautiful city, their winged shadows flitting across the giant, in-ground mosaics of the Third Circle, over olympic glass cabochons that contained enormous roses within, their petals splashes of color across otherwise dusky stone. And of course the bells rang: lighter and more somber in this Circle, like singing crystals.

In the distance, columns of smoke chugged into the sky from demolished ruins, almost-but-not-quite obscuring hundreds of Rankers from the griffins' vision. The nightmares appeared to have taken over the wealthy manors of the Eighth Circle for their own operations. They milled busily about, using their dark powers to reinforce the hideous wall of bones surrounding that part of the city. Shoring their defenses... One of the griffins, black with tufted ears, cocked his head. Was it a siege, then? If so, the king appeared to be winning.

The black griffin looked to his side at the smaller, pink female gliding there. The sun shone upon them and they were both overjoyed to have finally been given a purpose; an objective. It was difficult to be bogged down by heavy thoughts of war.

The breeze carried an odd mixture of char and something like the pleasant aroma of laundry detergent from the city's prized salons. It riffled through their feathers and the female canted her head into it.

"I hear warfare," she said, her voice soft with a French accent.

Kayle heard it too–weapons clashing with weapons, shrieks, the occasional battlecry or pumped-up primal scream–but it was contained. A small skirmish somewhere near, nothing more.

"Probably a few Rankers too slow to flee," he said. He pointed a claw down at a large, ornate building draped with the king's crest. Knights crowded the square beyond it, as did civilians, all mingling, intent on their individual tasks. A few paused to watch the two griffins' spiraling descent toward the landing platform on the building's roof, but only briefly.

Kayle scampered down the platform steps and gave himself a good shake before transforming into a strapping Irish lad in a sweatshirt, holey jeans, and beanie. He drew a lighter from his pocket and began clicking it open and closed. Mariah took the time to preen a little before leaping off the platform at him, chirruping playfully when he yelped and dodged to get out of her way. She transformed, running her fingers through her hair, smiling sweetly and looking much more refined than he in loose, pale trousers and an airy blouse with silver stitching. Kayle let her lead the way down into the building for their audience with the king. When it came to first impressions with royalty, it paid to be presentable.

They were in a bank–the City of Bells was rife with them–that specialized in the more common gemstones mined for use as the land's larger-denomination currency. As such, the passage doors were studded impressively with cabochons of onyx, opal, and agate. Guards patrolled all over the place–one, Sergeant Flaherty, who had been sent to fetch them, led them into the most secure chamber of the bank: the vault, wherein the king had settled for the time-being.

He awaited them, sitting tall in a finely carved chair, a voluminous sapphire robe draped like curtains over the arms, the back, obscuring his boots in a pool of velvet. The king's crown kept his thick curls from spilling across his face; a closely shorn beard, more stubble than anything, shadowed his face. The dark hair above and the beard below framed his eyes, causing them to stand out like lights. He held a scroll in one hand; it lay open on his lap. His chin rested on the knuckles of his other hand. Though his gaze was sharp enough–unsettling even; an intense stare that pierced them as soon as they entered–Kayle could tell that King Brody was supremely tired.

Mariah curtsied. Kayle promptly followed suit with a stiff bow.

An enormous white griffin stood from the wall, where he had blended in against the stark marble. Kayle started, wondering how Michael had gotten there before them. It had been Michael who, months ago, had met them at the shore of Pebble Embark and helped them to understand where they were, how, and why–and Michael had, mere days ago, directed them here. Despite the fact that Kayle and Mariah had been flying almost nonstop, it seemed that Michael had some secret edge.

The White Griffin's penetrating, neon-yellow irises remained upon Kayle and Mariah as he spoke to the king. "These are the ones of whom I have spoken." As ever, his mild, gentle voice rang with power, and bore the sort of weight that made warriors surrender, emperors kneel, masses weep. As ever, Kayle felt an uncanny combination of terror and joy in his presence, as if he stood before the world's best, most loyal friend, and that friend held a sword against his throat.

King Brody blinked and leaned forward. "The ones you sent Josiah to fetch?"

"No." Michael flicked his cat-like ears back in the negative. "They travel still, evaluating our fortresses and the regions you have liberated. This is Kayle." The White Griffin took two loping strides and was suddenly beside Kayle, who stiffened at his proximity to the fierce beast. Michael wound around behind him, his great head a good two feet above his own, and brushed Mariah with his feathery shoulder. "And this, Mariah. They are young griffins who can bring their skills to bear against the Rankers."

Brody's face cleared. "Ah!" He stood and went to greet them.

Kayle wondered how long it had taken Brody to perfect the royal stride–not an arrogant strut or swagger, nor a meek and shy mince, but somehow both confident and humble, proud and graceful. He was a man perhaps only four or so years Kayle's senior, but the facial hair and weariness in his eyes made him much older.

Brody shook their hands and said, "I am sorry for whatever tragedies befell you and brought you here, but welcome to the Land of Dreams." As he walked back to his seat, and the wooden folding-table before it, managing the train of his robe with the practice of a pro, Brody filled them in on his battles against gluttony, pride, and envy.

He briefly mentioned his unlucky encounter with lust, lifting aside his robes to show them the brace on his injured leg, and grumbled about being out of commission until it healed. The king kept it professional. There was no small-talk or personal stories, though Kayle thought that either would've made the man seem less immortal.

Brody draped his scroll open across the small table and tapped it. "And now, we've Greed," he said wearily. "The siege has been long, and it will be longer still. We aim to press in as soon as their supplies have run out."

"How will you know when their supplies have run out?" asked Kayle.

Brody gave him a clever little smile. "Because we've been taking them and redistributing them among the needy." He looked at the scroll again, examining a line of text toward the bottom. "Such is the price Greed must pay."

Suddenly remembering an important meeting he was running tardy for, Brody's movements became swifter and more decisive. He reached up and unfastened his ceremonial robe, which fell in a pillowy pile at his feet and revealed a similar but ankle-length and thus more functional cloak beneath.

Taking up a long bo staff adorned with a pair of violet feathers, the king said, "Greed's very nature ensures excess. He had already hoarded ample provisions before he barricaded himself away from us. But there are people in there with him who will need support soon if they are to survive."

"Who are they, Griffin King?" Mariah asked shyly, eyes respectfully downcast.

"Citizens we did not reach in time," Brody replied grimly. He slipped a bulky signet ring on a finger and let Michael drape a jeweled chain of office around his neck and over his shoulders with a grimace of mixed humility and disgust. "Greed had been here a long while before us. Many people were too far gone. Corrupted, turned into nightmares." He twirled the signet ring around his finger with his thumb, his eyes fixed inward on the ghosts of terrible memory.

"Because the Rankers seek to corrupt the dreamer?" Kayle asked, trying to order his thoughts. Brody nodded. Kayle frowned at a tiny, black neck-feather on the floor–not as black as his own, probably the king's. He wanted to know more–he and Mariah had been given more information in the past minute than they'd had in the months previous! But the king had shared all he knew. The burden of trying to uncover the secret plans of such a sinister enemy while defending the purity of an entire realm weighed heavy on Brody's shoulders.

"What I need now are wings," King Brody said critically, cool and solemn once more. "*Your* wings. You're the first griffin-hearted dreamers I've met in a long time. As such, you're capable of handling some special assignments. Rankers fear griffins, and we're specially equipped to handle them. I need you to fly across the land, observing, communicating with fortresses, liberated townsfolk, traveling merchants, displaced refugees, *anyone* who may provide an iota of information that may fill in the gaps in our knowledge. Until Josiah returns with his protege, ours is a constant battle of scales-tipping against the Rankers."

“What does this ‘protege’ have to offer that’ll turn the tide for us?” Kayle asked.

Brody glanced at the White Griffin. “All Michael will tell me is that he’ll bring us a hero–someone who will even the odds; give us an edge.”

Michael gazed unblinkingly at the wall above Brody’s head. “You know all you are supposed to know, young one.”

Brody seemed accustomed to such a response. He shook his head as if to jiggle away a bothersome thought and said, “We can discuss these matters further later. Now, I invite you both to join me. There is something I must do.”

Chapter Thirty-One:

A Man of Honor

"If you are going through hell, keep going."
–Winston Churchill

Brody limped along behind Michael toward another vault, this one set aside as the king's sleeping chambers. He touched *Fey* where the elaborate ear cuff spread along his jaw, steeling himself for what was to come.

It was a ritual he'd managed successfully only a few times, and at great cost of energy, after his meeting with Sylph. The idea had come to him in bits and pieces and clarified during his time in Goodwind. He'd sent a letter to Michael detailing his thoughts–it was, in fact, the reason the White Griffin was with him in the City of Bells; to lend his inexhaustible support for the trying but worthy task.

His "room," lit with a few candles, consisted of a cot, a few folding tables laden with field reports, his own notes, and empty goblets, and a traveling chest of clothes and various sundries. Brody went to the cot and eased himself back onto it, carefully lifting his injured leg to prop it on a pillow.

"If you wish to stay, please shut the door," he murmured absently, his mind already wandering around the task at hand and how he would confront the countless unique challenges that could arise. "After this task we will depart together and I will send you on assignment."

Kayle eyeballed the heavy, round, three-foot-thick vault door, then swung it shut and gave the spoked handle a few good wrenches. They were in almost complete darkness now, but for the candles and the strange, pearly, blue-white luminance of Michael's pelt and feathers.

"Please hold still and remain very quiet," Brody said. Mariah nodded her head, lips pursed, and sat where she stood, hugging her legs. Kayle followed suit, watching Brody somewhat marvelingly as if waiting for him to start speaking in tongues.

Brody fought a fond smile. He could tell that they were good kids. *Fey* showed him Mariah as a sun-catcher made of a rainbow of glass chips, or a lovely lace doily on a new housewife's table. Kayle left the impressions of the homey scent of smoke from a wood stove, and the brilliant flash of a firework right before it bursts with color. Brody wished he could've seen them fly in. There was something about seeing a griffin on the wing that enthralled and enchanted.

He shut his eyes and began taking deep breaths. *Fey* warmed the side of his face. He let his mind wander and drift as the paralysis of sleep crept over him. Over the past several months the elaborate ear-cuff had heightened his abilities. In this half-awake, meditative state, he could connect with the souls of sleeping dreamers. Sometimes the connection showed him nightmarish, but telling, images, sometimes he *felt* the connections like heat or chill against his skin, and at times he even absorbed the dreamer's emotions. He still didn't entirely know what this connection was *between*, but he suspected it was their souls.

After *Fey* had boosted his griffin power, it hadn't taken Brody long to realize that he had found the solution to one of his problems: he could now subtly warn reality of Ranker attacks. Josiah and Abram gave Brody frequent reports about their observations of reality. Violent crime continued to increase. Though neither of them had found any Rankers disguised as Sylph had been, no one doubted that Rankers were behind a lot of the incidents. The evidence was here, in peoples' souls.

Brody always strived to locate the souls of people with power, influence, and reach, who could use their wealth, connections, and resources to help those in need and combat the greedy, vicious nature of the Ranker-corrupted. The souls Brody came into contact with, however, were always random.

He frowned, nudging past spots of warmth in the blackness, examining cooler areas, but these were often no cause for real concern. He had come to recognize the *feel*, the *stench*, of Ranker corruption on a person's soul. It was like a burn on the skin, the odor of carrion on the air, or a painfully bright, red pulse. By investigating these souls, Brody could interpret the way in which the Ranker was manipulating the individual, and whether or not that individual was beyond redemption. Once, he found that a Ranker was picking at the bitterness in a young man's heart. His wife had just left him, and he was contemplating suicide. In these cases, Brody bounced from this person's soul to the soul of someone they were close to–a sibling, a best friend, a parent, or the like. In this instance, he had found the man's boss and impressed upon her heart that the man was suffering, carefully constructing and sharing subliminal images with her through their connection that would convince her to check on the man when she woke up.

Sometimes, however, Brody found an individual whose heart and soul were so poisoned by evil, that the Rankers used them to hurt many. These special cases required the utmost skill to handle. Brody found one of these individuals now.

Images came to him, faintly at first but clearer the closer he came to investigate: a wall of angry red with black veins that throbbed and grew points like thorns; the small face of a child with that same red oozing down over it like syrup until it was obscured. Brody penetrated deeper, immersing himself in the images so that he could untangle them. This was the work of Wrath. The Rankers had plans for this bitterly angry soul, whomever it was.

The harder he strained to puzzle out this person's intent, the greater the pressure Brody felt in his skull. But he was used to it by now. This was the easy part. Finally, he had collected enough data to understand that he sifted through the mind of a woman named Vickie, and that, because of some slight, she intended to go the local elementary school the following day, wait until the students were released, and then run down as many as she could in her car until someone stopped her.

Motives were beyond Brody. There were some things that escaped even the King of Dreams. And when a mind was this far gone, lost to the Rankers, there was nothing he could do to influence them otherwise. Instead, he moved from Vickie's mind out into the minds of those close to her, like counting links on a chain, and from their minds he reached out even further until he found a man of authority–a policeman, according to the images Brody picked up from him. *This* was the hard part.

Very carefully, Brody transferred images from his own mind into the other man's, influencing his sleeping thoughts, planting suggestive ideas and coaxing him into latching on to them. At first the man's subconscious rebelled automatically against his intrusion, and images fired rapidly against Brody, each sharp, like a piece of glass cutting through him. He felt his body tense up, heard himself groan through clenched teeth. His mind tried to awaken and spare him this pain. But with the experience of a martial artist switching his grip on a foe to a more secure hold, Brody subdued the man until he had finished leaving the impression he wanted to leave.

The next morning, completely unaware of what had taken place in his dreams, the policeman would feel compelled to take his partner and help manage traffic at the elementary school when the kids went home. Maybe he would even check in on that neighbor of his–Vickie-something. It had been a while since he had seen her tending to her beloved tomato plants in the front yard. Brody, satisfied, moved on.

He helped to prevent three more Ranker-inspired disasters, including a building explosion that would've killed the US ambassador in South Korea, before his anguished body finally forced him awake. It had been a fortuitous rest, though physically and mentally demanding, as always. Being in such close proximity with human souls, both those pure and bright and those soiled by evil, left his skin hot, his head feeling like it had been stuffed with air, his nerves buzzing like he stood near an electrical storm, and his insides churning like they were coiled into knots.

Brody sat up and hunched forward with his head almost between his knees, but he didn't feel as nauseous as usual this time; probably because he wanted to keep up appearances for the newcomers. Mariah had nodded off where she sat, and Kayle only had one eye open, though it was slowly blinking closed. Michael had been sitting over him like a guard dog. His brilliant yellow gaze warmed the back of Brody's head.

A question, the same question that often turned circles in his mind after these "naps," repeated itself once more in Brody's mind: Did Rankers create the evil in dreamers' souls, or was the evil already there and the Rankers just nurtured it? He thought of his father and Sylph and aggressively tore his mind away from such painful thoughts. He had to believe that there was just as much good out there as evil; that this wasn't a futile fight and that they had a chance at winning.

We have more *than a chance,* Brody reminded himself. *We have a prophecy. 'To purge the world, to end the blight, the King is coming with the night.' I will end this Ranker blight. It's already been written.* That comforted him. Everything was under control, events were unfolding to reveal an inevitable outcome. His job was to ensure that the outcome was in the dreamworld's favor, and he would do that to the best of his abilities.

Michael's warm breath huffed down into Brody's hair.

"I'm okay," Brody said, at the same time that Kayle stirred and asked, "What happened?"

Mariah woke up, smacking her lips, and Brody returned his crown to his head. "Warning reality. I have to time it right so that I visit different time zones each time I rest. The battle never stops–our minds are the Rankers' playing field and I must remain vigilant...even during naps."

"You were in other peoples' minds?" Kayle blinked at him.

"Not their minds, exactly. I was ghosting past their souls, hunting Rankers."

"Hunting...Rankers." Kayle grinned as if he relished the idea and Brody was put in mind of a crocodile waiting, still, just beneath the water's surface, for the gazelle to drink. He was glad that Kayle wasn't wearing a black cloak.

"Greed won't break for a while yet," Brody said. He probed at his temples to ease away the lingering pressure and leaned against Michael, whose rumbling purrs were like a deep-tissue massage. Brody felt himself sagging a bit before Michael propped him up with the crook of one large, sail-like wing. "We are seeking a token once touched by one of my predecessors. Once I touch it, I can bestow upon it some of my power, which will hopefully serve to help cleanse the city."

"And us, Sire?" Mariah asked, rubbing her eyes. "You want us to help you look?"

"No. I want the troops to see you–it'll bolster their spirits knowing that more griffins are out and about. Then we'll part ways and I'll have you fly to Changeling Fortress to the southwest. Inform them that Greed and I are still at an impasse. I will have my friend Abram send you with a satchel of classified documents. See that the master of the fortress gets them, and that he has copies sent to my council in the capital."

Brody waited for either Kayle or Mariah to question him, but they didn't–only stood there looking nervous. That alone made him want to embrace them. He was so accustomed to butting heads with dukes and magistrates and lesser-princes who thought him incapable because he was young and their weapons of choice weren't stained with an unsightly patina of old Ranker blood.

The door to the vault swung open, almost flattening Kayle, and admitted a short, round man in striped silks who, despite his cherubic features, marched at Brody as if on the warpath. Abram and Domine trotted on his heels, Domine growling something that sounded increasingly volatile in his native language. The man who had burst in stopped before Brody and drew himself up, his curly mustache and goatee trembling. Domine, behind him, reached his arms out as if to throttle the man from behind but Abram grabbed him and started to lecture him about diplomacy in hushed tones.

Brody took a deep, meditative breath, bracing himself, dredging up what he remembered from his brief etiquette lessons at the castle, and said cordially, "Good afternoon, Marquis. How go your hunts?" He hoped the double-meaning would not be lost on The City of Bells' rotund leader; it was both a common griffin adage, a "how-do-you-do" that he hoped would remind the Marquis of his status as Griffin King, and a means of subtly asking how the man's forays for supplies were coming along. Whether he understood Brody's courtly nuance or not, the Marquis blustered for a moment and then thrust a crumpled scroll under Brody's nose.

"According to your Councilman Isa, you have been channeling an outrageous amount of funds from my vaults to outfit your troops!"

"Yes," Brody said calmly.

The Marquis blustered again. "W-well! According to the Law, even the Griffin King must seek the permission of the provincial leaders before seizing control of their assets!"

"Not in a time of war," Brody said, trying to remain unreadable, keeping his voice low so that the Marquis had to check his aggravated breathing to hear.

"We are not at war!" The Marquis began to redden.

"War has not officially been declared, no. However, a volunteer army of more than five thousand constitutes a shadow-war, and all war-time laws apply except for those of drafting, mass-commissioning armor and weapons, and a few others."

The Marquis processed this with an extremely baffled expression, as if Brody could sink no lower in his eyes. "So. *So.* Loopholes, twisted words, and trampled oaths! That is to be your tone of rule, eh?"

Michael suddenly growled, his hackles rising jaggedly along his spine, his feathers puffing out. "You are warned; this man is your God-given king. Show him respect, for the great many blessings you have been given can be taken, this very moment."

The Marquis paled. Brody let Michael's words sink in a little. He wasn't sure whether it was the influence of *Fey* or not, but the White Griffin's shadow had seemed to swell and contort until it resembled something like a row of very tall men. Kayle and Mariah looked as if they didn't know what to do with themselves, as if they were a mere moment away from quaking in fear.

Taking the prophecy back from the Rankers and fulfilling it as the risen king who would *"purge the world and end the blight"* was an endeavor that required sacrifice, and that was still something Brody struggled to come to terms with. This war with the Rankers demanded finances and manpower. There was more than enough of the latter–brave, noble, dreamworld denizens were more than willing to fight for their king and their country–but finances were tricker to come by. As time wore on and the Rankers poisoned sections of the dreamworld, crops began to fail and trade to falter. The prices of food, clothing, and medicine had skyrocketed, and now Brody was demanding vast quantities of it to be directed toward the war effort. He may as well have been kicking his way into civilians' houses and taking the food directly from their tables. It pained him to do so; put a nasty taste in his mouth. But it was necessary for the greater good.

Brody said gently to the Marquis, "The funds are being taken in carefully measured amounts from your lesser vaults to purchase armor, a bedroll, and a sword for the warriors protecting your city–some willing enlistees from your own citizenry." There were no accusatory intonations in Brody's voice, but the Marquis still flinched as if he'd stepped on a splinter. "The rest of my withdrawals have been stored in my palace treasury to collect interest and serve as death-pay for the families of slain warriors. You are being recompensed with supplies from the Seat of Griffins–and clearly, Councilman Isa has forgotten his duties as Patron of Services. He should have informed you as soon as we began to enact the King's Right of Lex Belli."

Brody glanced at his two miraculously quiet friends and Abram nodded subtly and departed to send the council a stern reprimand–one of quite a few in recent months.

To the Marquis, Brody said, "My job is to ride the charger at the fore and stand the last in retreat. Mine is to inspire as a griffin and lead as a king. I am not robbing you but investing in our people." He paused, so that the faint sounds of laughing families and the shouts of drilling soldiers could reach them, and added, "Do you doubt them?"

The man didn't answer. Domine, behind him, looked ready to pounce if he didn't speak in the next few seconds. At last, he mumbled something, clasped his hands behind him, and said, "*Ahem.* Well. There is a little-known and well-guarded vault to the north, in the Fifth Circle just beside the glazier's shop. It is where we store our sunset opals. Shall I have someone guide you there later?"

Brody smiled graciously. "You are most generous, good sir."

The Marquis nodded, shrugged, then did both, still gazing awkwardly at the floor. "*Ahem.* Well..." He sniffed, removed a pocket watch from somewhere within his silks, gave it a fleeting scan, and said, "Good afternoon." He bowed and departed, nudging past Domine, who rolled his eyes, bit his lip, and snarled something vicious under his breath before following the man out. Mariah and Kayle switched amused looks.

Brody spun and went to his chest, rummaging within it and emerging with a neatly arrayed pile of gleaming light armor, setting it all gently upon his cot. Michael's tail twitched, the long feathers at the end fanning out. He moved to help Brody begin strapping on his pauldrons, talons ticking against the floor and the metal. Brody thanked him, handing back his riding cloak. Michael sat back on his haunches, letting the cloth drape across his claws, and nipped a few loose threads with his beak.

"Please join me as I go to patrol," Brody said to his guests. He needed to clear his head. A good, hard, unicorn-back ride would help chase some of his tension away. "Just long enough for everyone to get an eyeful. Then find Abram. He should be in the messenger's tower. Take the documents to Changeling Fortress. Sloth and Wrath have squatted in my cities long enough to begin poisoning the land around them. Some of them may never recover. They must have corrupted hundreds by now. Those papers detail preliminary attack ideas and are of vital importance. Do not delay." He tucked his great helm beneath one arm and accepted his bo staff from Michael with a murmur of thanks. He knew the White Griffin thought his rides unsafe–sometimes he even flew far above Brody's riding party, a white blob that made even the clouds look dirty.

In an undertone, Brody spoke to Michael. "Could you have word sent to my council that Isa is now in charge of bartering blankets and foodstuffs from the guilds for the warriors' families? He obviously needs more to do."

Michael cracked the swiftest of smiles. "It shall be so." He shifted his wings and Brody looked at them and then away, overcome by a heady sensation of deja-vu. Had he seen this conversation already take place months and months ago in those strange wings? He felt as if something were coming and each decision he made was a paving stone laid in the path toward that something. More and more often, whatever that "something" was made Brody feel unsettled; powerless, like he stood before a tsunami and it was too late to flee. He felt Kayle watching him, and so turned on his heel and left, still pondering Michael's wings as he clinked and clanked his way down the hall.

Brody strained to remember what he had seen in Michael's wings the day he'd ridden out from the capital–what inklings had there been of what was to come? He wanted, more than anything of late, to feel the embrace of his father, to smell his mother's perfume, and to feel young and loved again. He wanted to go back to school and become a lawyer and help people instead of sending them at Rankers and then identifying their remains later on the battlefield, hoping for at least a wedding ring to return to their family. He wanted a fulfilling night's rest that didn't involve running around trying to intercept nightmares, dancing around the jagged, acidic pools of corruption bubbling in peoples' deepest minds. But these were cravings that every griffin king before him had shared. Another part of his bitter, beautiful inheritance.

Mariah and Kayle whispered behind Brody as they followed him along and Kayle raised his voice to address the king. "What of the reports that mentioned a wandering Ranker, sire? What of Lust?"

Brody's mood took a sudden, steep plunge from melancholy into hot, savage hatred. His eyes gleamed a brilliant crimson and the ache in his healing leg throbbed.

"Sylph," he said through a carnivorous snarl. "She's ever on the outskirts, just beyond our reach." He swept past Flaherty where the sergeant held the door open for him, and down the steps of the bank into bustling activity–knights preparing for their patrol shifts or the change of the guard, warriors being shouted at by their superiors or managing supplies, camp followers flaunting their services, civilians scurrying to and fro to help however they could. Upon seeing their king, knights saluted and common citizens halted along their paths to stare in awe.

Wending his way along toward the stables near the outskirts of the Circle, Brody said, "We've a personal score to settle, she and I. Anything you hear that I may not have, inform me. She's the cleverest of them all and will be the trickiest to end."

There was more open space around the stables where knights wealthy enough to own a steed did their own calvary drills. Aydran came up on his jaunty paint, Khogar on her shaggy, dappled, mountain pony–Mariah, who had not yet seen a tribal, made a soft sound of adoration–and between them strode a proud, black unicorn. Mariah made another, louder sound of delight.

The spiraling golden horn twinkled in the sunlight as if it were a miasma of tiny stars. The nimble, deer-like body was garbed in a fine, tasseled blanket checkered red and yellow with little white griffins in profile on every red. The saddle, a lovely leather the color of almonds, had been stamped with talon-prints and bore the King's Crest in brilliant hues on the cantel. The unicorn switched its lion-like tail, pawed the ground with one cloven hoof, and stuck its head out to nibble at Brody's curls.

The king laughed youthfully and stroked the magnificent beast's cheek. "We'll get her, won't we, Dante?"

He stepped into the stirrup and swung easily up to settle into the saddle. He removed his crown, shook his hair aside, placed his great helm, and then pressed the crown down atop it so that it rested snugly on the slight rim around the brow. He nodded down at Kayle and Mariah.

"I look forward to when we next meet. May you fly on fair winds."

Without a perceivable command, the unicorn wheeled and took off like an arrow with a musical whinny, giving its heels an excited little kick. Aydran and Khogar were close behind. Mariah and Kayle looked at each other, then transformed and took flight.

After they had risen above the dust of the horses' departure, and after the clatter of horseshoes on stone had faded beyond their hearing as they wheeled far above, Kayle still stared in the direction of the patrol. He had never held royalty in high esteem, pompous gits that they were, but Brody... *That* was a king.

Chapter Thirty-Two:

Becoming Legend

"Character, not circumstance, makes the person."
–Booker T. Washington

For a year and a half, Peter had wandered, following Josiah around, filling up his three journals with sketches and snippets of information. All the while, he had been filled, bit-by-bit, with paramount excitement. On the lips of every civilian in every town they evaluated, every cart driver whom Peter and Josiah helped to unload provisions for rebuilding cities like Syranade, every knight at the fortresses where they flew to hear the latest news, was one name: Griffin King Brody of the Seven Virtues.

Though his main objective was to complete his journals, so that they would be ready for the hero Josiah told him they were intended for, Peter wanted to meet this king. He had seen enough of his handiwork; liberated towns whose citizens celebrated and honored their young ruler every night, stinking bonfires on the plains where burned the piled corpses of Rankers... Now, according to Josiah, he would soon meet the man behind the legend.

It was obvious that Josiah was eager too. As Peter had discovered, before Josiah had been sent to fetch him, train him up, and prepare him for meeting the White Griffin, Josiah and the king had become friends. Finally, they would reunite, if only briefly, at Stardust Fortress.

Stardust Fortress was situated just southeast of tribal lands near the coast. Peter and Josiah had flown over a vast inlet to arrive. Brody and his men had to have sailed straight across if they had been interested in haste. Sure enough, a fleet of ships floated in the harbor on the other side.

Josiah tilted his wings to slip nearer to Peter, shouting so as to be heard over the chill, misty, ocean winds.

"That's not enough ships for all of the king's forces. The bulk of the army must be marching around."

Peter flicked his ears to show he'd heard and peered down through his talons at the clipper ships with their many sails secured to their spars. He liked this area. The weather was more temperate, and the miles and miles of untouched woodland reminded him of home.

Stardust Fortress was a broad, squat structure built of large blocks of gray stone. Narrow banners emblazoned with the image of two twining serpents flapped heavily on the pine-scented breeze. Even gliding as far above as they did, seeking a landing platform, Josiah and Peter heard voices raised in cacophony. Josiah whistled in agitation, his black-tipped, spikey crown feathers lifting and lowering. Peter felt a little nip of worry zip through his own chocolate-brown plumage and pelt.

Folding his falcon-like wings, Josiah dropped, his tail and hind paws stretched out behind him. Peter followed suit, and the fortress seemed to gradually swell to fill his vision.

When they landed and transformed, looking around the foggy tower-top for an escort, a voice said, “About time! Come on, come on! We’re gonna miss the show!”

A grin split Josiah’s face. “Aydran!” He happily embraced the bard and the two exchanged pleasantries while Peter modestly adjusted the satchel he carried with his journals in it, lifting the flap to let Rexus out. The charlatan bounded to Aydran with a squeak, shinnying up his leg to nuzzle his neck.

When Josiah introduced Peter, Aydran gave him a helpless look and said, “I’d shake your hand, but then I’d have to let go of my money.”

“I thought you kept your bets in your viol?” Josiah said.

“I did until Domine found out that’s where I keep ‘em.”

“What did you wager on?” Peter asked.

“Whether or not Brody would win the Trial by Claw.”

“*What?*” Josiah stumbled past Aydran in a panic and slid down the ladder leading through the tower’s trapdoor without using the rungs.

“I know!” Aydran followed at a more sedate pace, his voice echoing within the tower. “Michael returns to the capital and suddenly our king is running around slapping cats!”

The Trial by Claw was a tribal custom that honored wit, strength, and courage, the three main attributes that guaranteed survival. Normally, it was a means for tribal cubs to prove their readiness to move into adulthood, or for petty disputes to be settled. For Brody, however, it was a chance to earn the respect of a few thousand additional warriors.

The local leaders had gathered at Stardust Fortress at the king's invitation to hear his plea for their aid. Being so mercifully removed from the Rankers' influence, sequestered safely away in the solitude of their mountains, meadows, and forests, the tribals and other local leaders proved difficult to convince. So, angry at their selfishness and ignorance, Brody had invoked a challenge to prove his might and demand their submission: the Trial by Claw. Normally, it was a quick grappling match, but the tribals, curious of this brave and well-spoken young man, had not pulled their punches. That didn't bother Brody. As the fight heated up, Brody relished the exercise and test of his skills. It had been a while since he'd had a good spar, and this tribal was a talented opponent.

Peter, Aydran, Rexus, and Josiah emerged on a balcony slick with recent rain. Domine and Khogar both sat on the railing with their legs dangling over the sides. Domine tapped his heels against the hewn stone balustrade in time to the drums beating a slow, steady rhythm somewhere below them in the bailey. Khogar's long tail lashed, betraying her anxiety, the colorful ribbons tied to it fluttering like streamers. Abram had his back to the spectacle, whispering an insistent prayer. He saw their arrival and gave Josiah a tight embrace, as if a familiar face would solve their issue.

"How is he? Holding his own?" Peter heard Josiah ask, then he was between Domine and Khogar, watching the scene below.

A huge crowd of onlookers cheered and pumped their fists, standing or sitting on wagons in a large ring around a scuffed and blood-patched circle of dirt and straw. Brody, his curly, dark hair limp, circled a giant of a tribal. Unlike Khogar, this was a lion, whose mane was braided and tied with charms. The humanoid lion wore a loincloth and leather wrappings around his hind legs. In either forepaw he held a hatchet, his brawny arms cocked in a master's pose, ready to strike. He lifted his lip to bare his long canines, his whiskered snout wrinkling in a growl.

Brody wore a pair of dark ketill pants, baggy around his thighs, tight at his calves, and some cloth shoes. His naked torso glistened with sweat, his muscles stood out in sharp relief as he panted for breath. Bits of straw were stuck to his back–he had fallen some time earlier. A long, red scrape ran from his shoulder to his sternum, creating a sort of "V" with the old scars across his collarbone. It was more difficult to see if the tribal had been wounded in any fashion–for one, he was covered with fur, for another, Brody fought with a staff rather than a blade. Brody gnashed his teeth and snarled back at the lion, his eyes two rings of smoldering red. Peter snorted an admiring laugh.

Domine looked at him. "Who are you?"

"Peter Malone."

"Oh." The titan returned his scrutiny to the bailey.

"Welcome," Khogar said, tugging on her ears with agitation when Brody narrowly avoided a sudden charge from the lion. "We have long expected your coming."

"Thank you. How's his Highness?"

Aydran squeezed in beside him, Josiah on the other side. The bard clicked his tongue against his teeth.

"Well, you see, what we have here is an S.O.L. situation." He closed one eye and pointed at Brody. "Outta luck," he moved his finger to the lion tribal, "and a great, big, shit. That's an elite, one of their best. They represent their entire tribe, like an icon. Supposed to be an honor, trading fists with one, but...tell that to the hunk of tenderized meat that's supposed to be their Griffin King."

The lion swung down with one hatchet, which Brody dodged, then crossways with the other. Brody arced and spun away as gracefully as a dancer, landing a good whack in the tribal's kidneys. The cat roared and snapped his slavering jaws in the air where Brody's elbow had been moments before. An excited smirk played fleetingly across the king's features.

"I should stop this," Abram muttered into his fist, practically biting his knuckles.

"It's just getting good," Domine protested distractedly.

"Oh, you know Brody. He'll work 'em a bit, then give a lecture that'll shame their grandcubs, then they'll all ride out together like something in a bard's epic." Aydran patted Abram's back.

Over the crowd's enthusiastic responses to the two contestants, Peter's sharp griffin hearing picked up occasional words exchanged between the pair. He tilted his head to listen, leaning on his elbows.

The tribal growled, "You fight well, human, but you are only flesh. I am fang and claw. Yours is the way of sword. Of stick. Mine is nature. Fire. Fire in here," he pounded his furry chest with the flat of one of the hatchets. "Put away your silly pretendings, cub. Practice your pouncing at butterflies until the rabbit is too slow for you."

"You would mock your king?" Brody showed his comparatively unimpressive teeth. A griffin's growl gurgled out from between them, garbling his voice somewhat. He struggled to keep his temper in check.

"The zebra's kicks teach our young to respect even the most unassuming of opponents. But in the end, the results are the same." The tribal sank fluidly onto all fours long enough to scoop up a pawful of blood-blackened dirt. "Blood upon the grass." He reached up and sprinkled the dirt over his mane.

"I am no zebra," Brody said. He touched his fingers to his own wound and streaked his blood across his face, forehead to jaw.

The tribal laughed and the two became inarticulate as they met and exchanged a flurry of dazzling strikes. The lion towered over Brody by four feet, driving his hatchets down to clap against the polished wood of Brody's bo staff. The king's arms quivered–he wasn't used to having to block so many downward blows–but the invisible wounds he'd dealt the tribal finally began to make themselves apparent in swollen bruises and cramped muscles that stiffened the lion's movements.

Then it happened–so quick that most didn't see the clever twist of the bo staff that intercepted the hatchets, sending them gliding down the shaft. Brody moved in while his opponent fumbled and landed a solid strike into the tribal's solar plexus.

The big cat lost his breath in a weak yowl and gave ground, but Brody followed through with a couple of sharp raps that knocked the hatchets from the lion's hand-like paws.

The success of his attack left Brody over-confident. The tribal lashed out with one paw, claws extended. Brody went back on his heels and half-turned to avoid it, but instead caught the brunt of the blow in his ribs with a meaty thud that all of his companions heard–even those *without* griffin-hearing.

Josiah cursed. Everyone on the balcony squashed against Peter to watch closely–even Abram.

The crowd gave a collective "*Oh!*" then became oddly still, as if the true dangers of their silly tradition had finally sunk in: what would happen if their Griffin King died here?

Brody grunted and winced, contorted sideways in the direction of his pain. Five new lacerations striped his side. But the young man forced himself upright and stood tall. The crimson seemed to leak from his irises to flood his pupils red. Peter frowned apprehensively. He had never heard of such a phenomenon before.

"You forget, tribal, that I, too, am a beast," Brody said.

In a shimmery flash of golden light, a black and white griffin replaced the king. Ramping up, Brody clawed the air with his talons, the fiery feather-tipped quills between his ears and wings standing on end and making him look even bigger. He spread his wings and screamed at the lion. The crowd appeared uneasy, as if they had forgotten what exactly being a griffin king entailed.

Domine whooped and shouted at Aydran, "I told you he would transform! You owe me two gold suns!"

The lion tribal seemed to be warring with his instincts: back down, as his bestial nature urged him to do, and risk bringing shame upon his people, or thrust his life into Brody's talons, to live or die as the king's mercy willed.

With a desperate roar of challenge, the lion bunched up his muscles like a tight spring and pounced. Brody launched to meet him. They met in midair, enveloped in a chrysalis of wings, and hit the earth hard. The pair somersaulted heads over tails, and Brody came up, human again, his bo staff pinning the tribal just under the chin where, with a bit of pressure, he could crush the lion's throat.

The drums went silent, but the cheers of the crowd shook the fortress windows.

"He did it!" Khogar shouted, her paws raised. "We won!"

Rexus chittered, running up and down the wall behind them and chasing his tail.

"This'll make a great ballad," Aydran said cheerfully, dropping some coins into Domine's palm. "Something like, 'Even in battles of tooth and claw the Griffin King prevails, for he has something no mere man has: a beak, two wings, and a tail!' I'll have to tweak it a bit."

Abram whispered a weak, weary prayer of thanks.

"Good, he did it," Josiah said, looking torn between relieved weeping and fury. "Now I can kill him for initiating this stupid custom in the first place."

Heedless of the sheet of blood curtaining his ribs, Brody spoke to the downed tribal in a low voice.

"Yield."

The tribal shook his head a fraction to either side; all that the bo staff allowed. "I cannot. My life is yours, Great King, Chieftain of

Many Thousands, Champion of the Prophecy. Take it or spare it, as our code demands."

Brody scoffed, the crimson leaving his eyes until they were their usual deep bronze-green. By now the celebrating crowd had noticed that Brody was speaking and had started to quiet. Brody faced them, raising his voice to be heard by all, leaving the tribal to roll onto his knees and slouch there.

"Your code would have me waste this warrior's life for the sake of tradition! Is loyalty so swiftly bartered and lost among your kind? I seek your aid, as I am owed, and instead find opposition because I am only human. Were tribals not made by man? Are you not the constructs of dreaming human minds? Am I not your king? Guardian of your lands? And what is a king if not a lion, devouring what beasts threaten his pride?

"Put aside your rituals, your exclusivity. Extend your hearts to your fellow dream creations. Fight for your homes, your lives, your brethren, for the masses crying for your help. Fight because it is right. Prove your honor, your worthiness, your virtue, to your king."

Chapter Thirty-Three:

The Problem with Diplomats

"It is necessary only for the good man to do nothing for evil to triumph."
–Edmund Burke

Josiah went to meet Brody and have him seen to, sending two guards up to escort Peter and the others to a private chamber. One of the guards was a slender man from the four-weeks-distant settlement of Wilkerson Shire, the other an older female snow leopard tribal with an age-whitened muzzle; a distant relation of Khogar's. They were left by a roaring fire with tea and biscuits, chatting about the fight's finer points.

The doors creaked open almost twenty minutes later and Brody entered, wearing a fashionable doublet, his hair still wet from bathing. He smiled warmly at them all, giving Josiah's breathless scolding no more attention than the tapestries on the wall.

"I mean, consider this: what if he'd clawed your intestines out?" Josiah ranted, shutting the doors behind them. "Hm? Literally pulled 'em right out. Three inches to the right and that's what would've happened. Then what? Would you two have played double-dutch with them?"

"Josiah, stoppit you old hen." Aydran chuckled from where he strummed his viol on a window seat. "It's over, you can stop fretting."

"What-ifs are only challenges whispered by our hearts," Domine said, puffing away on his pipe.

"What if you went to the kitchen and made me a sandwich, Domine?" Aydran said, fiddling a quick, plucky little tune.

Peter approached Brody. "That was...remarkable, Your Majesty."

"You must be Peter!" Brody took his hand and shook it, then winced and moved to sit down, propping a pillow between his wounded side and his arm. "I've waited a long time to meet you. Everyone's excited about this special mission of yours."

"They...are?" Peter poured a cup of tea and handed it to Brody who sipped as if it were nectar from Heaven.

"*Tch*–yeah!" Aydran cried. He struck a dramatic chord on his viol and said, in a narrative voice, "*A mysterious hero brought from the nether-realm of the Creators' Reality to turn the tide in the battle against the Rankers*. We're all holding our breath waiting to see this hero you find and what they can do."

"Whomever he or she is," Abram said, "Michael speaks as if they will be a Godsend."

"I trust Josiah caught you up while on your travels?" Brody asked.

Peter nodded. "You just reclaimed The City of Bells and Tall House is next on your campaign. It's a nightmare-sheltering zone–a haunted town of ghosts and murder–and it's where Sloth has nested. You've also been warning Reality when you can about Ranker strikes."

Brody bowed his head.

Peter hesitated, and pressed a dark hand against his chest as if trying to knead away the pain of sorrow. He examined his hands and said, "My goddaughter and I were looking into crime statistics. I was a veteran with a lot of time on my hands and she was a pretty popular counselor–we both saw the signs of something strange happening, but we couldn't figure out what or why. Then she got married and moved and started a family and she...she died not long after. I tried to continue our work, but...it was only when I got here that I truly saw the bigger picture."

Brody, deeply moved, set aside his teacup and murmured, "I'm sorry for your loss."

He might've said more, but a tumult of overlapping, arguing voices reached their ears from without. The griffins fell silent, cocking their heads, then Khogar and Rexus, then Domine, and finally Aydran.

Josiah and Brody looked at each other.

"What is *he* doing here?" Josiah asked, to which Brody responded with a "hell-if-I-know" expression.

The doors swung wide, admitting four humans and three tribals, all of whom ceased their loud bickering in Brody's presence. Meek obeisance was present in all figures but the man in front–Councilman Isa. He wore heavy, violet robes that draped unflatteringly over his bony body. A silver circlet finely inscribed with a braided pattern sat at his temples and a large, official-looking ring twinkled on one pale finger.

"I have only recently received word of your recruitment efforts," the councilman said in a long-suffering voice, not even asking after the king's condition first. "You have your volunteer army! Efforts to recruit imply that we are at war!"

Brody stood up slowly, taking care not to express the slightest twitch of pain. "You flew all the way up here just to slap my wrist?"

Isa almost spoke over him. "A significant threat to reality must be proven for true war to even be considered! The citizens do not need a war, not after what they've been through. It would...wrack the dreamworld! Trade and years of peaceful neutrality would be ruined!"

"If challenging neutrality means exposing Ranker supporters, then I'll gladly take that risk."

Isa rolled his eyes and took a frustrated breath through his nose. Domine and Josiah both grumbled at the disrespect and Brody heard a sour twang come from Aydran's villa as if the bard had just wrung its neck with outrage.

"If you are referring to the pharaoh of Tencina then I must remind you that he's given no indication–"

"And what have *you* to say?" Brody asked sharply of Isa's entourage.

One of the tribals, a puma wearing an old, colonial-style suit, looked at his companions before saying, "We tried to speak to 'im, yer Grace. We've already pledged our warriors..."

"But," said the representative from Druid's Hollow, a tall woman in a deep-green cloak, "we do agree that you've more than enough men for these remaining Rankers. We do not need war."

Brody's mouth became a thin, disappointed line. "Sloth and Wrath have held their stolen strongholds for years now. My reports tell me that for miles around Tall House, nothing lives. Animals have lain where they stand and starved to death. The stench of rot reaches even the mountaintops. The ghosts can be heard from here on a calm, quiet night. My people are suffering. And so are those in reality." He touched the beautiful ear cuff wending down along his jaw. "I've seen it. And the influence spreads daily.

"Wrath has left the corpses of the dead on stakes outside Raynarra. He has captured my scouts, skinned them, and made pennants with their hides. Each day he seeks some poor soul to torture–to even roam near his domain, one sees the fabric of the dreamworld twist and contort.

"And Lust," Brody's voice was rising, his eyes flickering red. He seemed to swell, the others, to shrink. "She wanders. And whatever sleeping soul she meets...she takes. You all advise me against war, but the Rankers have already declared war on us!"

A shocked, sickened, humbled silence deadened the room. Even Isa looked somewhat guilty. As if to help them save face, Brody looked at the cloaked woman and said, "Send your troops to Tall House. They should meet my men on their way there."

"You're sending soldiers out to Sloth already?" Isa asked in a much more dignified and courteous tone than that of before. "Why not to Wrath? They sound much more needed there."

"Because based on the reports Councilman Owf sent me, Wrath will be too risky to handle without myself being present. And according to General Amos, my countermeasures are not yet ready to be put into effect."

Brody suddenly sat down, looking pale, and then green, his eyes vacant. He held one hand against his ribs.

"Enough! The king needs rest. You can all pester him tomorrow!" Josiah ushered the councilman and the other local spokespeople out the doors. Abram went to check on Brody while the others moved to make their own departures.

"Sometimes I still can't believe that guy's a griffin," Aydran mumbled to Abram, who looked up from Brody's side long enough to reply, "Well, not every bird's a swan."

Peter was about to leave, lingering to wait for Abram who passed him with a polite smile and an invitation to get some dinner. Hot food and a warm bed sounded marvelous, and Peter looked forward to socializing with everyone. But he looked back at Brody, sitting alone, staring at the fire, and felt that he needed to stay just a bit longer.

"Why did your eyes change earlier? Go all red?" He shut the doors and lowered himself onto one knee beside Brody's chair.

Brody gestured to the couch beside him and said, "I was angry. Frustrated by the peoples' stubbornness."

Peter settled onto cushions patterned with Celtic knots and stuffed with something light, maybe feathers, and sighed comfortably. "They were *all* red. The centers, too. I've never seen that before."

"It's called bloodsense," Brody said. "Michael describes it as a righteous anger; when a griffin is driven to justifiable..."

"Wrath?"

Brody didn't answer, tapping his fingers rapidly against the arm of the couch. "I've been here almost three and a half years," he said, "obeying an ancient prophecy, eradicating powerful Ranker lords.". He reached up, took off his crown, and examined it by the firelight, tilting it in his hands. "And I haven't regretted one moment. But Wrath will be a test. My test."

"You seem far from wrathful to me," Peter said and at Brody's raised eyebrows, amended, "I mean the bad kind."

Brody tilted his head. He hadn't thought that there was a *good* kind of wrath. "I am bitter. And bitterness becomes anger if it sours for long enough. I worry about my parents and my body in reality. I thought that I wanted to be a leader, to live my ideals and inspire others to fight for theirs, but the further I go, the lonelier I feel."

"You have a great group of friends here with you," Peter said encouragingly.

"Yes. But still. I feel like..." Brody's eyes fastened in the direction of his ear cuff and rested there a bit before they shut in thought. "Like a rock on the very summit of a mountain with not even a cloud between it and the sky. It's beautiful, but it's cold. And day after day the winds erode a little more of the rock away."

Peter didn't seem sure of how to respond or what peace of mind he could give the young man. "Has Josiah checked up on you in reality? I know he goes there quite frequently."

"Yes, he has," Brody said, and nothing more. Cold fear threatened to choke the breath from his lungs. He didn't want to think or speak about the fact that the condition of his body had still not improved. He took a quick, deep breath and arose to his feet. Peter did likewise. An honest but sad smile that didn't reach Brody's eyes played about the king's lips.

"Speaking of which, I should check on Dante, my unicorn, before I rest. I could hear him whinnying all the way from the bailey. You must excuse me. We shall have to speak more another time."

Chapter Thirty-Four:

Apollo's Trail

"Some of the greatest battles will be fought within the silent chambers of your own soul."
–Ezra Taft Benson

A short time after his first meeting with King Brody, Peter met Kayle and Mariah on a dawn patrol flight. Like Peter, they would not be staying long. Their task was to fly between Brody and the land's fortresses, relaying top-secret messages. They had arrived in the latest hours of the night to bring the good news that whatever mysterious countermeasures the king had concocted for Wrath were ready. General Amos was having the supplies Brody had requested sent to the fortress nearest Raynarra. The news had lifted Brody's spirits greatly. He met with Isa and the local leaders now to discuss it, and the King's Six, his closest companions, were also attending. So Peter, left alone, had gone to Flaherty, one of the leaders of the volunteer army and one of the king's bodyguards, seeking a task. And here he was.

The trio of griffins soared over vast acres of untouched woodland, wondering what beautiful dreams played out beneath the boughs and in the glens. The sun had just risen, but its magnificent brilliance was blunted somewhat by the wisps of dawnward clouds dressed resplendently in hues of hot-pink and simmering-yellow.

They carried rain–the griffins scented it–and the winds would bring them in for a light shower by noon.

Mariah, on Peter's left, almost blended in with the eastern sky; her pale-pink coloration and ivory inner-wings mimicked the dawn clouds. Kayle, however, on Peter's right, looked like a patch of dark matter with indigo speckles in his wing feathers that winked in the daylight every now and then like stars. The pair of them had just finished telling Peter who Brody had been in reality–the horrible circumstances that had brought him to the Land of Dreams.

Peter let the story sink in and his heart stirred with pity. His silver eyes stung with tears. A burst of wind blew one back into the narrow, whisker-like black and white feathers streaming from his beak.

A small flock of geese flew by beneath them, honking conversationally. Kayle watched them go, curving his head down beneath his chest, his thick neck ruff stirring in the breeze.

"He's thinking of what comes after, you know," Kayle said. "The Seven Deadly are only the tip of the iceberg."

"So, he really is preparing them for war," Peter said solemnly.

"Aye. There's someone else out there. Behind the scenes. He's trying to find out who, but he's running out of time. He hasn't managed to capture a Ranker alive yet for interrogation."

"The Rankers have some sort of plan, something about 'pathmarkers' and crossing over into reality," Mariah said, "but every time he gets close to finding out some truth, the fight intensifies and the Rankers are all killed. Sloth, Wrath, and Lust are the only chances he has left to capture one alive." Mariah said. "Otherwise, by the end of all this, he'll be blindsided by whatever they've got planned next."

"Even if these foolish blighters aren't lookin' at the bigger picture," Kayle said, his cat-pupils narrowing in a stray beam of sunlight, "King Brody is. He has to."

Peter remained for another two months, long enough to see the king depart the fortress and join his massive army in a swift and sudden attack on Sloth. After that, as soon as Sloth recovered from the first blow and reared her ugly head, Josiah came to Peter with the news that Michael wanted them to move on. Peter had more pages to fill in his notebooks and there were more cities, towns, fortresses, and so on that needed to be evaluated and rebuilt.

Josiah assured Peter that they would return in time, if the battle with the Seven Deadly wasn't over in the next year.

The king overwhelmed Sloth in a month and a half. His zeal, his determination, his diligence, were anathema to the Ranker's lazy, noncommittal nature. Unfortunately, salvation had come too late for most of the citizens of Tall House—their very decayed corpses sprawled on streets and homes in poses that suggested they had fallen where they stood and starved to death, too overcome by the Ranker's influence to rise from their lethargy.

Most of the casualties on Brody's side were caused by the influence of the tormented spirits haunting the attics, bedrooms, alleys, and shadows. New ghosts acted out their deaths each day, even after Sloth went down beneath Brody's talons, luring warriors to jump from rooftops, drown in the nearby mire, slit their wrists, and poison themselves.

It was only when Brody found Great King Elex's chalice, channeled his own strength into it, and carried it throughout the entire town, Abram praying beside him the whole way, that the spirits settled. What survivors there were returned, having heard the battle from their camps deep in the woods, and joined in cleaning up. Most of the dead had to be cremated, as there was no time for individual graves to be dug, but afterwards the citizens said that the sun now shone on Tall House for the first time in uncounted generations.

The dead were honored, the injured seen to, a small group of warriors stationed in Tall House to help rebuild and await provisions from the nearest large metropolis, Starfall, and Brody departed once more. He rode Dante at the fore of his many hundreds, recognizable from any height and distance by sound if not sight. His trumpeters had no qualms about frequent, bold, royal salutes that sounded a challenge as they rang over the thunder of marching feet and drumming hooves. *We're coming for you,* they seemed to say, to any Ranker that cowered within earshot. *You're next.*

The king took one fourth of his army and sailed out from the inlet and along the coast toward the fortress of Apollo's Trail. The rest of the soldiers, led by Sergeant Flaherty, Marcus the gladiator, a samurai named Takeo-Kou, and an Amazon, Agave, would march overland to approach Raynarra from behind and pin it between them and the fortress. Though Brody would arrive at his destination sooner than the bulk of his forces did, he intended to use the extra time until they arrived to flesh out his plans and exchange news with the fortress keeper.

From the deck of his ship, Brody beheld the massive plume of smoke chugging skyward from Raynarra. By night, he saw thousands of red lights scattered across the scrubland around the city—the campfires of Wrath's army. Even across the considerable distance between them, even through the briny ocean wind and over the hissing expanse of blue-gray ocean, Brody felt, heard, and smelled Wrath as a sort of burning rash under his skin, a constant, mad chant, blood and brimstone. He had private misgivings about this enemy, for a part of him felt attracted to Wrath. Some latent, bitter creature that had lain dormant within Brody since his fight with the lunatic in the woods beyond his house, had lifted its head and curiously tested the air.

Dante, who stood on the deck beside him, never far from his side, snorted and shouldered against him as if to snap him out of his funk. Brody leaned against the unicorn, stroking the white and amber mane, and Dante swept his horn through the air in the direction of Raynarra as if to cut it from their sight.

Apollo's Trail Fortress was constructed on a high promontory and served additionally as a lighthouse. By far the most elegant fortress Brody had yet seen, it was tall and fluted, with waterspouts shaped into winged women and alcoves wherein sat golden griffins. Each wore a medallion on a red sash, bearing the name of a griffin king or queen. When Brody entered the fortress's bailey, which was more like a plaza than a militaristic courtyard, he beheld a large fountain capped with an image of Apollo in his fiery chariot driven by two stallions in gleaming steel. A covered colonnade obscured mostly by honeysuckle and climbing roses surrounded the bailey in a ring of beckoning shade.

Aydran, Khogar, Abram, and Domine gaped at the splendor around them, standing close at Brody's back. The knights Brody had brought with him would finish seeing to their ships, and unloading their supplies, and would enter the fortress through one of the tunnels carved into the base of the promontory. The dormitories and stables were situated in pockets that had been artfully sculpted directly from the stone and were nearly impossible to spot from without.

The fortress keeper here was Aramis, half man, half elf. He stood waiting before the fountain to greet them, his hands spread by his waist as if to embrace them. His shoulder-length, wavy locks, the color of myrrh and of a similar scent, were loosely bound and tied. His ears were slightly pointed, his eyes, crystalline violet in the outer iris and silver around the pupils, were distinctly elfin. Yet he was brawnier and more sun-tanned than the elves Brody had met, with more of a human's swagger than a full-blooded elf's glide.

Aramis wore a Romanesque toga, its train wrapped around his waist and then draped over one shoulder. He resembled a nobleman accustomed to enjoying the finer things in life, the dynamic keeper of a fortress unused to hardships. But Brody wasn't fooled. His griffin eyes penetrated the cool gloom of the colonnade. An assortment of dream-creations from men and elves to centaurs and sapient hyenas, and even a tall, bird-like creature with some sort of sharp-toothed dinosaur on a chain, wore the coppery colored armor of the Fortress of Apollo's Trail. They watched him intently, almost hungrily, and were unnaturally quiet.

"Welcome, Great Griffin King." Aramis performed a courtly bow. "Come, let us take refreshments in quarters beyond the sun's eye."

They entered the fortress through a pair of doors glittering with gold-leaf patterns and passed through a few corridors to a marvelously breezy sitting room that looked out over the sparkling sea. Brody could almost imagine that Wrath was not corrupting the land but a seven-hours ride away.

Dante, who would not be housed in the stables among common horses unless there was no room for him elsewhere, delicately reclined beside Brody's marble-framed chair and rested his head on Brody's lap. Aramis, who had made no remark one way or the other about the unicorn following them inside, smiled fondly down at the stallion, pouring them all wine.

"Has Wrath caused your fortress any trouble?" Brody asked, petting Dante's soft nose and accepting his wine glass.

"Not directly, no," Aramis said after a pause. "To attack this fortress, even with numbers, would be a fool's errand. We would see or hear an approaching army and it would be too much of an expenditure of effort to scale the cliff sides. But..." The keeper finished passing around drinks and sat with his own. "That's not to say we've felt no effects. About a year ago, two guards got into an altercation over a card game. One accused the other of cheating and before we could blink, he reached for his belt, took his dagger, and pinned his comrade's hand to the table with it."

Aydran flinched and grimaced. "Ouch." Brody noticed with mild amusement that the bard's wine glass was already empty.

"After we had received your command to end reconnaissance efforts, withdraw, and serve as a haven for refugees," Aramis went on, "we noticed nothing contrary. However, after the incident with the guards there began other...happenings. I witnessed one man speaking angrily to a wall. When I moved to take him away, I saw that both of his hands were mutilated from punching the stone. Another time, an entire wing of the fortress was awakened late at night by the sound of yelling. No, not yelling...hideous, primal screaming. One of our soldiers, in the throes of some mad dream, was found rampaging around his room tearing at his clothes, ripping his blankets asunder, smashing his nightstand to splinters with one of the drawers from his clothes chest. And it began to worsen about ten weeks ago, right when the fires appeared on the plains."

"The fires?" Brody asked.

"Campfires belonging to Wrath's allies, or 'jaded,' or whomever they are. We could just barely see them, off in the distance, and we knew they heralded Wrath's expansion. His numbers were growing. During a training exercise one morn, a soldier abandoned his waster to sink his teeth into his opponent's cheek."

This time everyone voiced their disgust. Aramis nodded sadly. "We had to convert our cells into quarters for invalids–those suffering most under Wrath's influence. We had to even postpone our drills, until the White Griffin came to us and blessed us with his power."

Brody sat straighter, almost brushing his hand against Dante's horn which, he knew from experience, would have set his entire arm to tingling for hours as if he'd grabbed hold of an electric fence.

"Michael's here?" His spirits lifted. He had long ago made peace with the White Griffin's random comings and goings but to have him present for their showdown with Wrath was welcome news, indeed.

"Presently he is away escorting your shipment from the capital," Aramis replied, with a curious expression betraying his intention to ask further in the near future for details of Brody's plans. "But yes, he will return."

"What of Wrath's allies? His 'jaded,' as you called them? Who and what are they?" Brody finished his wine and nodded when Aramis lifted the bottle and offered more. Aydran leaned forward, extending his own glass with his tongue sticking out between his lips.

"Bandits, highwaymen, creatures from nightmare whose appetites are slaked with anger and blood."

"How fares Raynarra?" Brody asked hesitantly. Aramis gave him a fleeting look–one of sorrow and accusation. Brody had to look away. Perhaps it *was* his fault that Wrath had festered for so long unchecked. Maybe Brody could have interfered earlier and helped save the however-many-hundreds who had become corrupted. It had to have been difficult for Aramis and his soldiers to watch the splendor of the land around them turn to desolation and ruin while they could only watch and obey their king. But Brody would not divide his forces to fight alone. Nor would he face Wrath until he was absolutely sure he could win.

Aramis remained standing, looking outside at the sparkling sheet of ocean. "Raynarra is fallen. Her refugees left long ago for the cities to the west still capable of supporting them. Those who remained...must be long gone."

They all became silent, mourning the lost. Brody felt as if his wine had turned bitter within him. Dante made a low, burring sound and nibbled at his glove.

"When Michael arrives with the catapults–"

"Catapults!" Aramis exclaimed. "You've sent for catapults!"

"Yes. And when they get here–"

"Then you knew," Aramis said, looking mystified, as if Brody had suddenly become some opaque nether-creature from deepest and most ancient dreams. "You knew months ago that Raynarra would be overtaken–that you would need to break in."

"I know Wrath," Brody said a little sharply. The keeper quieted and fumbled blindly down into his chair, bi-colored eyes round. "And Wrath knows war. I foresaw that defeating him would require more than simple steel. We would need stone."

"But I don't see the difference it–" Aramis's consternation was abruptly swallowed beneath a tirade of loud but distant warhorns followed by the pounding of what must've been elephantine war drums. Everyone started up to their feet, Khogar up onto her chair, her tail fluffed out.

"Those are the horns of the Blind Men," Brody said, and looked at Abram who added, "The nomadic mercenaries."

A clatter of hooves without heralded the arrival of a centaur, who looked thoroughly alarmed, the scruffy hair along his neck on-end, his thick, braided tail lashing. "Great King! Wrath approaches!"

Chapter Thirty-Five:

Battling the White Wyrm

"'Tell me, tutor,' I said. 'Is revenge a science, or an art?'"
–Mark Lawrence, *Prince of Thorns*

Brody was already out through the doorway when he heard Aramis protest, "He cannot possibly hope to breach our walls," to which the centaur replied, "He's brought one of his pets, sir. A moon wyrm."

Brody's trot became a sprint that he slowed to a sleek lope outside amongst the soldiers all fixated on the north. He flung himself against the battlements, shading his eyes and pressing his belly against the crenelated stones. A thick, dark ribbon, shifting as if made of ants, approached swiftly and would be at the base of the promontory in just shy of thirty minutes. Though it was a force to reckon with, Brody could tell that it was only about a sixth, if that, of Wrath's full army.

This contingent appeared to mostly be composed of men–the savage nomads of the moor; bloodthirsty weapons-for-hire who practiced hideous scarification for each soul they killed. They ran toward the fortress with individuals slowing to a jog when exhausted but quickly picking up speed again, spittle foaming their beards. In their midst rode a circle of five Rankers astride black horses that snorted fire and had scorpion stings for tails. Each used a spear to prod a pearly colored reptilian creature onward.

Brody, heart sinking, did indeed recognize it as a moon wyrm. It had a long, scaly, low-slung body and tail, with shovel-like foreclaws and a stout, powerful head full of rows of crushing teeth. Though this one was already a tad larger than a school bus, they were said to grow until they died–usually when one of their subterranean warrens collapsed on top of them, too unstable to retain integrity.

Brody watched the beast whistle piercingly and swipe at one of the Rankers, its eyeless head swiveling in the direction of the spear-point pricking its leathery hide. But it could only gallop clumsily forward. They weren't inherently evil, Brody knew, but they were dark creatures, like the hellish fish that swam at the bottom of the ocean. It was driven by one goal before all others–to tunnel, down, down into the cold and deep. When its snout touched the base of the promontory, it would burrow within and through...and bring the Fortress of the Sun collapsing down into rubble and bones.

The nomads chanted in unison while their trumpets blew and their drums beat, chanted something that sounded like the cries of a heathen god and reminded Brody of the bloodstained idol he'd found in the wilderness years ago. For the first time in recent memory, true fear quivered in his chest. He reached one hand up to touch the scars at his collarbone, but his glove met his breastplate instead.

Dante joined his side, his large eyes directed at the advancing army. He snorted and lowered his head until his horn pointed at them, pawing the ground with one cloven hoof. The others had gathered at Brody's back, with the soldiers of the fortress beyond them, uttering low oaths or prayers, but generally in various forms of distress.

"We don't have the numbers," Brody overheard someone say. "We can't beat them."

That statement, and the despair it sent fluttering through the soldiers, filled Brody with resolve in such a swift, burning wave that he felt his cheeks redden. *Bravery is for others.* His father's words climbed through decades of memory to ring in his skull. His eyes stung.

"We can!" he shouted, his voice echoing across the parapets. He turned, shutting out the chanting, the horns, the drums slung across the sloping backs of the oxen trundling behind the nomads, the squealing of the wyrm. He turned and looked fiercely upon his soldiers, his warriors numbering fewer than the charging army by a half and again.

"And as it is this day, so it shall be the next, and the next, until Wrath is destroyed. Who will bear witness with me? Whose own wrath is tempered by righteousness?"

His friends grumbled excitedly, eager to ride out with their king. Aydran raised the near-empty bottle of wine in toast, drained it in a few bold gulps, then threw it down at the blue-granite flagstones in a defiant, masculine sort of way. The bottle struck with a loud *clank* and rolled up against a battlement.

"Damn," Aydran said. "It was supposed to shatter."

Laughter rifled through the fortress and in seconds, the warriors had pledged their services, and their lives, to the young Griffin King.

Initially, Brody had had only the barest inkling of a plan. It was only after his words up on the walk, after he'd saddled up Dante, and after the fortress split its numbers with most joining Brody and some remaining behind, that the finer details came to him.

He adjusted his gauntlets, made absolutely certain that his fingers had full range of motion, and adjusted his posture to suit Dante's deer-like bounding. His knights clattered behind him. They curved down an inconspicuous trail toward the plains; more of a narrow ravine, really, with red stone rising high on either side of them.

Brody had seen that Wrath himself was not among the chargers. This was merely a welcoming gift to the king, a means of whittling down Brody's forces and evaluating his skill at thinking on the fly and fighting off a threat. Brody went over the plans he'd hastily detailed to Aramis before departure again and again. They required precise timing on everyone's part. He would have to trust the abilities of the men of Apollo's Trail.

They came out through a twisty curve that required their mounts to hop over some rocks and then they were out among the heather. Brody pulled Dante around in a wide arc, his men a sinuous serpent-trail behind him, and urged him into a gallop. The unicorn shrilled a whinny and stretched out his legs. Soon, the thunder of hooves roared behind.

When Brody came around the promontory, he saw that the nomads were a little less than ten minutes off and closing fast. His breath rasped harshly within his great helm. His heart pounded. Days beyond them, past unseen Raynarra, thunderheads churned dark and ominous in the sky. As he watched, the distant plum-colored clouds throbbed with a pulse of lightning. A gust of wind tossed his cloak out behind him and whistled through the cracks in his armor.

The nomads had spotted them. They abandoned their chant and bellowed a challenge instead. Their drums rattled out a staccato rhythm. The horns silenced. Dante lowered his horn. The men behind him roared. Two miles away. One. Brody's griffin vision picked out individual hairs in the nomads' beards. In the quarter mile before contact, all sound seemed to deaden; maybe it was only the blood pounding in his ears.

And then, when he was near enough that he could smell their sweat, Brody raised his bo staff. The sheet of glass in the fortress that served as the lighthouse light spun their way and tilted down. It reflected the sun full-on into the faces of the enemy, who faltered, throwing up their arms.

The centaurs fanned out behind Brody like spreading wings. They drew first blood, the razor edges of their greatswords glinting malevolently as the blades came arcing down. Hot fluids splattered against Brody's flank. He didn't look, bracing himself as Dante plunged forward and down, his horn goring a man and then swiping out through his ribs to cut another's throat.

The thump of colliding bodies, grunts, and screams arose behind Brody, but he had other targets. He led Domine, Abram, and six elves in a relentless drive toward the mounted Rankers and the moon wyrm, the latter of which had scented blood and was starting to panic.

The nomads Brody passed were ended in quick order by crushing blows from his stave, or Domine's blade, or the elves' daggers or arrows, or Dante's horn. The ones who had regained their composure somewhat and grabbed at him, trying to pull him from the saddle, were more often than not pulled down and trampled beneath the elves' silvery Glavherrian mares.

When they broke through into the ring of Rankers, none of them yet suffered any major injury. Though the mercenary nomads were excellent fighters in an ambush or one on one, they couldn't compare to armored soldiers on horseback. Brody felt more certain of his suspicion that they were but a sacrifice sent by Wrath to strain him.

The Rankers had seen them coming from atop their own nightmarish steeds. Apparently unaffected by the blinding lighthouse beam, one of them kicked his horse at Brody, in the clear space that had opened between them with their struggling wyrm and the nomads now tangling with Brody's comparatively meager forces.

The charging Ranker showed its teeth, spreading its jaws wide as if aiming to fix them around Brody's helm. Dante darted in low to plunge his horn in the nightmare horse's breast, bringing Brody in close enough to thrust his stave into the Ranker's mouth and out the back of its neck. Impact from Dante's horn meeting bone and then punching through it shuddered up to Brody's shoulders. The unicorn reared back, his horn crimson, and as they barrelled past, Brody rolled his wrist and flicked his stave so that the Ranker's corpse slid off it.

The other four Rankers were much more cautious. They stuck close to the wyrm, prodding it onward mercilessly, even though they risked driving it forward over their own men. Many of the nomads had turned their backs to the lighthouse and now set upon Brody's team, trying to steer them about so they would themselves be blinded in the light of their own scheme.

"Boy-King!" shouted a Ranker with a face like a hellish, half-melted mannequin's. "You are far from your nest, little chick! Come near, that you may know Wrath better!"

Wordlessly, Brody obliged. He guided Dante toward the Ranker that had spoken, then past him. Dante drew a line of red along the flank of the Ranker's horse in passing, and Brody swung high. The Ranker ducked beneath the strike and lashed out, its claws skittering across the armor over his side. He rode on, letting Domine engage behind him, and dodged the Ranker by the wyrm's hind leg as well, Dante fencing its steed's scorpion tail away.

They came 'round the wyrm, hopping nimbly over its long tail, to ride at the other two Rankers from behind. Brody managed to jab the nearest in the spine and then twirl his stave around and deliver an underhand-swing to its chin. The Ranker squealed in pain and lashed out, clubbing Brody in the face and throwing him back in the saddle. The Ranker snatched his cloak. With Dante cantering one way and the Ranker pulling another, Brody felt his feet begin to leave the stirrups. He tried to cling on with his knees and reached out with his staff to hook the reins and give them a tug.

The unicorn stopped suddenly, Brody levered himself and twisted to wrap his cloak around his arm, gathering some into his fist. Dante, now aware of his rider's peril, bucked, and Brody gave his cloak a sharp yank. The Ranker was dislodged and trampled beneath a Glavherrian mare.

The elves rode in a ring around the wyrm, loosing arrows into the nomads pressing toward them, always shifting. As he watched, one elf suddenly slid sideways as if falling, and shot an arrow up through the throat and skull of one of the Ranker's mounts. At the elf's command, his mare made a tight circle on the spot, dipping low so that he could pick up the spear the Ranker had dropped.

Another elf went sailing over their heads, striking the ground yards away, buried in the midst of the army. The Ranker that had thrown her, the one with the melted face, came limping jerkily around the wyrm, moving as if its limbs barely articulated. It snapped the elf's bow in one hand and discarded the pieces with disgust.

An elf in the moving ring gave another command and three of his companions turned their horses and made for their king. Seeing their approach, the Ranker rumbled a curse and quickened its pace toward Brody. Dante brought his forelegs together and flourished his horn as if posturing for a duel, but the Ranker feinted left and swiped right with its spear, cutting into the unicorn's knees.

Dante stumbled and the Ranker vaulted at Brody, sweeping him from the saddle. Brody turned as they went, like a feline aiming to hit the ground on all fours. He somersaulted over the Ranker and came up just in time to use his stave to redirect a powerful spear-thrust to his belly. He pinned the spearhead to the grass and stomped mightily on the shaft, breaking it. Then, warding the Ranker off with a pair of elegant swings from the stave, Brody swooped down to pick up the spearhead; a smooth, flat triangle of steel inscribed with an odd, red-tinted symbol.

"Let me taste your blood," the Ranker murmured, all malice and hatred.

As before, Brody held his silence. He would not be goaded into a blind rage. He held his stave in one hand, the spearhead in the other with its tip pointed toward his elbow. The Ranker circled to his right, Brody stalked to the left, tense, awaiting the tell–the physical give-away that would reveal the Ranker's intentions. However, he didn't expect the Ranker to drive its fist powerfully into the side of the wyrm thrashing behind it.

Brody shot the Ranker an uncertain look, shifting his weight. The moon wyrm threw its head up and keened at the sky. It tucked its snout in and dove at the ground, starting to tunnel down into it, its claws shoveling soil and rocks out behind it in lethal bursts.

"Don't let it escape!" Brody shouted to the nearest elf. In his moment of distraction, the Ranker moved. Brody caught the flap of its cloak in his periphery, turned, saw its hideous face two strides from his own, retreated clumsily, his mind blank in the broadside of the sudden attack.

Dante galloped out from the rising cloud of dirt behind the Ranker, his pelt still as satiny black as if it were dust-repellant. He drew his horn across the Ranker's back. Despite what had to have been an agonizing wound, the Ranker snarled and pounced at Brody. Brody swung the stave–a matador waving the red flag before the bull–the Ranker caught it. Brody pushed in, and sliced the spearhead across its throat, cutting its crow of triumph into a gurgle. Having slashed backhand, his arm caught most of the arterial blood. His gauntlet and vambrace dripped with it. The Ranker clutched at his breastplate, perhaps seeking solace in its pain, and collapsed.

Brody only then heard how his breaths heaved like hurricanes within his helm. He took the moment to mutter a prayer of thanks that he still lived. Dante, resting one foreleg on the tip of the hoof and trying to groom away the blood clotting at his knee, turned one tassled ear his way.

"Thanks for keeping an eye on me," Brody said. Dante swished his lion-like tail and snorted as if to say, *What would you do without me?*

A stone the size of Brody's chest hit the ground nearby. He frowned at the flying clouds of soil, trying to penetrate through to see the moon wyrm's progress. The remaining elves and two centaurs had positioned themselves near the creature's head, trying to jab it back out with their weapons. Domine held the back of one of its spade-like forearms lodged in his bear jaws and tugged every now and then like a dog on a rope. Despite their best efforts, the wyrm slipped under inch by inch and the harassment of the nomads nearest them all kept interfering with their focus.

Brody slid his stave into the loop on Dante's saddle and tightened his grip on the broken spearhead. He bolted toward the wyrm and swiftly picked his way up its tail, shuffling along its spine to its head. In a whistle of wind on folded wings, Abram dove past, forcing a nomad off the wyrm's tail.

It was like standing on the back of a very large mechanical bull. A few times Brody had to throw himself onto his hands and knees or else be flung off, and the dust in the air coated his mouth and stung his eyes. When he came near the digging foreclaws, he remained low, his weight dispersed as broadly as he could get it. If he fell off now, he risked being buried alive.

The proximity to the brain sent images breezing through the king's mind: a red-hot hand on flesh already burned by the sun. A pile of tangled string beginning to smoke and catch fire. Were these recollections of the wyrm's impressions of Wrath? Brody didn't know. He crawled over the shoulders and with a yelp, began sliding down the neck and into the tunnel the moon wyrm was creating.

Twisting himself around, Brody dug the spearhead into the neck. It caught on a bone or muscle, and he felt a pained cry vibrate through the beast's body. He looked down between his feet. There! He could just see the bony ridges at the base of the reptile's skull–its jaws flexed as it used its hard nose and forehead to smash through the bedrock it met. To kill it, and kill it fast, he would have to aim just right–to sink the spear into the soft spot where neck met head.

"Okay," Brody said to himself. He took two deep breaths, pulled the spearhead free, and fell.

Above the tunnel, the combatants were treated to quite a sight. The moon wyrm's large, sinuous body spasmed and began to thrash so madly that Domine was shaken loose and sent tumbling head over heels.

"His Highness!" Aramis rode forward, gazing helplessly at the carcass and the collapsing tunnel within-which its head was buried.

Khogar, standing nearby tending to an injured satyr, said unconcernedly, "Give him a few moments."

The decimated army of Wrath, those who had not fallen or fled, split their attention between their foe and the settling dust around the wyrm, just as curious as Brody's warriors to see how the king fared.

From the soft mounds of soil mantling the dead wyrm's shoulders Brody emerged, shaking his arms and legs clean, lifting his great helm so that a clod of dirt could fall out, revealing his dirty face. Dante trotted over and Brody leaned against him, removing his stave and clinging to it like a walking stick. Then he looked up and around at the hundreds of eyes and panted challengingly, "Come. Visit your wrath upon me. I've strength yet."

A few of the nomads flinched.

Aydran emerged into the ring around Brody, squeezing between two stricken warriors, and took one of Brody's arms, holding it aloft. "Warriors of Apollo's Trail, your Griffin King!"

The men roared their victory and with new energy returned to their skirmishes. But the spirit of the enemy had broken, and before long the nomads were retreating, chased down and killed, and once again, as he had promised he would, King Brody of the Griffins had triumphed.

Chapter Thirty-Six:

Wrath

"The wild still lingered in him and the wolf in him merely slept."
–Jack London, *White Fang*

In a little less than four months, Brody had purged the outlands of bandits, wraiths, goblins, and other allies of Wrath. Each night, fewer and fewer campfires glimmered and soon the myriad stars and comets once again reigned supreme in the evening sky.

Some had fled to Raynarra's very walls, where Brody would not risk pursuit until the rest of his army arrived, which, he suspected, would be soon. Those of the fortress held him and his Six–four with Josiah and Rexus gone–in high esteem. He had earned their formidable loyalty. If he'd commanded them to leap from the highest tower, they would have, trusting that he would be there to catch them on the way down.

Michael had long since returned and honored Brody with a blessing for his victory against the moon wyrm. The battle had been unofficially dubbed that of "the red spear." Michael had encouraged them to feast and celebrate the fallen, of whom there had been a surprising few, and they did just that. Word soon reached the council and cities far and wide of Brody's miraculous success, and gossip spread like wildfire–until one could believe that Brody had single-handedly fought ten dragons. Letters pledging support, official scrolls recording generous donations of food, arms, and medicine made by minor kings, flocked in on the wings of messenger falcons.

And then one day Michael came bearing important news.

Brody half-reclined on a sort of couch on a balcony, his view a panorama of ocean and sky just begging to be enjoyed on griffin wings. But at the moment, he was deeply submerged in a book. It wasn't an official writ or an expository text on law. For the first time in years, he read a work of fiction—a heart-wrenching tale about a bumbling youth determined to travel through the astral realms in search of his own soul so as to reshape it and change his fate. Brody didn't understand all of the references, but it was a captivating read all the same.

A bouquet of pale-yellow tea roses and a teapot sat on a small tray near him, their scents mingling with the wind and the watermelon that Dante nibbled at by his feet. In a room somewhere close by, Brody heard Aramis playing a harp and beautifully singing a slow, somber song in the elven language.

At a break in the story, Brody closed his eyes and just absorbed all he could feel, smell, and hear, letting the book rest, open, on his chest. He knew that anything imagined by men would fall short of the real thing, but he couldn't help but wonder if this was what Heaven might be like.

Aramis had insisted that during Brody's stay he be treated well, and like a proper king, and Brody admitted that this was the most well-rested he had felt since his days of training back at the castle. But still...he frowned to himself. He grew more and more weary of late. His sleep did not restore his energy, and even when he transformed into a griffin, he felt sapped of much of his strength. Perhaps it was stress, perhaps the onset of depression, perhaps an indication of how his body fared in reality, comatose almost five years now. Whatever the reason, he could not dwell on it. He had two Rankers yet to defeat and after them, who knew what would come?

"Worrying is a sign of weak faith," Brody said aloud. He needed to hear himself say it. Dante neighed softly as if in agreement, lifting his head with a large slice of watermelon in his mouth, the rind like a broad, green smile. Brody laughed.

"Wise words." Abram stuck his tabby-striped griffin head around the doorway of Brody's room. "'Be still and know that I am the Lord,' as the Good Book says."

"Abram!" Brody said warmly. He sat up. Michael stuck his head around as well, and Brody stood, his smile falling. "Is there news?" Even Dante had snapped to attention at the appearance of the White Griffin, his dainty golden hooves tapping against the floor as he brought them neatly together beneath him in a squared stance. He shook his soft, feathery amber-streaked mane and nickered.

"I bear news," Michael confirmed, "and it is this: your army has arrived. On the road they met General Amos's shipment, hence the extra time they took. Both are ready and await you north of Raynarra on the violet." The violet was an expanse of hilly moorland covered in purple heather. It provided various locations that would be excellent for catapults. "However," Michael added, "Wrath musters his troops to meet them."

"What?" Brody felt a switch flip in his brain. He slipped inside between Michael and Abram and started removing armor from his armor stand before he'd even comprehended that he was doing it. As he began buckling and latching the pieces together on his body with the aid of Abram's nimble talons, he mentally rehearsed his plans and challenged them with potential obstacles.

Michael remained outside, his talons resting on the railing, his wings half-open. "Shall I relay a message to your generals?"

"Yes." Brody turned to let Abram adjust the armor against his torso. "Tell them to get in position. I'm on my way."

"It'll take Aramis and his troops about an hour to saddle up, ride out, and attack from the south," Abram said.

A cold chill fluttered near Brody's diaphragm. "Yes. They know what they're supposed to do. Wrath will be evenly matched, numbers-wise. We'll be able to keep him on his toes until the others come."

"What about not-numbers-wise?" Abram asked with concern, his cat-like griffin eyes searching Brody's face.

Brody held his gaze sternly but unreadably and was glad to put the great-helm over his face.

Abram handed him his stave but didn't let go of it until after he'd said, "I know you harbor misgivings about facing Wrath. We've traveled together long enough, you and I, for me to know when something troubles you. How fares your spirit?"

"Once I find whatever reliquary stores the tainted essence of King Kel the Smokewing, and once I cleanse it, I'll feel better," Brody said. He moved to stoke Dante's cheek and bid the unicorn a brief farewell.

"You've fear," Michael said, not accusatory, never that, but sympathetic, kind, gentle, like a veteran of many battles speaking softly to a young recruit, "because you are mortal. And for this, the temptation may be very great. But remember what makes you king." And he sprang up onto the railing and dove off of it, soon a white line gliding away to the north.

Brody departed soon after Michael had, by way of the same balcony. He flew high, where the great winds that shaped the clouds sent him shooting like a bullet over the world. For a while he watched Dante trying to follow him below, a black ant sprinting across the moor, but he soon left the unicorn and the fortress far behind.

He took the minutes of peace before he reached Raynarra to steady and prepare himself. He didn't look below at the wasteland of Wrath's influence, at the bones and charred earth, at the mound of still-smoking carcasses where they had piled and burned the enemy dead after the cleansing of the moor.

Instead, Brody drifted peacefully among palaces of cumulonimbus; fluffy towers whose capitals only leveled off when they reached the top of the atmosphere. He knew it was time to descend when the carpet of clouds below him turned sullen gray as if stained. He arrowed down, the wind whistling shrilly through his quills, and landed on an area of the clouds near a small gap. The clouds were cold and squishy beneath his talons and paw pads, like soggy cotton balls. Through the gap, he saw Raynarra's wall, and with a heavy sigh, he looked above and around him at the serenity of the heavens, then dove through the hole, illuminated by a shaft of sunlight.

He tilted his wings and fanned his tail, leveling out about a mile above the city, absorbing details as he went. What he could glimpse of the streets between the red-shingle rooftops spoke volumes of the grim state of the place.

The homes and shops were dark with doors smashed in and shutters hanging from windows. The streets were laden with filth: overturned carts, strewn clothing, gray bones, collapsed timbers black with ash. Monsters slunk about, hissing up at Brody as his shadow crossed over them, not just Rankers, of which there were many, all filing in organized lines to Raynarra's main gates and northern ramparts, but nightmarish beasts as well. Some, Brody could name: zombies, werewolves, ogres... Others were the demonic spawn of mankind's worst nightmares, beings that could only be described as fears and hatreds given physical form.

The dead rotted where they'd fallen, their remains scattered into sundered fragments, but Brody saw that there yet remained survivors. What he saw gave him little hope, however. The living Raynarrans jabbered madly from within gibbets, badly starved, their hair falling out in patches, covered in suppurating sores. Others showed signs of having undergone public torture, tied to poles and suffering from horrendous wounds.

Brody saw these and worse as he flew over the city and a rage such as he had never felt before filled him from beak to tail. He shook with it, his guts writhed with it. A gurgling growl rumbled in his chest. His eyes became red with bloodsense. A part of him urged him to rescue those miserable, suffering captives, rescue them with a quick death.

This is what they'll turn the dreamworld into, Brody thought. Mingled horror and fury gathered in his chest like a dark thunderhead. *This is what they'll do to my kingdom and all of my people.*

A half-dead woman slumped against a wall, her mouth moving sluggishly as she spoke to herself. As Brody's shadow touched her, she lifted her head, her bloodshot eyes rolling vaguely in his direction. Brody dove down closer to her before he knew what he was doing, talons reaching as if to take her up.

A flood of black cloaks filled the square around the woman and Rankers leered up at him. They all wore human disguises. One, a sandy-haired young man who could've been a surfer-dude that Brody might pass at the beach, wiggled his fingers up at Brody in a mocking wave. It was unnerving to see all of the masks hiding the horrors beneath; faces that maybe belonged to any number of dreamers from reality, faces so very like the ones that belonged to Raynarra's mutilated citizens. He could not rescue the suffering without being swallowed up by that mob.

Brody clenched his talons, struggling to fly in place. Their false eyes were upon him, filled with scorn. Their sneers were sharp with hatred. Brody looped a little closer, the Rankers grouped tighter together, and he whimpered helplessly. Somewhere beyond he heard a sergeant shouting a chant and a company of warriors responding in kind at rhythmic intervals. His men. Them he could help.

Brody glowered down at the Rankers and thundered a terrible roar coupled with a hawk's scream—the battle cry of a griffin. They jeered and one said, "We'll be here when you get back!"

'To purge the world, to end the blight,' the words of the prophecy streamed through his brain, the words as rhythmic as a primal drumbeat, a reassurance; a promise. *'The King is coming with the night.'*

Brody, winging the last mile or so to where he saw his troops' standards snapping in a dry wind, felt as if his muscles were tight enough to wrench his own bones out of socket. His people had suffered terribly. Innocents had been slaughtered–just as that hiker had been, long ago in the woods near his house. And the Griffin King was powerless to bring them peace. A messy knot of fury and grief tangled around his insides. His red eyes glowed in tandem with the hot flush that spread beneath the feathers of his face. Then he would bring them justice, if nothing else.

His army was like a blanket of glittering pinpoints, armor winking in the weak sunlight. The standard-bearers stood tall, proud, and very young at the fringes, the mighty catapults waited in the midst. Sword-and-shield men stood in the very front–they were the ones exchanging war-words with the sergeant on horseback pacing before them, his rank denoted by the large metal badge on his chestplate. Then there were the ranks of support fighters wielding maces and greatswords, then archers, and then the very few magic-users powerful enough to make an impression in combat.

Upon seeing their king and the pale flash of his inner-wings, the army let loose with a resounding cheer that caused the small stones scattered about the wasteland around them to bounce. Brody landed beside a catapult on his hind paws, touching his talons to the boulder resting in its bucket. Hundreds of words and names had been scraped into its craggy surface with chisel, claw, or knifepoint.

My family; My wife Amelia; Freedom; The Golden Griffin; Truth; Doing Right; A Good Death...

Months past, Brody had instructed General Amos to build four catapults and send them and their payload to Raynarra when ready. Brody's troops were to carve their ideals, their reason for fighting, into the stones. He was glad to see that they'd managed it along the way.

"Righteous wrath," he murmured. He sprang up to perch atop the catapult's frame, looking out over his soldiers, at a sea of expectant faces and round eyes. Someone, Ranker or victim, screamed behind Raynarra's walls and Brody saw an unsettled ripple roll through the troops.

He raised his voice. "When you see these stones bring down the walls, remember not to lose yourself. When these stones open the gates, remember the faces of your loved ones. When these stones, into which you've channeled your very essence, your soul, lead our charge, remember why you fight with me, and not the Rankers!" Brody paused. The army was silent, as if absorbing his words.

"Some of you may have fought alongside my predecessor, King Uriah. But not like this. Wrath will make you take foolish risks. He will lead you to rage. You will abandon your brothers-in-arms to satisfy your own delusional vendetta, and you will die. Let us fight. But let us do so together, with grave purpose. Let us kill, but to bring peace, not wrath."

Brody saw Michael, like a white star, standing beside Sergeant Flaherty to the west and he felt an incredible stirring of deja vu. He had seen this battlefield before, seen a black-and-white griffin speaking to a great many as he was now, in the White Griffin's wing. The old sense of something rushing at him, some heavy burden, returned. Brody swayed dizzily. Then a loud, playful voice shouted down to them from the ramparts.

"Now where's the fun in all that?"

Wrath had arrived.

He wasn't much to look at–his hair was oily and stringy, hacked unevenly so as to keep out of his eyes. He had a short, tangled beard, and what skin wasn't covered by dented, stained plate armor was heavily scarred and patched rash-red and fish-bone-white. He leaned comfortably against the battlements of one of the bartizans over the gate, grinning at them.

"We finally meet, King Brody." Wrath dipped his head. "I'm pretty pissed that you killed my pet. You know how difficult it is to catch moon wyrms? We lost a lot of Raynarrans to exhaustion just diggin' holes deep enough to find the damn thing."

Brody ignored the barb in Wrath's words, replying before he could feel the sting.

"Perhaps, had you been present, you could have stopped me."

Wrath gave him a slow, crocodile smile. "Oh, child. As you are about to learn, a king should never leave his castle."

"I have questions, Ranker, questions you will answer!" Brody shouted.

"Now is not the time for words," Wrath said, his voice low and dangerous. "I see you've brought me a gift." He gestured at the catapults.

Brody felt the bloodsense throb in his veins. He felt too small for it–as if he must burst. "I bring you uncertainty!" His hackles went up, a roar echoed beneath his words. He heard a mumble of approval move through his warriors and turned to them once more, one last time before battle.

"What do you fight for? *I* fight because you–" he whirled, wings half-open, to stab his beak at Wrath "–are the serpent in shadow; you are the whisper in the dark! I fight because you are Rankers, nightmare filth, and I am the Griffin King, protector of dreams!" His army exploded with battlecries–Brody felt them vibrate through the wood of the catapult. "Fire!" he commanded, leaping down out of the way.

The catapults creaked and groaned, their arms swinging up, driven by powerful cords of twisted sinew. The boulders sailed through the air, beautiful in their deadliness, and struck the walls and gate of Raynarra with resounding explosions of demolished masonry. Chips of stone and metal burst into the air like confetti. Brody saw the remains of a few Rankers too slow to retreat flip grotesquely to join the rubble, their robes flapping.

Brody's bloodsense gave everything a red tint, as if all was bathed in the shadow of a lunar eclipse. His senses were sharper than he ever remembered them being. He felt famished; starving for something more than food, thirsting for something more substantial than water. They heard the gates as they were wrenched apart and when the dust had settled enough to bring back decent visibility, the army charged forward, weapons uplifted, met partway by a flood of Rankers determined to at least delay their getting inside to Wrath.

Brody tried to get a sense of the pulse of the battle. Would it be an attempt by Wrath to decimate their numbers and slay the Griffin King? Would Wrath try to escape? Would the Rankers employ clever, roguish tactics within, among the alleys and shadows, or tear into them with savage brutality? Could they expect any nasty surprises? Secret weapons? *Fey* sent Brody an image of a black cloud of smoke lit from below by a massive fire. He saw a wooden stake splintered on a shield and a beautiful marble statue falling, hitting the ground, shattering, revealing that it was hollow and full of blood. As usual, he couldn't decipher any exact meaning, but Brody felt that the Rankers were betrayed by their own spell, that Wrath had rendered them fools and that somehow, Wrath would fall.

A mage from Starfall strode past, her hands raised, her lips pressed tight, conjuring a shield around the fore of the army, even though they were now too distant for her to see them. Some of the troops had made it in–Brody now stood near the very hind of his army. Flaherty appeared beside him, and Brody reined in his blood-sense enough to not lunge at the man in surprise. He clacked his beak with irritation.

The marine hadn't appeared to notice–but he did lose his train of thought at seeing the king's completely red eyes, and stammered a bit before blinking forcefully and saying, "We heard your call before you joined us. What happened?"

Brody thought of the dying woman, curled up by the wall. "Kill any wounded you find," he said. "Any of the Rankers' playthings."

Flaherty frowned uncomfortably. "We...we have medics, my King."

"Not for these," Brody said solemnly. His heart ached. "They are beyond repair. The best we can do for them is end their suffering."

A Ranker had somehow made it around or through the army in more-or-less one piece and stood gawping at Brody as if it couldn't believe its luck. While the king's head was turned toward the marine, it raised its dagger and thrust it at the thick collar of red-orange feathers around Brody's neck.

"Sire!" Flaherty pointed and made to lunge forward and interpose himself between the weapon and its target, but Brody whirled with a horrible scream and had torn the Ranker to pieces in seconds–before it could even make a sound. Flaherty, and the other soldiers who had witnessed the remarkable feat, were very obviously impressed and intimidated. But Brody didn't notice. With the first warm splash of blood on his talons had come a berserker insanity, and he swam readily into the current, letting it carry him away.

He half-ran, half-flew in the fray, lost in the battle, savage and carefree. He laughed and he wept, though he could not have said why later, and then he angered that his tears blurred his vision. He passed one of the boulders they'd launched where it lay nestled amongst ruined rubble and touched it in passing, leaving a bloody talon-print. He ripped through the enemy, crowing his euphoria, lost in a cavalcade of visions real and imagined.

Sometimes, certain sights and sounds broke through his blood-sense to tap against the smothered, rational part of his mind. He heard a pair of war horns ring piercingly through the air and echo through Raynarra's spoiled streets. The quavering, intimidating wails of the horns of Apollo's Trail. Had the others come? How much time had passed?

He saw Abram soar overhead and heard him shout down to him, but his words were mere noise to Brody, who only briefly raised his tail in greeting. He saw Dante spring past like a buck across a stream, his pelt almost as dark as a Ranker's cloak.

Brody sought something, anything, that spoke out to him as once belonging to King Kel the Smokewing as he tore through the city. At one point he felt something strike his wing, hard enough to drive him to the side a few steps. He looked at it and saw that it was an arrow.

Brody laughed and broke the shaft in his beak, pouncing toward the figure crouched beneath the eaves of a house and just raising its bow to shoot again. It was a Ranker, but a Ranker unlike any Brody had seen yet. It looked up, saw him coming, and laughed–a sound like a pipe being unclogged. It looked like a man. A thick, black, tarry substance leaked from its eyes and mouth, oozing between its teeth, out over its lips, shining in the daylight showing opaque through the storm clouds. It was more monster than human, all its empathy gone, functioning solely on whatever dark forces drove the Rankers, forever corrupted by Wrath.

Brody felt some of the bloodsense leave him in the face of the tainted dream-creation, once a healthy, happy Raynarran. Fleetingly, he wondered what *Fey* would show him of the dream-creator's mind if he searched for it in his sleep. What had happened to the man or woman in reality, whomever they were? What trial had they failed to overcome in their everyday lives that had allowed Wrath to poison their mind?

The Ranker saw his hesitation and shrieked, stabbing at him with a fresh arrow. Brody recoiled, but not fast enough. The steel tip pierced his shoulder, grated across the bone, and tore out through the muscle, becoming lodged there. He loosed a yowl and instinctively spread his wings. The Ranker, startled at the sudden flash of white feathers within the immense span of Brody's wings flinched, and suddenly disintegrated into a cloud of ash with naught but a shout.

Before his confusion could sink in past the pain spreading down his limb, Brody was joined by the female mage he'd seen earlier. Hot purple flames curtained her hands–she held them up, stalking cautiously forward to look around him and make sure she'd hit her mark. With a satisfied nod, she smiled at Brody, who nodded gratefully back. She saw the arrow in his shoulder and was about to address it when a movement in their periphery made them both crouch low.

From Raynarra's high house, once the seat of the city's mayor, arose a flock of chincrest wyverns, their scales glimmering gold and red. One of them dove down at Brody and the mage, its hind claws out and reaching. Brody hissed and took a cat-like swipe at it with a talon. Griffins were generally much brawnier than wyverns and a show of force was often enough to scare them off. These ones, however, had the influence of Wrath behind them.

The one harassing Brody distracted him with its venomous jaws while another darted in, quick as a bat, and pinned the mage down hard against the ground. She screamed and Brody went to her, shouldering hard around his own wyvern, tearing the arrow from his wound in the process, but the other had already lifted partly into the air, dragging the mage by her arms. Every time she began to mutter a desperate incantation, the wyvern threatened to drop her, forcing her to abandon her spell for one that could catch her should she fall.

The first wyvern managed to get a mouthful of secondary feathers. Brody's volatile bloodsense returned in an explosive swoop and he savaged the brute's face and throat with a flurry of his claws, then leaped up after the second, which was now a good forty feet up and still trying to climb, obviously straining against the weight and wriggling of the mage. It made a double take down its spine, slashed the sharp tip of its tail at Brody's eyes, and after Brody had flinched away, he saw the wyvern's talons empty, and the mage tumbling through the air below, too terrified to scream, too disoriented to spellcast.

Brody chirped his helplessness and dove, the wind streaming over the cocoon of his wings like water around a fish. He stretched out his forelegs, spread his claws, kept his tail straight out behind him like a rudder. His tunnel vision only showed him her–her eyes meeting his as she fell, a symbol of all the lives he had failed to save. Then she struck the edge of a rooftop with a sharp crack and bounced off to hit an awning, bringing it down around her like a shroud. Brody had to barrel-roll with a flit of his tail or else meet the same fate, his beak missing the rooftop by a feather. He landed ungracefully by the mound of cloth, wood, and broken wares, listening for a heartbeat, but there was nothing–only the stench of too much blood. She was dead.

Brody's feathers and fur stood on end. He looked up at the wyvern flapping off to seek another victim and gave a murderous barn owl shriek, bunching his muscles to take off in pursuit, but something huge and whiter-than-snow fell upon him, pinning him down securely against the ground.

Brody squawked and struggled, snapping his beak blindly–then he felt a painful nip in his ear and heard Michael's cool, commanding voice.

"Calm yourself and be still!"

He did.

"Michael?" The bloodsense began to leave him–the red mist in his eyes to dissipate. Michael held him firmly, a restraint and a shield, protecting him as sanity slipped back. Brody looked at the dead mage and swallowed down a throb of guilt. Then he turned his gaze upward.

The bloodsense had hidden much from him. Twelve wyverns circled above like vultures where before he had seen but one. Three wyverns lay dead around them, when he only remembered slaying one. In fact, there was a broad avenue of carnage wending back along Brody's footsteps. This was what bloodsense gifted the Griffin King.

Kayle, the black griffin, hovered nearby, staring in shock at the devastation. Brody figured he and Mariah must have returned after their latest sojourn to report and joined in the battle.

Michael spoke again. "Know thyself. Return to thine heart. What feel you?"

Brody focused his senses inward on his own body and realized how terribly weak he was. The bloodsense's dual-edge had left him as frail as a rabbit kitten. The arrow wounds in his wing and shoulder ached intensely and he had other injuries that he had no recollection of receiving.

"I'm...hurt," he said.

"Patience," Michael said, stepping off away from Brody. "Seek out Wrath, young king. You are more than a beast driven by passions. You are a man, governed by higher virtue. Find yourself again–consort with your spirit. Then go." His hot, radiant eyes flashed and he took off, scattering the wyverns with a haunting, ethereal warcry.

Brody did as told, meditating, delving through the chaotic layers of his physical form to the thoughts beneath and beyond. His ideal–his identity–the things that truly drove him and kept him grounded. His father, his friends, the faces of the dead, these were his councilors. He stifled impotent rage beneath their voices and summoned forth his ideals. Justice. Virtue. Bravery.

Bravery is for others, his father had told him.

He transformed and found himself kneeling as if in prayer, his cape spread around him, his armor shining dully like wet fangs, one hand wrapped around his bo staff. The wounds that he'd collected in griffin form shifted and settled across his body. Though muted somewhat by his metal plate, the pain duller, more manageable, arrowheads and sword tips had found the seams and gaps in the armor or punctured it in places, the injuries to his wings transferred to his upper back and sides. He was weary, yes, injured. But he had strength enough.

Brody opened his eyes and lifted his head–and saw a shadow thrown up on a wall by firelight some distance away beneath a stone archway. The shadow could only belong to Wrath–Brody recognized the compact body and mounds of armor. He stood and hurried after it, forcing in deep breaths to relax and prepare himself, and moving languidly in the hope that some energy could regenerate.

He wound his way through the bones of the city, past brown flowerbeds, cracked stone angels whose eyes glowed white as he passed, shops whose contents littered the smashed-in doorways like strewn organs. The bulk of the fighting roared behind him–here, it was as quiet as Syranade's cemetery had been.

Wrath's shadow led him into a wide area near the city's far wall. It was, or had been, a serene location with a few elderly apple trees and benches and vast barrels filled with a rainbow-variety of colors for dyeing cloth. The air smelled of the many fruits and oils used to make the different hues. Wrath stood still and calm with his back to Brody as if examining the bricks in the wall before him separating the dyeing yard from the street beyond.

"Are you fleeing?" Brody asked.

The Ranker turned smoothly, as if he stood atop a lazy Susan. A black mist billowed around him. He replied expressionlessly, "Wrath knows no cowardice."

"No. Only foolishness." Brody grimly inclined his chin.

"I am not the fool." Wrath's face broke into a manic leer. Blood oozed out between his teeth. Brody blinked and it was gone. "You have pursued the epitome of malice, the manifestation of brutality, away from any candle flame of hope."

Wrath tilted his head. “Flee? There is no place I would rather be.”

Chapter Thirty-Seven:

A Patient Man

"What goes around comes around. And sometimes you get what's coming around[...]And sometimes you are what's coming around."

–Jim Butcher, *Grave Peril*

Wrath moved first, lifting his arms, both his hands wrapped around the hilts of long, wicked-looking knives. Brody hefted his staff up in a sort of one-handed golf swing and clipped Wrath under the chin, but it didn't seem to faze him. The Ranker sliced at him with a dagger, Brody jumped aside and jabbed behind him with the butt of his bo staff as he went. It connected with Wrath's tasset, his dented, pock-marked hip armor, with a grate of wood on rusted metal.

Brody danced away, evaluating Wrath's reach and the reckless passion of his fighting style, and felt a stinging stripe along the back of one arm where the knife had nicked him. He pressed his free hand against it, holding his bo staff out like a shield toward Wrath, who didn't appear in any hurry to end the fight.

The Ranker touched one wrist to his red and white chin, where a swollen, purple bruise developed. Brody's strike had been hard enough to fracture bone, and Wrath's voice came slightly distorted as if his tongue was too big for his mouth.

"This is what comes of interference–war."

Brody looked hard at him. "Wars end."

"And you will be the one to end them?" Wrath scoffed. "No. You're going to come with me. In pieces, if you must."

This took Brody by surprise. He blinked and lowered his guard, then blinked again and took a step back into a fighting stance. "Why?"

"So that the prophecy can be shaped in our favor!" Wrath came in low, leading with one dagger hooking upward toward the seam between Brody's poleyn and cuisse, the second dagger held backhand and ready to follow up with a slash to the neck. Brody deflected with his staff, trying in vain to land significant strikes of his own, wholly absorbed in redirecting Wrath's blades. The knives knocked against Brody's stave so swiftly that they put Brody in mind of the hungry beak of a woodpecker against the bark of a tree. He didn't realize that he'd been driven back until his spine hit the brick wall.

"That isn't how prophecies work," he grunted disdainfully, fighting to keep his frustration from turning into loathing and then madness. "What will be, will be." He struck like an adder, a feint that drove Wrath to lift his arms and deflect a weapon that wasn't there.

Brody ducked and stabbed up into the pressure point in Wrath's armpit where his armor gapped, a strike that should have torn muscles. Wrath howled in pain and seemed suddenly driven to greater viciousness. He wrenched Brody's stave away with such force that Brody had to let go or risk his arms being dislocated. Then he dropped his knives, and grabbed Brody by the neck, all so swiftly that Brody had to fight panic to catch up.

With his two giant, hairy hands, Wrath ripped Brody's pauldron from his shoulder–and sank his teeth through cloth and flesh. Brody gave a strangled cry, feeling Wrath's jaws strive to meet through the thick muscle of his deltoid, feeling warm blood blossom down his arm between skin and vambrace. The pain intensified–he felt it climb up his neck and down to his fingers and dug the thumb of the hand not trapped against Wrath into the Ranker's eye.

Wrath tried his best to tear a mouthful from Brody's shoulder but had to let go with a yelp or risk losing the eye. Brody's blood wept from the Ranker's grimacing mouth. The sight of it offended the king.

"'What will be, will be,'" Wrath spluttered, scornfully mimicking Brody's words. "Shall I tell you what will be? A Dark Griffin, fighting for the Rankers. A dark king to sit upon an iron throne."

"And what of your leader, Garrett?" Brody asked, trying to staunch the red flow from his injury with the torn remains of the tunic around it. His voice was frail. The wound hurt terribly. "Would you unseat him?"

"Yes, you think yourself so clever for knowing our secrets, don't you? But you don't know them all." Wrath jumped at him and Brody, deprived of his stave, raised his fists–but it was only a taunt. The Ranker chuckled malevolently. Old martial arts lessons slowly crawled from memory, but Brody's collection of injuries was bringing him down. He needed to think outside the box, to be patient and find an opportunity.

Brody reached out into a broad, knee-high barrel beside him, one of many in the vicinity, and scooped a handful of the orange dye within at Wrath. Wrath dropped one knife, his hand flying up to catch the incoming glob, which splattered against his fingers and then into his face. He scrubbed at his eyes, snarling a vile oath in a voice pinched with pain. Brody moved quickly, kicking the weapon aside–it hit a bucket and knocked it over–Wrath turned toward the noise, his streaming eyes screwed shut.

Brody glanced thoughtfully at the bucket, then darted for the other dagger, the one still in the Ranker's grasp, his arms turned inward, the important veins and tendons of his wrists sheltered toward his body. Wrath heard, twitched his blade up where it could find the gap between Brody's breastplate and plackart, but the strike was tentative and slightly off–Wrath still struggled to clear the dye from his eyes.

When Brody's forearm met Wrath's just above the wrist in a clang of armor-on-armor, stopping the thrust, Wrath suddenly pushed eagerly against him like a shark scenting blood. Brody planted his feet, shifted so that he could wrap his fingers beneath the armor over Wrath's shoulder blade, and swiftly brought the Ranker's arm back, keeping a tight, close hold of the elbow. He pressed until he heard the bone pop out of place, then peeled the knife out of Wrath's limp hand and moved to create distance between them, collecting his bo staff.

Wrath's face was livid, twisted so that he looked more monstrous than human, his disguise slipping so that his features seemed horrifically melted. Brody glimpsed hair that writhed like snakes, a mouth filled with rows of sharp teeth, bulbous eyes with white, glowing pupils.

"The nightmares behind me are legion, child. Our schemes are beyond your ken." Wrath forced his shoulder back into place. His heel brushed the bucket that Brody had knocked over. He took up his first dagger, the one that he had dropped, and, faster than was possible, had pinned Brody fast against a giant barrel of water meant to fill the dyeing tubs. Brody had to drop his staff again to wrap his hand around Wrath's wrist, struggling to keep the Ranker from punching the dagger through his armor and into his vitals. Wrath had Brody's other arm pinned high over his head, the second dagger glinting above them like a lethal star.

"You'll be holding your guts in your lap when I've finished with you, boy," Wrath murmured, his stinking breath, like battlefield carrion, hot on the king's face. "And then, I'm going to make you eat them."

"Beware the wrath of a patient man," Brody snarled, the sweat of his struggle running down his cheeks. "Especially if that man is the Griffin King!"

He let Wrath go and twisted aside. The Ranker's dagger drove deep into the water barrel and became lodged. Brody dropped the other knife from his trapped hand overhead, intending to catch it in his free hand, but Wrath intercepted it and held the knife as if surprised that a fresh weapon had been deposited so helpfully into his grasp.

With all the dregs of his remaining strength, Brody wrenched the Ranker's arm around and caused Wrath to stab himself with his own blade, just beneath the right collarbone.

Alarm and pain first paled then reddened Wrath's rashy face. Brody shoved him, forcefully guided him back toward the barrels of dye. Wrath lost his footing on the fallen bucket, tripped, and tumbled into a barrel of blue dye with a great splash. There he remained, his energy spent, too weakened by his injury to heave himself back out again. He groaned with pain, every inch of him coated in thick, blue liquid.

A large pair of flapping wings gusted Brody and Kayle landed, his black pelt glossy with the perspiration of combat. Mariah wasn't far behind. She took a brief look at the humiliated Ranker and her bright-green, feline eyes sparkled at him.

"Are you well, Sire?" Kayle asked Brody, maroon eyes searching.

"Better than," Brody replied. He glared at Wrath and, even senseless as he was by pain and paint, the Ranker seemed to shrink at feeling the weight, the disgust, and the dark oaths behind that royal gaze.

Brody smiled at Kayle. "We've captured a Ranker."

The extent of Brody's injuries were such that he would be out of the fight for a while. Michael helped him to ensure that Wrath was taken securely into custody and assisted him in overseeing a few more vital tasks before the White Griffin guided him to his war tent. It stood just far enough away from the city that the stench of destruction could not reach it. Khogar and Domine chatted wearily but happily around a cooking pit–the snow leopard tribal proudly brandished a new, crimson wyvern skin. Dante grazed nearby, his horn pristine and his cloven hooves spotless.

Brody greeted them, but Michael didn't allow him to linger. He was herded into his tent and helped out of his armor. Michael tended to his injuries and departed and Brody, bathed and in fresh clothes, fell upon his cot and slept for ten days.

When he finally awoke, Brody felt the passage of time in his stiff limbs and in the weakness of his bones. He was back in Apollo's Trail–someone must have brought him there–and he was ravenous. There was a small mosaic-topped table beside his bed. He eased himself up and began cramming the fruit from the silver tray atop the table into his mouth. While he ate, he tried to remember if he'd had any significant dreams, or if he could remember experiencing periods of wakefulness in the past ten days that he could collect details from.

They must have found King Kel's item of power, or else they'd still be battling Rankers. He strained his thoughts. Hazy images that were perhaps a mixture of memory and *Fey*'s power slowly drifted through his mind: a silver sickle–the moon? A scythe?–an icicle lit red by the setting sun behind it; a night sky smattered with stars, which fluttered and became a cloak of black velvet that twisted and looped into a noose.

Brody bit the inside of his cheek and grimaced, forcing himself to chew the next strawberry a little slower. The breeze wandering in through the open balcony doors chilled him, so he stood to change out of his nightshirt, feeling the strain of tense muscles, spots of dull pain–his body reminding him that he had been unwell.

He studied himself as he changed into a simple, soft, red, gold, and black embroidered tunic, taking stock of his wounds. There were puckered, red scars at his shoulder and ribs where the arrows had struck him while in griffin form. The knife wound he'd gotten along the back of his arm was a long, pink line just beginning to fade into a pale scar. There was a raw, purplish ring around his neck as if someone had, at one point, lassoed him or tried to throttle him with a rope, and sundry other scratches and burns that he didn't remember receiving in the battle for Raynarra. The bloodsense had blinded him to much of the goings-on. He wondered how much worse he would have fared had he not worn armor, or not been protected by the berserker strength of his griffin form, and shuddered.

Laughter trickled in from outside his room; high and honest. Brody found his bo staff and crown and once he had finished dressing he took the tray of fruit with him out onto the balcony. From there, he could see the furthermost southern edge of the main courtyard and glimpsed his companions, and Kayle and Mariah, conversing heartily about something that had even old Abram doubled over with mirth.

He watched them awhile, smiling. Khogar in her new tunic of red wyvern skin tapped her goblet against Domine's, who sported a great bald patch in the middle of his wild hair that was just beginning to grow back. No one looked in too bad a shape, and if any nursed a bad injury then it was in no place that Brody could see.

His thoughts turned and he set the fruit aside, tapping his fingers on the balcony railing, pondering whether or not he should obey his own sudden whim.

He decided on the affirmative and re-entered his room, going through to the door. As he'd expected, a guard had been posted just beyond, a man of middling years, clean-shaven, the auburn hair beneath his helm braided in the elven style. When the door to Brody's chamber opened, the man looked upon him with relief and joy barely maintained by the professionalism of his training.

The guard saluted him, and Brody greeted him and said, "Would you please escort me to where Wrath is being detained?"

Wrath's cell was deep below ground–a chill, dark room of stone with a door of thickset iron imbued with binding spells. Brody thought the door overkill. In the light of the torch held by the guard, he could see that the Ranker was thoroughly chained to the wall, wrapped up like a mummy in metal links. A fire golem in the form of a large mastiff had been conjured to sit directly opposite the prisoner, watching unblinkingly, ceaseless in its task.

"Thank you, knight," Brody said to the elf, who stared at the unresponsive Ranker with frightful intensity and loathing. "Please, allow me some moments alone to converse with him." The elf hesitated, looking at Brody as if to protest, then merely shifted his weight, nodded, passed Brody the torch, and departed as far back along the corridor as privacy required.

Brody waited patiently for the Ranker to acknowledge him, taking the time to study him. His complexion was waxy, his hair in greasy strands, his eyes downcast, cheeks sunken and partially obscured by a patchy beard. All else was hidden by the chains. After a few mutually silent minutes, Wrath spoke in a raw, croaky voice too low to carry farther than the distance between them.

"You are not impotent in your rage. The Deadly Seven have broken." He fell silent, motionless, but Brody waited and he went on.

"Rankers have underestimated griffins time and again." Now he looked up and the torchlight made his eyes shine like a cat's green discs. "But *you* overestimate your longevity. We have time. We have the patience of the stones."

"You'll need it," Brody said smoothly. "You will not be leaving this place. We will wring whatever information we can from you as water is wrung from an old cloth."

A lusty smile flickered across Wrath's dry, cracked lips. "Do as you will. But there are forces behind me that are beyond the imagination of any of your kind and, like an asp from beneath the rocks, we will strike the moment you bare your heel."

"Then I suppose I shall have to stick to flying," Brody said, lifting his head imperiously. Wrath shook his head slowly with a clink of metal links.

"Childish bravado. You feel it, just as I smell it on you."

The torch trembled a moment in Brody's hand. The flame danced. The fire golem twitched its ear at him. Wrath, his head still bowed, smiled broadly. Brody could see his cheeks riding up.

"Fight well while time remains, Great Griffin King," the Ranker said.

Chapter Thirty-Eight:

Mounting Secrets

"And the eyes of the sleepers waxed deadly and chill,
And their hearts but once heaved, and forever grew still!"
-Lord Byron, "The Destruction of Sennacherib"

Time moved ever forward, inescapable in its unyielding crawl, and all were forced along before it–even the Griffin King. The Ranker's words remained a thorn in Brody's side even weeks later as he rode Dante through Raynarra, helping to evaluate whether or not the city could be salvaged. He felt the passage of time as a weight that pressed ever more belligerently against his back.

After he sent a report to his council and received a reply in which they advised him to begin rebuilding efforts, Brody lost himself to new distractions with no small amount of relief. He hired builders from the closest settlements and paid them, not with money, but at their request with seeds, timber, iron, and cloth that they could bring back with them to their people. To a backdrop of sawing, hammering, the shouted commands of foremen, and the lowing of the oxen pulling carts loaded with debris or corpses, Brody and his Six kept a sharp eye out for important documents like the Ranker letter from Crystalia.

The army needed something to do, so Brody had them join in on the rebuilding efforts and Raynarra was swiftly shrugging out of its grim shroud to emerge with an air of promise. No new reports arrived detailing where Sylph hid, and Brody knew that his frustration was making itself known to his friends. His consolation prize was in the information Wrath divulged before the Ranker expired.

There weren't many who managed to meet the requirements of the rigorous program that trained the "Vigil;" an elite cluster of warriors, spies, and assassins who pledged complete and unyielding loyalty to the Griffin King. But their methods brought results.

The man who came to Brody after his final "meeting" with Wrath stood with his hands together, fingers spread, one of which displayed a large ruby ring. His fingers were long and slender, like they belonged on piano keys, not around the bitter implements of interrogation.

In a low, careful voice, the man said, "The Ranker has given us the locations of small outposts nearby wherein he kept important information. He describes them as heavily guarded, the documents stored high in a tower locked away in a vault box."

Vault boxes were heavily enchanted items that could only be safely opened at the touch of their owner and a spoken command. Should a foolish thief attempt to chance their luck and break into one, he or she would find the vault booby-trapped and suffer any number of terrible consequences. Compared to having to waste any amount of time trying to figure out what the password could be, Brody decided that breaking in was a necessary risk.

The first box was opened by a wind golem that thinned itself to a razor-edge and shot itself into the keyhole, slicing through magic and mechanism. The lid had sprung open, making those in the vicinity flinch, watching from behind the safety of their shields. With a pop and fizzle the dying magics sparked and incinerated the neat sheaf of documents within almost instantly.

But Brody urged his Vigil to try again, all the while feeling that time was slipping away–that he was reaching the summit of some mountain, the climax of a story. He couldn't have explained, even to himself, why he felt this way, but there were a few who seemed to sense his anxiety. Dante made more frequent efforts to seek him out and nuzzle him, laying at his feet and resting his gentle, horned head on Brody's knee. Khogar stood at arms-length when Brody gathered his Companions to speak, her cat perceptions sensitive to the king's tension, ears flat, eyes privately concerned. Domine had taken to fidgeting irritably in his presence, as if he itched.

The second outpost had been gutted, as if the Rankers had departed hastily and abandoned it to the elements. The third bore fruit. Though ramshackle and abandoned, its security room and vault boxes were intact and ripe for the plunder. Under Brody's command, and despite pushback from Councilman Isa, the King's Council had commissioned a rather expensive inventor in the kingdom to create a new golem. It had only taken the man a little over a week to concoct something with the mechanical intelligence of a metal golem and the nearly microscopic form of a creature straight out of the *Terminator* movies that Brody had been fond of as a youth. Its minute, robotic frame arrived to them in a small metal canister delivered by messenger bird.

Once Brody opened the lid and coaxed the tiny creature out onto the lid of the vault box, it clicked, chirped a chirp almost too high-pitched for even Brody's griffin hearing to detect, found the seam between the box's lid and body, and set to work.

It had been designed to function as a bacteria, to work systematically to destroy the vault box's magical defenses. Within minutes, Brody tilted his head at hearing a series of small hisses, like drops of water on a hot skillet, and the lid sprang open. Someone came forward to collect the triumphant little golem, and two guards moved at the same time to shield Brody from the potential hazard of unleashed magics, but Brody shrugged them away with a stern command and used the tip of his bo staff to ease the lid open the rest of the way.

Within lay a neat stack of small scrolls sealed with blackish-red wax. Brody scooped them out, ignoring the grandmotherly concern exhibited by his guards as they grumbled at his shoulders. His companions came forward from where they'd been pressed against the hewn-stone wall with bated breath.

"What are they?" Aydran asked, but Brody had already torn one open and stretched it flat upon a nearby tabletop to reveal several detailed charcoal sketches. Everyone became completely silent as they studied the human figures streaked against the ivory parchment. Brody felt first confusion and consternation. He didn't recognize the faces, nor could he read the symbols beside them. Some had a messy scribble slashed through them. He handed it to Aydran and broke the seal of the next while Abram leaned close to the bard to mutter thoughtfully over the illustrations.

Brody shook the second scroll open and felt his heart skip a beat. *This* face he recognized. It was his own; an eerily precise, life-size sketch of Brody's face from perhaps twelve years ago. Everything, from the shape and set of his eyes, to the beginnings of the scar at his collarbone just visible at the bottom of the page, to his serious but curious expression–everything had been almost lovingly captured on the parchment.

He touched a few lines of symbols by the illustration of his temple. Questions sprouted in his mind: Had they been watching him this long? Taking notes? Studying and observing him like he was some new, dangerous creature? Had his beacon been so bright that even years before he had arrived in the dreamworld a griffin, they had known he would be a significant threat? That he would become a king?

He glanced at the first scroll. It had passed now into Khogar's paws and the tribal blinked curiously down at it. Were these, then, other targets? Other victims? Khogar seemed to be of a similar mind. She touched each of the sketches in turn with her silvery paw as if performing some sort of ritual, her whiskers twitching as she whispered something soft and gentle to the unknown figures.

Domine had taken up the third scroll and opened it, then held it at arms-length with a startled grunt. "What manner of beast is this?" he growled. Abram looked over the titan's shoulder and paled noticeably–piquing Brody's curiosity.

He joined them and Domine allowed him to take one side of the scroll. Everyone else, including the guards, gathered in close. Within, splashed across the parchment in thick, black streaks, smudged in places where the charcoal had broken and been smeared by the artist's hand as if they had created their work in some impassioned frenzy of emotion, was a four-legged monster of a sort that none of them had ever seen.

It was like something once beautiful and powerful, a glorious creature embracing the highlights of creation, that had been tragically twisted and tortured so as to belong in man's deepest, most anguished nightmares. It was nearly indescribable in its horrificness.

Half of it seemed to be made of smoke, as if it had been born from a cloud of ash. Its wings were skeletal, like a dragon's, with sharp spikes along the outer edge that could deal lethal wounds should the creature slash close past something in flight. The tail was extremely long and whip-like, and the bones pressed out against lizard-like skin and thick, glossy feathers. Worst of all was the face. It resembled a human skull with slightly elongated, sharp-toothed jaws. Horns curved at its brow, the sides of its head, where the skull met the neck, and tusks stuck out from beneath the empty eye sockets. A thick, black liquid, like ink or tar, ran from its mouth and eyes and smoke billowed out from where its ears should have been. Everything about the monster was pain and suffering.

"This is a Dark Griffin," Brody said, speaking slowly and carefully to disguise the fear that wanted to quiver in his voice. "This is what they wanted to turn me into."

After a pause soured by tension, Aydran said in an uncharacteristically subdued manner, "Well thank God they didn't."

"One scroll left," Abram said, reaching into the box. Brody set the Dark Griffin scroll down and took up the last, breaking its seal and unraveling it carefully in case it, too, bore an unpleasant, startling image. But he needn't have bothered. This one was covered in a strange script; each glyph a rounded symbol surrounded by spikes and dots.

"It's in a code or a different language," Brody said. He rolled it back up and tucked it into his belt. "Maybe Michael can crack it." He lifted his head to the hole in the stone wall meant to serve as a window. It was darkening to dusk without. He scented the glowing moon irises as they opened to soak up the lunar rays and spread their glittering pollen. He scented the mist rising from secret streams and heard the high squeaking of bats. A smattering of blue and white stars, and a few golden pinheads that were other suns had just begun to emerge through the gaps in the moon-silvered clouds.

"But it grows late. I would rather not linger here."

They departed as swiftly as they were able, riding for their camp some six miles distant. The party was silent the entire way. Even back among their tents they treaded lightly, unaccustomed to the weight of soundlessness away from the army. Brody's troops made for the capital now. Six of the Deadly Seven were dead and the last had dropped beyond even the wildest rumor. Sylph had, it seemed, vanished. Now it was Brody and his Companions once more, digging for answers in Wrath's derelict hovels before rejoining the knights and finally returning to the palace after almost five years.

As Brody climbed into his cot, Dante stuck his horned head in through the tent flap. Observing Brody for a while from his large, doe-like eyes, the unicorn entered the rest of the way, circled once, and lay down. Brody smiled and snuffed his bedside candle, settling back and closing his eyes.

He missed his castle. He missed his home. The two had become synonymous over the years, when the nearest thing to home had been the dusty, dangerous road. Sleep seeped over him like a heavy blanket or a dark fog and his thoughts wandered. His dreams had been enigmatic of late. He'd found it becoming more difficult to delve into the sleeping minds of others and send them advice or warning, as if he were distracted by a murmur and left confused and aimless. He awoke weary and sore and wondered if only his desire for vengeance was all that kept him going, and no longer a kingly obligation to duty.

Vengeance. Such a word. Retribution. Revenge. Payback.

Brody's dreams that night were tinted red and blistered with heat. He walked the Hall of Paintings in his castle, studying the likenesses of those who had ruled before. Behind each figure in its frame was a strange, vaguely humanoid shadow as if a man stood just the other side of a curtain. The further he moved down the hall, the nearer he got to his predecessor King Uriah, the closer and closer that shadow became.

A blonde-haired woman waited at the end of the hall, her back to him. A question sprang into his mind, and he asked it of her.

"Where is your base of operations?"

The dream changed. He walked home from school, touching his hand to wizened tree trunks that he hadn't seen in half a lifetime as if to reacquaint them with his presence. Sylph walked past him alongside a seasonal brook, turning stones over with her foot. Though he couldn't *see* it, Brody sensed that there was another presence nearby, watching.

Sylph bent to lift a snake that she had startled to movement, letting it twine around her wrist, crooning to it. Brody's flesh prickled with hatred.

"What power allows you to cross over into my world?"

Again, the dream changed. He stumbled along a dark sidewalk glistening with rain. Vehicles sped past, college students stood in the doorways of restaurants and pubs, laughing cheerily, their words a garbled slur to Brody's ears. He smelled the alcohol on his own breath. Sylph stood right beside him, supporting him.

"What are the pathmarkers?"

When she didn't answer, he mustered all of his focus and felt the strands of the dream fray like stretching ropes. He drove her hard against the wall beside them, one hand knotted around her long, silky hair.

"Speak, you evil bitch!"

She emitted a horrible shriek and threw him back, away from her. There was a squeal of brakes, the flash of headlights, intense pressure as if his entire skeleton were being forced out through his skin.

He was in a hospital bed. His mother and father–how aged they looked!–spoke out in the hallway with a doctor who shook his head and gestured at his own torso as if explaining something about internal damage. Brody sat up and moved slowly toward them, dragging along his I.V.

"It's a miracle he's lived this long," the doctor said gently, "but there's been so much deterioration. There's nothing we can do. He's shutting down."

Are they talking about me? Brody wondered. Something fell behind him. He turned and saw a canister of pills roll toward him. But the room was empty. He stalked forward, glaring into the corners, at the gap beneath his bed, at the curtains drawn at the window.

"Where are you?" he growled. His query was met with silence.

Then one giant claw wrapped around him and a hideous, masked face, painted like a harlequin's, snaked over his shoulder on a sinuous neck and whispered, "Right behind you." Those claws squeezed and Brody felt himself spinning into a dark abyss. He saw something below him; a sea of waves…an island of forsaken, pitted rock…a fortress lit with thousands of candles and reeking of Rankers.

Then Brody awoke and heard Josiah just outside his tent, summoning him. Dante nibbled persistently at Brody's ear, and he suspected that the unicorn had been attempting to rouse him for quite a bit now. He sat up, stroking Dante's velvety muzzle and stretching sore muscles. His nightmares clung to him still, though Dante's strange, pure magic slowly warded them away. *Fey* seemed unnaturally cold against his cheek. He took a moment to shove back his premonitions and hide his remaining uneasiness, then stood and opened his tent flap, grinning at his old friend.

"Josiah! It's been too long!"

Rexus jumped, chattering, from Josiah's shoulders to Brody's, twining his weaselly body around Brody's neck and pressing his head against Brody's jaw. But Josiah looked weary and forlorn. He smiled, but the expression was weak. He looked distracted by weighty news, and as if he struggled against tears.

"What's wrong?" Brody asked with concern, lifting his arms subconsciously as if to reach out and catch Josiah should he collapse. Josiah blinked rapidly at him.

"Michael is here. He wishes to speak with you about...that Ranker letter that you wanted him to translate. He's on the cliff-side just east of here." He took a pair of long steps and embraced Brody, his king, his friend, tightly. Even after Brody had returned the squeeze, Josiah remained latched on. Heat radiated off of him as from the body of someone in great anguish of spirit. Brody wrestled with his alarm.

"Josiah? What's wrong?" he asked again.

A moment longer and then Josiah released him, smiling with whatever false cheer he could muster. "Nothing. It's...it's good to see you again, that's all."

Brody hesitated, trying to read further, trying to pick through the cracks in Josiah's words, but his friend said quickly, "Better hurry. Don't want to keep Michael waiting." He stuck his arm out, elbow cocked, Rexus jumped to it like a trained parrot, and the pair soon vanished into the morning mist around their campsite. Brody heard a collection of loud, powerful wingbeats, and a scarlet griffin feather came spinning lazily from the sky to rest, stark and lonely, against the grass.

Chapter Thirty-Nine:

Final Preparations

"Has this world been so kind to you that you should leave with regret? There are better things ahead than any we leave behind."

–C.S. Lewis

Brody puzzled over Josiah's behavior all the way to where Michael awaited him. He hadn't spoken to his old friend in quite some time, busy as the scarlet griffin was with showing Peter around.

He frowned to himself, automatically using his bo staff to nudge aside a fir branch laden heavily with needles as Dante cantered along a deer trail. The saddle was his second home now–he adjusted his weight and stance with nary a thought as the unicorn blazed his trail and as his own mind swam with confusion.

And who was Peter, anyway? A dreamer who took studious and diligent notes on the dreamworld and its denizens...why? For the first time, Brody acknowledged the events that seemed to be taking place behind his back and wondered at their purpose; at why he had been kept in the dark.

Then Dante sprang over a lattice of tree roots and out of the forest onto a marvelous cliffside vista. Behind them, Brody could now clearly see the jagged mountain range upon whose highest, cloud-hidden peak squatted the abandoned fortress of Skybridge. In the distant east sparkled the enormous lake that skirted tribal territory. Ahead the bells and carefully sculpted, blown-glass towers of the Kingdom of Bells and Union Town glittered. And sprawling below them to the west beyond the alders, maples, and aspens that dazzled with fiery autumnal beauty, stretched the valleys and vales of the druidic clans.

Michael, his white pelt and feathers almost blinding in the sunlight, reclined, leonine, near the edge of the precipice, his talons dangling off of it. Even laying down, his head was nearly level with Dante's. One ear turned back to listen to them. Brody dismounted gracefully and approached on foot, one hand resting on the shoulder of his unicorn, who walked alongside him.

"Josiah said you've deciphered the letter?" Brody asked hopefully, his worries muted in the presence of the powerful and enigmatic griffin.

"Yes," Michael said softly. "It is done." He stood and Brody realized that he held an oiled-leather tube in one of his talons. Michael dropped it carefully into Brody's hands and Brody tried to tame his movements into something a little less eager as he popped open the lid and shook out a sheaf of parchment: the coded scroll from Wrath's fortress; translated. He read through the letter once, then again, puzzling out the strange dialect and picking apart the Rankers' lingo.

"'High General Garrett has already initiated the Crossing...'" Brody read aloud, "'Even now he walks the world of the creators and sows the seeds of discord, preparing the way for the rest of our troops. He remains ever-vigilant for the griffin-hearted, lest they chance to interfere...' So it isn't just the Seven Deadly crossing over, it's all of them–it's an army!" Brody looked up at Michael in alarm. "*All* of them, en masse. Would they wage their war in reality?"

"War has always found its choice battlegrounds in reality," the White Griffin replied, unreadable. Brody considered. There would be no magic to aid humanity in the cold darkness of reality. No transforming into a griffin. But *how* were the Rankers stepping over? What power aided them? He read on.

"'Use the pathmarkers to find the location of our base of operations... Send word to our allies that the first shall be located at the southern coast and will call to them once established. Let them march as a scourge through the false king's lands, razing his cities to the ground...' The pathmarkers are clues! Or...coordinates?" Brody read the remainder of the letter to himself, lips moving soundlessly. "But it doesn't divulge the location of their base or the identity of their leader beyond a name and title. High General Garrett, hmmm..."

He looked up. Michael gazed impassively out over the world, gleaming like a star. Brody wondered at his silence, impatient, and remembered Josiah's odd behavior earlier. A cold, creeping worry climbed his backbone. He tried to ignore it.

"No matter. We've enough here to act with finality. We will fight, and finally purify this land. I'll go to the council. They'll not approve of a declaration of war, at least Isa won't..." he grimaced at the thought of arguing with the arrogant, disagreeable man. Dante, sensing the turmoil of Brody's emotions, stepped closer so that Brody could comb his mane.

"Perhaps you could intervene on my behalf?" Brody asked Michael hopefully, giving Dante a gentle pat across the withers. "They'll listen to you." He waited, but the White Griffin did not respond. Brody would not be deterred, however, and he stubbornly held his silence, waiting, taking deep, calm breaths.

The griffin shifted so that he sat facing Brody, his neck arched gracefully like a swan's, beak almost touching his breast, and eyes veiled.

"You've one further step on your journey. One final test that awaits."

That cold worry became an icy fear that almost strangled away Brody's voice and sapped the strength from his limbs.

"One further? Before what? What do you mean?"

"Before your eternal reward and everlasting peace."

Brody stared at him, his spirits crushed, suddenly drained of energy. His vision blurred with tears and his legs shook so that he had to lean against Dante or else fall.

Michael, watching him, his eyes suddenly brilliant with compassion, said heavily, "He weeps; oh, how he weeps for you."

Brody didn't ask him what he meant–there was only one question scorching his mind, beating in his chest–the one, powerful question that all humans dread to ask.

"I'm going to die, aren't I?"

Michael, after a pause, dipped his head. Dante whickered.

Brody sank to his knees, squeezing his hands into fists that he then pressed against his body as if to hold back the geyser of anguish threatening to gush from his soul. Everything he had ever felt before;

every terror, every sorrow, his every pain, was paltry compared to this. His strength was suddenly as a child's; his wisdom as insubstantial as wind; his courage as yielding as a blade of grass to a boot. The lines of the prophecy played through his mind, but they were no longer encouraging. Now, they seemed mocking, each word stinging in his brain.

'Eclipsed the sun, corrupted all, a King shall rise, a King shall fall.'

"But..." He clenched his teeth together until his jaw ached. He had been about to say that he was supposed to defeat the Rankers, that he was meant to fulfill the prophecy, but his throat tightened, and he didn't trust his ability to keep the quiver of cowardice from his voice.

"Why?" he asked instead. As if that one word had been a cork removed from a bottle, all of his emotions bubbled up and he started to shake. "Did I do something wrong?"

"Not at all," Michael said softly.

"Then *why?*" Brody's voice cracked and tears trickled down his cheeks. Fear, betrayal, anger, confusion, all twisted around inside of him in a knotted mess. Dante whickered and nuzzled his cheek but Brody didn't feel it. "This is..." All of his questions left him as if vacuumed away. He bent forward and clasped his hands before him as if to pray, but he didn't have any more strength. In the back of his mind he'd always thought he would defeat the Seven Deadly, stop the Ranker plans, fulfill the prophecy, and go back home. But back to what? Josiah's reports on his condition hadn't been promising. What quality of life did he have to look forward to back in reality? No. This had always been his fate. To die here. A second wave of tears sprang to his sinuses.

"The prophecy continues to unfold, child," Michael said. Brody took a tortured breath. His lungs felt like they had shrunk.

The White Griffin continued, still speaking in that patient, comforting voice. "Your race is won. You have fulfilled the tasks set out for you. Your soul is ready to depart its broken vessel. Now comes the final step, the most difficult test for every griffin ruler. You must leave your crown for the next individual fated to sit the winged throne, and trust that all is in control; that all plays out as it is meant to."

Brody sniffled and didn't respond. His insides turned somersaults, his helplessness gnawed at him, grinding at his bones.

Michael came one step nearer and spoke down to him, his breath as warm and comforting as sunlight. "Do you think the journey over, young king? No. This is but the closing of a book and the opening of another. You face the beginning of a path whereupon countless many before you have stepped, and it is not a path of dirt and shadow, where rocks await to turn your ankle. It is a golden path, a brilliant path, and at the end..." He dwindled off and Brody looked up into his face. Michael's eyes gleamed with a loving light that Brody hadn't seen there before. It reminded him painfully of his father, somehow.

"Words cannot describe," Michael finished.

"W-when?" Brody asked, drying his tears with the heels of his hands. "When will it h-happen?"

"Soon, child," Michael said. Though he stood but a step away, the White Griffin was too far for Brody to appeal to, to seek solace from; his ways too different. But then he looked up and saw that Michael's wings were open, spread so as to eclipse his view of the realm. Hundreds, if not thousands, of images raced into his eyes, past his vision. They came too fast for him to register, but a feeling of peace embraced him. His tears fell freely now, but they were not of sadness.

"What should I do?" he asked, and his voice was strong. He found his feet.

"Fight until the very end," Michael said, his wings folding closed. Dante leaned against Brody with a soft snort. Brody nodded. He squeezed the letter in his hand and mounted the unicorn. Before turning 'round back along the path, Brody turned his head to look at Michael, who perked up his ears attentively.

"Please...will you retire my council? I would like a new one chosen for my..." he swallowed hard around the golf ball in his throat, "my successor. People who are loyal, fresh, obedient, and strong."

"I shall select them myself," Michael said.

Brody bowed his head and let Dante canter back into the tree shadows. Behind him Michael murmured, "Farewell, King Brody the Gallant." Then he gave a mighty lion's roar accentuated by a piercing eagle-shriek–a griffin's call–a tribute, a salute, to a young man who had ruled well.

"What is it I'm to do?"

Brody could tell that Abram was frustrated. This was the first time in five years that they would be apart. Perhaps he could sense Brody's sorrow, some of the anguish that had driven Brody to meet him in his own tent, in the wee hours of the morning, away from their other friends.

"Have I done something to upset you?" Abram asked, his voice wounded. It brought the sting of tears to Brody's sinuses–helpless tears that could not be shed, lest they betray him.

He needed Abram in the capital city to reassure the people, in case his body finally failed in reality before he could return himself. He needed Abram to be a shepherd and lead the flock, to use his compassionate heart and gentle understanding to speak peace unto those who would grieve. To stand ready as a counselor and to welcome whomever came next to sit the throne.

"I want you to help Michael," Brody said lamely.

"Michael doesn't need help!" Abram cried. Brody heard Domine grumble in his sleep in one of the nearby tents at Abram's raised tone. "And why are you changing the council at a time like this? Couldn't it wait?"

"No," Brody said shortly. He finally looked away from the wall of Abram's tent and fastened his deep, amber-green eyes intently on Abram, frowning. He saw the agitation on Abram's face; the unyielding loyalty and unflinching courage that would have him giving his last breath in service to his king and friend.

Abram must have seen something in Brody, too. Concern dropped like a cloud across his features and he put a fatherly hand on Brody's shoulder. "What aren't you telling me, son?"

Brody almost told him, then. The age-old urge to confess arose, hard and bruising in his chest, up into his throat. But he couldn't give it voice. To share this, his final secret, to give it power with his words and breath, would overcome him. Instead, he stepped forward and embraced Abram tightly.

"Thank you for standing beside me."

Abram patted his back gingerly at first, as if frightened. Then he wrapped his arms tightly around Brody, stroking the back of the king's head like a father comforting his child. "Always," he said quietly.

When Brody released him and stepped back away, he saw the weight of understanding, a sting of suspicion, deepening the lines on Abram's face. For the first time, Brody saw how much the man had aged in the years they had journeyed; how gray was his hair and stooped were his shoulders. Though he was a griffin, he was no warrior...his gifts were much more priceless: wisdom, comfort for the downtrodden, compassion for the suffering soul whose sword-arm needed strengthening and whose shield needed the dents taken from it.

The pastor began to weep, tears trickling down his cheeks, lips trembling, breath hitching. "F-fear no–no evil..." he said, lifting his hand to grip Brody around the back of the neck, looking deeply and severely into Brody's eyes, "for He is with thee... His rod and staff c-comfort thee. He–He prepares a table before thee in the presence of thine enemies. H-He anoints thine head with oil..."

Brody closed his eyes. This was his father's favorite psalm–he remembered hearing him recite it in the dark, early morning hours from his bedroom when the demons from the war haunted his father most. He whispered the last verse with the pastor.

"'Surely Your goodness and love will follow me all the days of my life, and I will dwell in the house of the Lord...forever.'"

"Amen," Abram said, his voice now so harsh, his breathing so broken, that it sounded like a snarl. He rested his forehead against Brody's, clapped his hands twice against Brody's arms, and then abruptly withdrew, his footsteps receding through the dry, late-summer grass outside.

"Wait, where's ol' Abram?" Aydran asked. He plucked his viol in a spunky way from the back of his white-and-chestnut horse, which leaned against a tree with all four of its legs crossed. He watched the others work, dismantling their tents, trying to economically place the items in their packs so as to preserve space. "I mean, who's gonna keep an eye on me?"

Domine stood and stretched his back with a growl, his spine popping. He pointed at Aydran with the stem of his pipe. "Will you help us or just sit on your skinny ass like bump on a rock?"

Aydran held up his finger. "First of all," he turned his hand so that he pointed down at his steed. "This is a *horse* and he's been gaining weight, thank you. Secondly, it's 'bump on a log.'"

"What is?" Domine glared.

"The expression you're looking for–bump on a log, not rock."

Domine spun to look up at Brody, who had just finished strapping his saddlebags onto Dante and climbed into the saddle. "Where *is* Abram?" He sounded exasperated.

"On an errand for his king," Brody said, in a tone that heavily implied that he would say no more on the subject. Domine tilted his head at Brody in an uncannily ursine way, unsettled, perhaps, at the barely perceptible strain in his voice.

"You hear that? I'm all yours!" Aydran flashed Domine a charming smile.

"The poor man probably needed a break," Khogar said mildly, attaching the beautifully stamped leather reins she'd recently tanned to her horse's bridle. Aydran started playing his viol in time to Khogar's actions. The tribal's whiskers twitched and she primly ignored the grinning bard.

"Let's move out," Brody said. His throat tightened. He would miss his friends; the laughter, the encouragement, the feeling of having companions at his side who loved and respected him.

Domine gave him one last concerned look, then climbed atop his dark stallion and followed Khogar out of the clearing at a canter.

Chapter Forty:

King Brody the Gallant

"You never know how much you really believe anything until its truth or falsehood becomes a matter of life and death to you."
–C.S. Lewis, *A Grief Observed*

On the path to the Seat of Griffins, Brody immersed himself in the scrolls they had taken from Wrath's last stronghold–especially the letter that Michael had translated. He attempted to translate the symbols on the other scrolls using the letter as a code breaker but hadn't discovered much of use so far.

"Remind me what we found out, again?" Aydran asked, ducking so that a large fir branch they passed wouldn't sweep off his bard's hat.

Their mounts cautiously picked their way along a very narrow path carpeted with stones, long-abandoned shells of some kind, and pinecones–some as large as Brody's head. It was dim here in the shadows cast by the behemoth branches intertwined above them and blocking enough of the sky so that only a few meager sunbeams made it through to inform them that it was still daytime. The gloom, though peaceful, wasn't entirely pleasant. Not many birds saw the enclosed and dimly lit place as attractive for nesting. The absence of their song left only the secret, mysterious noises of an ancient forest–creaking trunks, rustling undergrowth, the skittering pawsteps of some passing critter.

Without looking up from his work, Brody said, "The Rankers intend to cross over into reality, and the pathmarkers are clues intended to guide Ranker allies to their 'base of operations.' The first pathmarker will be along the southern coast–most likely at Pebble Embark."

He thought of the day, five years ago, when he had arrived on that golden beach, washed upon its shores like a bedraggled chicken, and wondered if there was intentional irony in the Rankers' decision.

A maple leaf large enough to be a child's blanket landed on the path directly in front of Dante, almost spearing itself on his horn. Dante shied a little, his cloven hooves dancing, his tasseled ears spinning. Brody looked up to see a cat-sized red squirrel scampering from branch to branch. None of their mounts much approved of this forest. But this lonely path was the quickest way back to the capital city and the Seat of Griffins. They would cut through the Misty Pass, realm of the elves, within the month, but until then they had to stomach these primordial woods–home, perhaps, to mankind's wilder, harsher dreams.

"And when we get home, we'll make a plan of action, aye." Aydran deftly spun so as to sit side-saddle and look back at Brody. "So why are you staring at those scrolls like a scholar with no girlfriend? What else is there?"

Brody rubbed at the tunic and mail over his scars as if absently rubbing away a dull pain. "Where *is* their base? Who is their leader?"

Fey throbbed dimly with warmth at his cheek and he transferred his touch to the intricate metalwork of the elaborate ear cuff. If he focused, he could see the multitude of images that *Fey* sent him: an icicle dyed red in the setting sun behind it, a coppery griffin's feather, a bouquet of flowers bound with blue ribbon, a joyous smile framed by tear-streaks. But ever since seeing the images in Michael's wings, those generated by *Fey* had been too many and too bizarre for Brody to pay much mind. His thoughts were too turbulent and his heart too unsettled.

"I thought Garrett was their leader?" Aydran asked tentatively. "He's the one addressed in all their letters?"

Brody deciphered another symbol and added it to the key he was making with a few scratches of his quill. "Everything we've found about Garrett refers to him as the 'high general,'" Brody mumbled distractedly. "High generals answer to someone..."

They lapsed into silence for a time, dismal in the dreary dark of the ancient trees, trees that, Brody considered, had probably been wizened in King David the First's time. Aydran strummed a slow tune that was somewhat smothered by the gnarled roots, mounds of soil, and thistle thickets and Khogar, leading their party, hummed along.

Noon passed, and Brody began having to rely on his griffin vision to read and write by. Domine spoke low behind him–he tilted his head to hear.

"You are agitated," the titan rumbled.

Fey sent Brody a rather poignant impression of a tight, warm embrace and he winced, thinking of his parents. He wished with an intensity that burned that he could have seen them one last time and bade them farewell. A few of the lingering sensations from Michael's wings returned and peace once again seeped over him.

"I'm homesick, that's all," he said to Domine. "I miss my parents. My friends."

"Why?" Domine asked. He sounded honestly bewildered. "Are we not your friends? Your family?"

Brody smiled down at Dante's saddle horn. "You are," he said. "But sometimes among my kind the bonds of blood hold us fast, even when we're separated by leagues. Our families shape us well into maturity."

"And this...makes you stronger?" Domine, a man among his people when still a child, raised to adulthood by the elements and the bitter hardships of solitude, could not understand. But Brody thought of his father's wise parables and sage advice with grateful fondness.

"Yes... They made me stronger."

Ahead, Aydran and Khogar argued over whether or not their army would disband now that all captured holdings had been brought back under control.

"We've still one of the Seven Deadly to find," Khogar said patiently.

"Yeah, I remember that bitch," Aydran replied. "But she moves too fast. We'd be better off sending some Eyes after her, making it a covert operation all sneaky-like." He strummed some danger music on his viol.

"She will be found," Khogar said, as if to reassure Brody. "The viper, the wind, the truth, all are swift and all must rest."

Brody considered his personal vendetta against Sylph as if he stood opposite a great chasm from it. The rage that had driven him so forcefully had drained away like water after Michael's news. What did it matter anymore? He would soon join his ancestors beyond this world of ghosts, grievances, and vengeance. Now, he sought only rest, and a few final answers.

Eventually he had pieced out enough of the Rankers' strange script to begin transcribing the notes on the scrolls into recognizable sentences. He ran his fingers across the line of text near the illustration of his face, his lips moving soundlessly, hungrily, as he read, *The Dark One requires that we play on his fears, then shape them into Sin.* Beneath this was a list of the seven Ranker lords and ladies and one final bit of instruction as if it had been afterthought: *Reports mention a heavy influence of idealism. Apply your powers towards weakening this foundation.* But Brody ignored this. He was transfixed by the first three words. Who or what was the Dark One? Another of General Garrett's titles? Another name for Wrath?

There was nothing of import in what comments there were on the page bearing the charcoal illustration of the Dark Griffin. He turned impatiently to the last page, the one covered in sketches of human figures. The pale parchment tore slightly at his hasty grip. There was a small heading at the top. The best he could make out was something like, *Master's Chosen*, though he couldn't be sure. Next to each sketch was a label or something similar that varied from person to person: *Dark Soul, Dark Soul, Griffin Hearted, General Garrett's Own*... Who was the 'Master?'

With a grunt of frustration Brody scoured the notes for something, anything, he had missed. He found a line of smudged script almost hidden in the shading of the shoulder of a young man's portrait. He scribbled the translation above it with feverish quill-strokes, then read what he had written: *The Dark One has expressed great interest in him and requires that High General Garrett begin the Crossing as soon as the moment proves opportune.*

The Dark One. High General Garrett. Two separate entities.

"*Halt*!" Brody shouted. Dante stopped immediately, locking his long, deer-like limbs and lashing his lion-like tail uneasily. The others yanked on the reins and their mounts dug in their hooves, whinnying indignantly and tossing their manes.

"What's wrong?" Aydran asked, a little peeved at having his viol shoved against his nose. Brody felt their eyes and their alarm. Domine's stallion huffed behind him and Domine grumbled something at it in his own language.

"There's someone else in charge," Brody said. His heart thudded in his chest like an elephant stomping its legs. He felt breathless, exhilarated at pulling aside the veil in the shadows to expose this Ranker secret, horrified at what it meant.

"Of what, High King?" Khogar asked from the front, turning her shaggy pony about.

"The Rankers!" Brody spoke hurriedly even as his mind raced along a myriad of paths. What to do with this information? It changed everything–their plans, their strategy, his goal as king, all needed to transform to accommodate what Brody now knew to be a powerful and imminent threat.

"Someone other than this 'Garrett' governs our enemy?" Domine asked.

"*Yes,*" Brody said emphatically. *Fey* was warm on his cheek but Brody didn't know whether this was because of the flush rising in his face or not. Images pressed in on his mind as the cuff responded to his stress: the flash of a black pelt, a ruby in the shape of a heart that transformed into a drop of blood, a shattered sword half-buried in the grass.

"Well...well this is..." Aydran was speechless. "Who... I mean... *Who can control the Seven Deadly Sins?*"

"Someone incredibly formidable," Brody replied as he rolled up the scrolls and stuffed them away. He considered taking *Fey* off as another round of images came to him, distracting in their detail.

"Good," Domine growled. "Finally, a worthy foe."

"The hell's every Ranker been up until now?" Aydran cried.

Domine shrugged. "Paltry."

"What shall we do with this information?" Khogar asked.

Brody had dismounted and moved to squeeze between Domine's horse and the cluster of vine maples beside the trail to the clear space behind their party.

"I'm going to transform and fly to the capital. They're going to gather their allies soon, if they haven't begun already and we need to muster our own armies."

"Gooooood!" Domine practically roared.

Dante had managed to rear up and turn on the spot and was trying to shoulder past Domine to get to Brody.

"No, my friend," Brody said–*Fey* was almost too hot now on his jaw– "I'll return as soon as I can."

"Go, fly! We'll make camp the next clearing we find," Aydran said.

Domine cried out when Dante shreed and redoubled his efforts to pass. Domine's stallion nipped at the unicorn, ears flat, but Dante ignored it, using his horn to prick the horse's side until he'd managed to prod it far enough aside to make it by.

Brody's companions had joined him in chiding the unicorn, shouting in bewilderment at the sudden, rabid change in his demeanor. Brody held his hands out, suddenly fearful of Dante, those cloven heels and that sharp horn. But the black unicorn pulled up short, his pale mane bristling on his arched neck.

Domine had just dismounted to check his mount's grazes when a large tree branch fell from far above them, rolled off a lower bough, and landed against the trunks with a rustle of pine needles.

"Whoa," Aydran said, "That must be one heck of a large..."

Brody looked up instinctively, his eyes lifting even before his head was tilting on his neck. *Fey* sent him an image of a giant spider with its legs stretched across its web. But it wasn't a spider spread across the trail above them.

A dozen beautiful, winged Rankers hovered in a ring overhead like marionettes on strings–a frozen mural of surreal magnificence and crushing doom. And in the midst of them all was Sylph in her true form, each of her four talons wrapped around a tree trunk.

As quick as a blink, Sylph dropped and pinned Aydran to a tree through the chest with the broken branch. Brody made a sound that was part scream and part gasp–the crunch of his friend's ribs, the spurt of arterial blood that splashed across Sylph's harlequin face, were agonies that he felt in the depths of his soul.

Even as the others stirred to action, Brody saw Sylph kick aside Aydran's horse, breaking its two front legs, and heard her murmur into the dying man's face: "A bitch, am I?"

Aydran gurgled something, his teeth limned red, his flesh as white as a bone, and then his head fell back against the tree. He breathed his last.

Sylph left him where he stuck and turned slowly to face Brody. With one step she shattered poor Aydran's viol into chips of wood and twanging strings. With another, she broke the neck of Aydran's horse where it thrashed on the ground kicking up a cloud of dirt. Then the twelve angelic Rankers fell, and there was only chaos.

Chapter Forty-One:

Righteous Wrath

"He that falls obstinate in his courage [...] who, dying, yet darts at his enemy a fierce and disdainful look, is overcome not by us, but by fortune; he is killed, not conquered..."

–Michel de Montaigne

Brody's view of Sylph became blocked when Domine sprang from his horse, tumbled across the ground, and came up the mountain bear, almost ten feet tall on his hind legs. He roared fiercely at the enemy; a sound that vibrated in Brody's rib cage.

One of the Rankers slashed Domine's stallion across the throat with its sword and the horse died instantly, 1500 pounds of muscle dropping to the earth–now nothing more than meat. Domine turned and lunged at the Ranker. With one sweep of a paw, he almost tore one of its wings from its body. Then Sylph stretched her serpentine neck above the melee, grinning nastily down at the titan. She extended her forelimb toward him and Domine roared again.

"Go!" Khogar shouted from somewhere at the other side of the battle. "Fly, Great King!" Two of the Rankers tried to get at Brody, but Domine spread his paws across the trail, and they had to pull up short, snarling, swords raised.

Brody turned, half-mad with panic, excitement, ferocity, and sprinted a decent length away like a crazed rabbit. Then he heard Domine grunt in pain and he stopped. One of the Rankers had severed the titan's left limb just above the paw–fresh blood spouted against the uniform brown and green of nature and joined the treacherous pools turning black and slick in the soil underfoot. The other Ranker swiped at Domine and sliced a deep wound in the dark, curly pelt. Domine's defiant, pained cry made Brody flinch.

In the instant that he stood there, the young king thought of his father, who had never left a comrade behind, alone, to force upon the foe one final glare before being pierced upon the enemy's bayonet. Brody glanced at Aydran, dangling from the tree, thought of how the bard's last vision had been of Sylph, but how he had died with his friends around him, avenging him as best they could, as he must have known they would–as he would have done for them.

And Brody turned on his heel and charged back to the fray, Dante a black comet stretching beside him, chin low and horn down, long legs out for the plunge. The flapping wings of the foe, their strikingly black robes, were his sole focus, his entire world. He lifted his chin and his eyes shone crimson. He readied his bo staff. If this was how it was to be, then he would have it no other way.

Dante ducked beneath Domine's outstretched, shaggy limb and sprang up, parrying a blade with his horn. White sparks danced on contact.

Brody appeared around Domine's other side, his posture fierce and challenging. Sylph saw him and her red smile stretched to frame her eyes. Coiling her neck over and around the flapping wings and flashing swords of her comrades, she reached out at him, claws spread.

Domine, his mutilated limb pressed tight against his chest, stretched his jaws wide and sank his teeth into that grasping arm, tearing a chunk of flesh from the bone with a brutal jerk of his head, but Brody could tell that he was weakening. Sylph screamed–a prehistoric sort of sound–and focused instead on the titan, striking with her shark-teeth bared like a cobra.

A Ranker brave enough to meet Brody's challenge faced the king head-on, declaring itself with an arrogant flap of its impressive, feathered wings. Brody was reminded of a vampire bat baring its fangs, bloated with its sanguine meal; a vicious pike dragging a swan's carcass to the depths of a lake. With an impatient growl, Brody yanked *Fey* from his face and threw it into the midst of bodies.

The Ranker stabbed in, blade angled so as to catch Brody's liver, but the king was quicker. He jabbed his bo staff at the Ranker's face like a halberd. The end smashed through the nightmare's eye socket and a portion of its face shattered like porcelain to reveal something like a skull made of smoke beneath. The Ranker cried out–a scream that made the earth quake as if it writhed with terror. Brody's own voice rose in response and his eyes were as crimson as Josiah's feathers.

He drove the Ranker back, controlling it, master and orchestrator of its pain, then gave it a contemptuous flick so that it slid off the end of Brody's stave and into another Ranker coming in from the side, knocking it down. A third Ranker swung its sword down to cleave at Brody's skull and he wisely disengaged, but a little too slow. The sword severed his staff cleanly in two–and the jarring impact knocked Brody's hands free of the wood, leaving his fingers cramped and sore.

Dante came to his rescue, giving the two fallen Rankers a good kick with his cloven heels for good measure and dueling with the sword-wielder, his glossy black neck shining with sweat that emphasized the long, supple muscles therein. Another Ranker came in low, bowled Brody over, its weapon lost or abandoned in favor of a closer ground-game.

As he fell, Brody wrapped his arms and legs around the Ranker so that its tackle turned into more of an awkward nose-dive. As the breath rattled out of his lungs and he fought to suck in air, Brody managed to feel some triumph at hearing the Ranker's alarmed grunt. Its wings almost knocked his legs free from around its back, but Brody locked his ankles tight and repositioned his knees.

The Ranker sat back, forcing itself free of his arms, and Brody managed to quickly throw his arms up over his face to block its formidable punches and hammer fists. Once it realized that this tactic wasn't working, it slipped its hands under his guard and fastened them around Brody's throat, squeezing like it was trying to separate his head from his shoulders. Brody coughed and it was suddenly a struggle not to panic. He was losing control–it had been a while since he'd had to fight his way up from the earth, to earn his way to even ground. It would be a mistake, however, to obey his instincts and waste energy attempting to pull away from the Ranker or push it off. Old jiu-jitsu lessons sparked his muscle memory. He yanked the Ranker in close, breaking its grip, and rolled over on top of it.

He was within arms-reach of his broken bo staff now and he took one of the halves and smashed it down across the Ranker's face once, twice, a dozen times, over and over again until its mask had cracked and disintegrated into fine fragments, until its wings fell limp and twitching and its struggles to unseat him weakened. Its terrifying, dead, shadow-skull was now exposed. Something about it spoke to something primal within Brody, that very human part of him that feared the silent darkness beyond the campfire and was unsettled at the sight of a cemetery on a stormy night. A chill of ancient fear lifted the hair on his arms like a frosty fog.

So Brody leaned forward and screamed his hatred down into those twinkling eye sockets until heat burned the frost away and the lion roar of a griffin had finished rolling around his teeth. He snatched up the other half of his stave and sought another upon whom he could project his wrath.

He passed Dante, intercepting a sword to the unicorn's flank by breaking the arm that held it, and in return Dante gored a Ranker through the collarbone before it found Brody's unprotected back. He glimpsed Khogar's silvery pelt and saw a ribbon of tattered tail ribbons before wings filled his vision and his two staves clattered across the back of a hand until it imploded and abandoned its weapon.

But as well as he fought and as considerable as his skills were, Brody's opponents steadily sapped his reserves of energy. Those whom he had considered incapacitated, or at least debilitated beyond recovery, returned to engage him repeatedly. Killing just one required strength and time that he didn't have.

Finally, his reactions slowed just enough to allow a sword-hilt to connect with the back of his head, rattling his teeth and blotting his vision. He thought that he heard his skull crack, and he smelled something like ozone, then the worst headache of his life splintered through his brain to his temples, down into his cheekbones, throbbing in his molars. He fell, dropped like Domine's horse had, as if he were but an empty husk.

He didn't remember hitting the ground, only drifting in a semi-conscious state as if stuck in that space between waking and a soft, gentle dream. Something fell near enough his face that it filled his unfocused vision–something that thrashed and tried to rise until half a dozen swords gored it into minced meat. He heard a death-cry and saw a pool of silvery blood spreading toward him.

"Dante?" he whimpered. His voice was muffled to his own ears. Hot tears ran across the bridge of his nose just in time to meet the silver blood warm against the side of his face. He felt himself being lifted and propped against a knuckle-like tree root. His mind slowly started to clear and he reached a trembling, un-coordinated hand back to touch his head. It came away coated a pie-bald red and silver. His curls were sluiced with it.

They had dragged him off the trail a short way into the trees, away from the carnage. He turned and tilted his head, trying to glimpse his friends, to see if Khogar or Domine were still alive, but the bushes and brambles blocked his view. As the seconds ticked by, bitter doubt set in, and instead of clinging to hope, he reached instead for strength. It almost eluded him, but he managed to collect a few shreds before shock could set in.

Seven of the beautiful Rankers still lived, some even in spite of grievous wounds. They stood in a vague circle around him, facing out, their right hands reaching across their waists to rest on the hilts of their swords. They were as still and watchful as statues. Sylph paced slowly, comfortably, a few feet in front of Brody, still in Ranker form, limping on the limb that Domine had bitten through. By Brody's medical reckoning she should have bled out by now, but for a Ranker such as Lust, feeding off of the sins of billions, her wound was obviously but a bothersome trifle.

She grinned at him, crooked red lips and serrated shark teeth, but it was a dangerous sort of smile. The rictus smile of someone beyond furious attempting to control themselves.

"Behold, the fallen king with his furrowed brow, the griffin in the man a broken mask," Sylph said in a tone jagged at the edges like a veiled weapon.

Brody met her purple-rimmed black eye sockets, his breathing just beginning to return to a steadier rhythm.

"Sylph," he said grimly in greeting. A sudden, beyond-hot spike of hatred slashed through his heart. He quelled it to something more restrained, but let it remain, flushing his limbs with power.

Sylph twined her neck in a disturbed way, like the wriggling of a snake's body after its head is severed. She brought her painted mask lower, to his eye-level.

"Why do you still seek familiarity?" Her breath was like a sweet perfume, a luring scent to trap unwary men, but her snake-like tongue flickered out at him, and nausea made Brody's stomach churn. "Hmm? I am older than the griffin kings, older by far. I am not your silly paramour, not the girl whom you called Sylph, who watched as you stumbled along discovering your deeper truths."

Brody sat up a little straighter. He realized that he still held half of his bo staff in one hand, its wood blackened and just beginning to crust with whatever passed for blood in those angelic Rankers. He didn't want to draw Sylph's attention to it, so he tucked it a little beneath his thigh and said softly, "You are not lust any more than I am virtue. You are just one of its familiar faces."

Sylph tilted her head as if mystified. "You are so very like your father. Had you seen him then, in the jungles of war, you would have recognized me in him more than yourself." She stretched a wide, thirsty smile.

"You would have made me a Dark Griffin," Brody said. If she would bring her face closer, he could find a place for his half-a-bo staff through the bottom of her chin.

"That was the original plan, yes," Sylph said casually, pausing to run her tongue along the deep wound in her limb. "You had such potential. If we could only have harnessed your bitterness, your hatred, coaxed it hotter..." She nodded, her lips stained with her own blood. "Yes. You would have been a most powerful weapon–nigh-unstoppable, so the Ancients vow." She glanced at the back of one of the angelic Rankers as if seeking validation, then gingerly attempted to put weight on her torn leg. It took none and she hissed–a rough, wrathful sound. Her malevolent eyes dragged slowly to him.

"But you've gone too far, now." Her head began to rise, her neck to arch higher and higher like a cobra about to strike. "Better to begin anew; better I seize your kingdom now while it reels over your death and take the next bumbling griffin ruler as soon as their feet touch the dreamland shores, that their soul may fester under my care and give birth to the Dark Griffin. I am as patient as the earth. By inches we crawl across these lands and encroach upon these dreamscapes, but they are ours, all the same."

Brody felt warm blood stream down the back of his neck from his head wound and fought off a sudden cloud of light-headedness, fluttering his eyes to clear away the film that seemed to have dulled them.

"Your body has been shutting down," Sylph said gently. "Do you feel it? Have you sensed it?" Her crimson lips peeled away from her fangs until he could see where they anchored in her gums, long and narrow like pencils. "This will be your father's greatest nightmare," she said, and her voice seemed to echo up from a well. "He shall bury his child."

Her head snapped forward like a striking rattlesnake, fangs parted to close around his head. Brody fell to one side and the bark beside him exploded into splinters and dust. He thrust up with his bo staff into that cloud of debris and felt it meet resistance. With a growl he gave an almighty shove–felt great drops of hot liquid splash against his arm.

Sylph's yelp at smashing her face against unyielding tree trunk became a shriek of alarm. She drew back, pulling free from the staff. A fresh wound marred her long neck–a jagged hole gaped in her smoky gray flesh. She shook herself with a series of sharp, anguished cries like the keening of a wild animal. A few of the other Rankers had turned to observe, expressionless, betraying no concern for their leader.

Brody fought to stand, a struggle such as none he'd overcome before, his muscles straining and quivering. Sylph said something garbled in perhaps a different tongue and sent him tumbling across the clearing with a swat from one of her claws.

"Bah!" she exclaimed scornfully, and Brody felt her footfalls thudding through the earth. He pushed himself up onto his arms, but that was all he managed before Sylph sent him flying with another shove. "You would strike *me?* Fool!" Sylph spat after him, a touch of hysteria in her voice.

This time Brody fetched up on his side against a soft barrier of ferns, their fronds draping over him as if to check whether or not he was okay. Brody was uncertain, himself. His ribs ached as if a few had cracked and his mind was muddied. He couldn't quite collect his thoughts.

"Where is your ideal now, O King?" Sylph's mocking words came as if from a distance greater than the clearing allowed. He saw her approach and came up on his knees, fists up. She scooped him up, and slammed him down against the earth, pinning him beneath one of her spidery hands. Her claws scraped the dirt. "What good are your sage words and your meager attempts to defy your nature?"

With her other hand, she sliced a rent into his chest at his collarbone, directly opposite the old scars. His skin cried out with fresh pain, his mind rang with it; with alarm at the battering he had absorbed.

"Abandon your paltry hopes, for if you knew who stood behind us, you would despair!" Brody thought that he almost detected two voices speaking Sylph's words simultaneously. One was Sylphs's own, and the other was deeper; more malignant, ancient, and immortal. Something about it reminded him of Michael and he could imagine that he felt a *presence* a bit like the White Griffin's. He had an image of a pure spring that had been fouled, a bright light that had been snuffed. And then, oddly enough, he remembered seeing this entire moment play out in Michael's wings years ago, as exactly as it had now. The archangel had known Brody's fate–it had been written at his birth, and greater hands and a wiser mind had steered him to this moment.

He thought of his upbringing, of his father, of the ideals he had sought. He thought of the Griffin King Prophecy, of the vision he'd once had of the coppery colored griffin, of the hero that Peter Malone had been charged with finding. *A King shall rise and a King shall fall.* He thought of how glorious it was that he had played such a valuable role in paving the way for someone even greater than himself and he smiled, flushed with sudden warmth at the thought that he would soon go to a place prepared for him by One who saw and knew all, where his weak body and ages of suffering would pale to insignificance compared to the wonders and adventures that awaited in the Kingdom Beyond.

Sylph shook him and his blissful moments of peace faded into a near corner of his heart. He had accomplished much, Brody thought. He had lived well, as his father had. But one task yet remained before him. He turned his head and looked straight up at Sylph.

"Will you yield," she asked, "Or will you even now cling to the vestments of your so-called saints, Brody Red-Eye?"

He gazed up at her a few moments, studying her monstrous face, seeing her loathing, her desire for his death, her lust for his pain. He wrapped his hands around two of the long fingers of the claw she had pressed against him. They were bony, but strong, like tree limbs. She glanced at his hands, and smiled at their comparable size and frailty, the blood running slower from the wounds in her neck and limb.

Sylph had mocked him, had savored the pain that the truth brought him: that his father had summoned a Ranker so powerful that it commanded legions.

But Brody understood the full truth of it now–in fact, he'd understood it ever since the bloodsense had overtaken him in the battle against Wrath. His whole life he had thought that an ideal had to be some pure, perfect thing and that he had to become some pure, perfect person. His whole life he'd sought out that untarnished perfection in others and been bitterly disappointed. But that wasn't what made a man. That wasn't what made a Griffin King.

An image came slowly to him now. His eyes hardened on Sylph's face.

"You remember him," Brody said softly. Sylph tilted her head. "You remember the fear you felt."

Through their contact the image came to him. Sensations of awe and uncertainty welled up in him. He saw the black wolf with her bloody paw prints, stalking confidently through the snow, come up short as she beheld a man slouched beneath heavy burdens, dressed in martial rags, a rifle held loosely in one hand, face smeared with greasy paint and smile a nightmarish, bloody rictus. Brody saw some of himself in the man–in the jawline, the nose, the flinty spark in the eyes–and for the first time since learning that his father's bloodlust had summoned Sylph, he felt that he truly understood his father and that they were equal.

"That's why Rankers fear the griffin-hearted," Brody said fiercely. Wrath trickled into his heart, but this time it didn't shame him; this time, he embraced it and absorbed it like liquid energy. "There's darkness in each of us, yes. And sometimes that darkness is like poison. But the reason you couldn't break my father," Brody sneered, "the reason why Wrath couldn't break me, is because we *take* that darkness. And we *own* it." By the expression on Sylph's horrible face, Brody knew that the images he beheld had blossomed in her mind as well. Her crimson mouth was open, the serrated teeth bared, as if she were frozen in fear.

"For all your powers of darkness, you Rankers forget that *we* made *you*, not the other way around. And people like my father, like me? We *take* our nightmares, our fears, our failures, that darkness in the corners of our hearts, and we turn it against itself. We use it as fuel to feed the one thing, whatever it is, that drives us forward and makes us indestructible–an ideal."

Sylph eased away from Brody a bit as if scandalized. He dug his nails into her skin and held her stare. "You know it. You saw it. You saw that, even as my father lusted for blood, there was something greater that drove him; that stood behind him."

The Ranker, his father's Ranker, tugged away from him, but he held tight, letting her drag him forward and up onto his knees. The wolf stared, frozen, at the man, who grinned knowingly at the wolf, and behind him an entire forest burned with a raging fire, all-consuming, purifying the land.

"And I am his son," Brody said, his voice strong, clear, and ringing. "And like his own ideal, mine stands thus: I will fight for others, no matter how many Rankers I draw in, because despite all of humanity's flaws..." his pupils flooded crimson with bloodlust. "It's worth it."

He leaped high, transforming into the black and white griffin, the sudden beating of his wings making Sylph cringe. In his periphery he saw the nearest Rankers spin and rush towards them but, uncaring, he reached up and clawed at Sylph's face. One of his talons felt as if it caught on her mask but she shrugged him off and coiled her neck away.

A blade pierced his wing. With a screech he let himself sink back to earth, transforming as he went, and drove all of his weight down directly into the face of the Ranker who'd attacked him. Surprised at his rapidly shifting forms, the Ranker blundered to stab at him again, but too slow. Brody drove his thumbs deep into its eyes, stood, and delivered a fatal stomp down onto its ruined face. He took its sword and returned to Sylph. She appeared ready now, her stance fluid, shifting, like a cat's, spitting rabidly at him, her every fang bared.

Brody ran boldly at her, deflected one of her claws off of his fresh blade, and sliced deep into the back of her forearm. She whirled, he became the griffin and warded her back with a snap of his beak, sharper now that he was armed again. His exquisite griffin hearing betrayed the approach of another Ranker behind. He flicked his ears back, pounced away, then pirouetted back behind it and in two stabs of the beak had severed its head.

Then Sylph charged in again and he transformed, crouched low. She floundered over him and he shoved his sword up. It parted the flesh between two of her ribs, too far to the side to take an organ but enough to frighten her away.

Their battle tore the earth and snapped trees and thundered through the forest in horrid echoes. Sylph managed to catch him across the face with the heel of one talon, tossing his head to one side. Blood streaked from his nose. He stumbled in a circle, his wrist going to his lip where it had split on one of his teeth. A Ranker caught him unawares, stabbing him from behind. Its sword drove through his back just above the waist and came out above his hip bone. An appendix wound–perhaps large intestine. He cried out at the screaming agony, brought the Ranker down with a jiu-jitsu sweep, and punched his sword down through its throat.

He felt hot, as if fire burned through him, wild like an animal, hungry for something more than food. Sylph charged. He transformed, flapped his tattered wings, came down on her back, transformed again, buried half of his blade in the meat just above her shoulder. Her left limb went limp. She collapsed, scrambling, and he dove and somersaulted clear, weaponless. With a curse in some foul language, she kicked him, launching him through the trees to skid into a large bed of pale mushrooms.

One of the four remaining Rankers pursued him, its white wings spread beautifully like a dove's, its eyes as cold and stinging as an arctic wind. It landed before him, studied him expressionlessly for a moment, and cast aside its own weapon, taking him up by the throat and shoving him brutally up against a tree. Brody heard Sylph coming–he broke the Ranker's hold, charged in low to bring it down, but it had expected this and sidled clear, pounding one fist down against the wound in his back.

Brody roared his outrage and struck at its face–a feint–but the Ranker caught his arm and struck him in the midsection, then again, again, until Brody's legs gave out. It flipped him over onto his back. Another Ranker appeared and raised its sword to drive down into his heart. He transformed, knocked the Rankers aside with paws and wings, stood, and killed them both.

Sylph was nearly upon him. He transformed, took up the sword, braced himself, and rammed it beneath Sylph's breastbone just as she threw her bulk at him. Her screams were deafening, as sharp and piercing as daggers in his ears. Brody grimaced and gave the sword a tug, but it was stuck. The last pair of angelic Rankers swooped in, their movements frantic. Brody tried to engage but one clubbed him in the neck with the pommel of its sword and for an instant he felt weightless; insubstantial.

"No," he mumbled through gnashed teeth, "Not yet." He released the sword, vaulted up, and it was as if his griffin wings had manifested, sprouted from his human shoulders to aid him aloft this one final time because somehow, he had reached Sylph's high, arching neck and wrapped his bloodstained hands around it. The weight of him forced her low with a strained gurgle. His feet touched earth.

One of the Rankers struck him in the ribs. He dug his fingers in tighter as if trying to tear through her flesh. The other Ranker stabbed him in the belly but he hardly felt it. Blood the color and consistency of tar oozed out over his hands now. Sylph wailed furiously. She struck blindly at him with her one good foreleg and accidentally got one of the Rankers, spearing it on her claws and flinging it away. Then she toppled, almost but not quite on her side, pinning the last Ranker beneath her. Brody dealt it another of his powerful stomps...and then he and Sylph were alone, locked in their final struggles, their pants and gasps the only hushed sounds now, a din of susurrations and whispering breath.

Sylph weakened. Brody transformed and clenched his talons deeper in her neck, loosing a guttural lion's roar when her head wandered in his direction. He saw her as he had before–the costume she had worn when they'd first met: golden-white hair, blue eyes, a taunting smirk on bright red lips.

Her mouth twitched, her jaw worked. When her lips parted, crimson saliva welled out over them.

"Yes," she gurgled, croaked, looking up at him. "Yes, I see him now..." The muscles of her neck convulsed. She shut her eyes a moment and when they opened again there was one last glimmer of defiance there. "There will be war."

Brody snapped his beak and Sylph saw the man, the king in him, unafraid; challenging.

"Yes," he replied. "Yes, there will be."

Chapter Forty-Two:

The End of the Beginning

"If we find ourselves with a desire that nothing in this world can satisfy, the most probable explanation is that we were made for another world."

–C.S. Lewis

A humble robin recognized the omens of King Brody's death first. It heard the faint sigh on the wind, saw the ravens circling and croaking their lament, felt the icy breeze as if the sun had left them to weep. With a whistle of alarm, the robin dutifully spread the news, that the Land of Dreams would know its tragedy and grieve.

Peter wrote in his journals some ten miles distant, observing a sphinx sunning herself on a stunted tree down in a shallow red canyon. A small bachelor herd of satyrs sprang past crying the sad news of Brody's death. For a few moments, Peter only sagged in shock as the satyrs leaped gracefully from ledge to ledge to the canyon floor, overcoming their instinctive fear of the alert and waiting sphinx to fulfill their obligation and share their melancholy tidings. Then Peter stuffed his materials into his satchel and threw it across his shoulders, transforming on the run and clumsily launching himself into the sky with a clap of his great wings and a shriek to let Josiah know of his departure if Josiah was nearby.

The odors of blood and ruptured innards and the strange, foul, sweet stench of Rankers led Peter, fifteen minutes later, down through the darkening treetops of a forest and into a clearing. First he had to navigate the carnage, his silver eyes scouring the deepening shadows to identify bodies. Placing his talons delicately, his long beak clicking his agitation, Peter found a few faces that he recognized. The bard, the tribal, the titan...companions and confidantes of the king.

They had not been dead long. A familiar wound ached in Peter's chest–memories of the World War and the brave, young lives extinguished as quick as a gunshot; open eyes, porcelain faces, purple lips, and contorted limbs the final indicators of a defiant death. He saw that now, again, in these soulless husks, these good soldiers who had laid down their lives in service.

Peter tracked the carnage through the trees until he found what he hunted for: a black and white griffin's body, all tattered feathers and ruffled fur, stretched out beside the sinuous, serpentine remains of a large Ranker.

"Your Highness," Peter choked out, bounding to Brody's side and cooing softly over him as if to ease his passing, for he saw that the young king was not dead yet, but dying, suffering from terrible wounds. Peter raked the earth with his claws in helpless anguish, his tail lashing to strike his flanks.

Brody opened his eyes. They were so glazed and bloodshot that their original hue was indiscernible. They rolled sightlessly and his beak opened. "Who...?" he groaned. His voice was hoarse. His breath wheezed and whistled as if there were something wrong with his lungs.

“It’s Peter Malone.” Peter transformed and laid a hand against the sweat-oiled feathers of Brody’s shoulder. Blood had turned the dirt under his knees to black mud.

Brody was silent. He felt his wounds as bright stars of flame torn into his hide. Visions–dreams? Hallucinations?–ran rampant in his mind. A vast, terrible, otherworldly something moved like a dark storm cell just beyond his comprehension. He saw the disharmony left in its wake: birds flying into fire, serpents devouring themselves, wild animals birthing stillborns or half-formed mutants swiftly abandoned. Though he couldn’t quite identify the…*something* lurking in a nearby dimension, he felt that he recognized it; had brushed near it his entire life.

With his medical mind, he assessed his injuries. His insides had been breached. Sepsis could be a slow killer, but blood loss would take him before then, if not at least strike him mercifully insensate. He felt Peter stroking his neck as if he were a dying pet, but he couldn’t move away.

“Are they all dead?” he asked. He thought of Aydran, speared on the end of a branch and smirking crimson at Sylph. Dante’s silver blood streaking his night-dark pelt like comet-tails.

“They’re gone,” Peter said after a pause. Brody said nothing. How could he have doubted them, years past? Doubted their loyalty? What happened to dream-creations that died?

“‘To sleep, perchance to dream,’” Brody said. The patches of light and dark across his vision twinkled as if seen through dewdrops. “But maybe we dream to wake up… Did you know that babies dream when still in the womb?" He turned an ear toward where he thought Peter to be. "What do you think they dream about?"

Peter searched for a response, his throat tight. He didn't want to speak, only listen. "I don't know, your Highness."

Brody's ear twitched and his eye rolled toward the man's voice. "I think they dream about an in-between place. Simple dreams, maybe, but the purest kind of all–the sort that keep the good threads of this place from fraying. Maybe they are whispers of the Golden Griffin, words that, as they grow, only their deepest thoughts will remember when they dream."

He felt himself stiffening, his wings falling open, his tortured muscles cramping, but he was unconcerned. This was but a step on a journey. "Well, the Land of Dreams is an in-between place. It's where we make choices as we sleep, right or wrong choices that affect the outcomes of our lives."

Peter, who suddenly felt that he was the recipient of a deep, secret truth, murmured, "What is the Land of Dreams in between?"

Brody paused again before replying, as if listening to another sound, one Peter could not hear. Then– "Us and Him."

Peter suddenly felt very small. He knelt, humbled in the bloody mud, his silent tears dripping down into Brody's shaggy feathers.

Brody, meanwhile, found himself losing his struggle not to drift away from himself. At moments, he seemed to be looking down on himself. At others, he felt a strong pull to go and examine one of the white spots on a nearby alder, as if each speck of nature, each leaf and twig, were a riddle that he was finally capable of puzzling out. He felt that he could sit and stare at the sunbeams dancing through the swaying tree tops for eons. But a pang of urgency called him back to himself. There were things Peter needed to know. Words came to him as if spoken in his ear and he repeated them as he could.

"You must intercept the pathmarkers. Starting at Pebble Embark. Something is coming more terrible than any nightmare. It will make orphans of children, widows of women, murderers of men." The sense of supernatural malevolence crept against him as if bidden and he squeezed his eyes shut. "But there is only one thing to fear, and it isn't death."

Mustering all his strength, Brody tucked his head in until his beak touched the claws of his talon. He murmured, "My gift, as I return to dust." The old vision of the copper-colored griffin fritzed through his memory. With an intense force of will, he transformed, and rolled onto his back. In his hands he clutched five dark, lethal griffin's claws–razor-sharp sickles.

Peter watched helplessly, hands outstretched and hovering as if to hold Brody down. The king was as white as milk, except for the violet of his lips and the scarlet staining his teeth. His curls were mussed and filthy with a caked mat of blood from some obscured head wound.

"Give these to him," Brody said, "My successor." He remembered the customs his tutor at the castle had spoken of–the significance of this bequeathment. He hoped that whomever came next would understand too. Words spilled into his mind again.

"This next is for you, Peter Malone, and you only..." Brody almost didn't recognize his own voice. It sounded strange. Peter was alarmed as well. He drew back some, squelching in the mud.

"The face of the future king will be familiar to you. Protect him, even should it cost you your life–but let not your love for him smother him from his destiny. He will be the two-fold king, hero and champion, Rankerbane, the bridge between worlds and the strider of memory.

"Where he steps, new life will grow. Where he glances, fools will cower. Where he fights, the earth will shake. Where he flies, darkness flees..." He stopped suddenly, and he felt very hot–feverish.

"You can't go," he heard Peter sob. "We need you!"

Everything Brody had accomplished, everything he had *become* flickered through his mind's eye, and he took the time to treasure them, feeling less and less tangible, less and less concerned with fleeting, mortal events. He saw himself, a child, sitting on the sofa, snug between his mother and father, drowsing and listening to the crickets chirping out in the moonlight beyond their porch.

He saw himself and his friends around a bonfire, celebrating his last day home before college, singing along to the music on someone's truck radio. He saw himself rigorously debating with a professor, his classmates becoming nonexistent as he lost himself to his words, honed his skills, tempered his zeal with logic.

He saw himself being crowned King and beholding the marvels of the dreamworld with wonder. He remembered the respect and love of his companions, and, with a final pang, he remembered the first time his homesickness became acceptance–he had finally found his calling, found a place to which he belonged. Not as a healer, a surgeon, or a lawyer, but as a leader and a protector. He stirred. Had he seen all this, so long ago, flash through Michael's wings?

"We still need you..." Peter said again. Brody felt him trembling with sobs.

"Not now," he said, smiling. "Not anymore. I've finished my race. I've done my part. Now it's your turn. Blessings upon you, my friend."

His final meeting with Michael trickled back to him–not the words they exchanged, but the images that he beheld in Michael's wings. Before, there had been too many to process. But now they poured back into his mind, and he managed to catch a few. He beheld rolling fields dazzling with dew and as green as young life itself; himself sitting on a hillside, silhouetted by a sunrise behind him but his teeth flashing in a broad smile; he saw faces, warm and kind, hands reaching out to welcome him; he saw an ocean of crystal or glass; a mansion carved from exquisite gemstones; a huge lion carefully grooming the tiny head of a lamb sleeping between its paws.

Whatever or wherever it was, wherever these images came from, it was a place even more beautiful and profound than the dreamworld, though something about it was similar.

Brody turned his face into the sun, then remembered he hadn't been able to see the sun for the thickness of the canopy. This was something else, something brighter and warmer. He walked toward it; didn't look back. "If you see my parents before I do," he said, wondering if Peter heard, "Tell them that I lived for a reason, and as bravely as I could... My father will understand..."

Chapter Forty-Three:

Long Live the King

"Since it is so likely that children will meet cruel enemies, let them at least have heard of brave knights and heroic courage."
–C.S. Lewis

And so passed Great Griffin King Brody the Gallant, 75th ruler of the Land of Dreams. His was a solemn procession that wended its way along the tiers of the capital city three days later.

As the pallbearers guided the horses bearing the casket in the hearse-carriage through the city, that all of its citizens may lament, Peter watched from a lofty perch. He sat, in griffin form, atop one of the crumbling stone cross beams of the palace's ancient court-yard, his keen gaze observing the king's funeral train from afar. They would circle back, he knew, to lay the king to rest in the secret tombs hidden in the mountains behind the castle, but Peter would not be made privy to the sacred rituals thereafter. He had a different task ahead, anyhow.

"His spirit has gone," Michael said. The great, ghostly griffin stood precariously atop a column beside him, like a cat on a bedpost. "His body perished. All that remains to us is a memory, a facsimile created by the love of his people."

Peter recognized many in the crowd below; people and crea-tures that Brody had affected profoundly in his lifetime: Skâlger, Lord

Puddle, warriors from his army, ambassadors he'd charmed, civilians he had rescued and given purpose.

"You must leave post haste to find the prince and intercept the Ranker pathmarkers at Pebble Embark." Michael turned to gaze at him now. Peter felt the heat of his brilliant, yellow-white pupils. He had told Michael everything Brody had told him–everything except what Brody had divulged to him exclusively–but he felt that the White Griffin knew even that. He had given Michael Brody's talons, which Michael had sent to the crafters at Boiling Point Mountain, and told the White Griffin of the dark force Brody had sensed approaching.

"Yes," Michael had said. "Calamity awaits on the horizon."

Now, he leaped gracefully across the gap between them, gusting Peter with a scent like spring rain from his uplifted wings. Peter finally looked at him, softly clapping his beak, apprehensive at Michael's nearness.

"You will know him, the new prince," Michael said slowly. "He is Jonathan, son of Esther He'klarr."

Peter ramped up with a whistle. "Not Esther my..." Old memories from many years gone by returned to him in a rushing tide: saving a woman's life in the War long ago when he had still been a boy; being wounded; a difficult labor and a life-changing birth.

But now this? Could it really be so? Esther's son, the next king? Would he look like her? Peter felt giddy, recalling Brody's final words and instructions; that Michael had long ago charged him with preparing his journals for a coming hero. Everything was falling into place.

"Jonathan. It's a good name," Peter remarked, elated, unable to keep his talons still.

"He will be scared and angry, bitter and alone. Show him the way," Michael said gently. "I've selected your squadron, who will accompany you on this important journey." He pointed skyward with his beak. A flock of griffins wheeled there, their calls loon-like, haunting and bereft.

Peter recognized most of them as the fresh, young council members that Michael had spent the last few days busily recruiting. He had no idea of where the former council members had gone or, really, why they had been replaced. He hadn't been present when they had been dismissed. The other two griffins above were Kayle and Mariah, whom he had met frequently, if briefly, on his sojourns with Josiah.

"The Black Griffin and Mariah shall accompany you as your confidantes and protectors of the prince," Michael said. He indicated the distant gates leading out of the capital. "The rest of your men, warriors all, await beyond. Their leader, Flaherty, shall obey your every command."

Peter nodded, eager to be off. He stood up, arching his back, then cast Michael a curious look. "What about you?" He would have appreciated the powerful griffin's support in facing whatever dangers they might confront on their search for the prince, their hunt for the pathmarkers.

Michael's ears laid flat. His eyes flashed. He lifted his head, cutting a proud, grand profile, his eagle stare fierce and unafraid. "I shall announce that we are at war. Allegiances must be tested and old alliances rekindled. The wheat shall be separated from the chaff." He didn't look at Peter, but his words were directed at him.

"You will find allies on your journey, in unexpected places, and you will meet resistance too, for many quail in the shadow of war."

Peter searched out King Brody's casket. It was almost at the lowest tier now. Even from this distance he heard the howls and tears of those beholding the funeral train as it passed them. Yes, Peter knew a thing or two about war. He knew its sting, its stink, its thrill and its chill. He knew that dark days awaited them all, both here in this wondrous Land of Dreams and in reality.

His silver eyes developed specks of a griffin's gold, of a sad joy. Though he had been but the humble son of a humble man, of no great significance in the reality of his birth, the impact Brody had made on the world and in the hearts and minds of all who knew him, would leave an eternal mark on the Land of Dreams. Across the dreamworld that day, folk raised their glasses in Brody's name. In Syranade, Rega, the bard from the Fortress of Ice, sang a soulful rendition of Aydran's ballad detailing the victory against Gluttony. In Crystalia, the miners unveiled the completed quartz statue of Brody to tumultuous applause, the crystal sparkling as sapphirous as the wing of a jay, shot through with ribbons of glittering gold. In Raynarra, a little girl held her parents' hands as they prepared to return to their city. Tugging away, the girl stooped, shifted aside a discarded bit of canvas, and lifted a long, black-and-white feather that could only have belonged to their beloved Griffin King.

Yes, there would be War. But because of King Brody, they were prepared. He had slain the Rankers' Seven Deadly; their mighty leaders. He had destroyed their stolen fastnesses and decimated their swollen ranks. And his efforts, his accomplishments, both modest and mighty, had paved the way for a boy who would become a man and a king the likes of which the dreamworld had not seen in millenia. For, as his father had once hoped he would, King Brody the Gallant had led with wisdom, fought with courage, and lived with purpose...as do all who possess the heart of a griffin.

ABOUT THE AUTHOR

I first realized that I wanted to be an author when I was in middle school. Stress, peer pressure, and other personal struggles drove me to desperately escape to wondrous new worlds between the covers of books. I took comfort from such authors as Jim Butcher, C.S. Lewis, Markus Zusak, Christopher Paolini, and D.J. MacHale. These same writers inspired me to begin writing my own stories, in the hopes of creating worlds that others could "visit," just as I visited Narnia, Alera, Alagaesia, and so many others.

I later obtained a Bachelor of Arts in English and graduated magna cum laude. I am now a teacher with a masters in teaching and I teach art, social studies, and creative writing to third and fourth grade students. I also meet during my free time with high-school-aged students and help them to overcome writer's block and edit their stories. When I'm not teaching or writing, I'm world-building, meticulously detailing the world in which my stories take place.

www.ingramcontent.com/pod-product-compliance
Lightning Source LLC
Chambersburg PA
CBHW030603310726
48979CB00003B/547
9798218766290